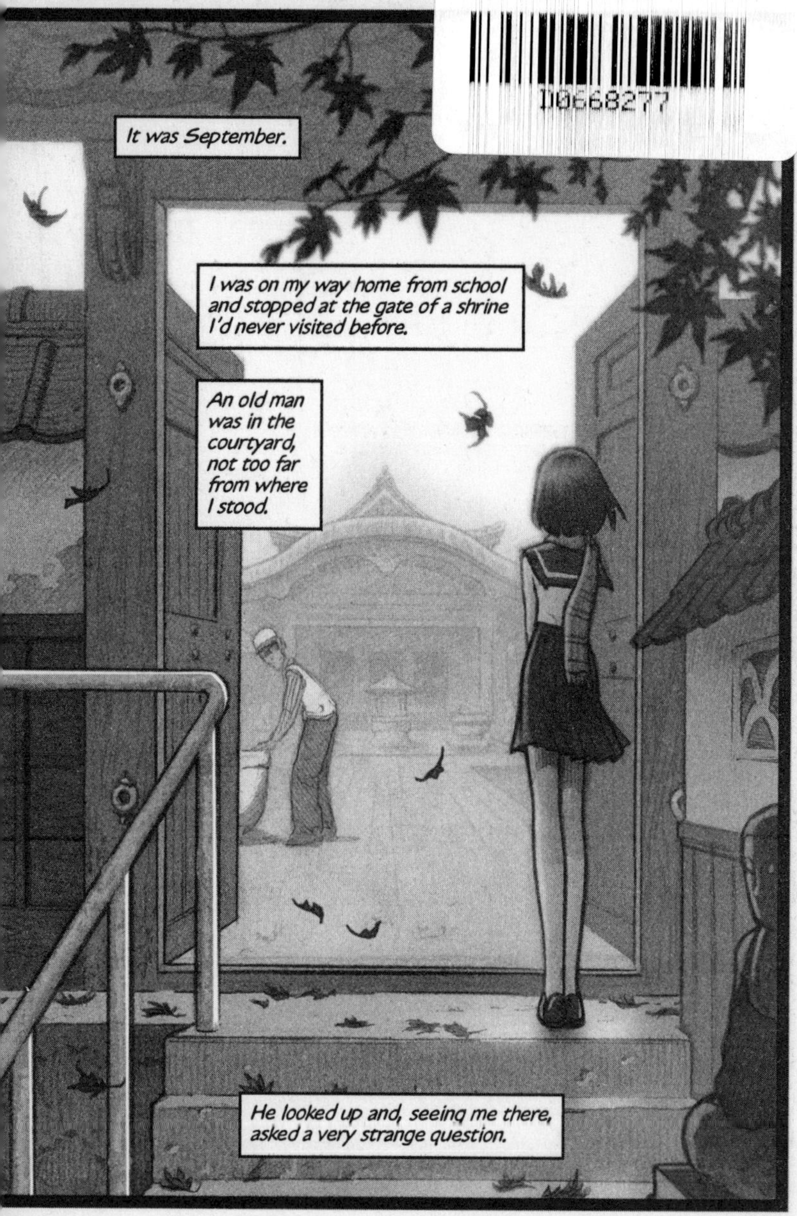
It was September.
I was on my way home from school and stopped at the gate of a shrine I'd never visited before.
An old man was in the courtyard, not too far from where I stood.
He looked up and, seeing me there, asked a very strange question.

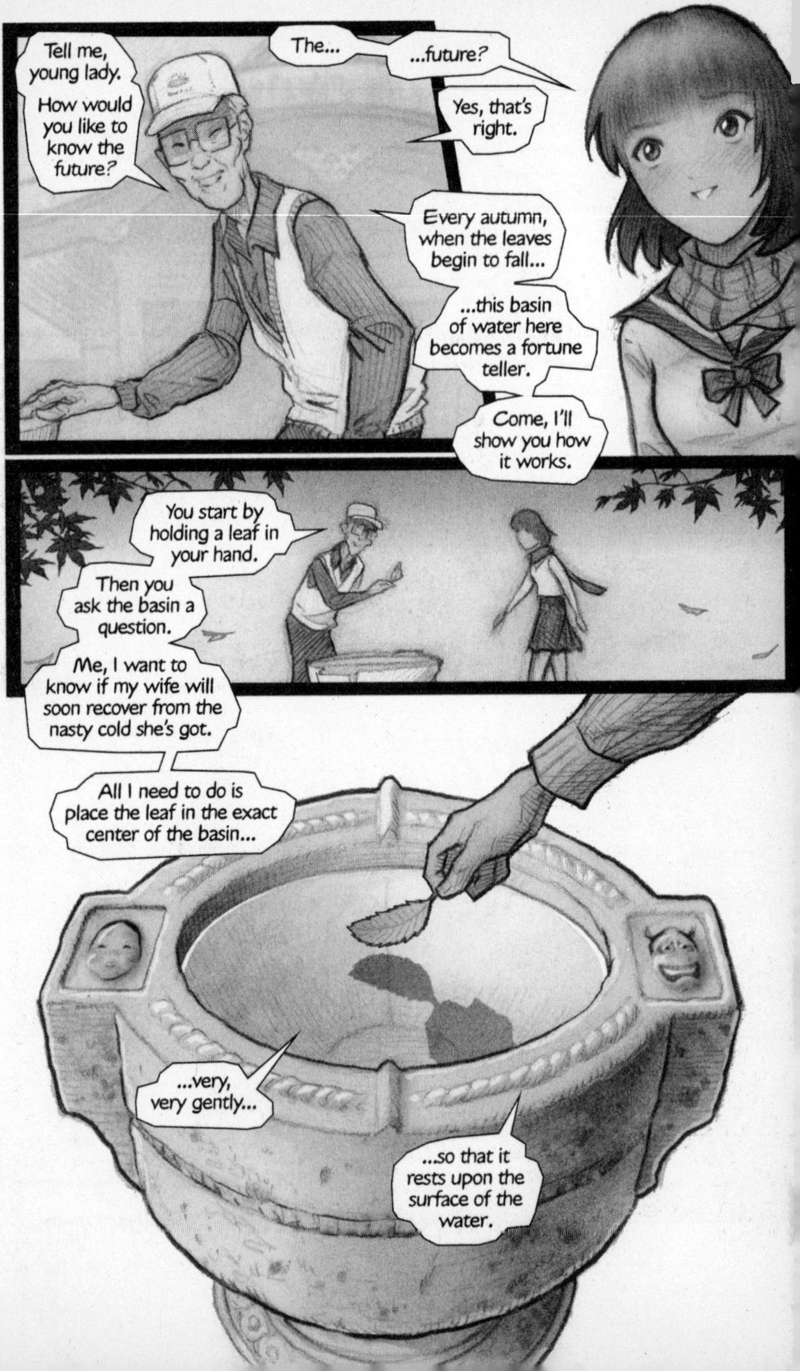
Tell me, young lady.
How would you like to know the future?
The...
...future?
Yes, that's right.
Every autumn, when the leaves begin to fall...
...this basin of water here becomes a fortune teller.
Come, I'll show you how it works.
You start by holding a leaf in your hand.
Then you ask the basin a question.
Me, I want to know if my wife will soon recover from the nasty cold she's got.
All I need to do is place the leaf in the exact center of the basin...
...very, very gently...
...so that it rests upon the surface of the water.

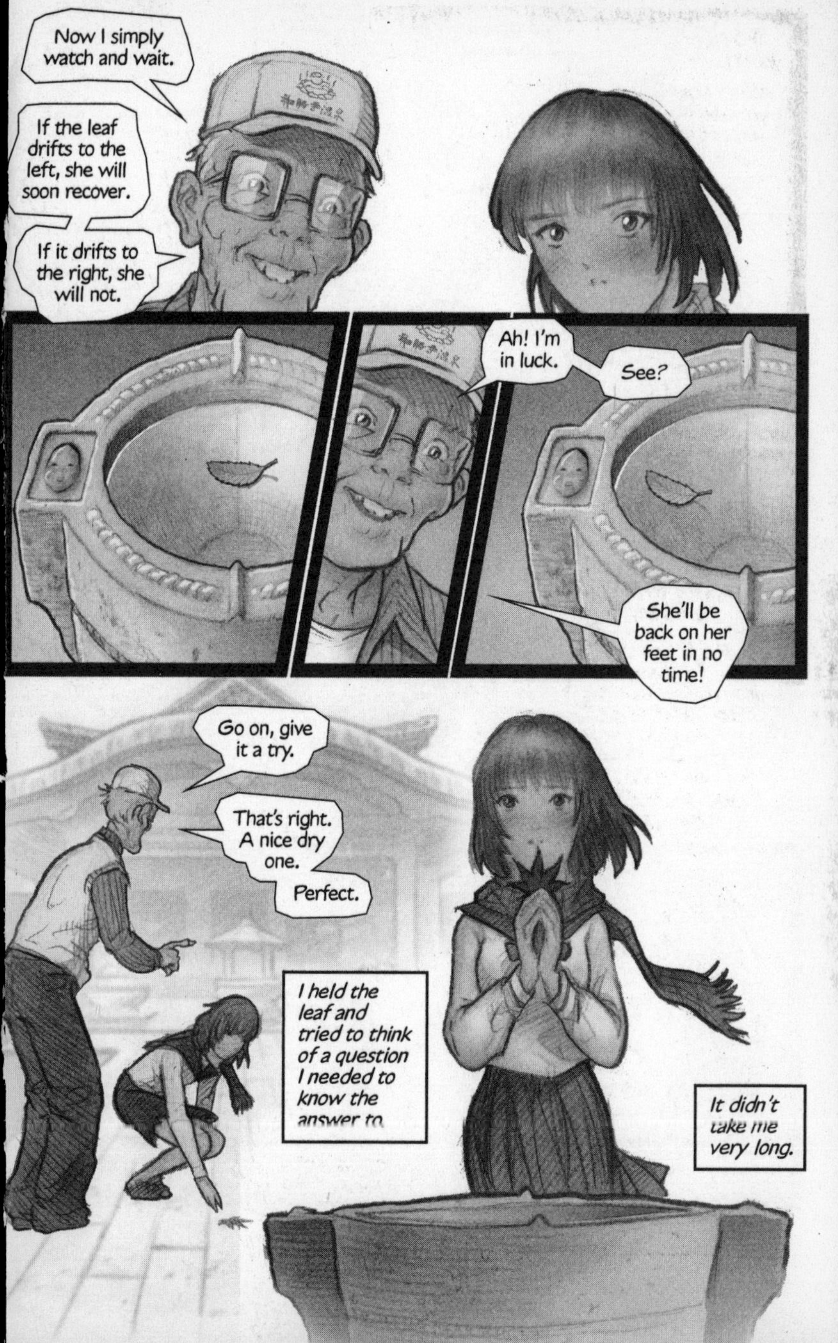
Now I simply watch and wait.
If the leaf drifts to the left, she will soon recover.
If it drifts to the right, she will not.
Ah! I'm in luck.
See?
She'll be back on her feet in no time!
Go on, give it a try.
That's right. A nice dry one.
Perfect.
I held the leaf and tried to think of a question I needed to know the answer to.
It didn't take me very long.

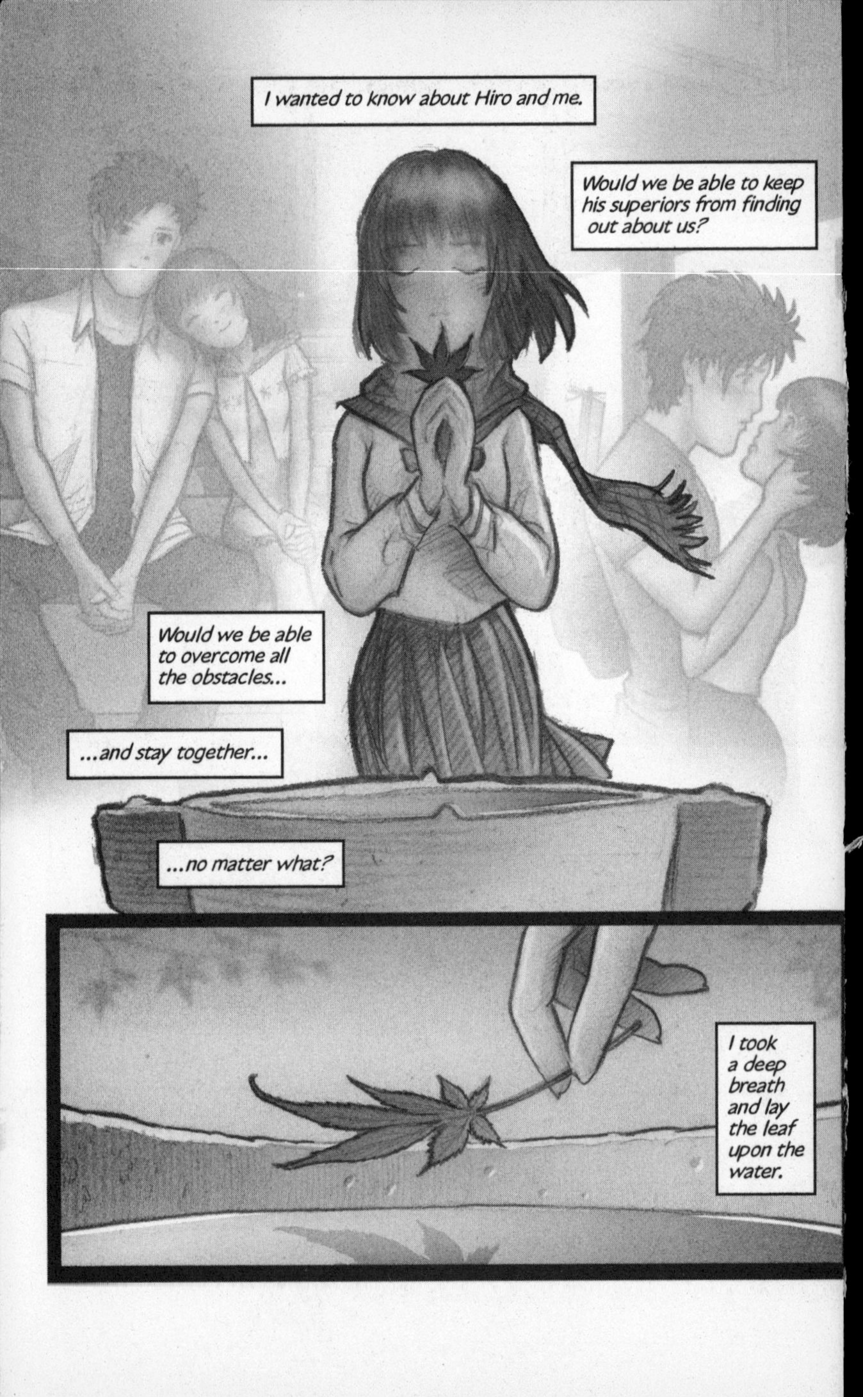
I wanted to know about Hiro and me.
Would we be able to keep his superiors from finding out about us?
Would we be able to overcome all the obstacles...
...and stay together...
...no matter what?
I took a deep breath and lay the leaf upon the water.

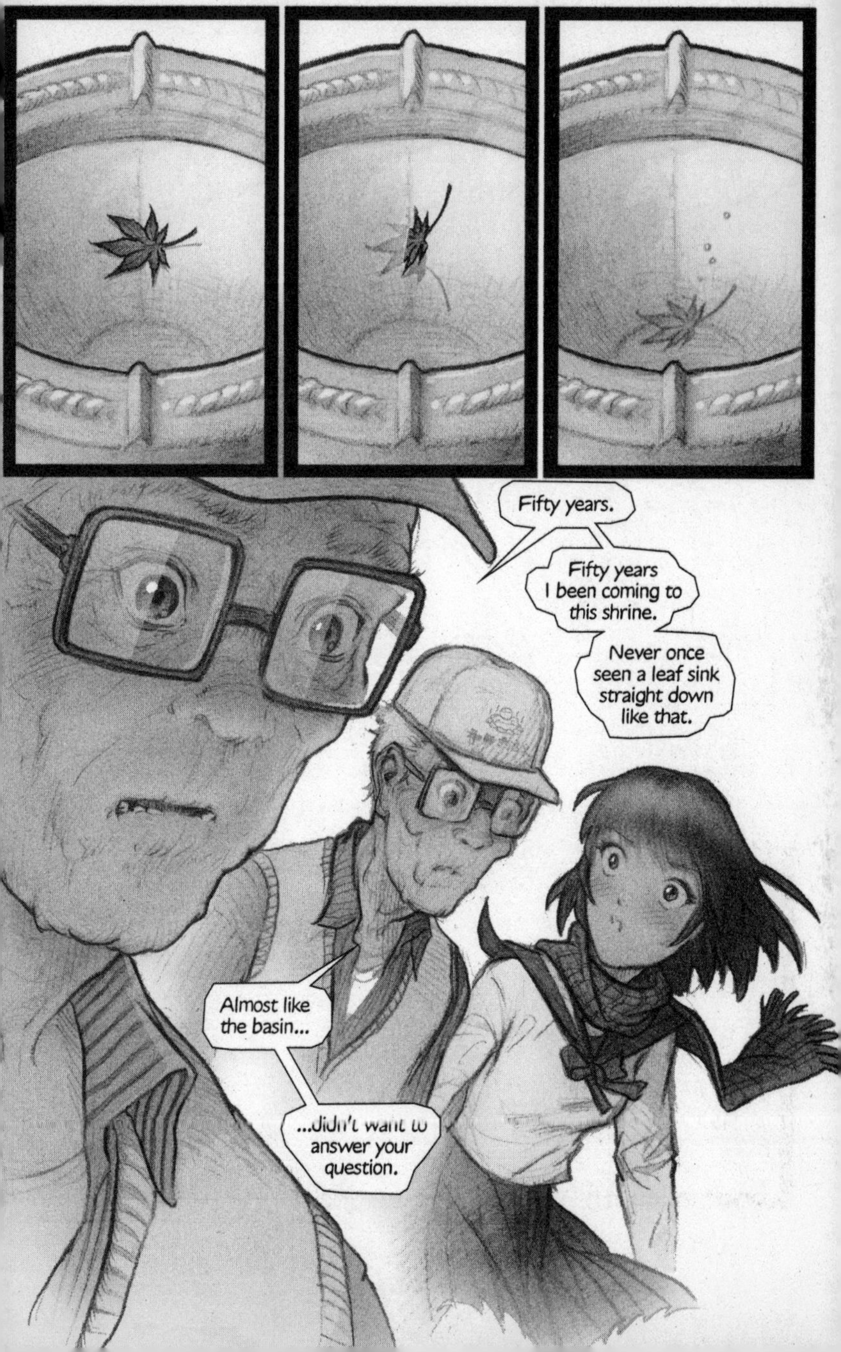
Fifty years.
Fifty years I been coming to this shrine.
Never once seen a leaf sink straight down like that.
Almost like the basin...
...didn't want to answer your question.

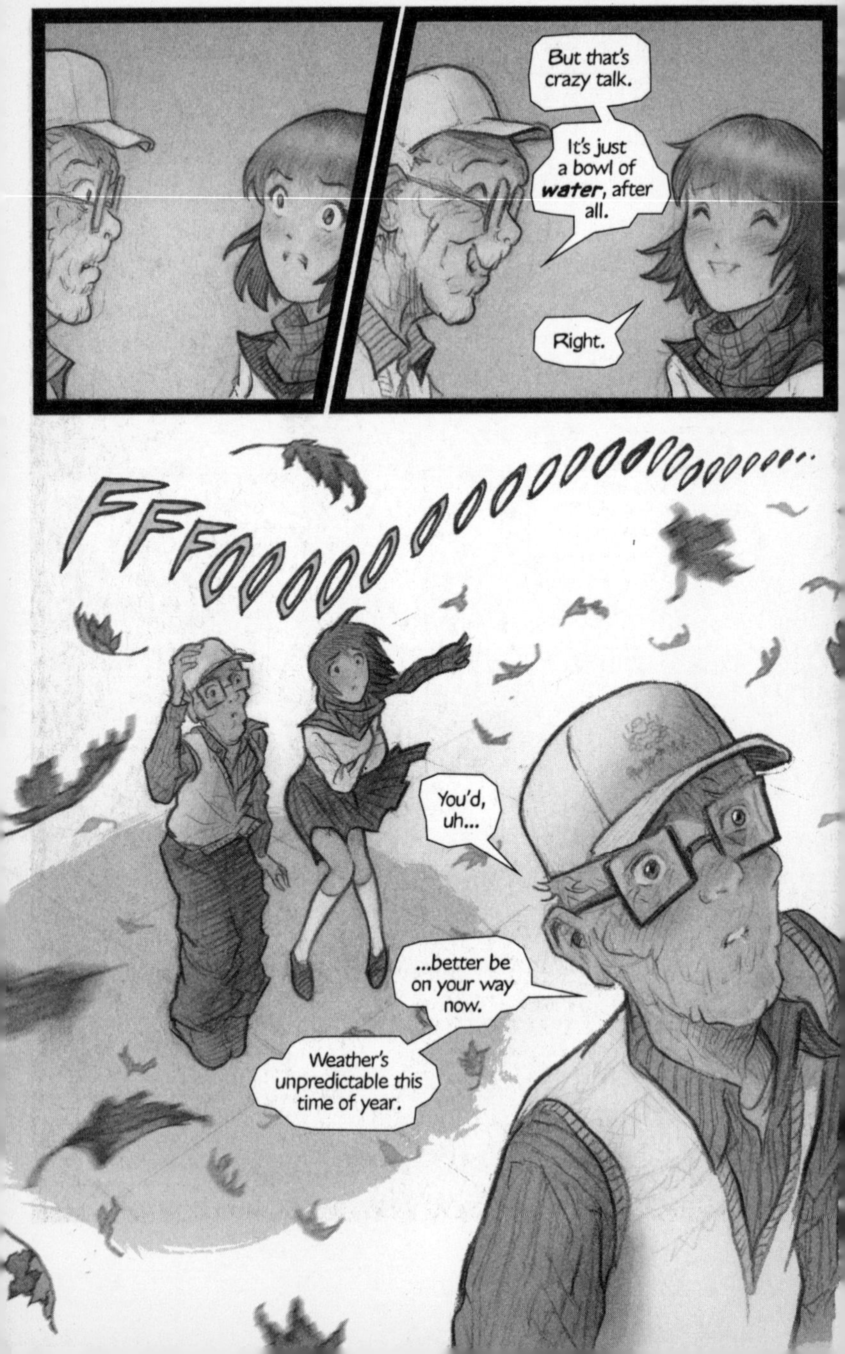
But that's crazy talk.
It's just a bowl of ***water***, after all.
Right.
FFFOOOOOOOOOOOOOOOOOOOOOOOoooooooo...
You'd, uh...
...better be on your way now.
Weather's unpredictable this time of year.

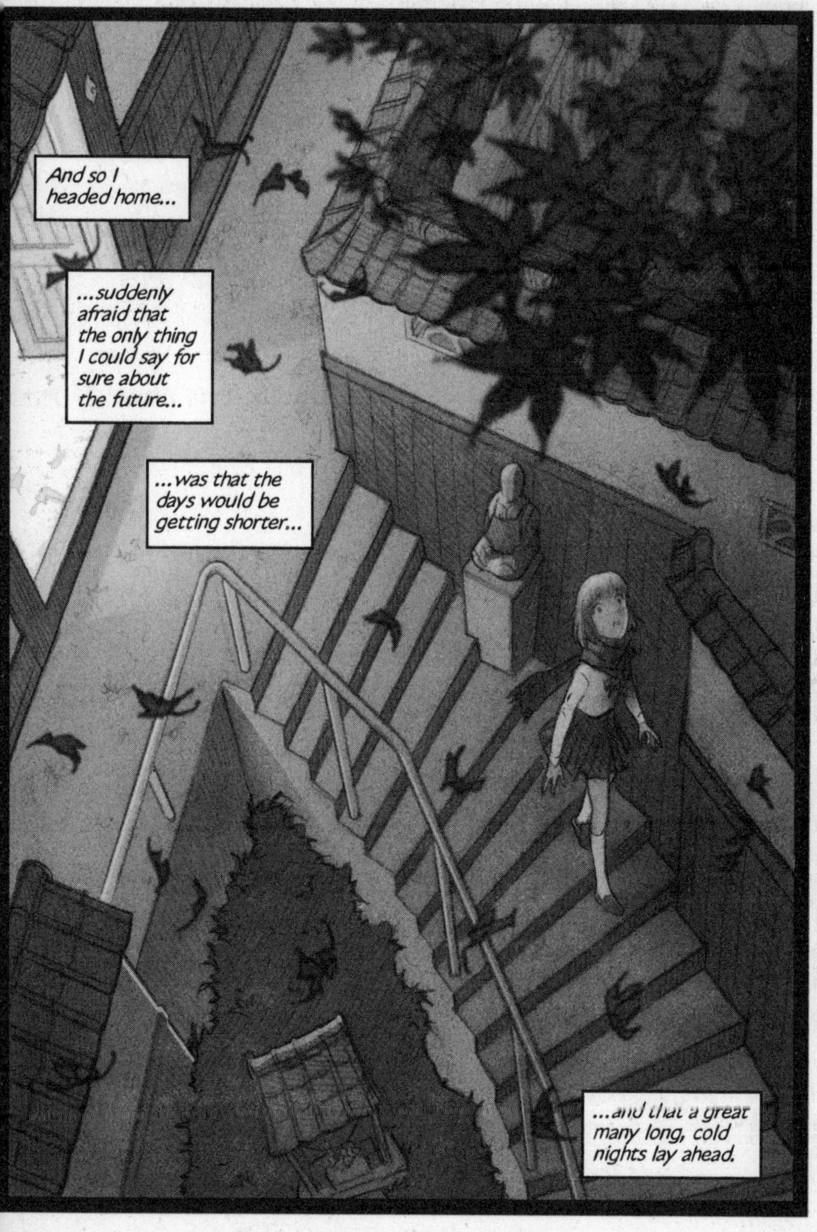
And so I headed home...
...suddenly afraid that the only thing I could say for sure about the future...
...was that the days would be getting shorter...
...and that a great many long, cold nights lay ahead.

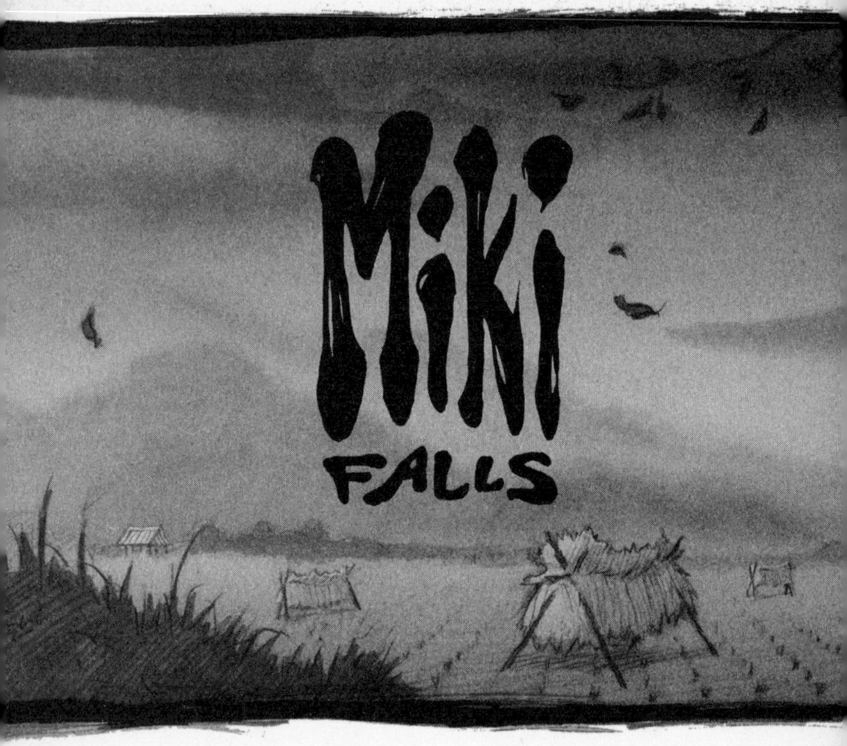
MiKi
FALLS

MARK CRILLEY

HARPER TEEN
An Imprint of HarperCollins*Publishers*

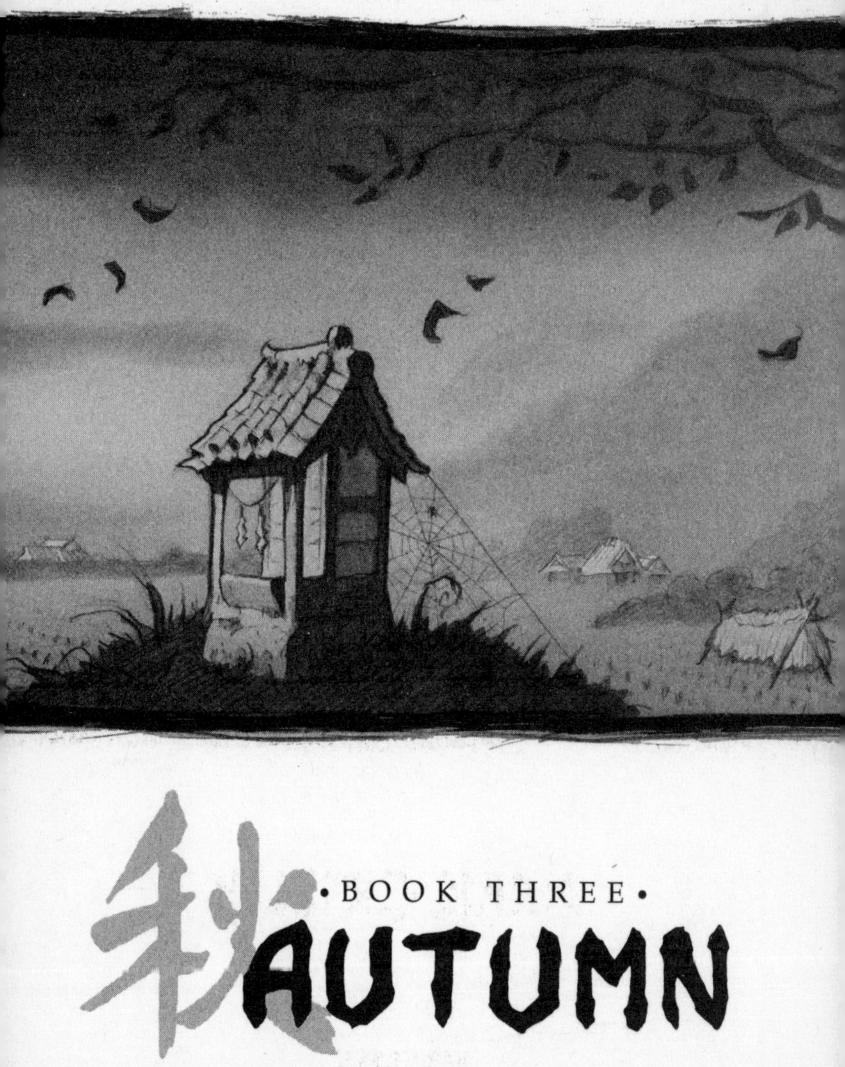

秋 ·BOOK THREE·

AUTUMN

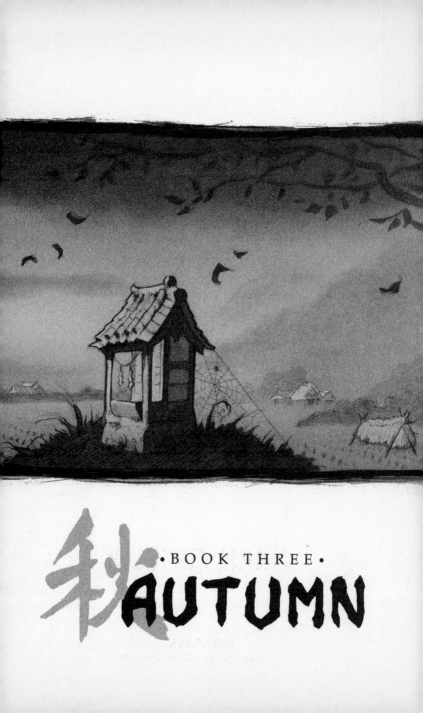

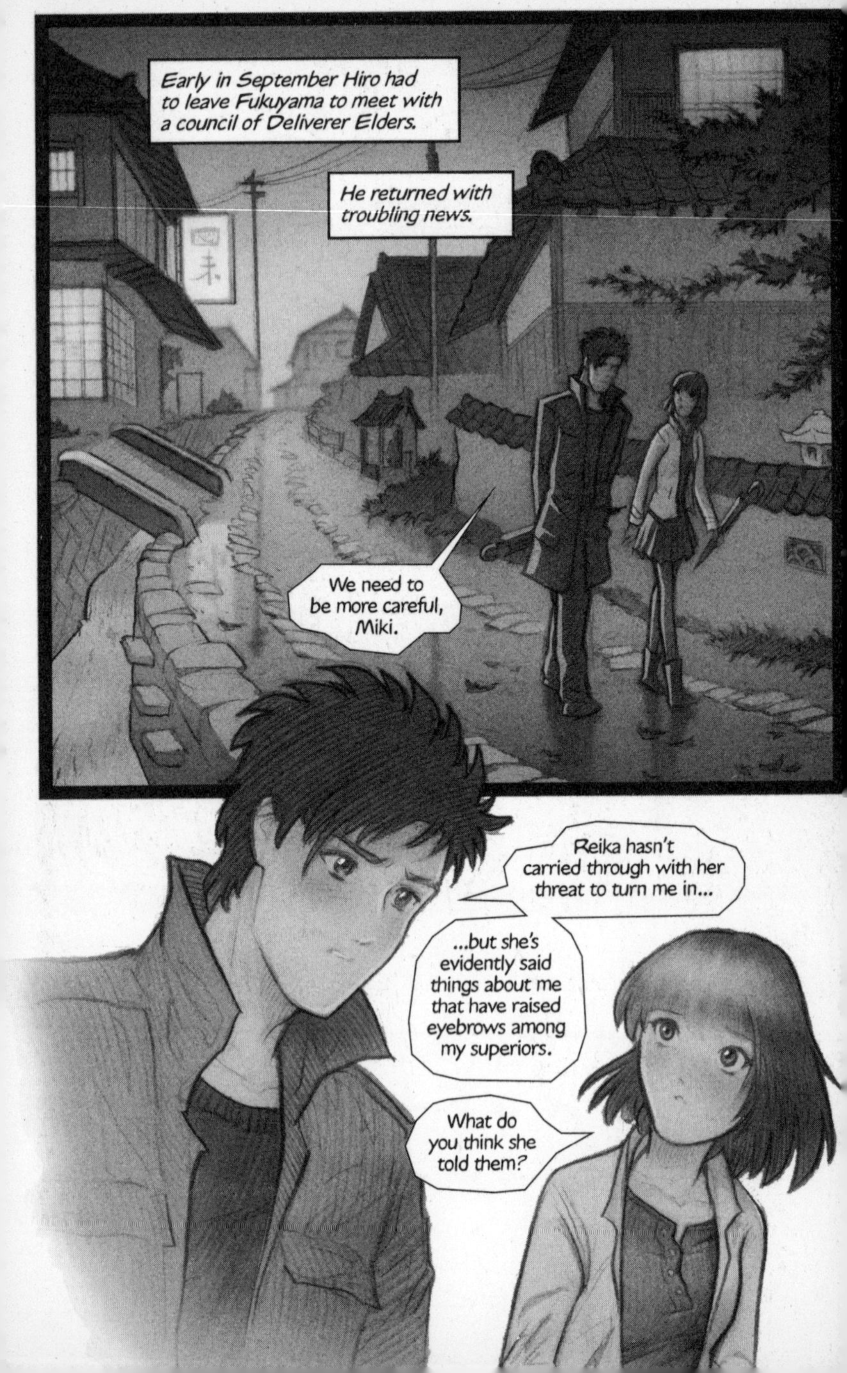
Early in September Hiro had to leave Fukuyama to meet with a council of Deliverer Elders.
He returned with troubling news.
We need to be more careful, Miki.
Reika hasn't carried through with her threat to turn me in...
...but she's evidently said things about me that have raised eyebrows among my superiors.
What do you think she told them?

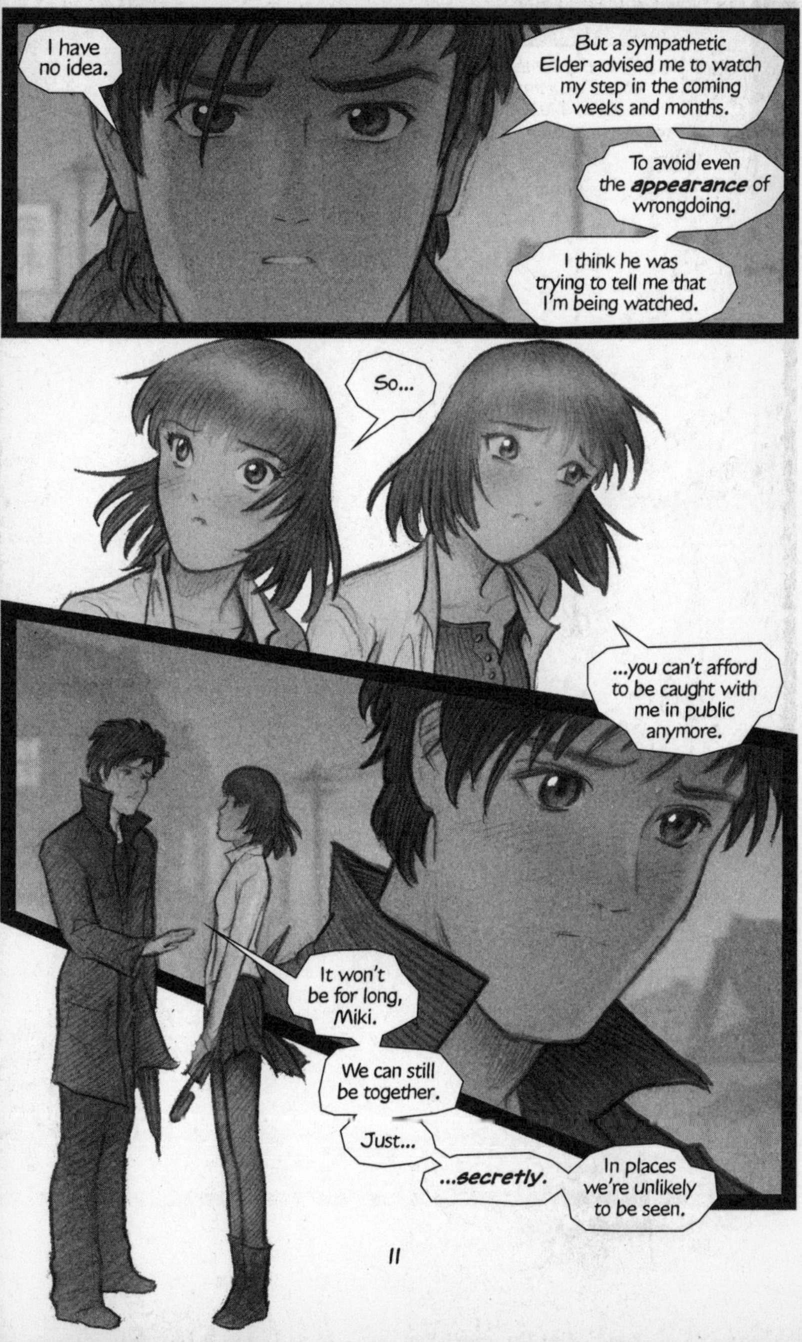
I have no idea.
But a sympathetic Elder advised me to watch my step in the coming weeks and months.
To avoid even the *appearance* of wrongdoing.
I think he was trying to tell me that I'm being watched.
So...
...you can't afford to be caught with me in public anymore.
It won't be for long, Miki.
We can still be together.
Just...
...*secretly*.
In places we're unlikely to be seen.

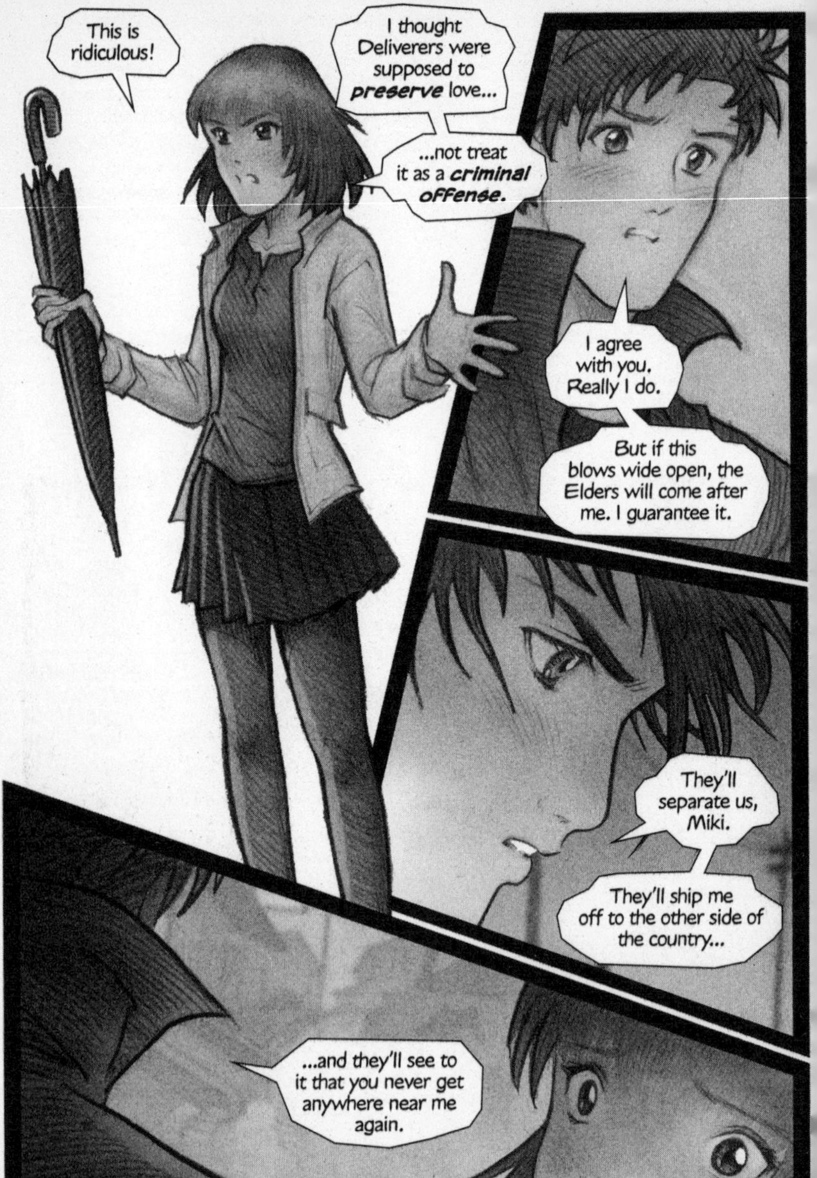
This is ridiculous!
I thought Deliverers were supposed to **preserve** love...
...not treat it as a **criminal offense.**
I agree with you. Really I do.
But if this blows wide open, the Elders will come after me. I guarantee it.
They'll separate us, Miki.
They'll ship me off to the other side of the country...
...and they'll see to it that you never get anywhere near me again.

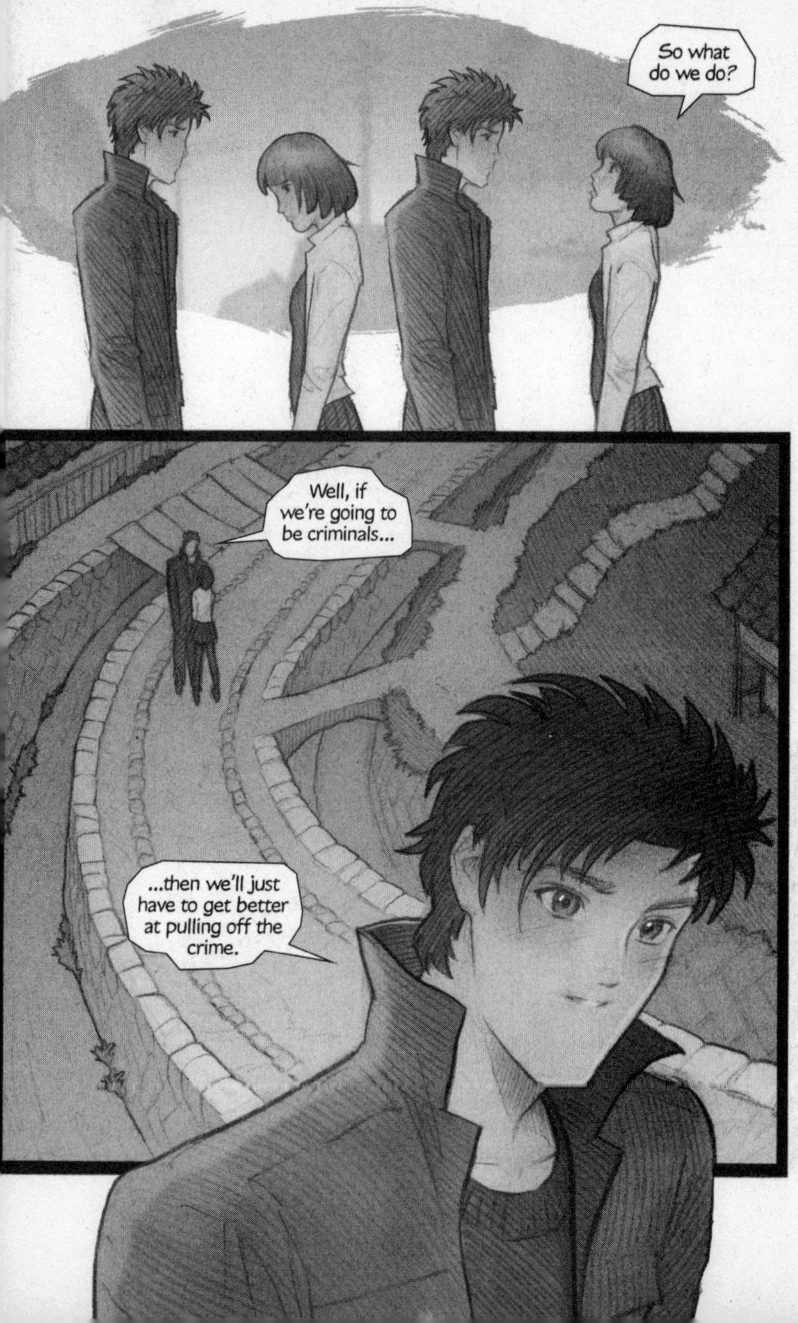
So what do we do?
Well, if we're going to be criminals...
...then we'll just have to get better at pulling off the crime.

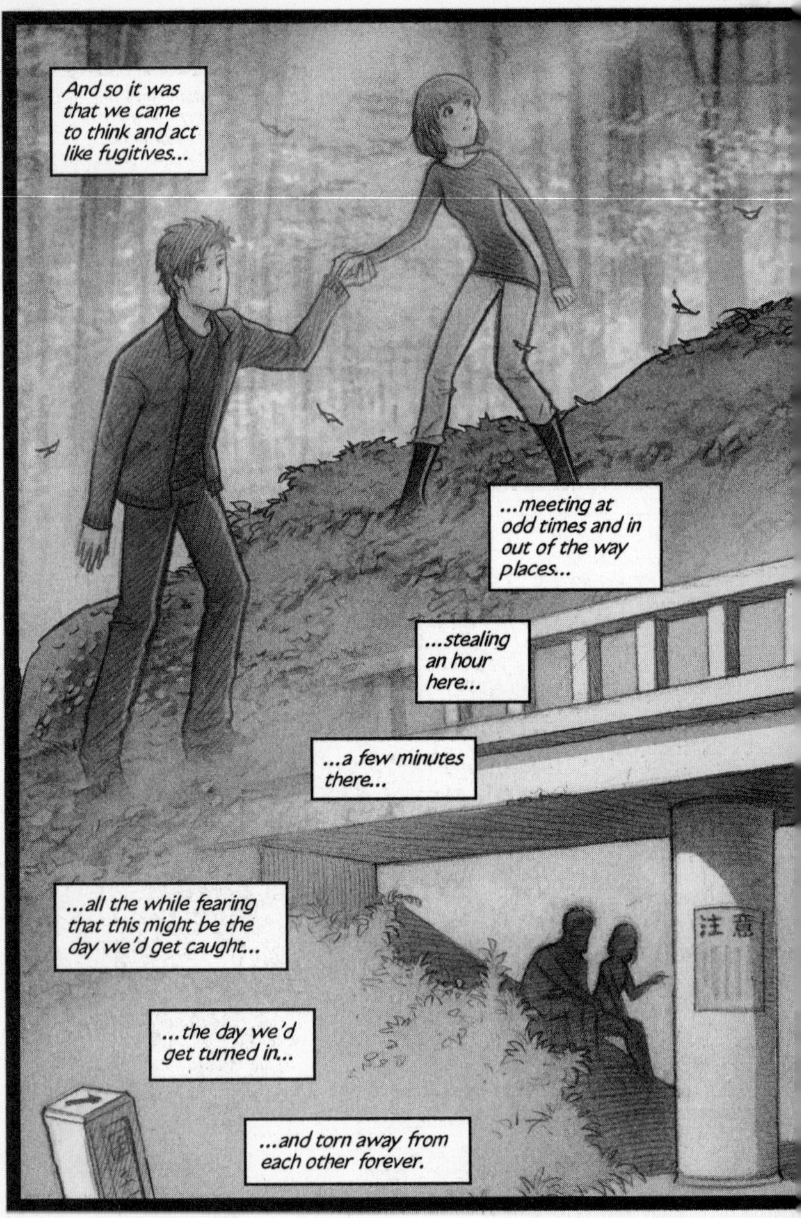
And so it was that we came to think and act like fugitives...
...meeting at odd times and in out of the way places...
...stealing an hour here...
...a few minutes there...
...all the while fearing that this might be the day we'd get caught...
...the day we'd get turned in...
...and torn away from each other forever.
注意

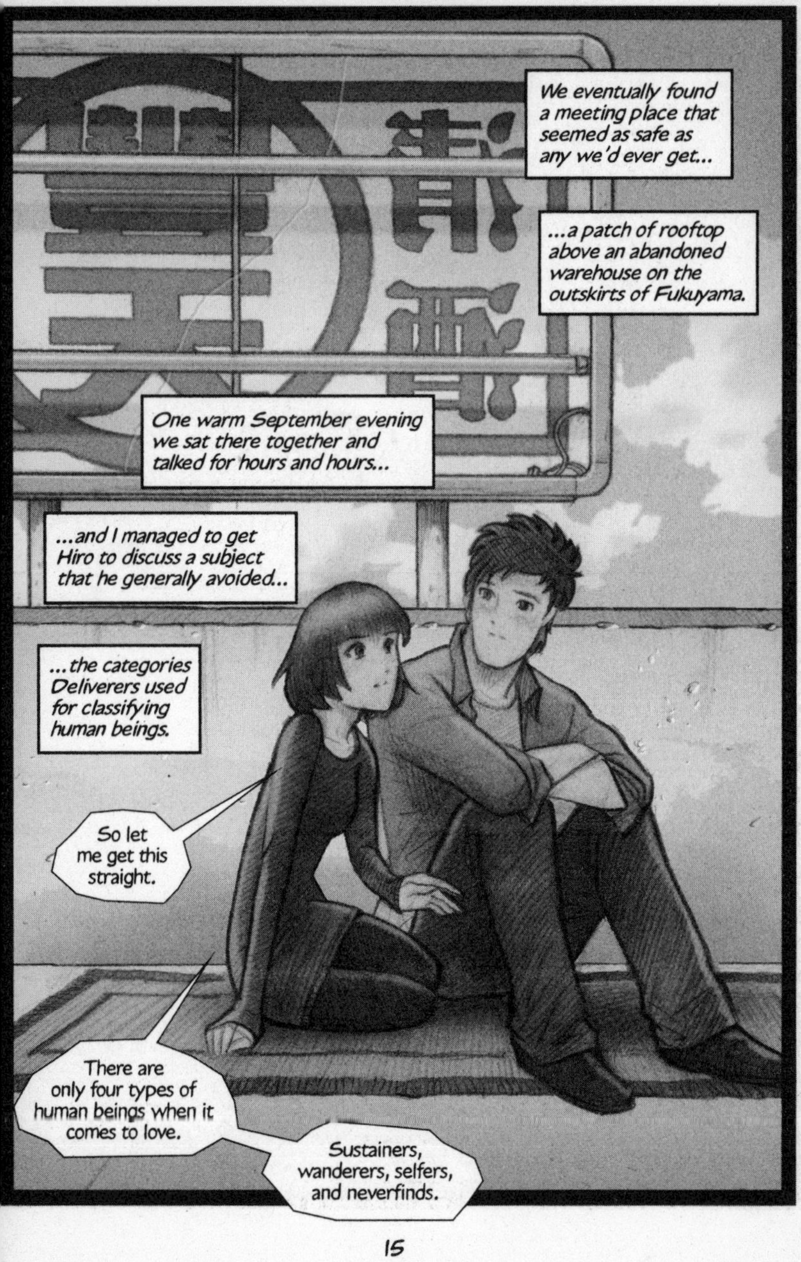

We eventually found a meeting place that seemed as safe as any we'd ever get...
...a patch of rooftop above an abandoned warehouse on the outskirts of Fukuyama.
One warm September evening we sat there together and talked for hours and hours...
...and I managed to get Hiro to discuss a subject that he generally avoided...
...the categories Deliverers used for classifying human beings.
So let me get this straight.
There are only four types of human beings when it comes to love.
Sustainers, wanderers, selfers, and neverfinds.

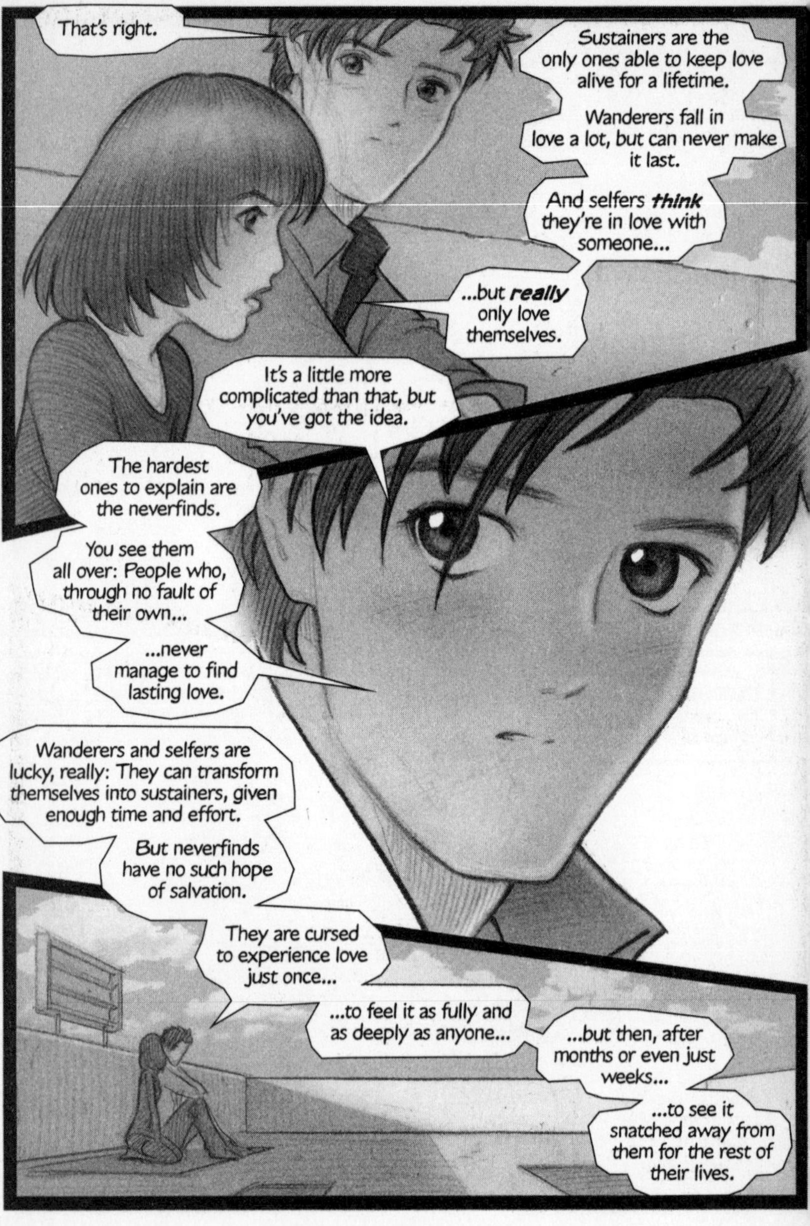

That's right.
Sustainers are the only ones able to keep love alive for a lifetime.
Wanderers fall in love a lot, but can never make it last.
And selfers *think* they're in love with someone...
...but *really* only love themselves.
It's a little more complicated than that, but you've got the idea.
The hardest ones to explain are the neverfinds.
You see them all over: People who, through no fault of their own...
...never manage to find lasting love.
Wanderers and selfers are lucky, really: They can transform themselves into sustainers, given enough time and effort.
But neverfinds have no such hope of salvation.
They are cursed to experience love just once...
...to feel it as fully and as deeply as anyone...
...but then, after months or even just weeks...
...to see it snatched away from them for the rest of their lives.

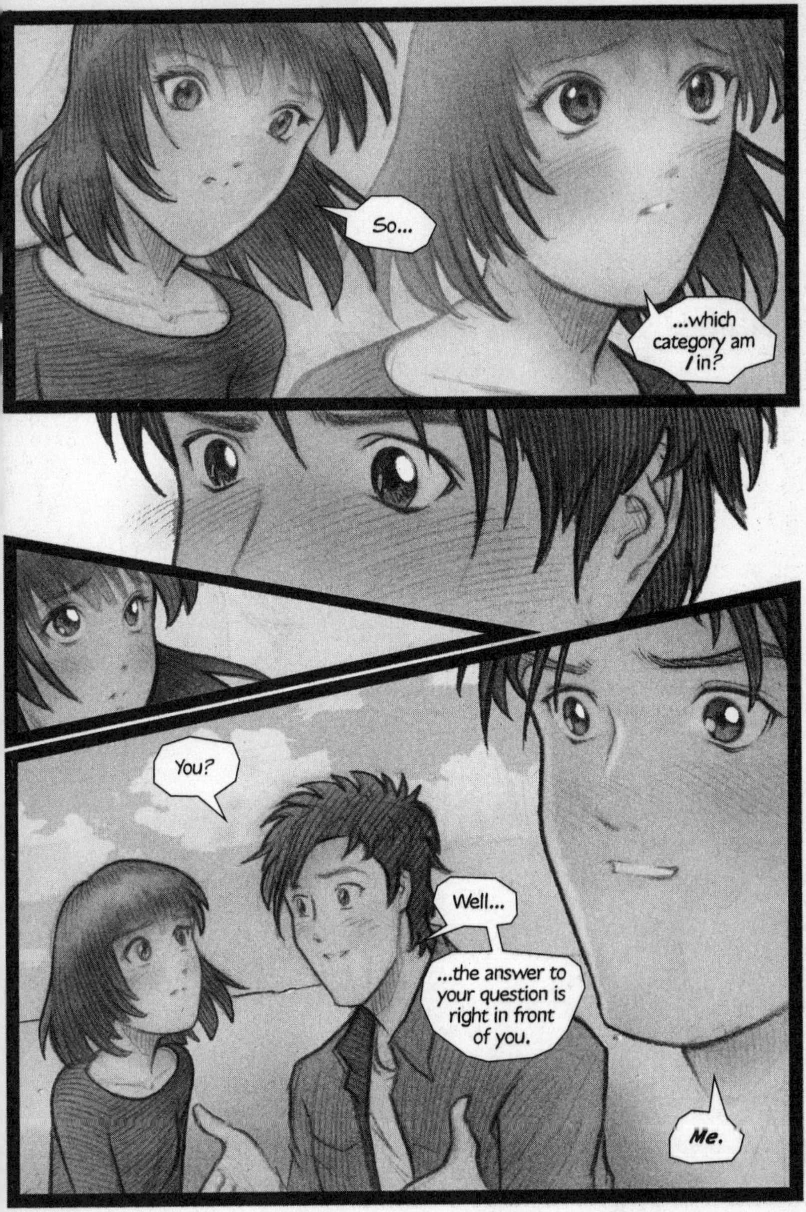
So...
...which category am *I* in?
You?
Well...
...the answer to your question is right in front of you.
Me.

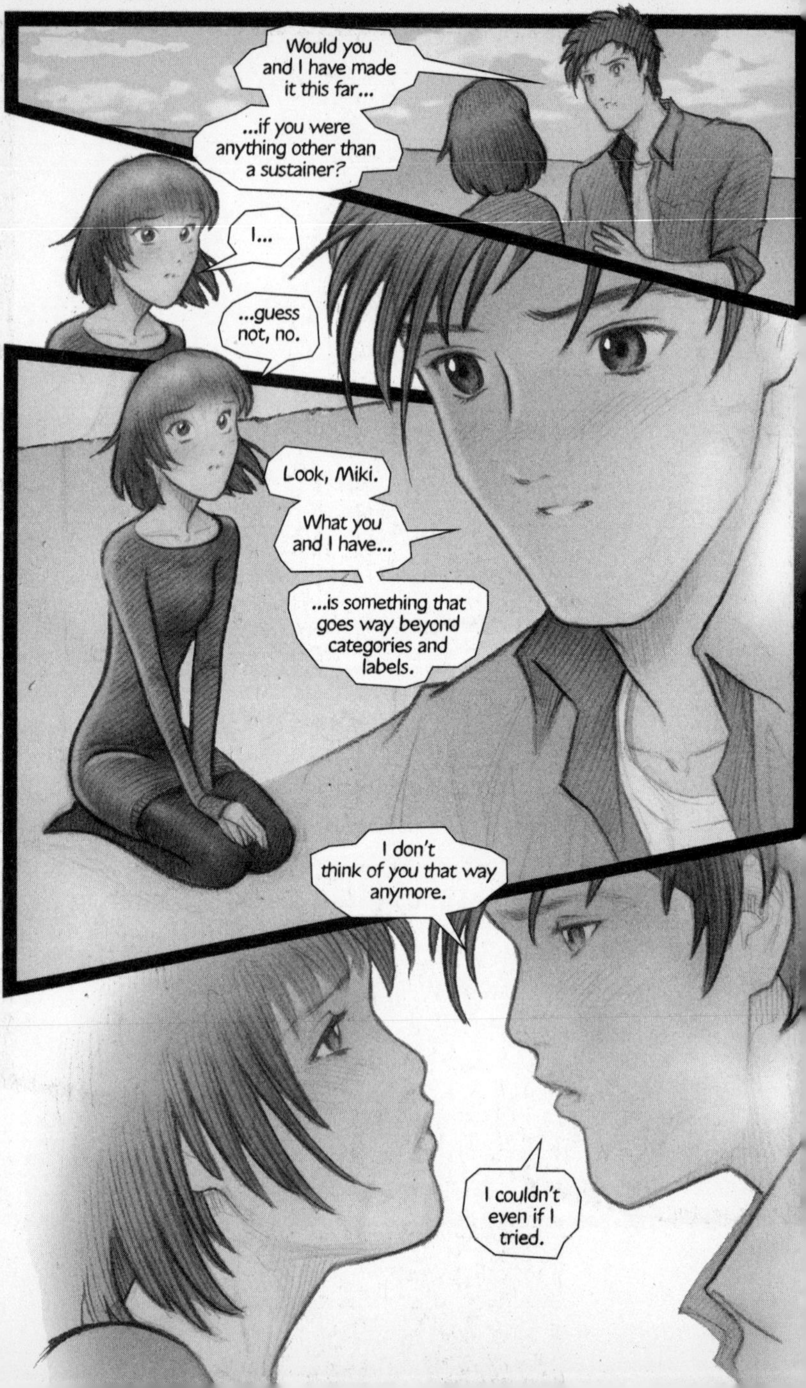
Would you and I have made it this far...
...if you were anything other than a sustainer?
I...
...guess not, no.
Look, Miki.
What you and I have...
...is something that goes way beyond categories and labels.
I don't think of you that way anymore.
I couldn't even if I tried.

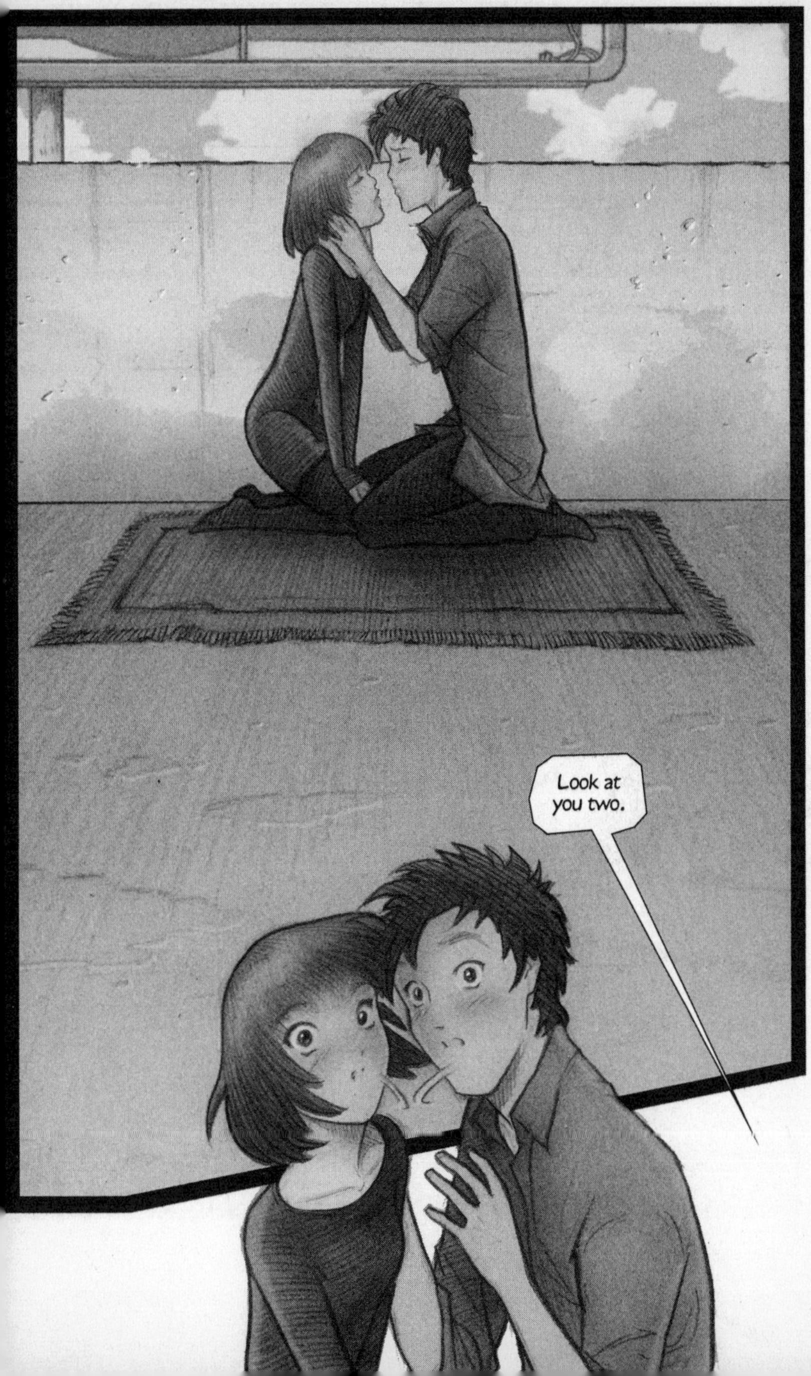
Look at you two.

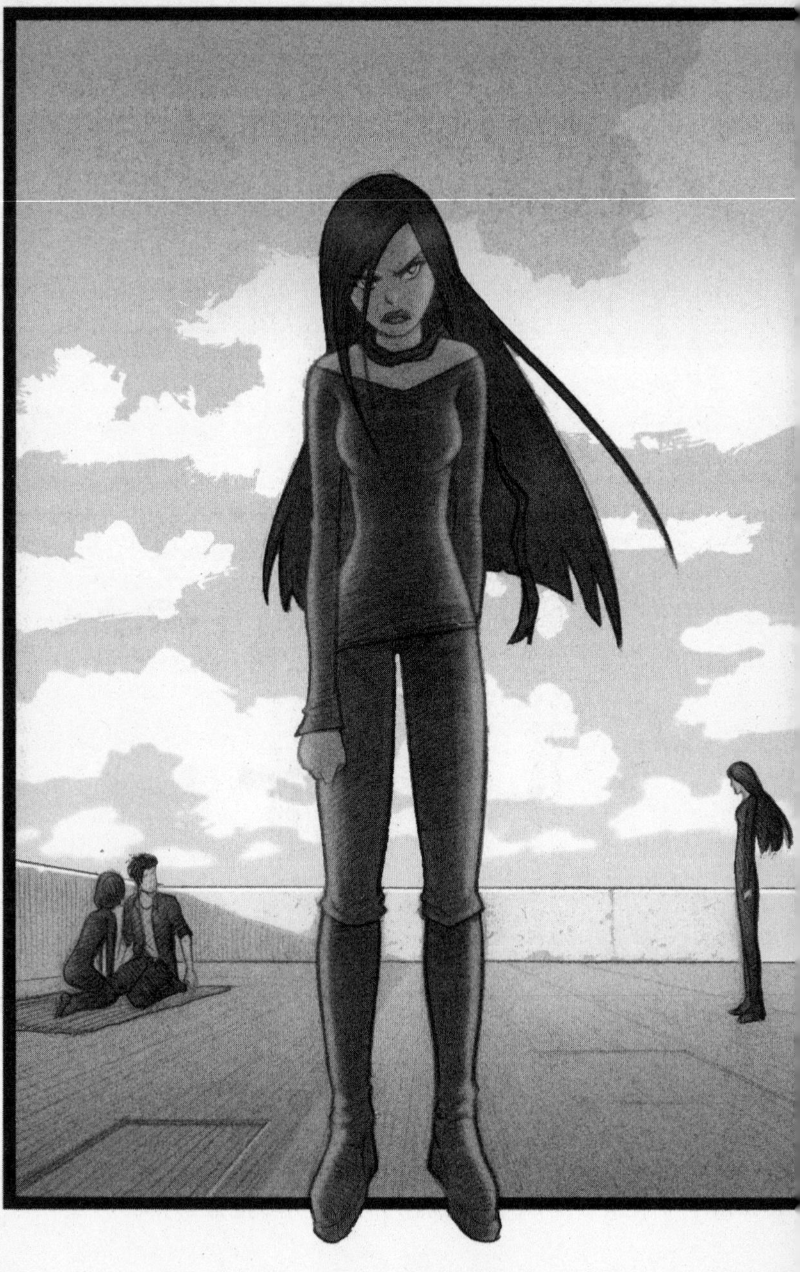

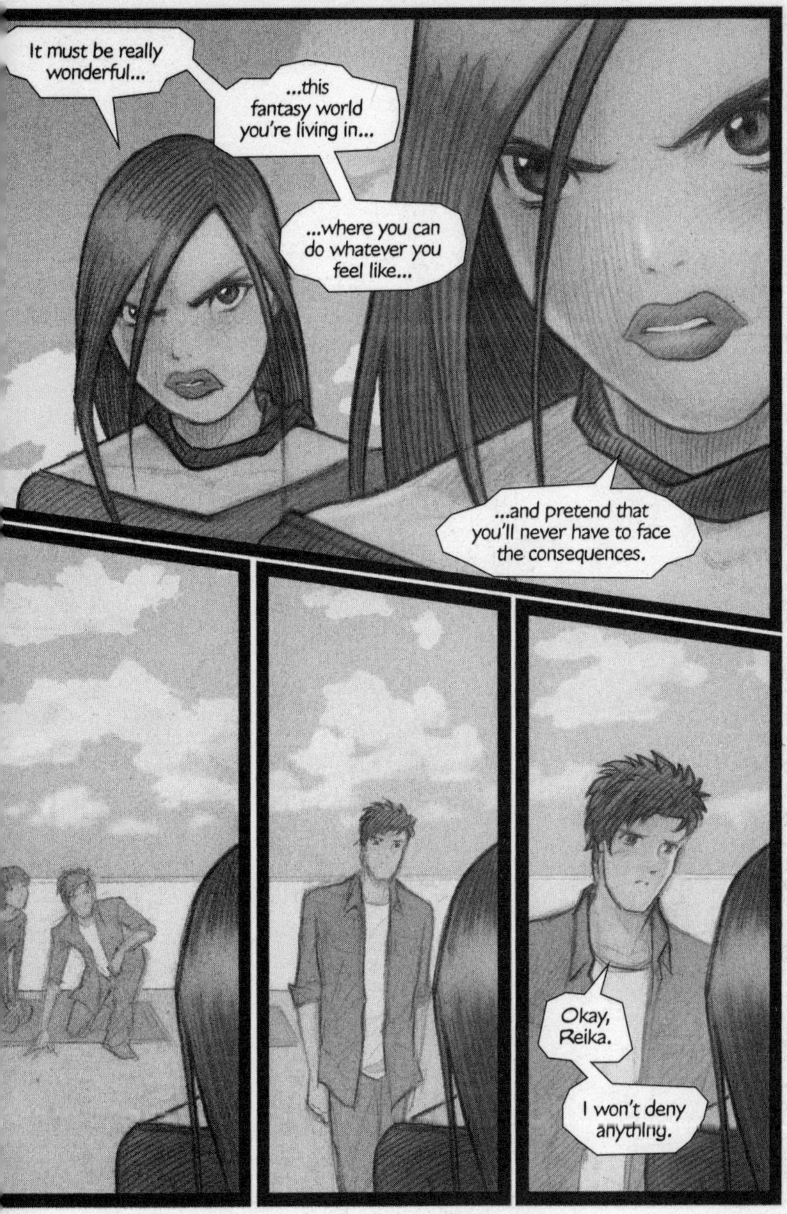
It must be really wonderful...
...this fantasy world you're living in...
...where you can do whatever you feel like...
...and pretend that you'll never have to face the consequences.
Okay, Reika.
I won't deny anything.

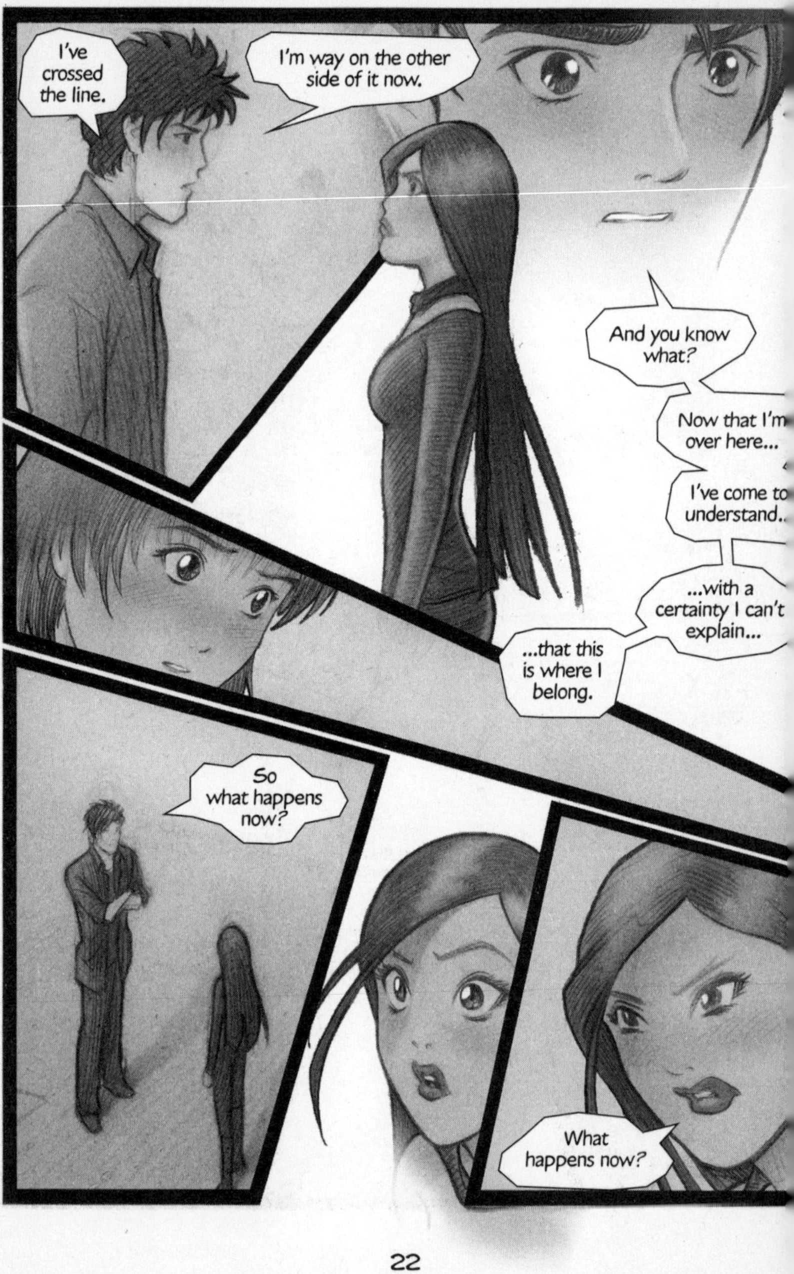
I've crossed the line.
I'm way on the other side of it now.
And you know what?
Now that I'm over here...
I've come to understand...
...with a certainty I can't explain...
...that this is where I belong.
So what happens now?
What happens now?

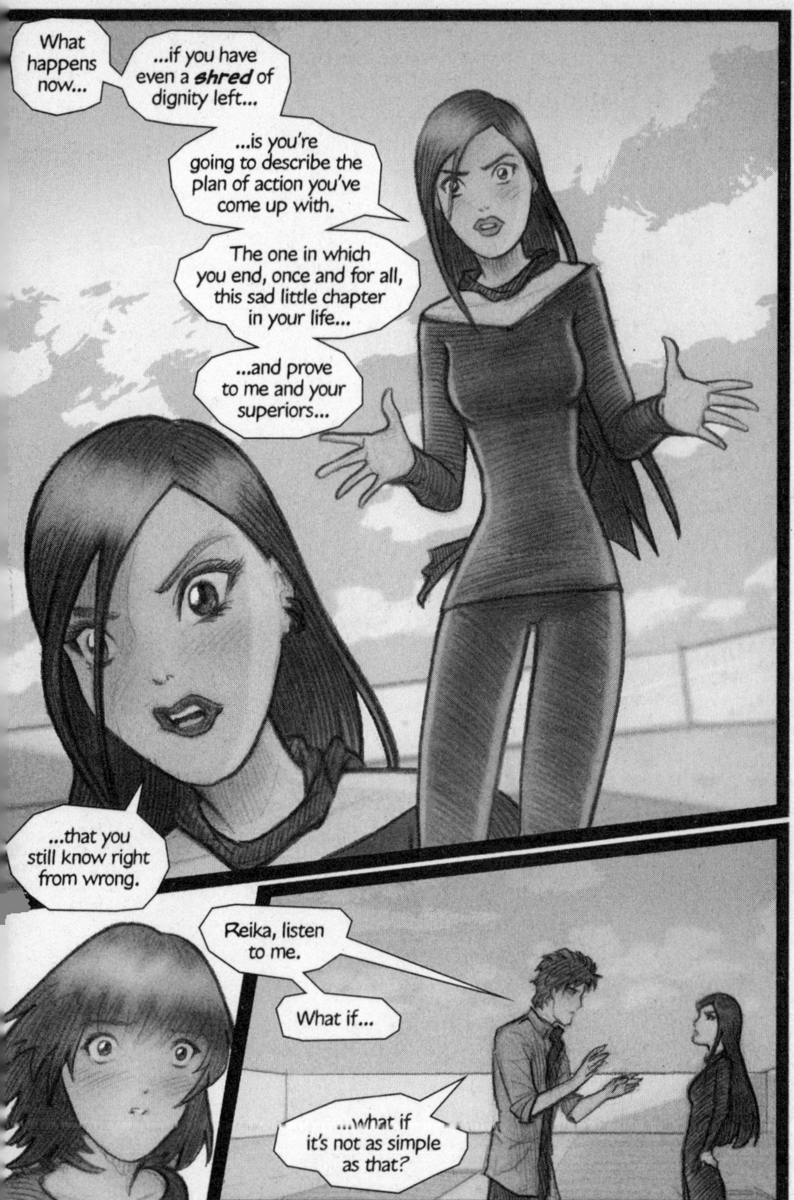
What happens now...
...if you have even a *shred* of dignity left...
...is you're going to describe the plan of action you've come up with.
The one in which you end, once and for all, this sad little chapter in your life...
...and prove to me and your superiors...
...that you still know right from wrong.
Reika, listen to me.
What if...
...what if it's not as simple as that?

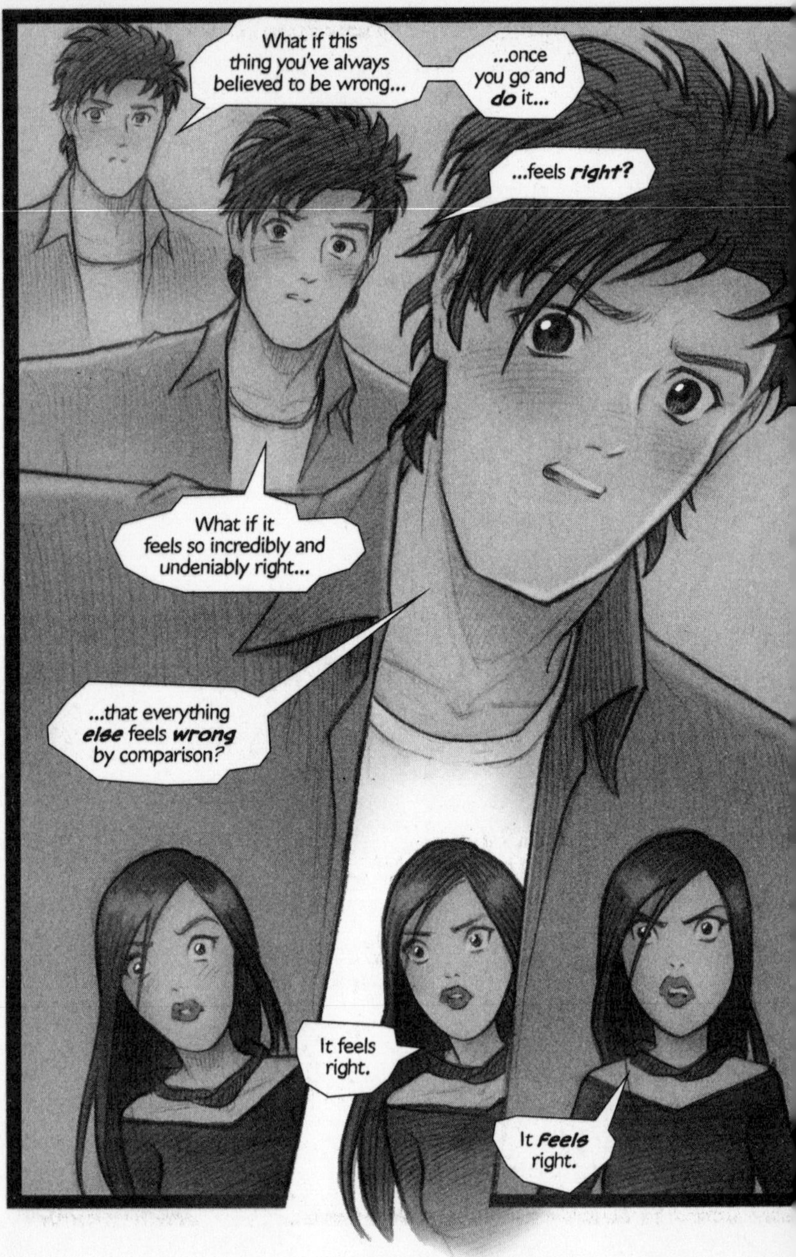
What if this thing you've always believed to be wrong...
...once you go and *do* it...
...feels ***right?***
What if it feels so incredibly and undeniably right...
...that everything ***else*** feels ***wrong*** by comparison?
It feels right.
It ***Feels*** right.

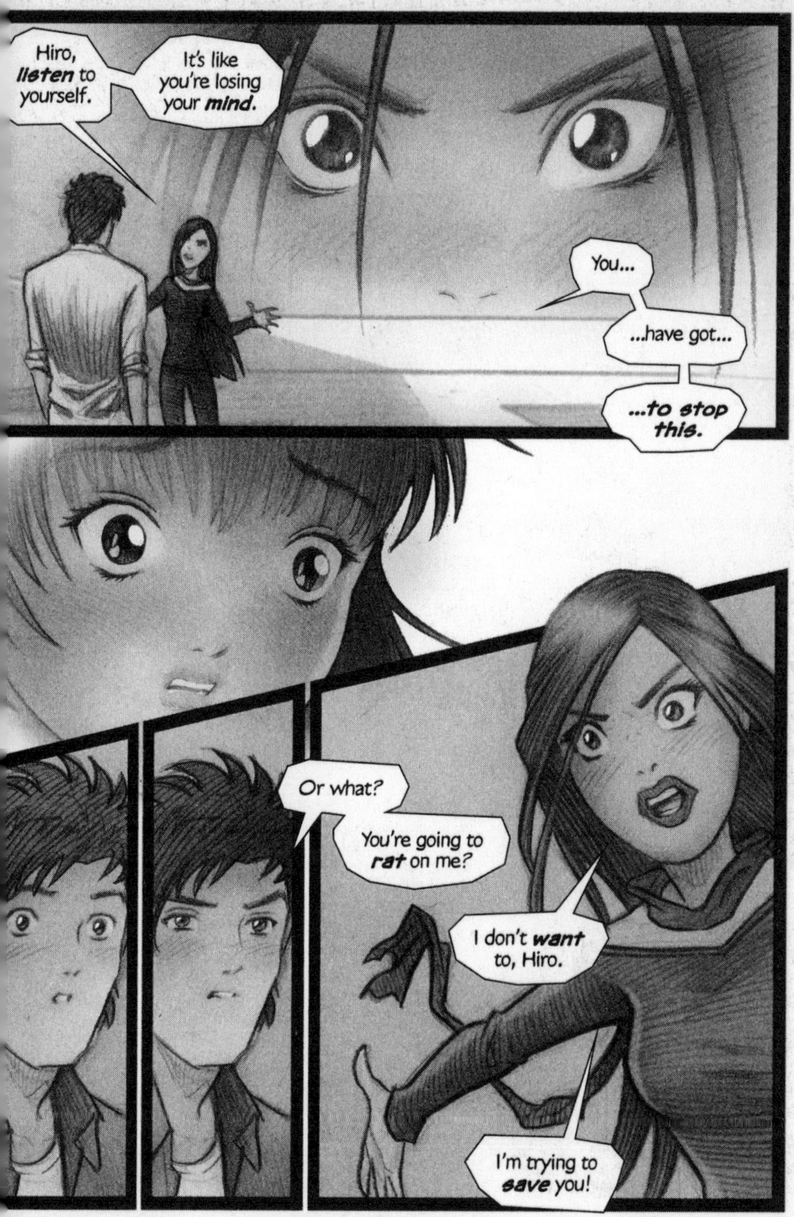
Hiro, ***listen*** to yourself.
It's like you're losing your ***mind***.
You...
...have got...
...to stop this.
Or what?
You're going to ***rat*** on me?
I don't ***want*** to, Hiro.
I'm trying to ***save*** you!

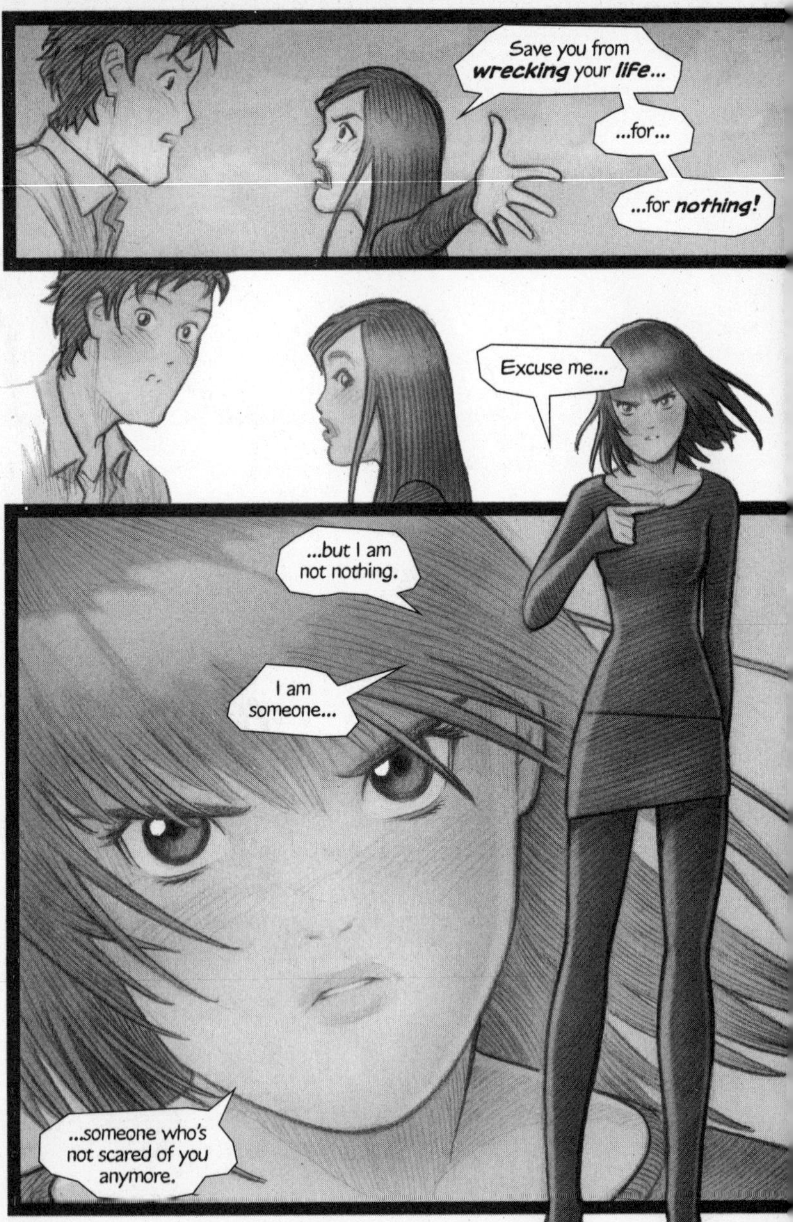
Save you from **wrecking** your **life...**
...for...
...for **nothing!**
Excuse me...
...but I am not nothing.
I am someone...
...someone who's not scared of you anymore.

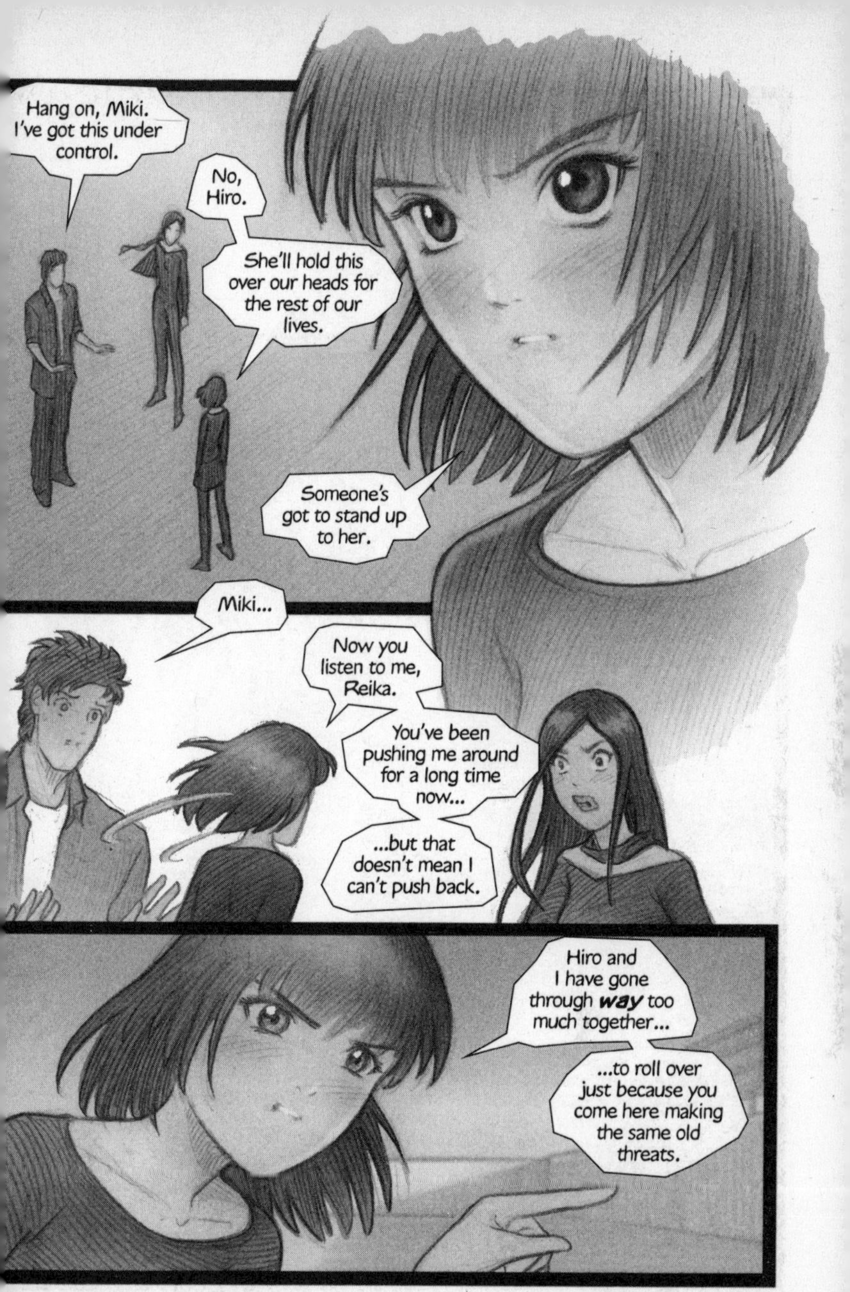
Hang on, Miki. I've got this under control.
No, Hiro.
She'll hold this over our heads for the rest of our lives.
Someone's got to stand up to her.
Miki...
Now you listen to me, Reika.
You've been pushing me around for a long time now...
...but that doesn't mean I can't push back.
Hiro and I have gone through ***way*** too much together...
...to roll over just because you come here making the same old threats.

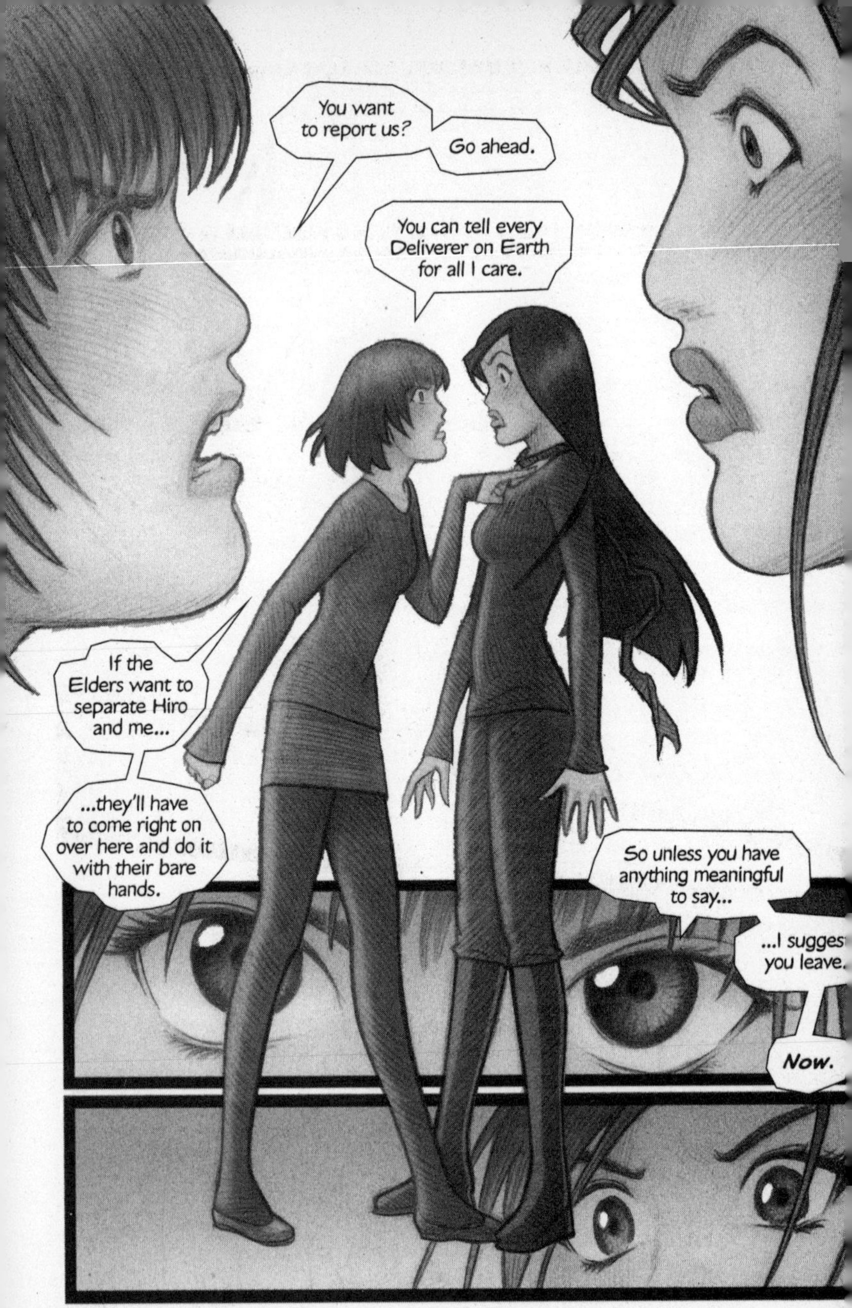
You want to report us?
Go ahead.
You can tell every Deliverer on Earth for all I care.
If the Elders want to separate Hiro and me...
...they'll have to come right on over here and do it with their bare hands.
So unless you have anything meaningful to say...
...I sugges you leave.
Now.

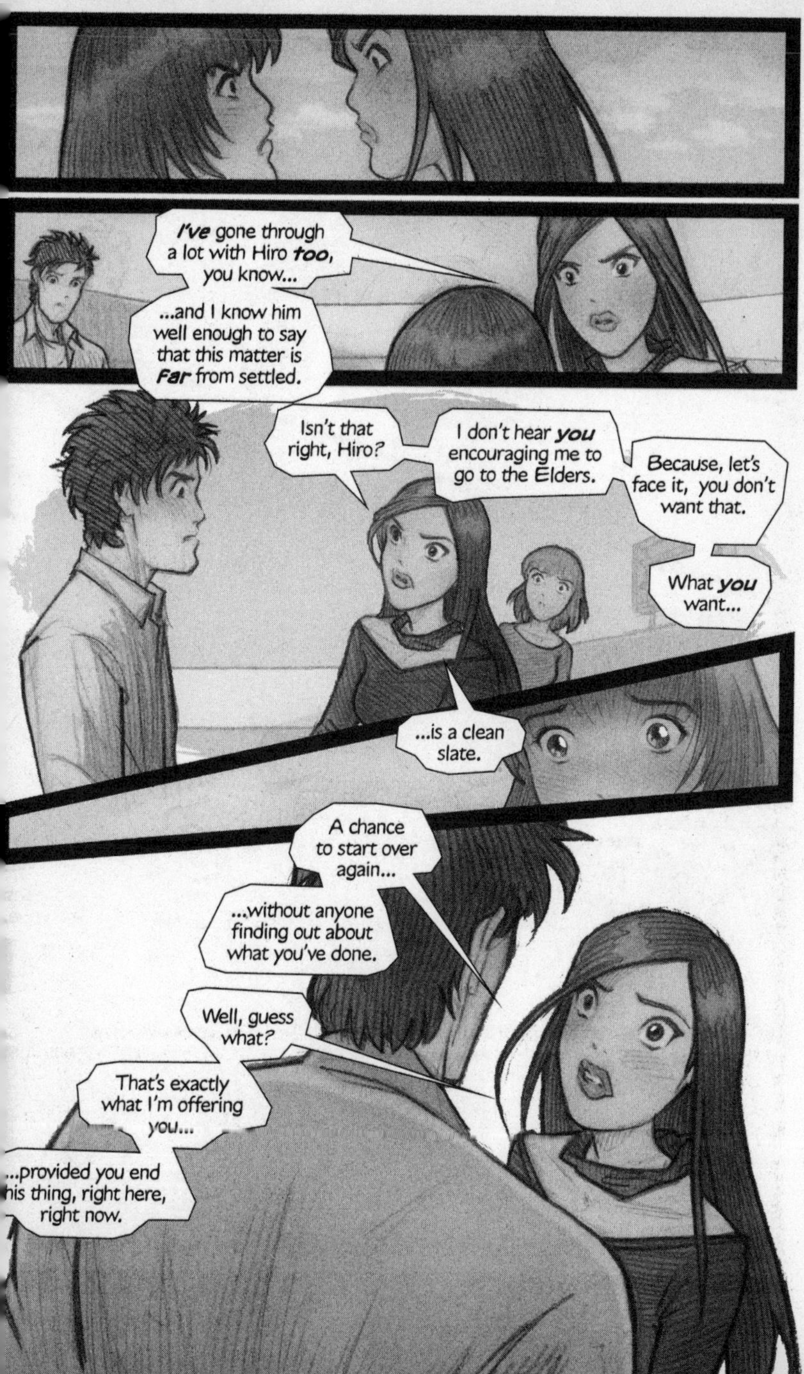
I've gone through a lot with Hiro *too*, you know...
...and I know him well enough to say that this matter is *far* from settled.
Isn't that right, Hiro?
I don't hear *you* encouraging me to go to the Elders.
Because, let's face it, you don't want that.
What *you* want...
...is a clean slate.
A chance to start over again...
...without anyone finding out about what you've done.
Well, guess what?
That's exactly what I'm offering you...
...provided you end his thing, right here, right now.

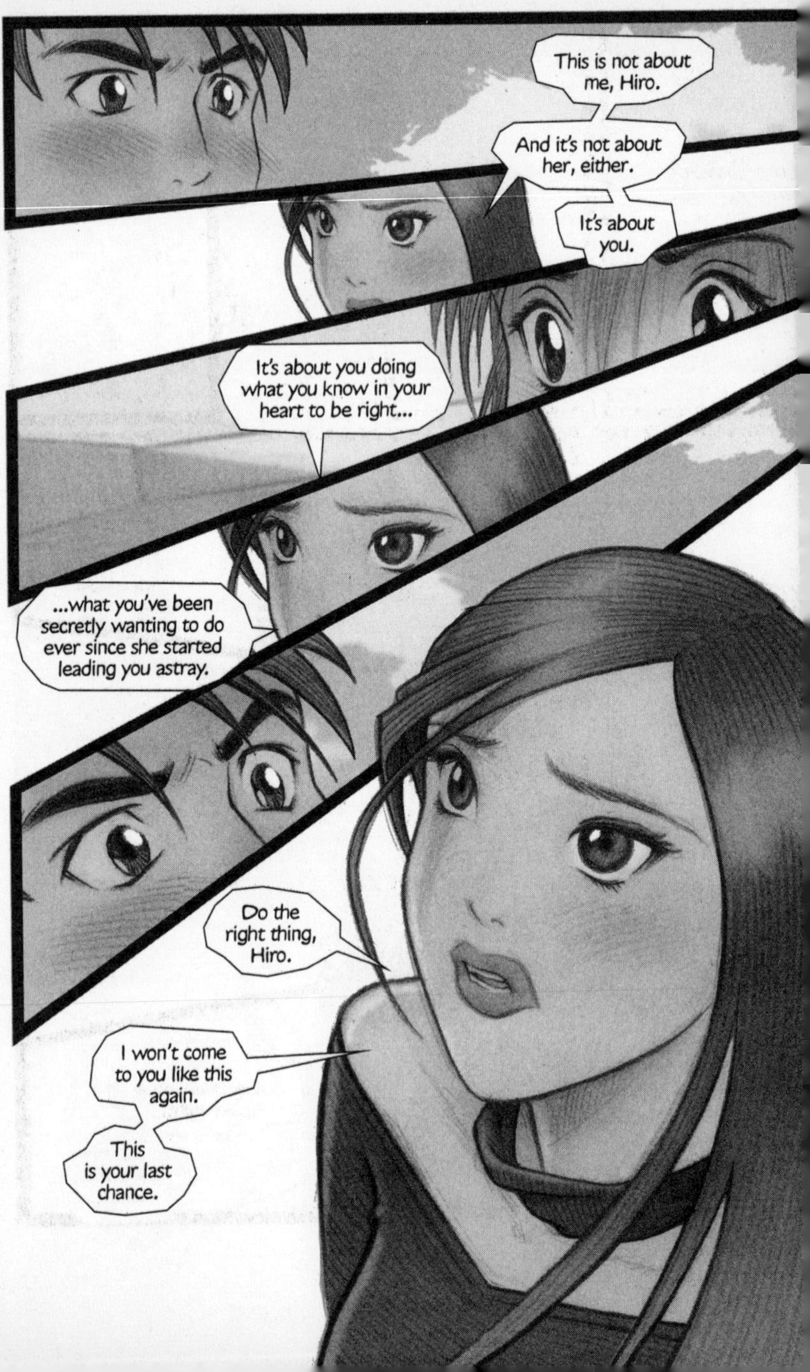
This is not about me, Hiro.
And it's not about her, either.
It's about you.
It's about you doing what you know in your heart to be right...
...what you've been secretly wanting to do ever since she started leading you astray.
Do the right thing, Hiro.
I won't come to you like this again.
This is your last chance.

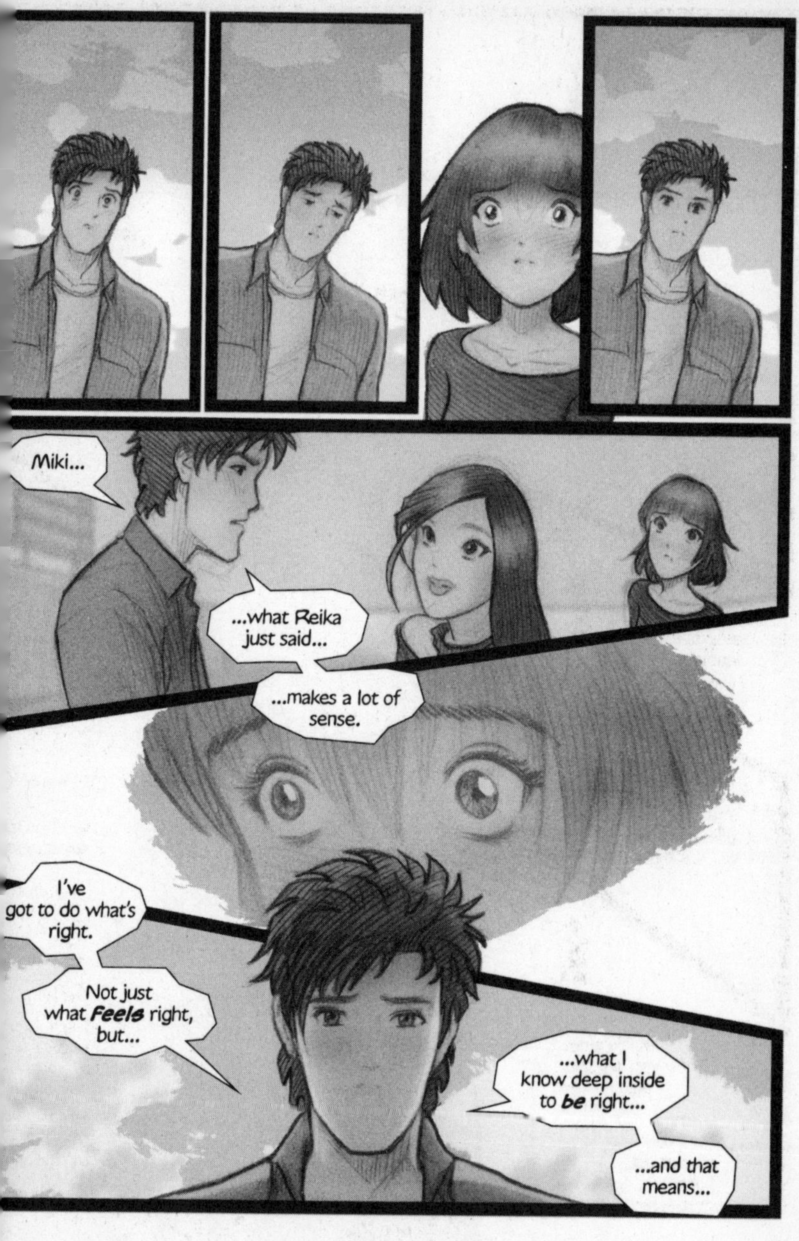
Miki...
...what Reika just said...
...makes a lot of sense.
I've got to do what's right.
Not just what *Feels* right, but...
...what I know deep inside to *be* right...
...and that means...

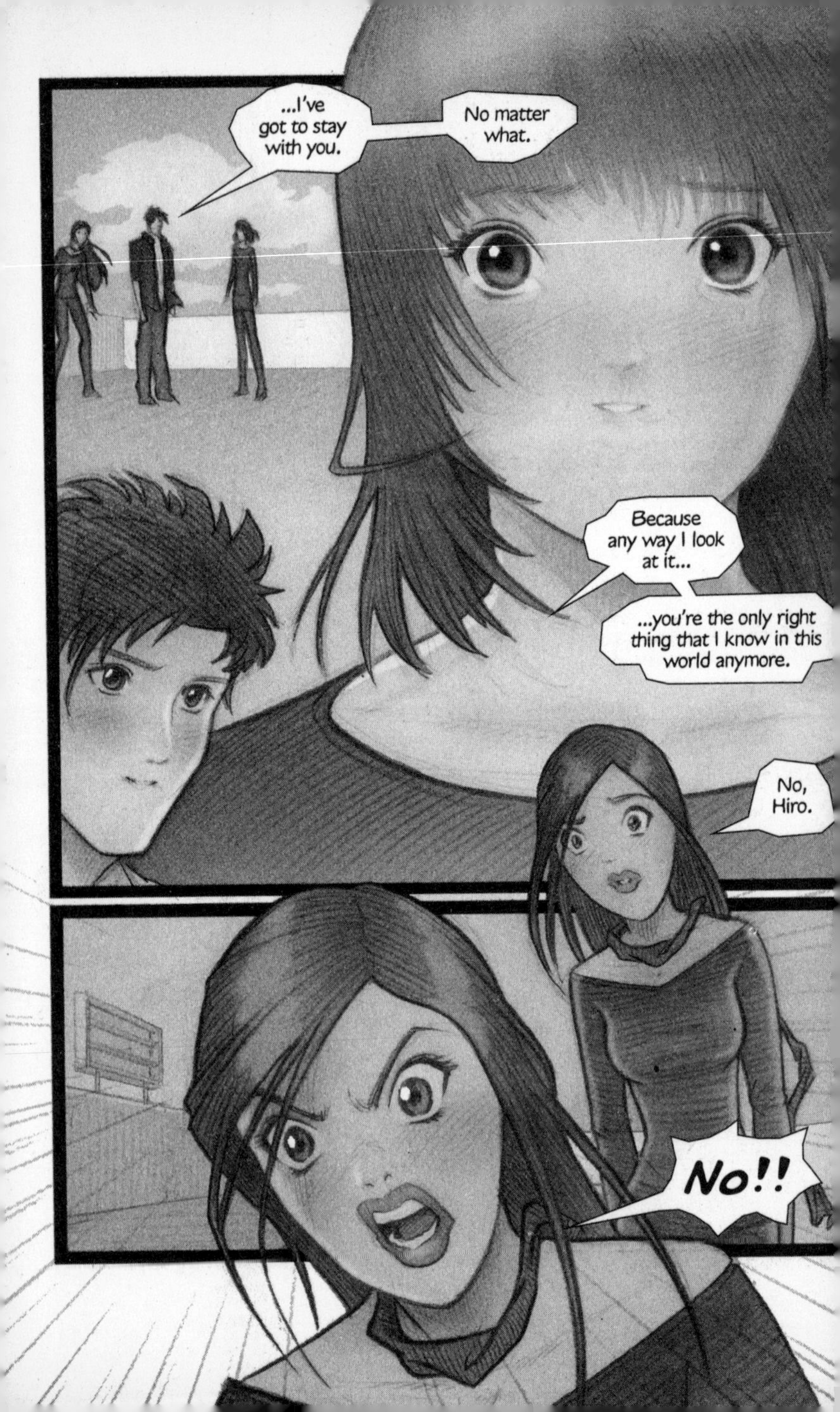
...I've got to stay with you.
No matter what.
Because any way I look at it...
...you're the only right thing that I know in this world anymore.
No, Hiro.
No!!

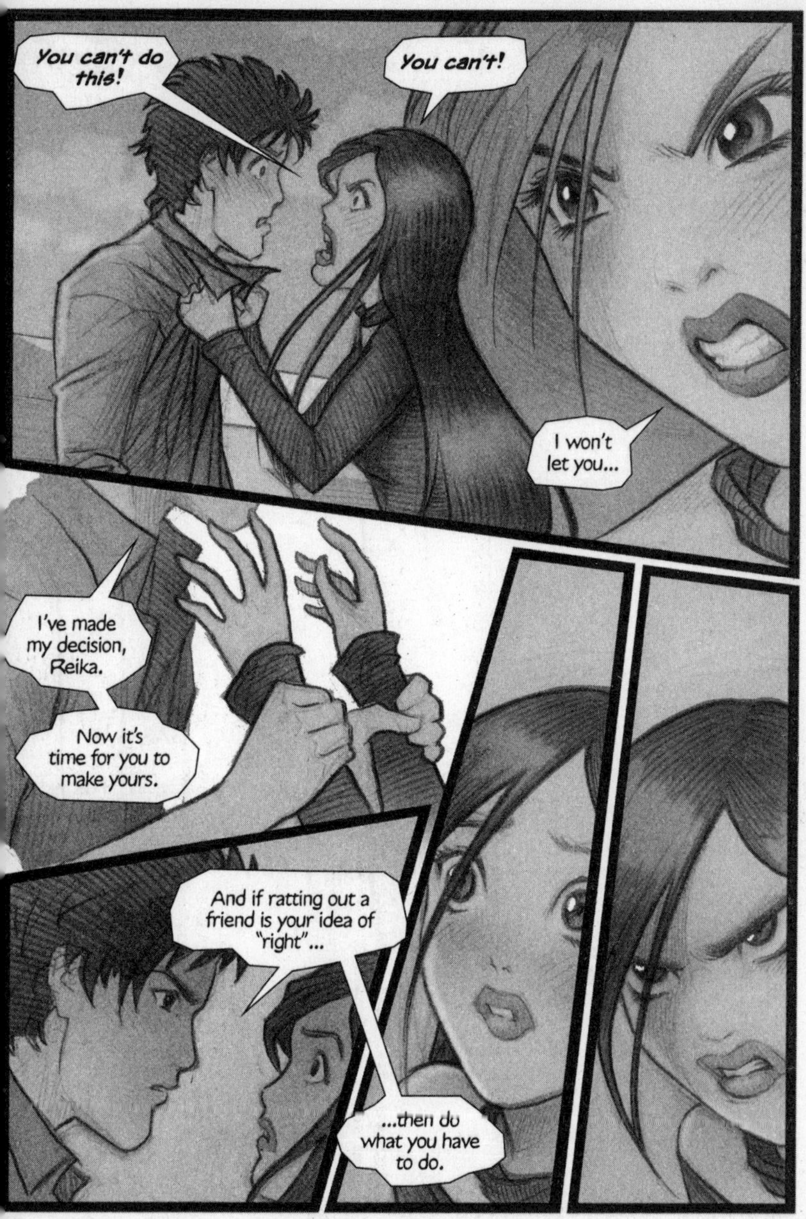

You can't do this!
You can't!
I won't let you...
I've made my decision, Reika.
Now it's time for you to make yours.
And if ratting out a friend is your idea of "right"...
...then do what you have to do.

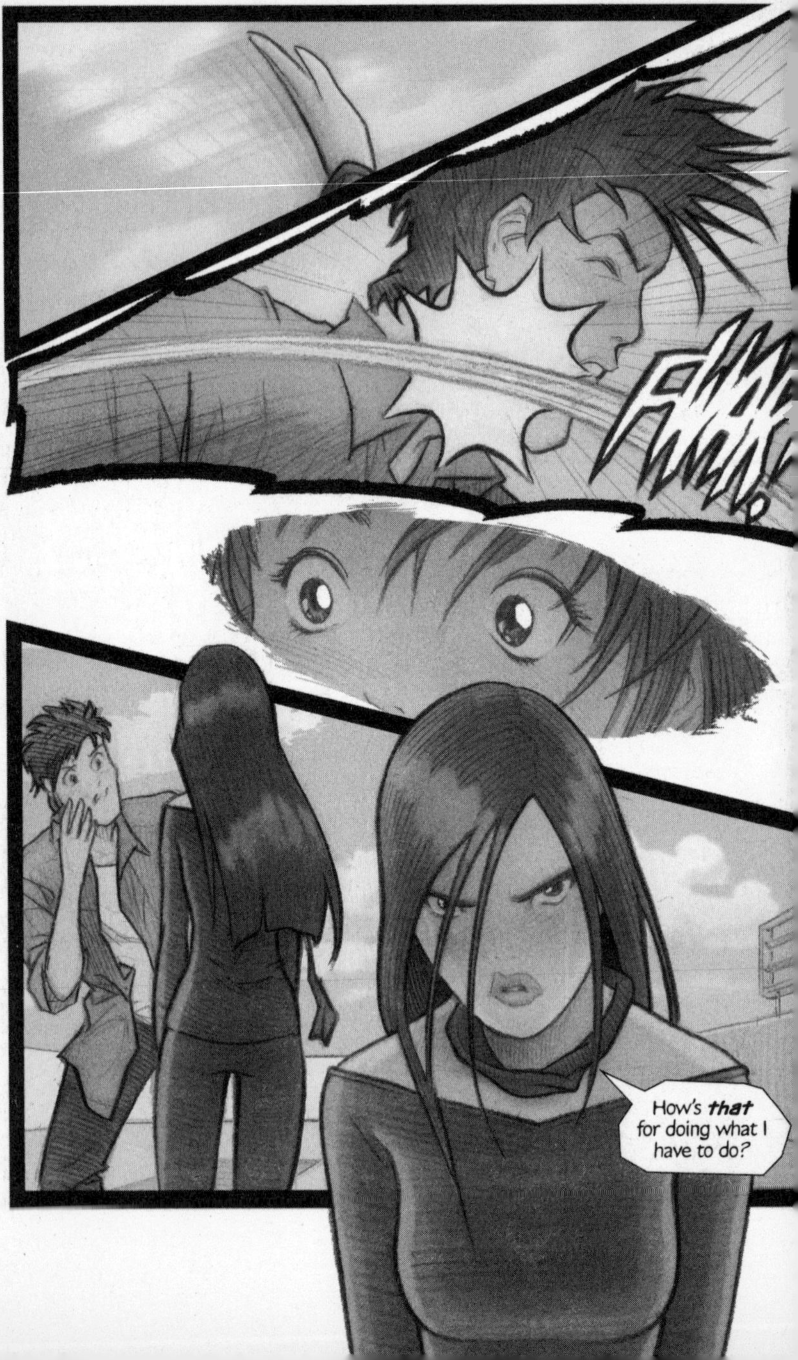
How's ***that*** for doing what I have to do?

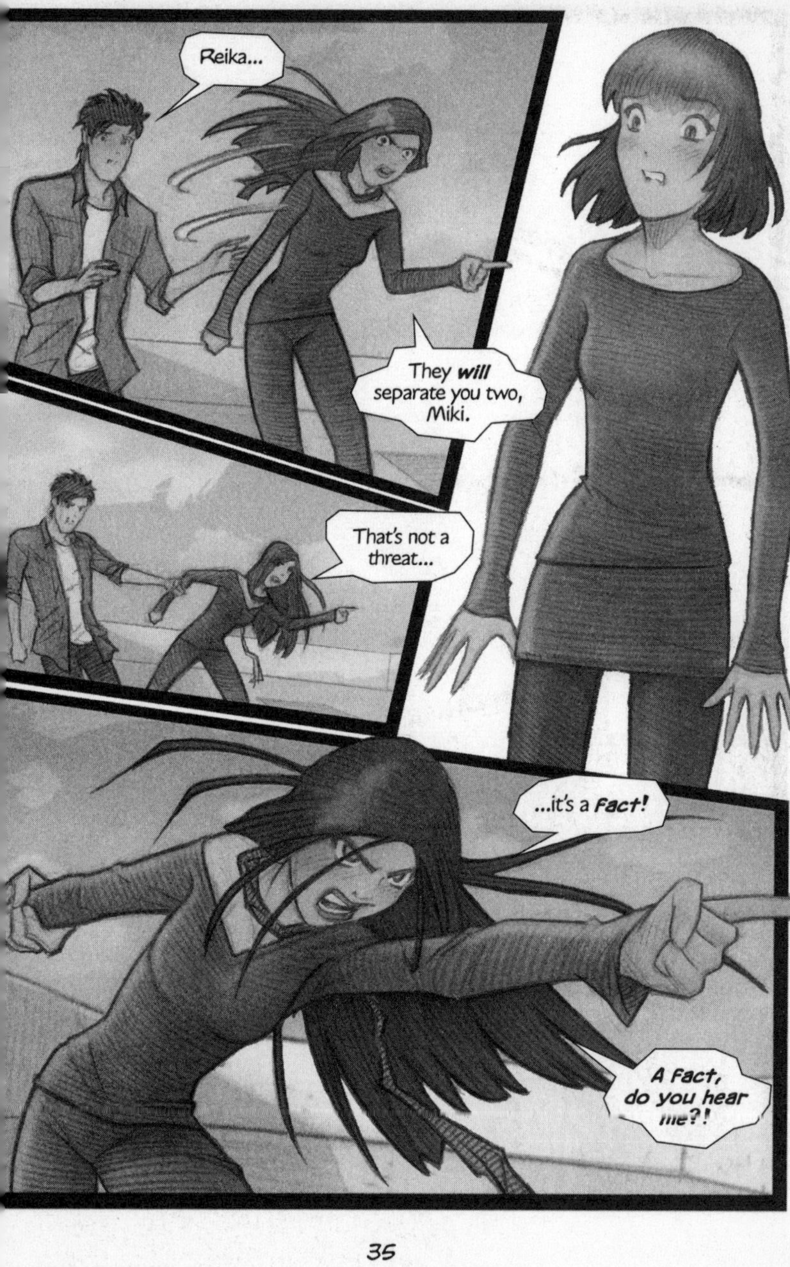
Reika...
They *will* separate you two, Miki.
That's not a threat...
...it's a *fact*!
A fact, do you hear me?!

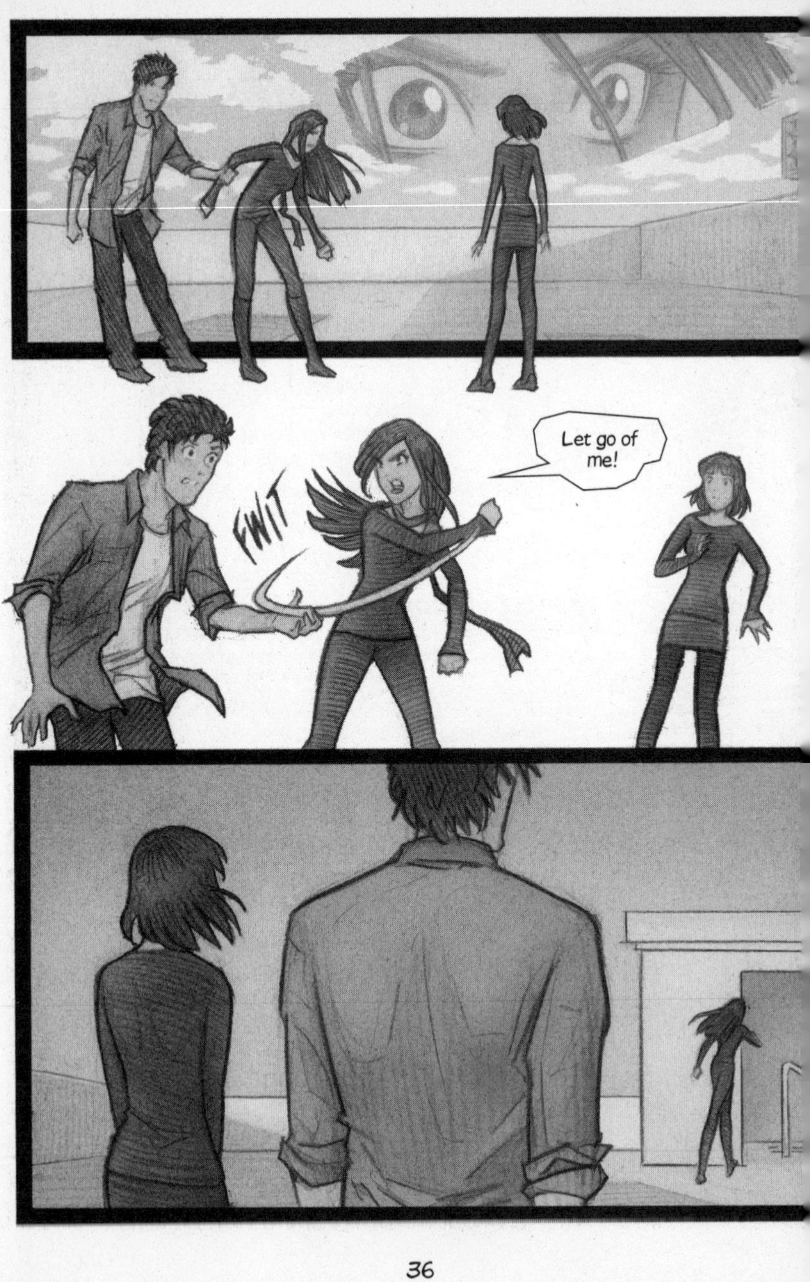
FWIT
Let go of me!

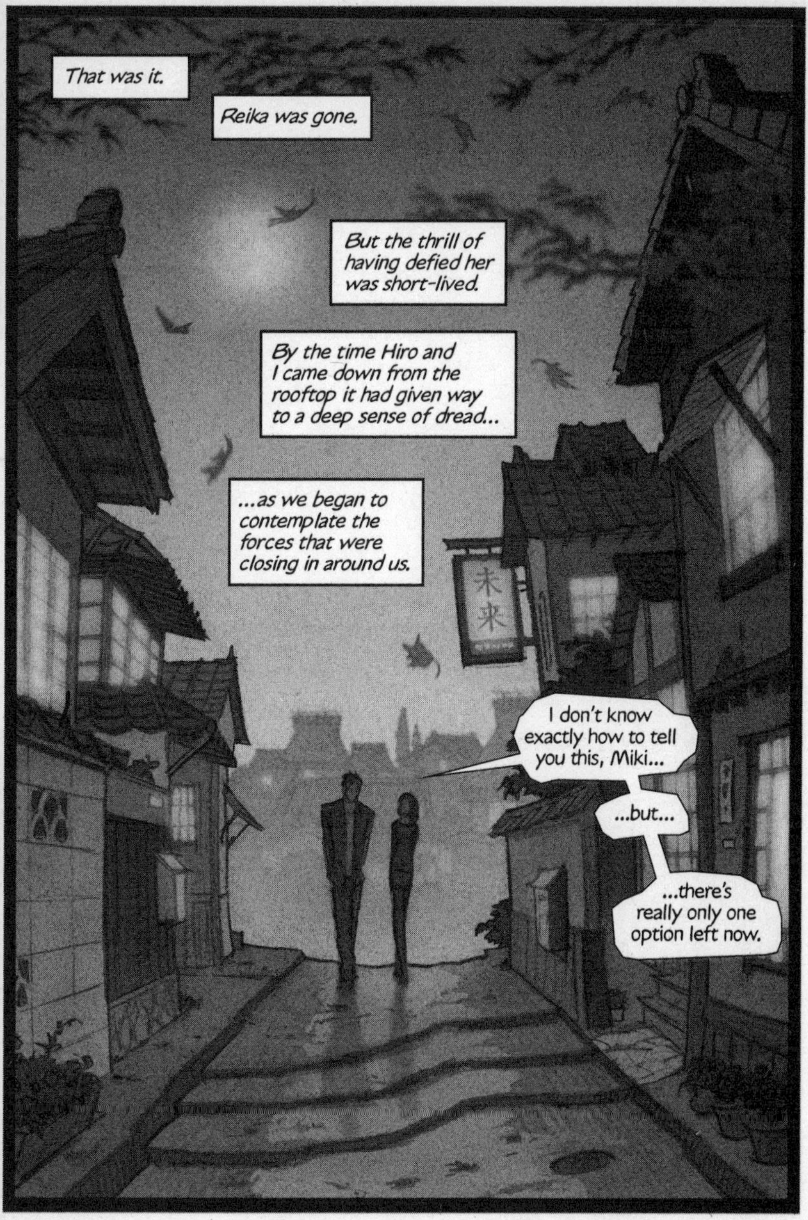

That was it.
Reika was gone.
But the thrill of having defied her was short-lived.
By the time Hiro and I came down from the rooftop it had given way to a deep sense of dread...
...as we began to contemplate the forces that were closing in around us.
未来
I don't know exactly how to tell you this, Miki...
...but...
...there's really only one option left now.

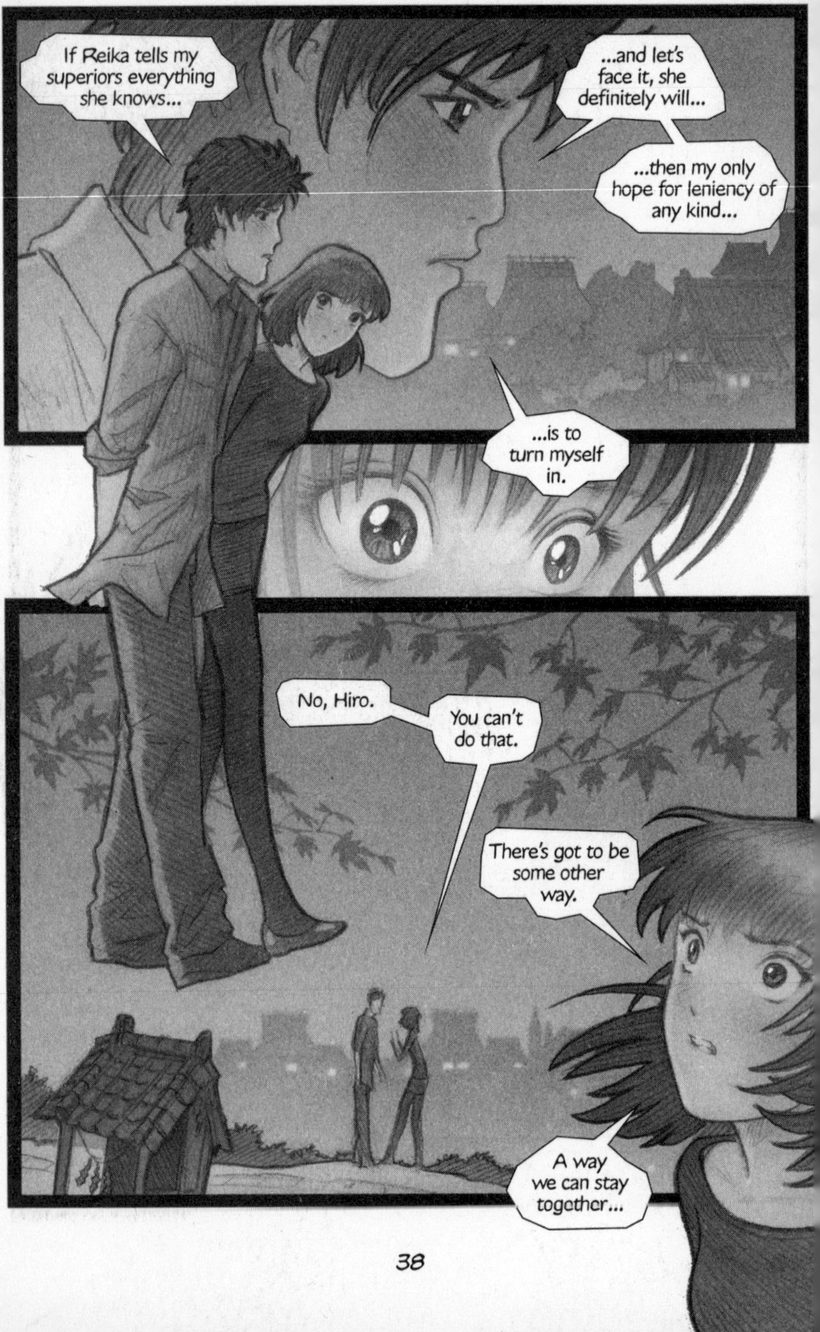
If Reika tells my superiors everything she knows...
...and let's face it, she definitely will...
...then my only hope for leniency of any kind...
...is to turn myself in.
No, Hiro.
You can't do that.
There's got to be some other way.
A way we can stay together...

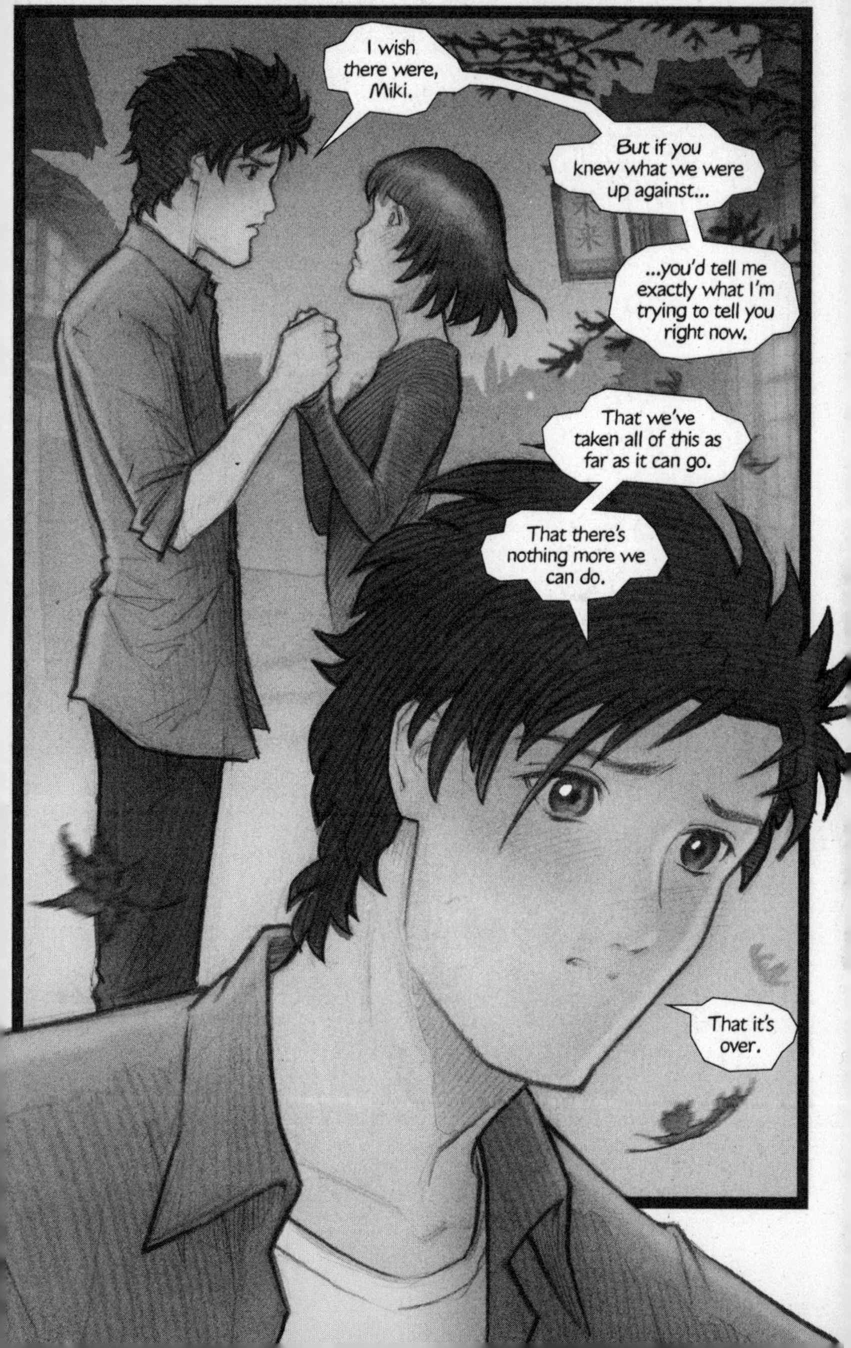
I wish there were, Miki.
But if you knew what we were up against...
...you'd tell me exactly what I'm trying to tell you right now.
That we've taken all of this as far as it can go.
That there's nothing more we can do.
That it's over.

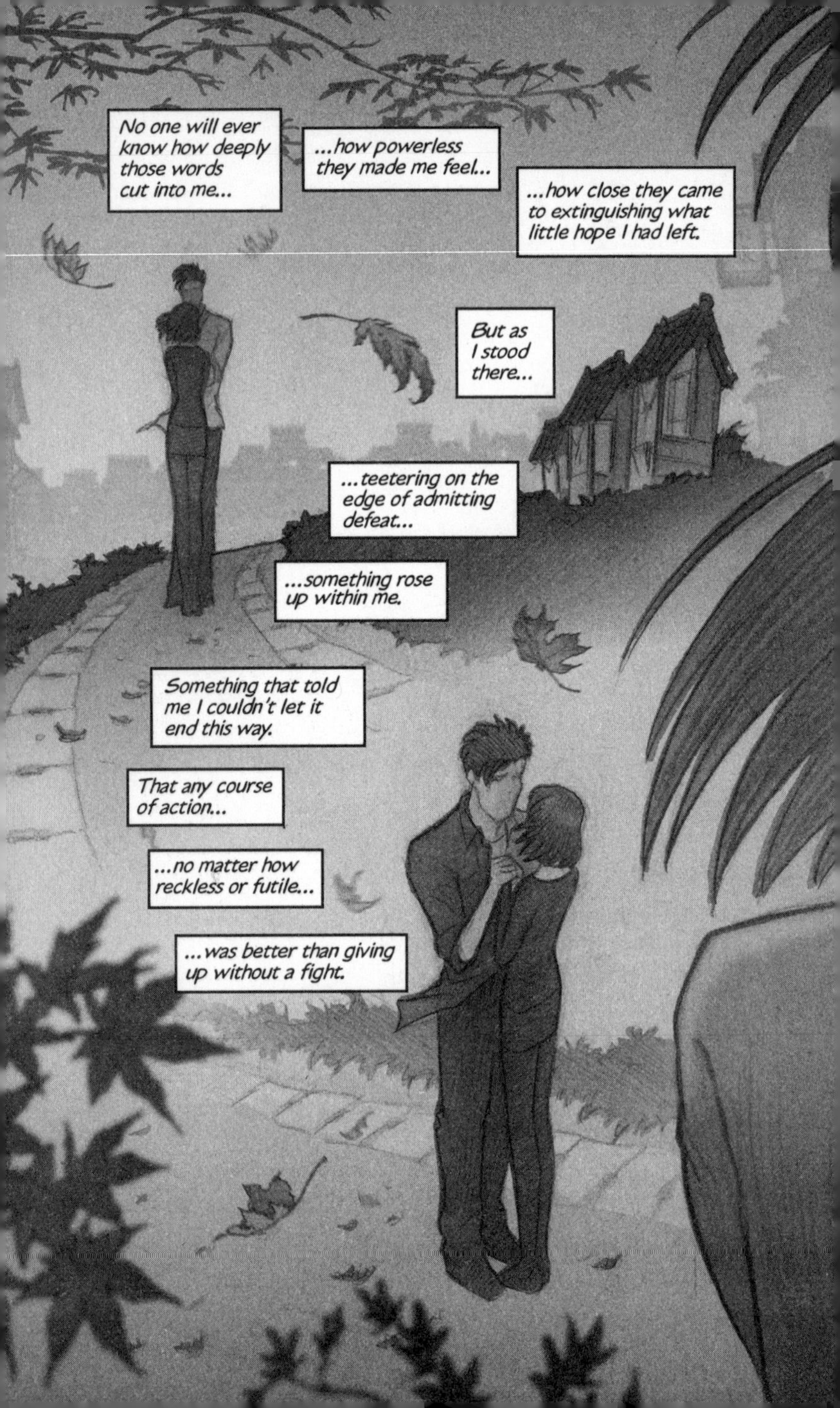
No one will ever know how deeply those words cut into me...
...how powerless they made me feel...
...how close they came to extinguishing what little hope I had left.
But as I stood there...
...teetering on the edge of admitting defeat...
...something rose up within me.
Something that told me I couldn't let it end this way.
That any course of action...
...no matter how reckless or futile...
...was better than giving up without a fight.

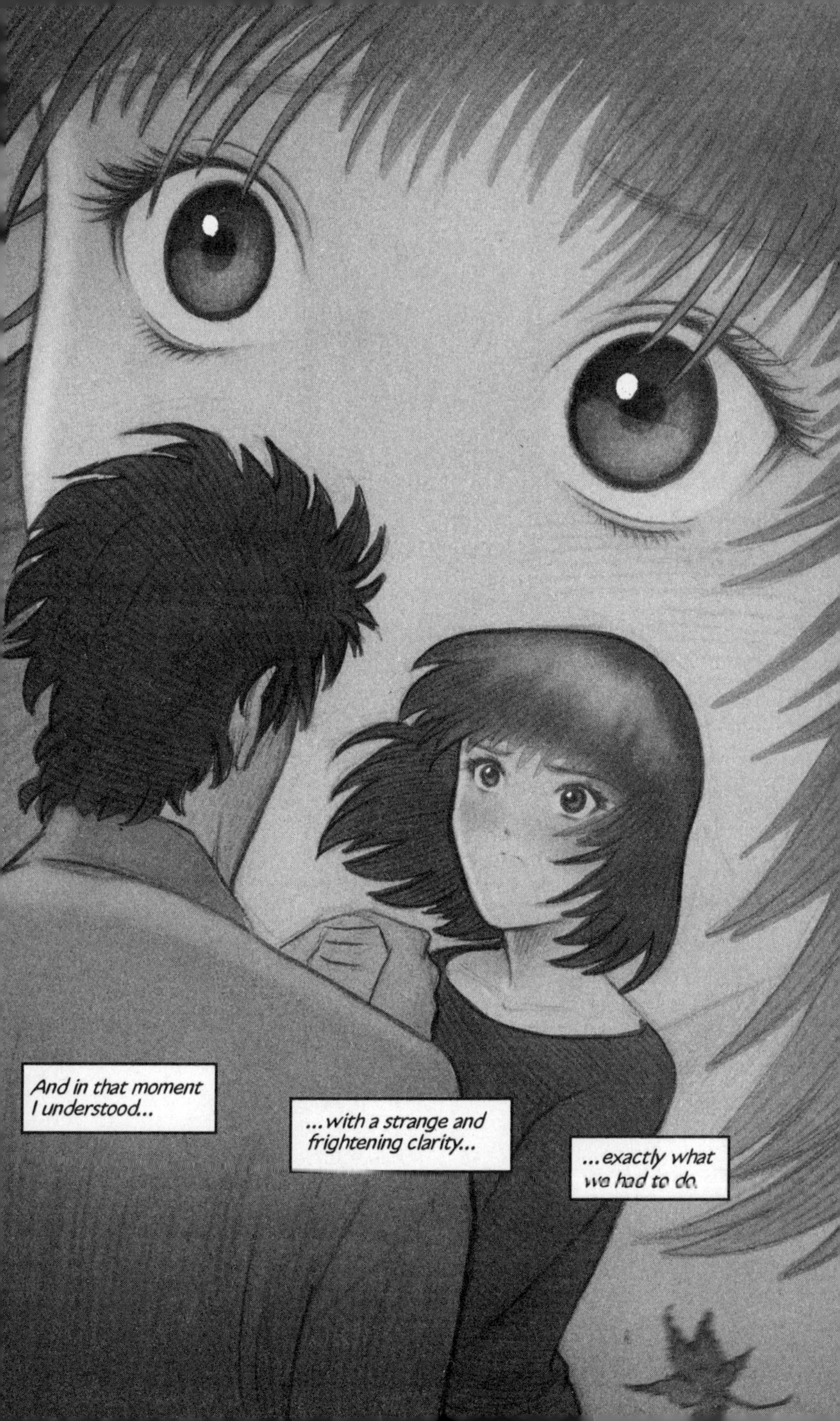
And in that moment I understood...
...with a strange and frightening clarity...
...exactly what we had to do.

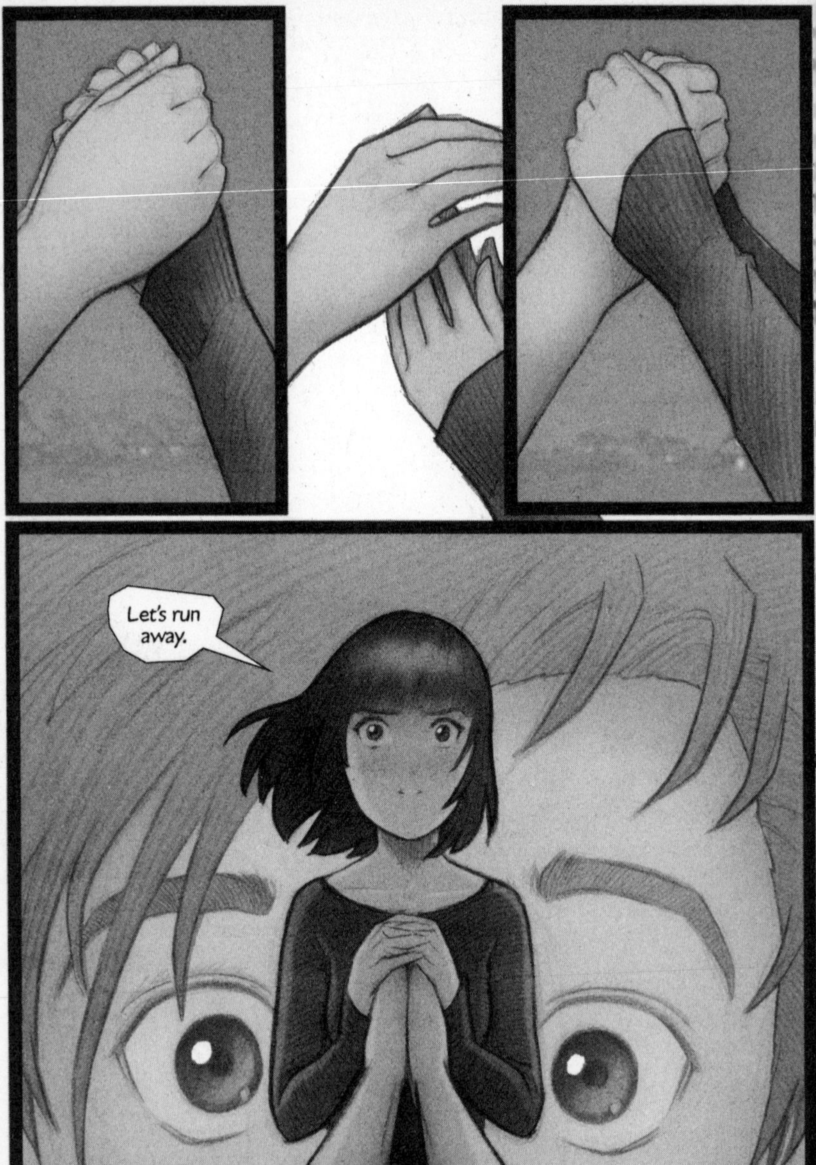
Let's run away.

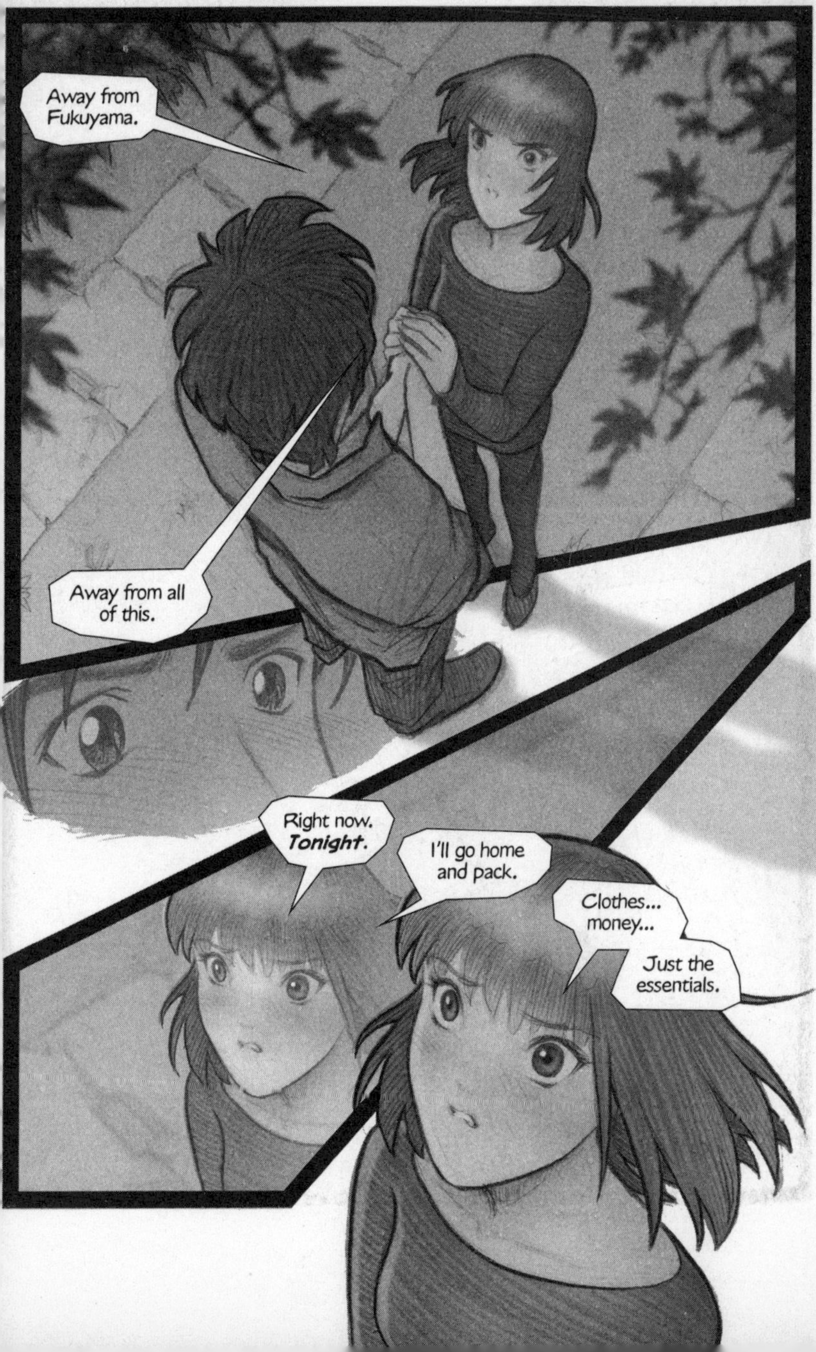
Away from Fukuyama.
Away from all of this.
Right now. *Tonight*.
I'll go home and pack.
Clothes... money...
Just the essentials.

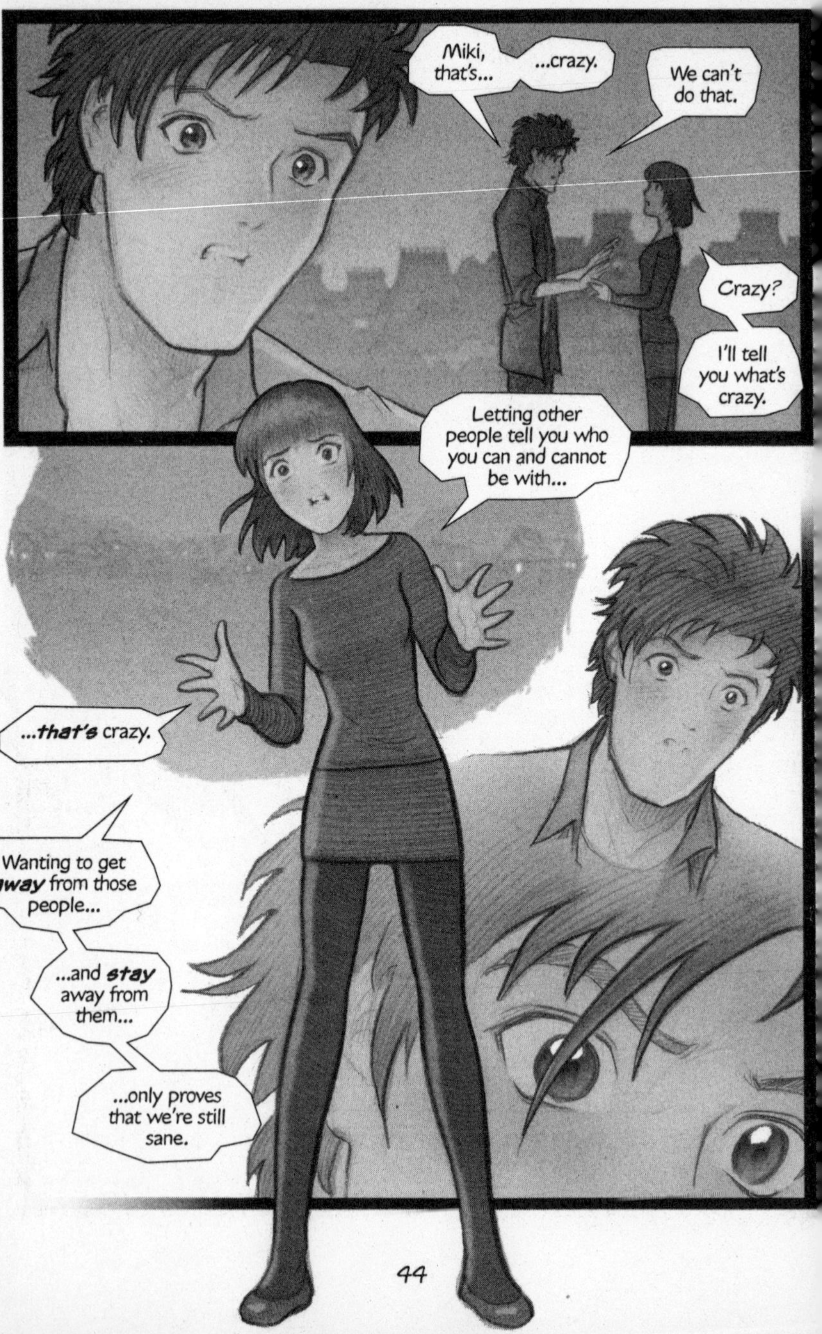

Miki, that's...
...crazy.
We can't do that.
Crazy?
I'll tell you what's crazy.
Letting other people tell you who you can and cannot be with...
...*that's* crazy.
Wanting to get **away** from those people...
...and **stay** away from them...
...only proves that we're still sane.

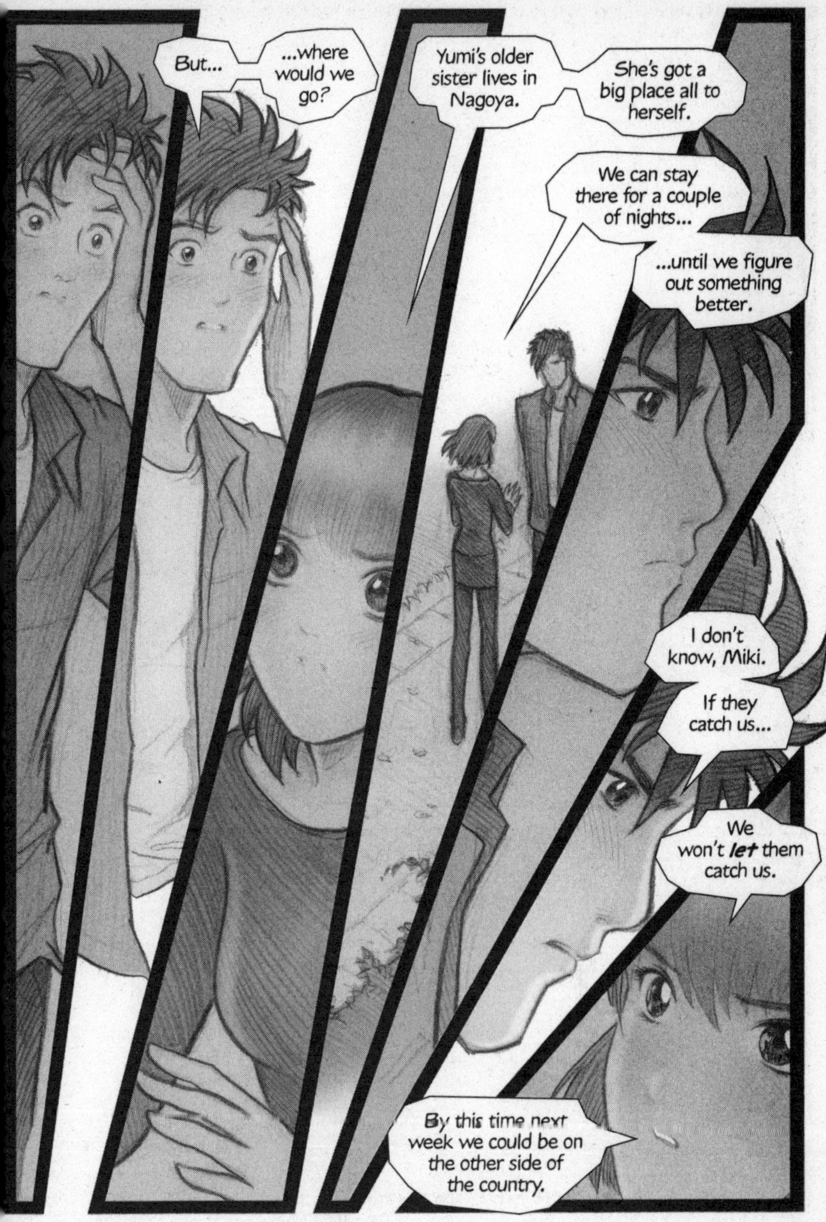
But...
...where would we go?
Yumi's older sister lives in Nagoya.
She's got a big place all to herself.
We can stay there for a couple of nights...
...until we figure out something better.
I don't know, Miki.
If they catch us...
We won't *let* them catch us.
By this time next week we could be on the other side of the country.

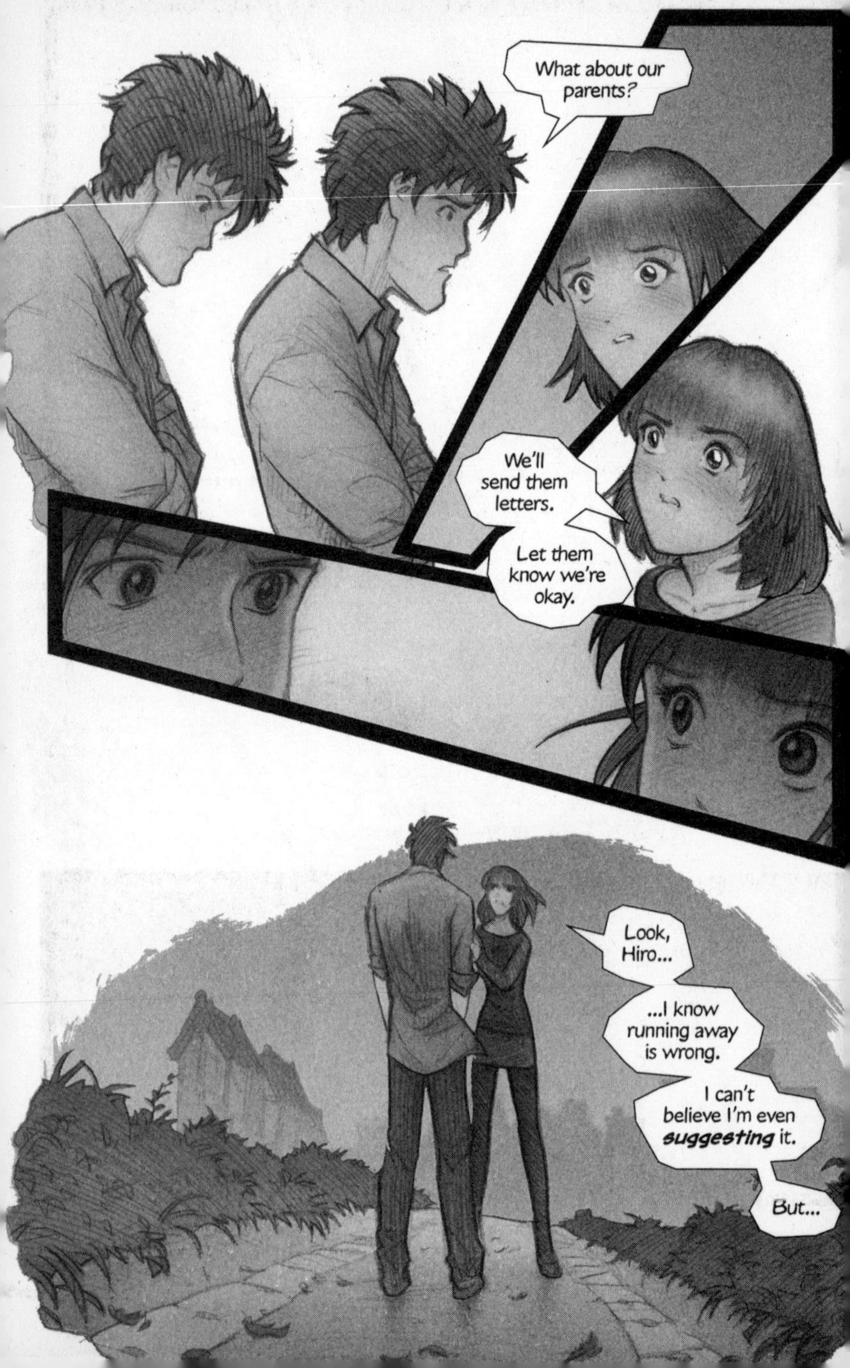
What about our parents?
We'll send them letters.
Let them know we're okay.
Look, Hiro...
...I know running away is wrong.
I can't believe I'm even *suggesting* it.
But...

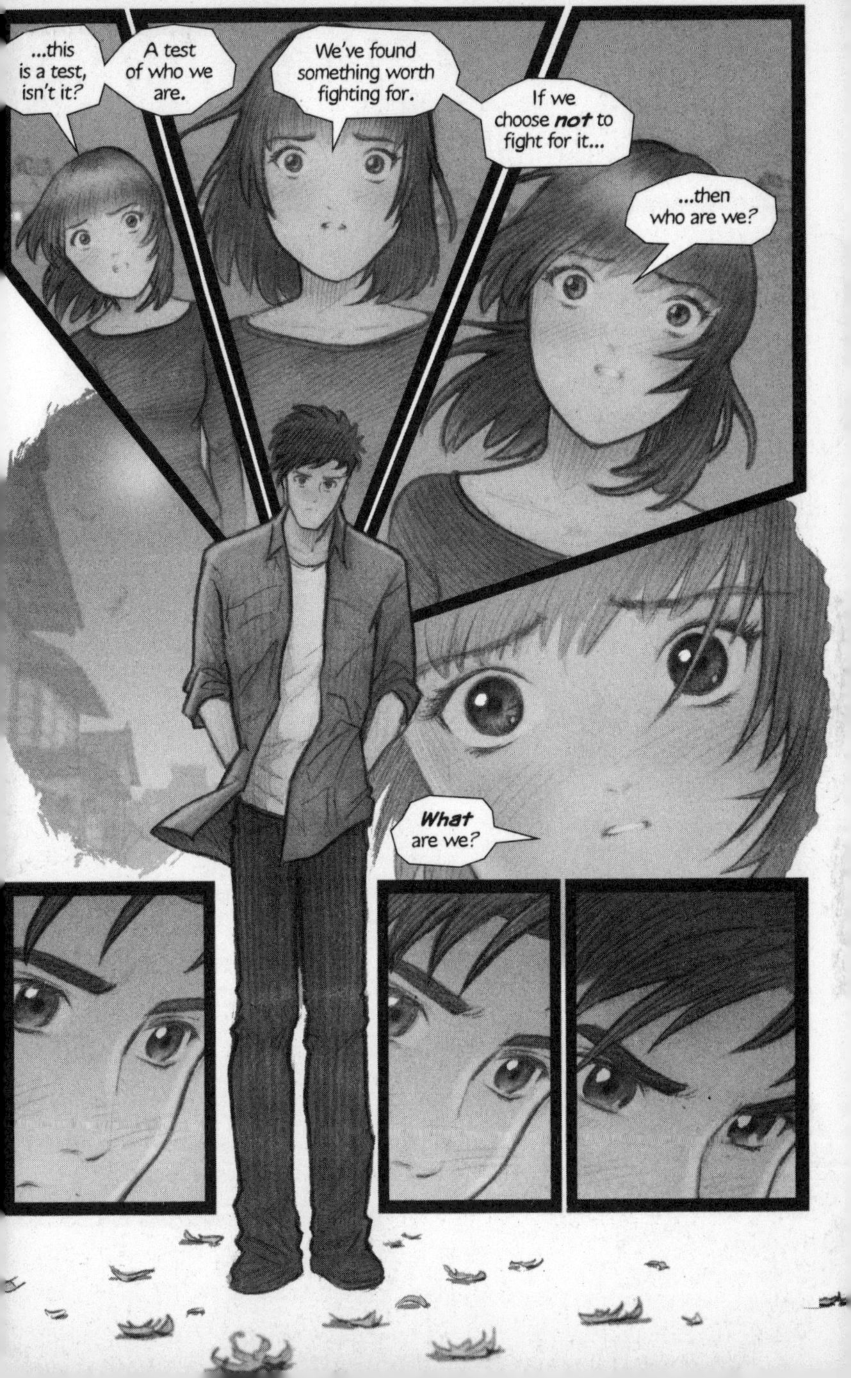
...this is a test, isn't it?
A test of who we are.
We've found something worth fighting for.
If we choose ***not*** to fight for it...
...then who are we?
What are we?

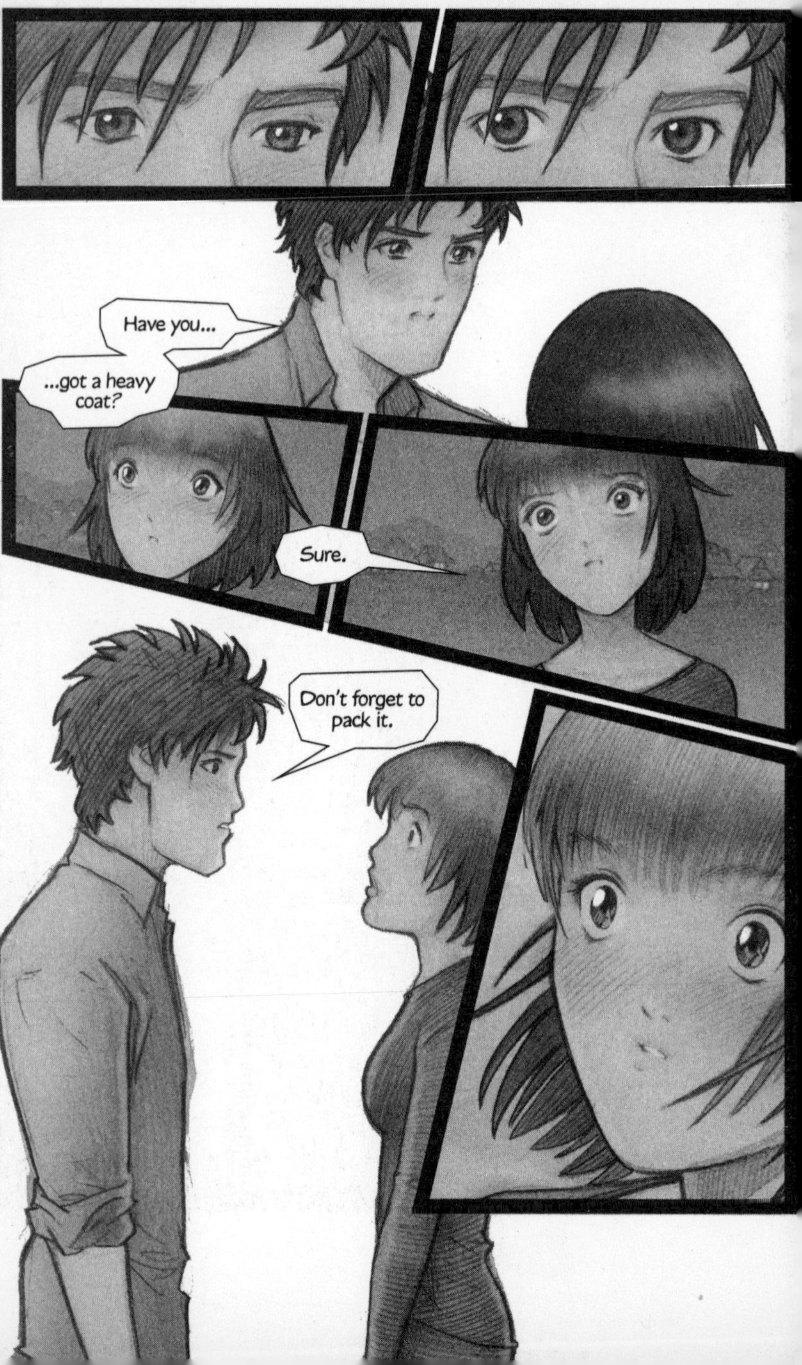
Have you...
...got a heavy coat?
Sure.
Don't forget to pack it.

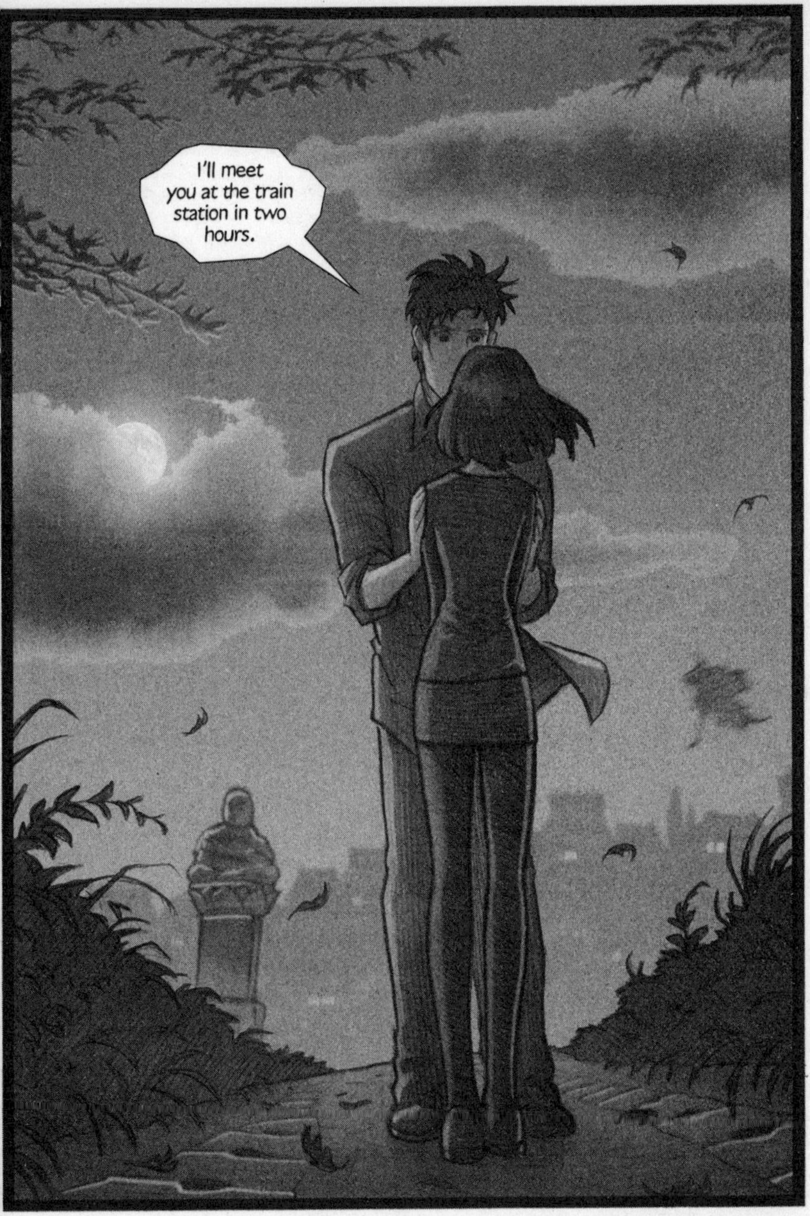
I'll meet you at the train station in two hours.

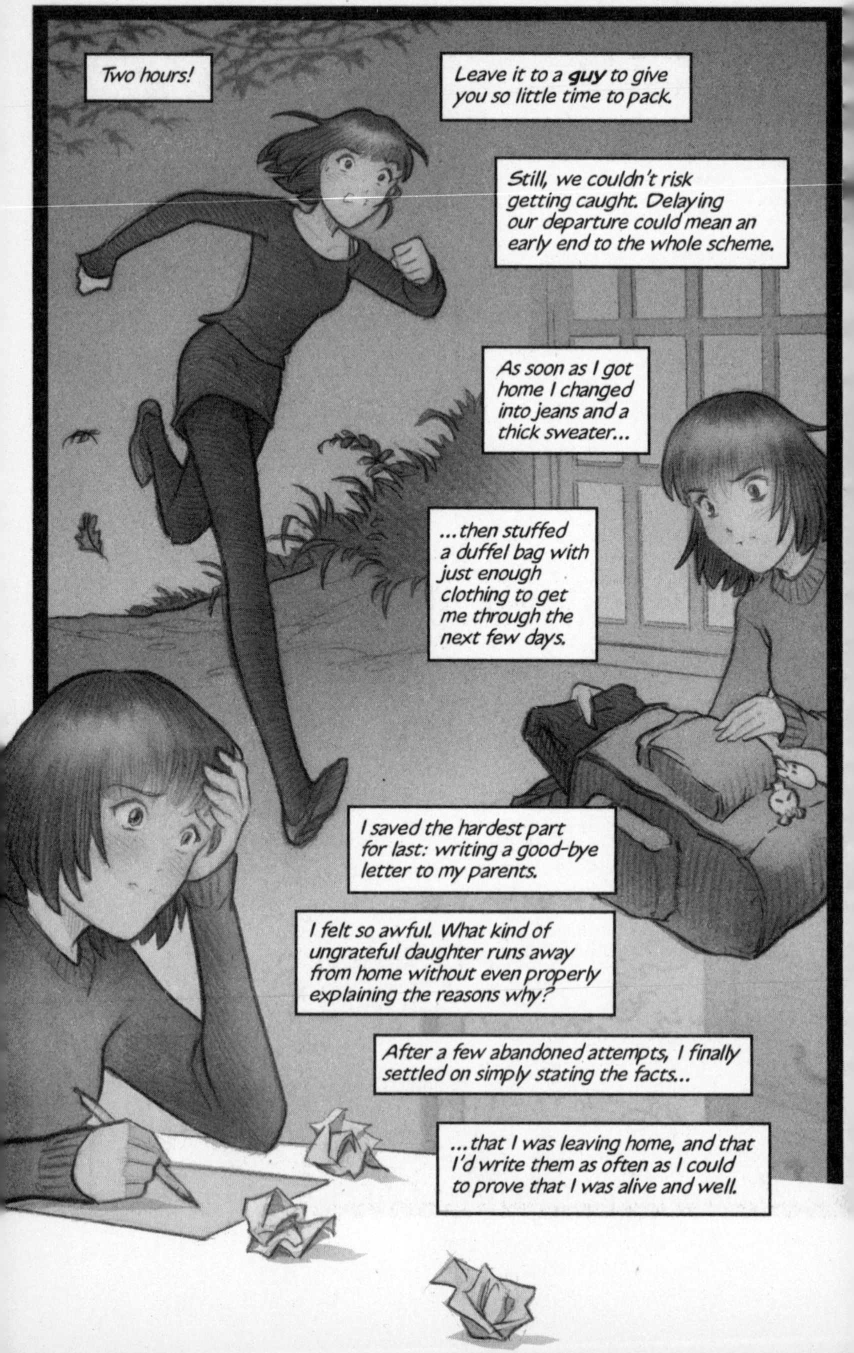

Two hours!
Leave it to a **guy** to give you so little time to pack.
Still, we couldn't risk getting caught. Delaying our departure could mean an early end to the whole scheme.
As soon as I got home I changed into jeans and a thick sweater...
...then stuffed a duffel bag with just enough clothing to get me through the next few days.
I saved the hardest part for last: writing a good-bye letter to my parents.
I felt so awful. What kind of ungrateful daughter runs away from home without even properly explaining the reasons why?
After a few abandoned attempts, I finally settled on simply stating the facts...
...that I was leaving home, and that I'd write them as often as I could to prove that I was alive and well.

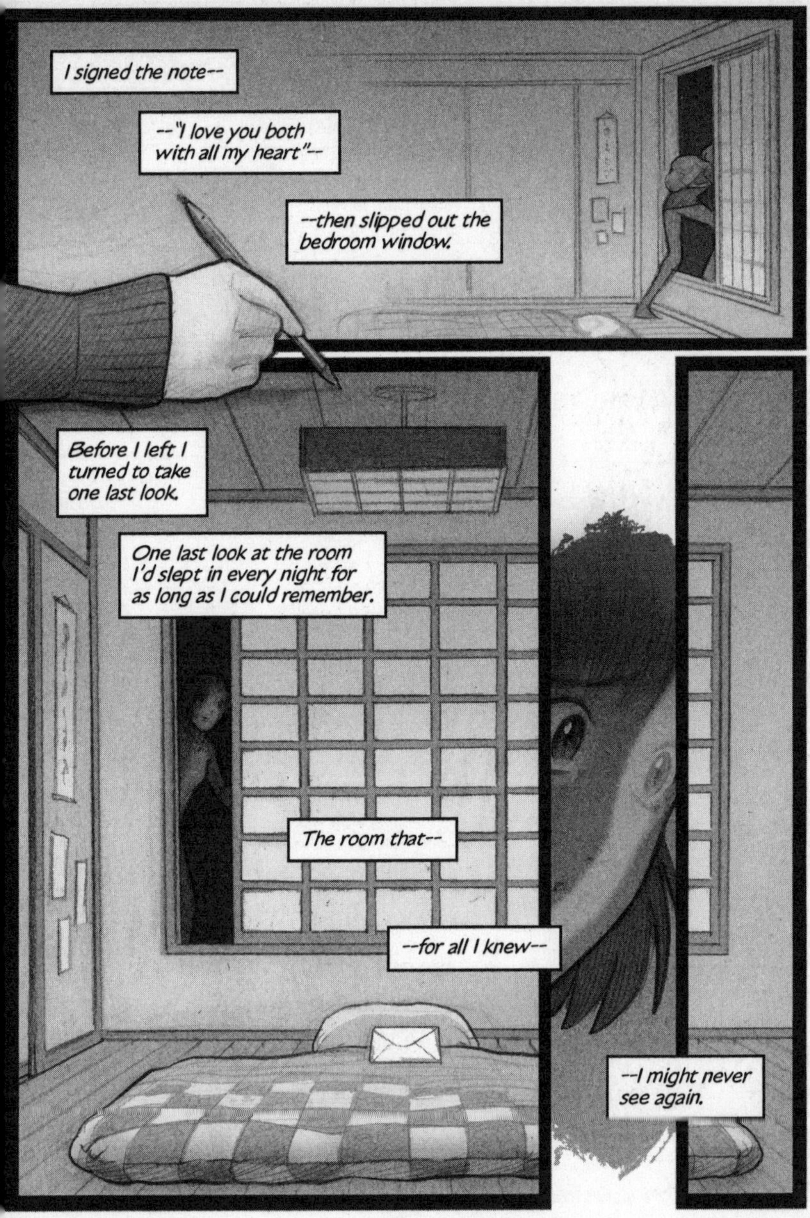
I signed the note--
--"I love you both with all my heart"--
--then slipped out the bedroom window.
Before I left I turned to take one last look.
One last look at the room I'd slept in every night for as long as I could remember.
The room that--
--for all I knew--
--I might never see again.

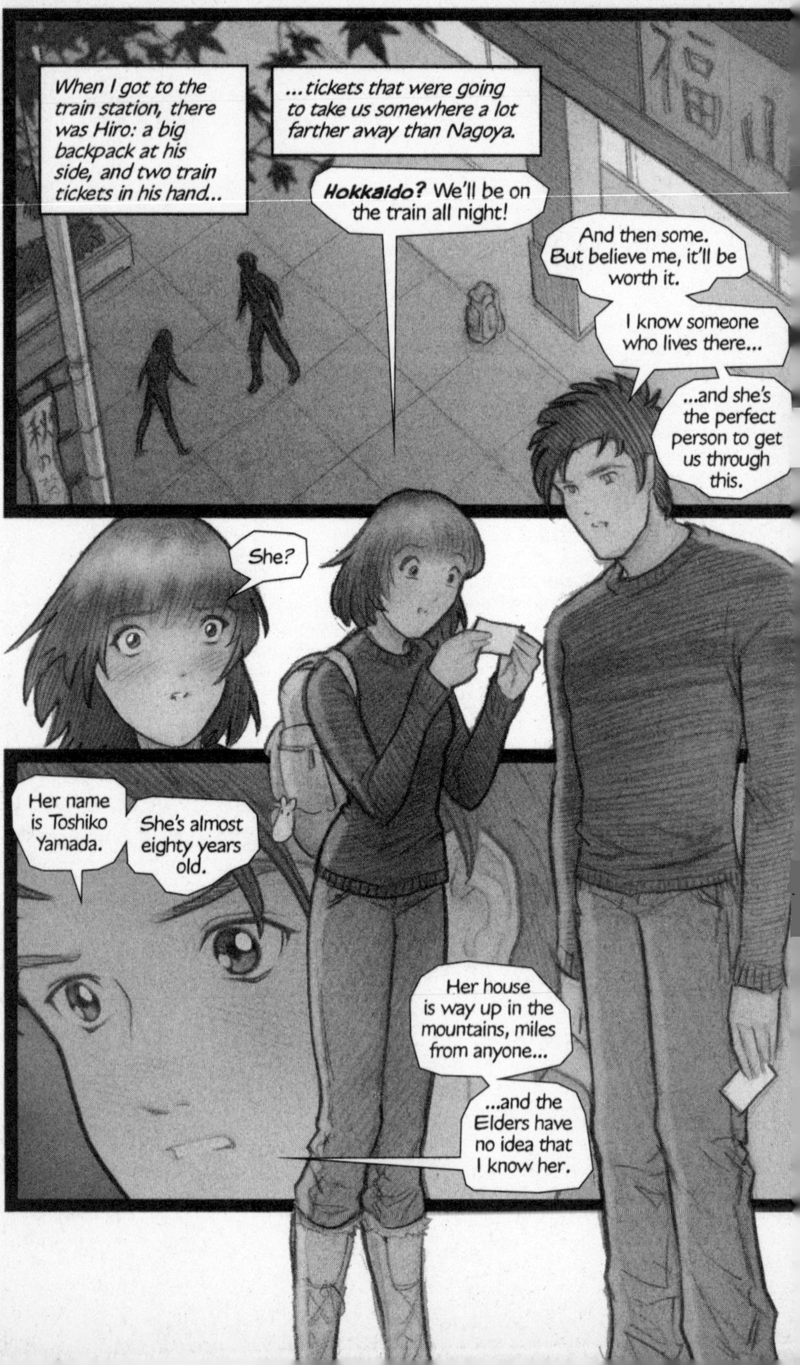
When I got to the train station, there was Hiro: a big backpack at his side, and two train tickets in his hand...
...tickets that were going to take us somewhere a lot farther away than Nagoya.
Hokkaido? We'll be on the train all night!
And then some. But believe me, it'll be worth it.
I know someone who lives there...
...and she's the perfect person to get us through this.
She?
Her name is Toshiko Yamada.
She's almost eighty years old.
Her house is way up in the mountains, miles from anyone...
...and the Elders have no idea that I know her.

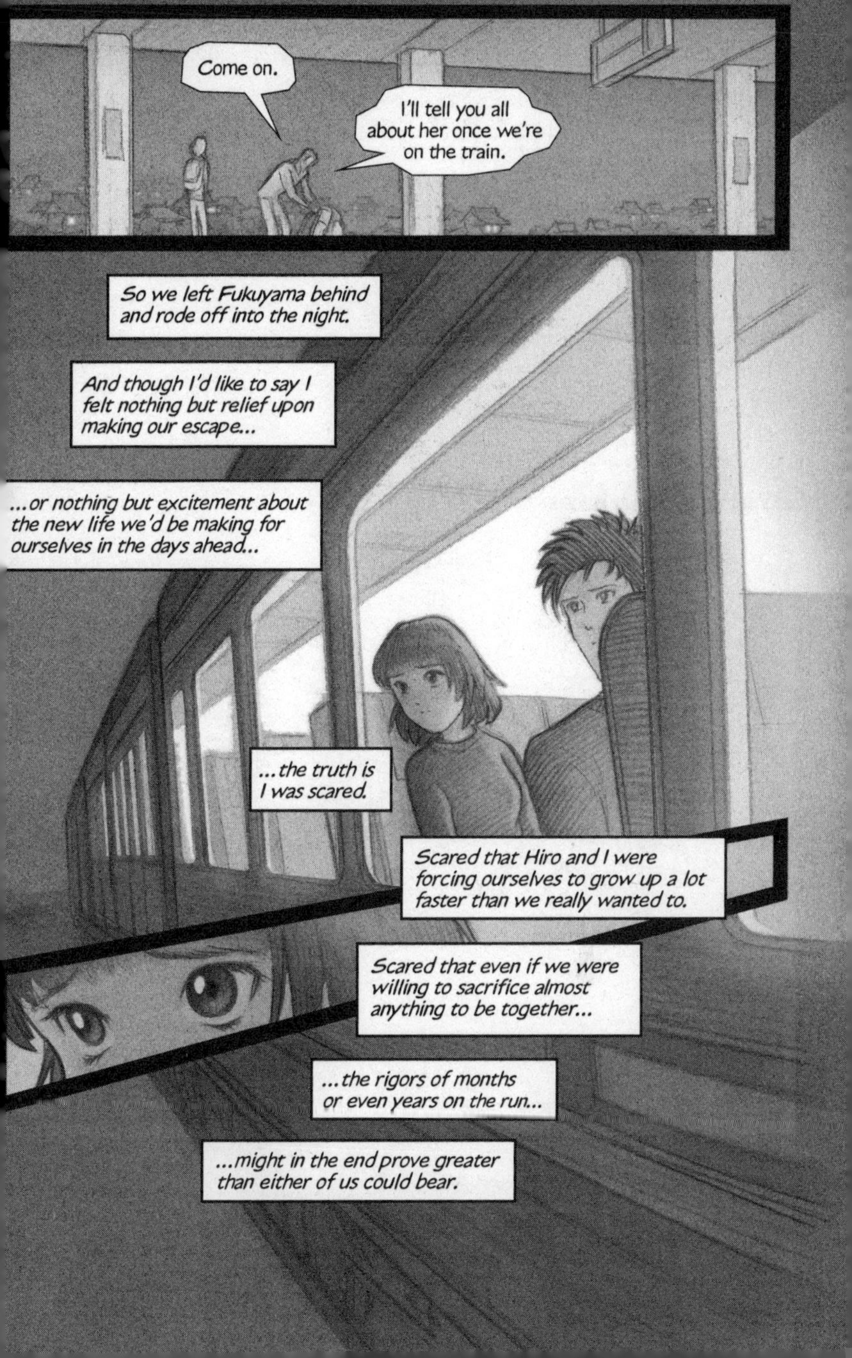
Come on.
I'll tell you all about her once we're on the train.
So we left Fukuyama behind and rode off into the night.
And though I'd like to say I felt nothing but relief upon making our escape...
...or nothing but excitement about the new life we'd be making for ourselves in the days ahead...
...the truth is I was scared.
Scared that Hiro and I were forcing ourselves to grow up a lot faster than we really wanted to.
Scared that even if we were willing to sacrifice almost anything to be together...
...the rigors of months or even years on the run...
...might in the end prove greater than either of us could bear.

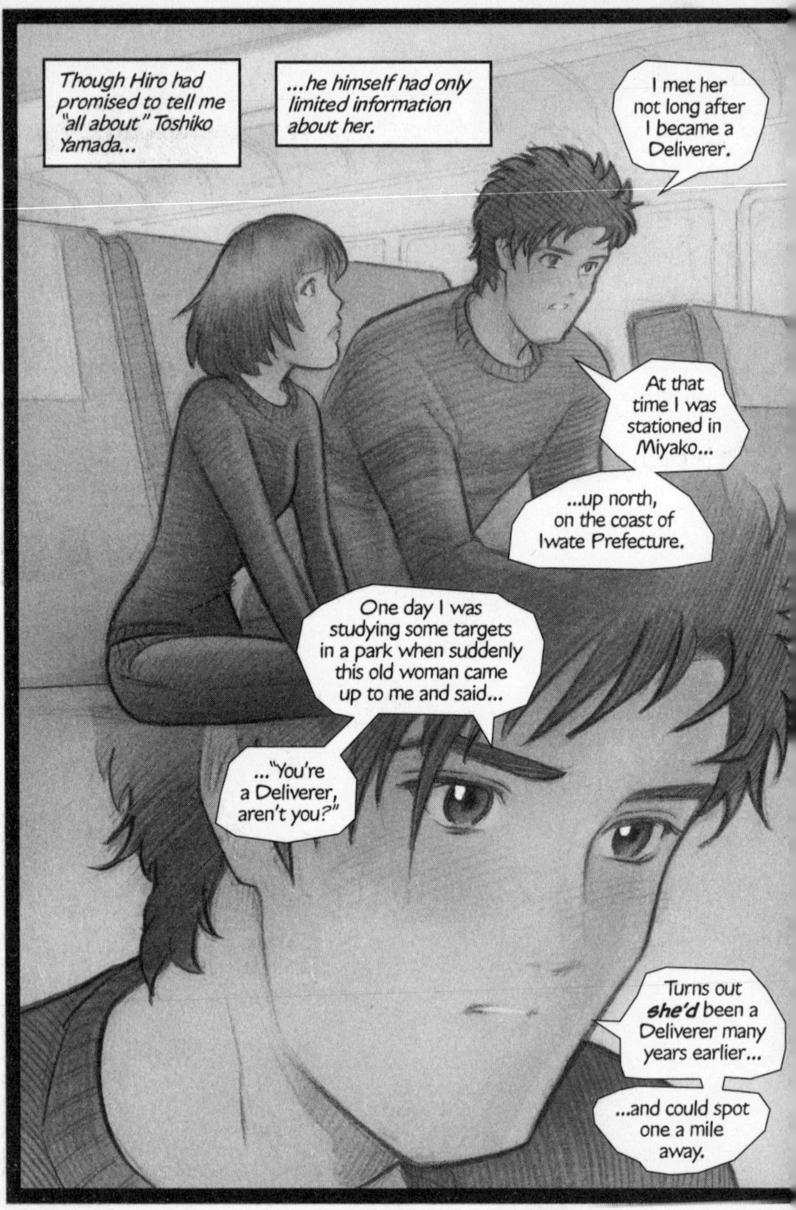
Though Hiro had promised to tell me "all about" Toshiko Yamada...
...he himself had only limited information about her.
I met her not long after I became a Deliverer.
At that time I was stationed in Miyako...
...up north, on the coast of Iwate Prefecture.
One day I was studying some targets in a park when suddenly this old woman came up to me and said...
..."You're a Deliverer, aren't you?"
Turns out *she'd* been a Deliverer many years earlier...
...and could spot one a mile away.

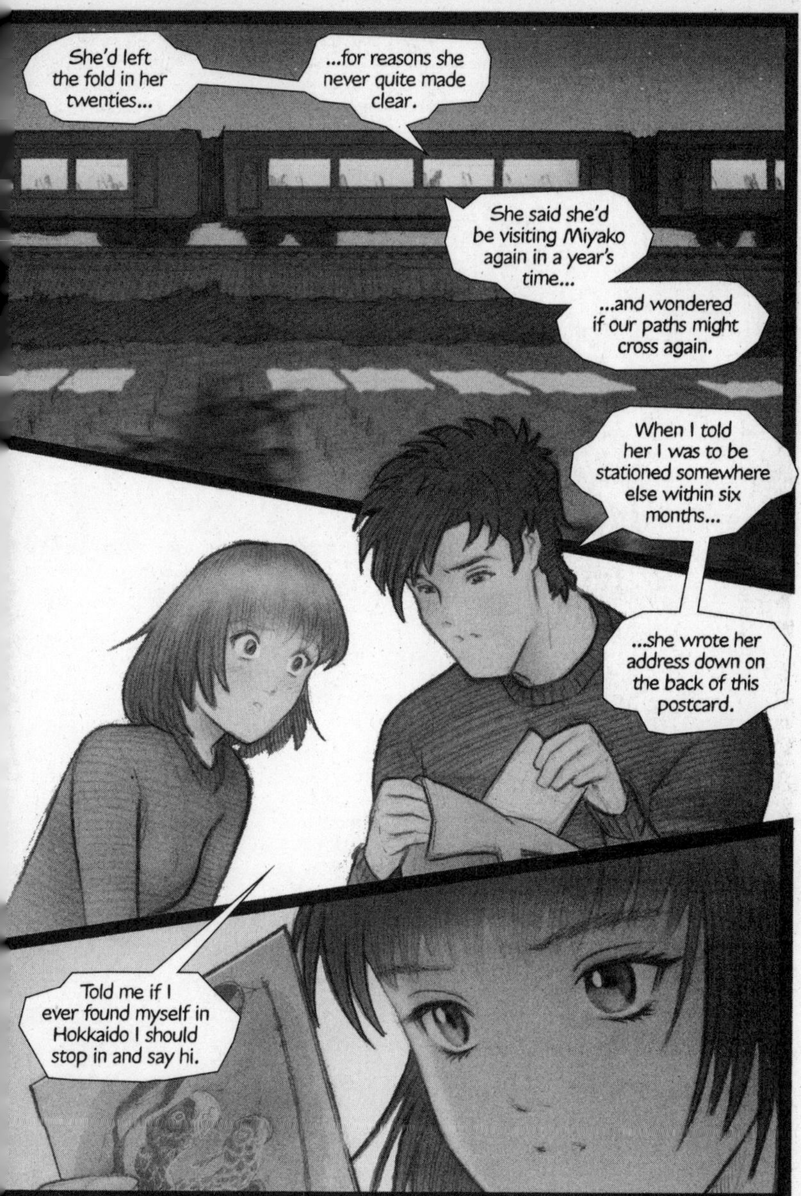
She'd left the fold in her twenties...
...for reasons she never quite made clear.
She said she'd be visiting Miyako again in a year's time...
...and wondered if our paths might cross again.
When I told her I was to be stationed somewhere else within six months...
...she wrote her address down on the back of this postcard.
Told me if I ever found myself in Hokkaido I should stop in and say hi.

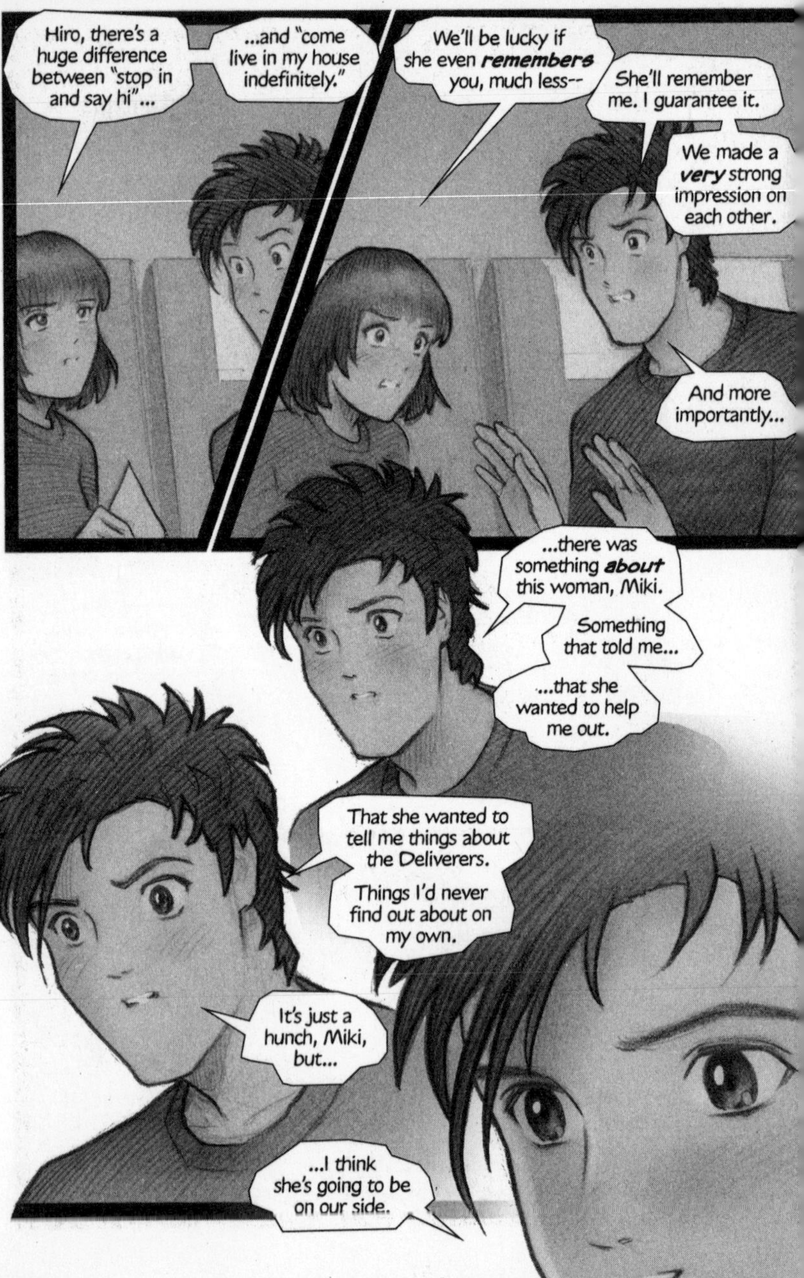

Hiro, there's a huge difference between "stop in and say hi"...
...and "come live in my house indefinitely."
We'll be lucky if she even ***remembers*** you, much less--
She'll remember me. I guarantee it.
We made a ***very*** strong impression on each other.
And more importantly...
...there was something ***about*** this woman, Miki.
Something that told me...
...that she wanted to help me out.
That she wanted to tell me things about the Deliverers.
Things I'd never find out about on my own.
It's just a hunch, Miki, but...
...I think she's going to be on our side.

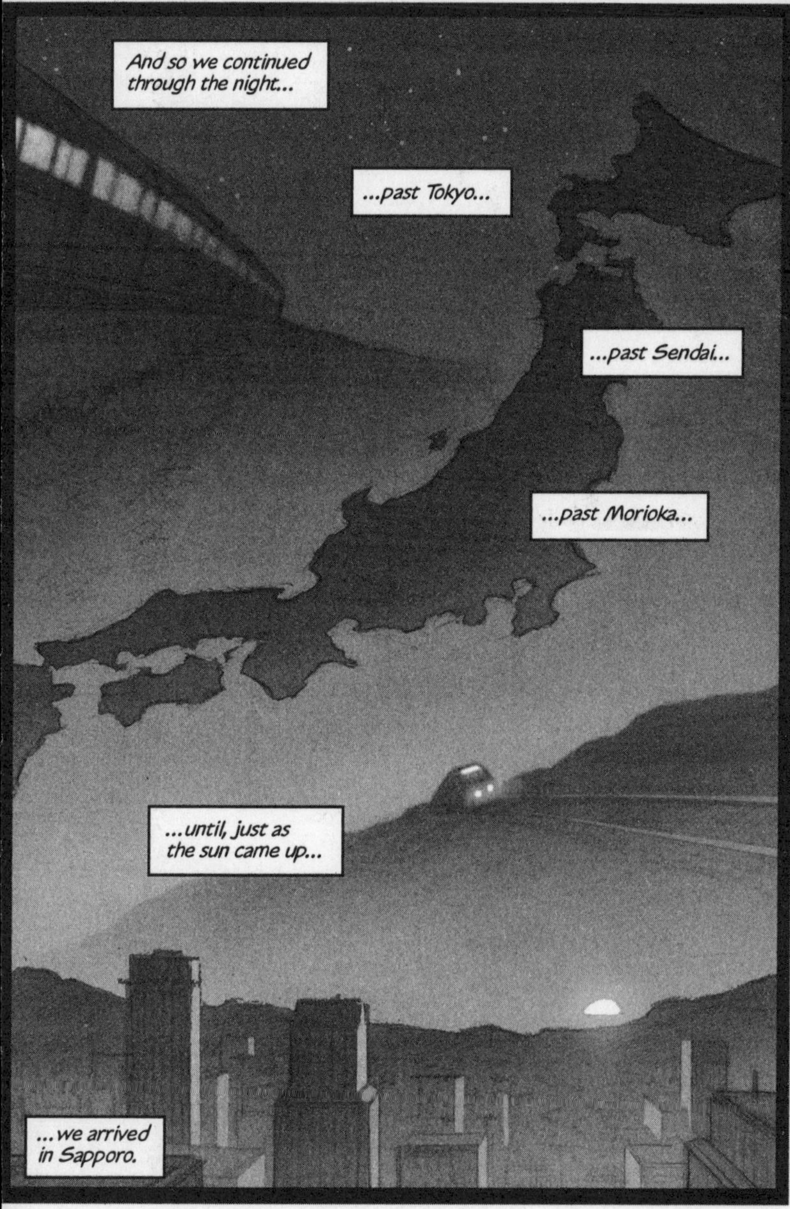
And so we continued through the night...
...past Tokyo...
...past Sendai...
...past Morioka...
...until, just as the sun came up...
...we arrived in Sapporo.

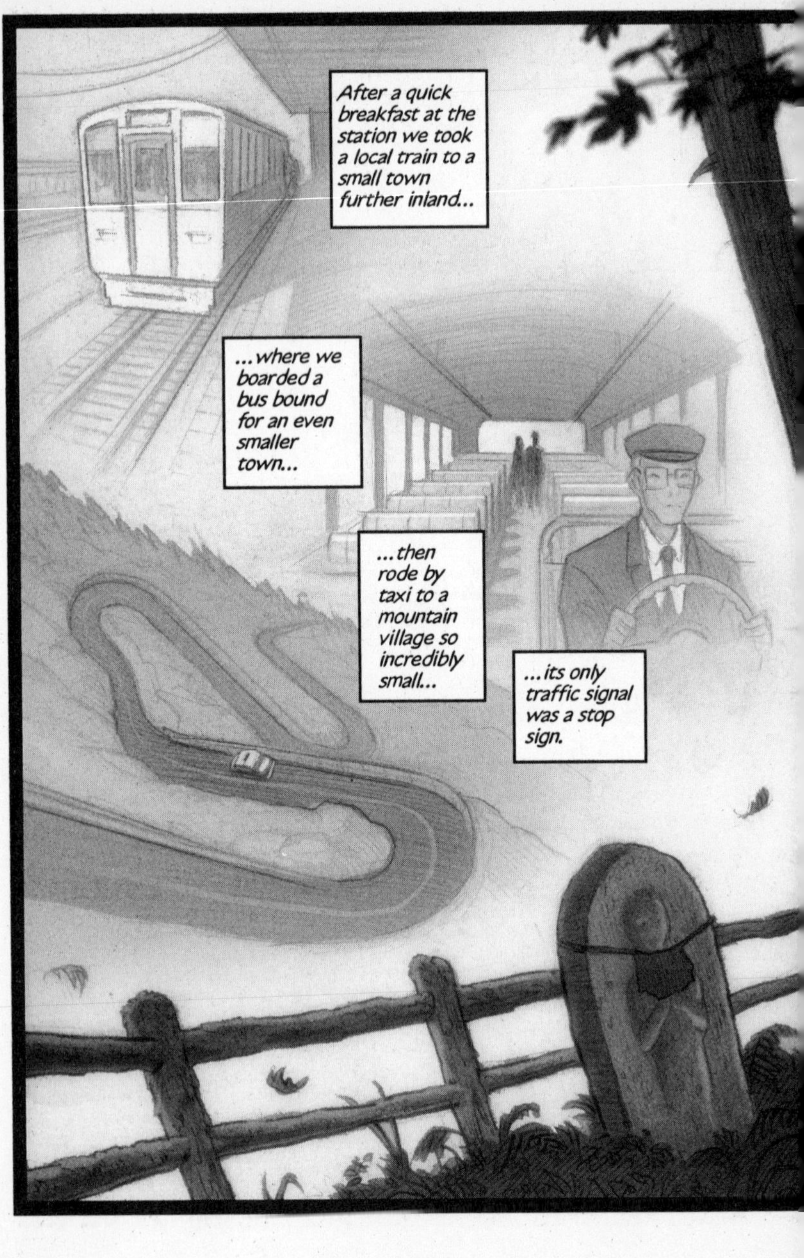
After a quick breakfast at the station we took a local train to a small town further inland...
...where we boarded a bus bound for an even smaller town...
...then rode by taxi to a mountain village so incredibly small...
...its only traffic signal was a stop sign.

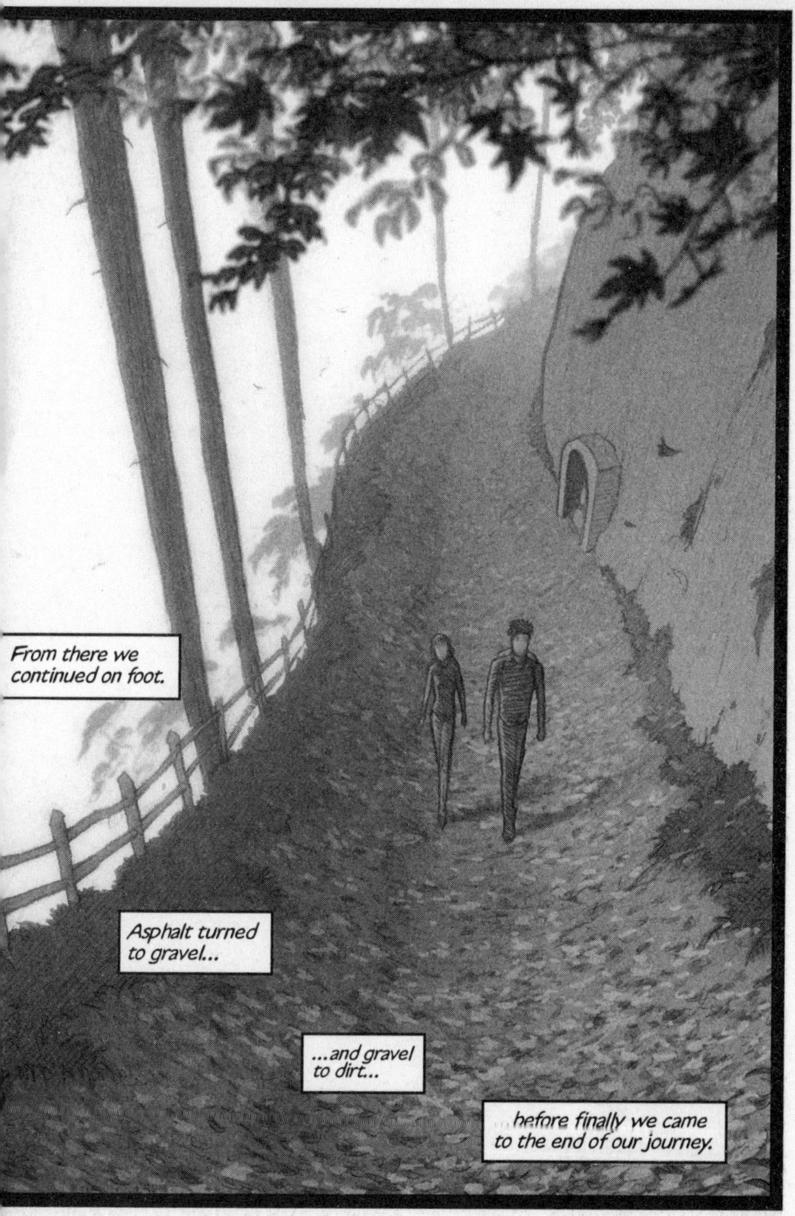
From there we continued on foot.
Asphalt turned to gravel...
...and gravel to dirt...
...before finally we came to the end of our journey.

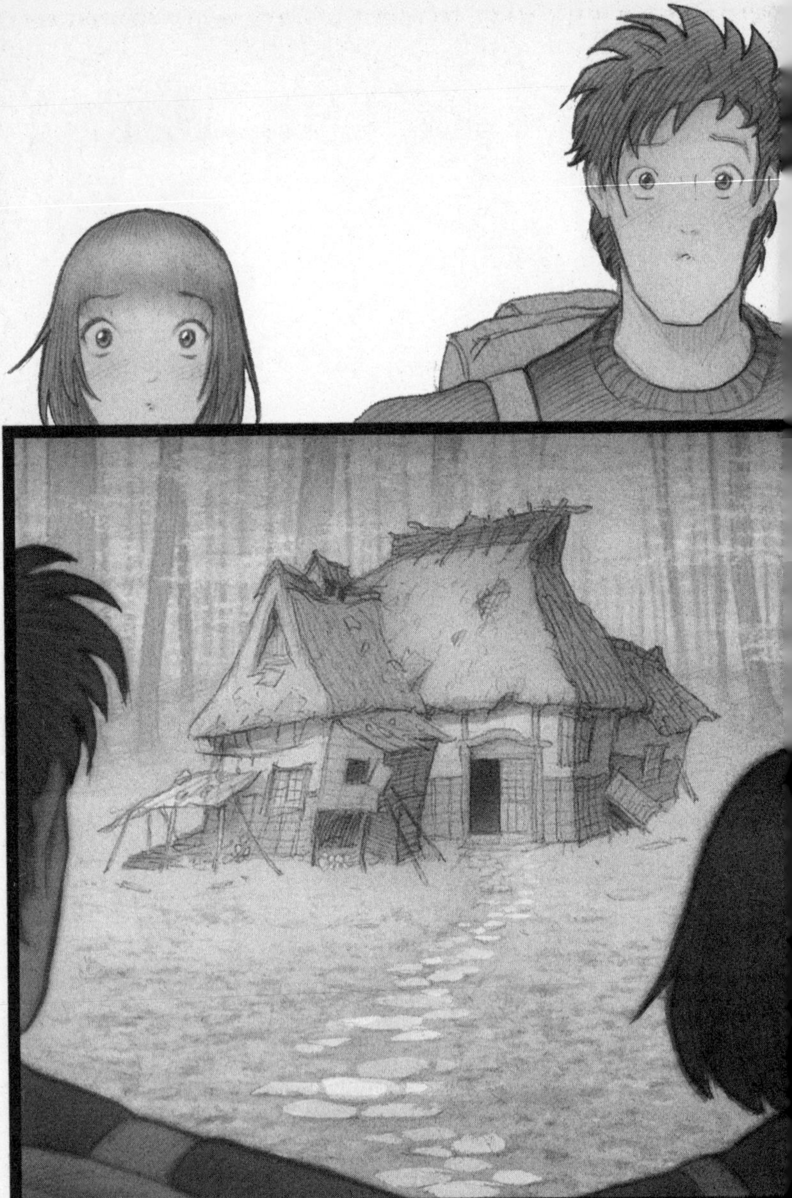

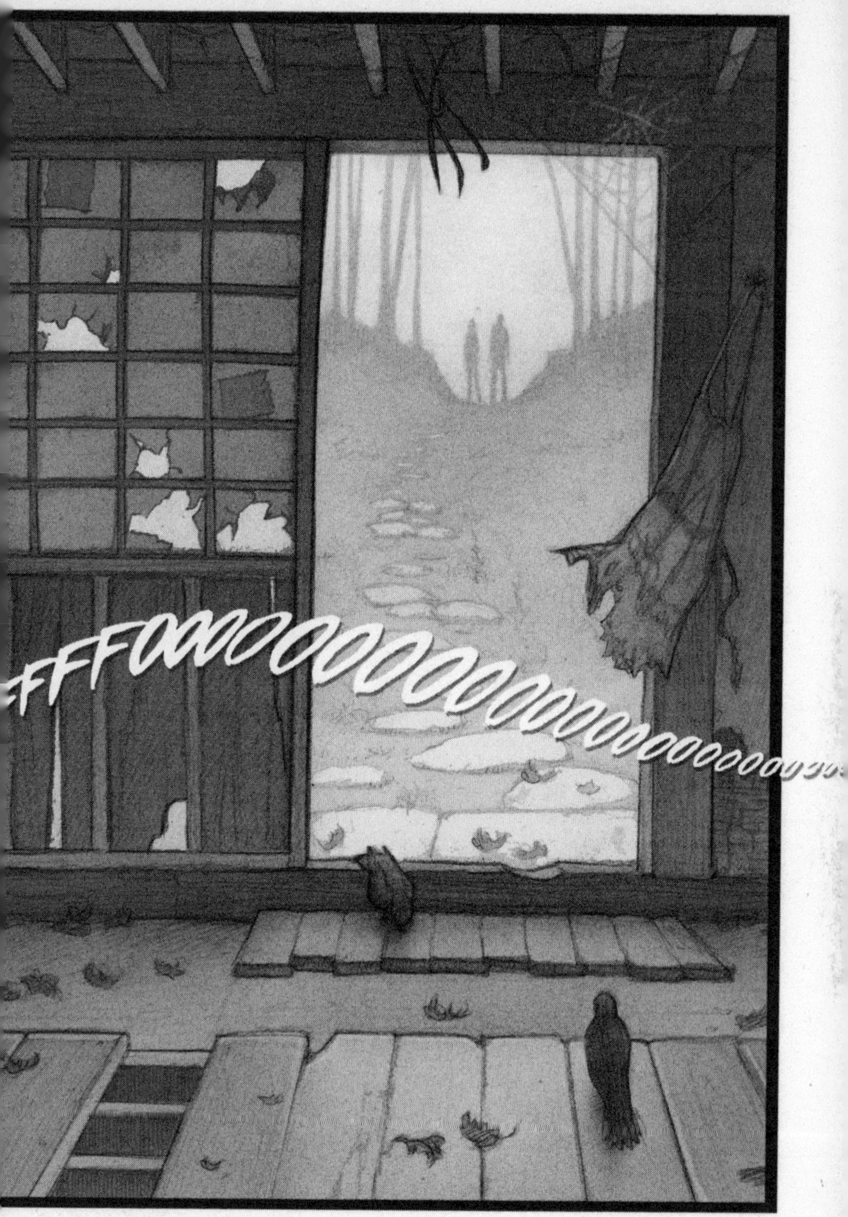
FFFOOOOOOOOOOOOOOOOOOOOOOOOOOOOOO

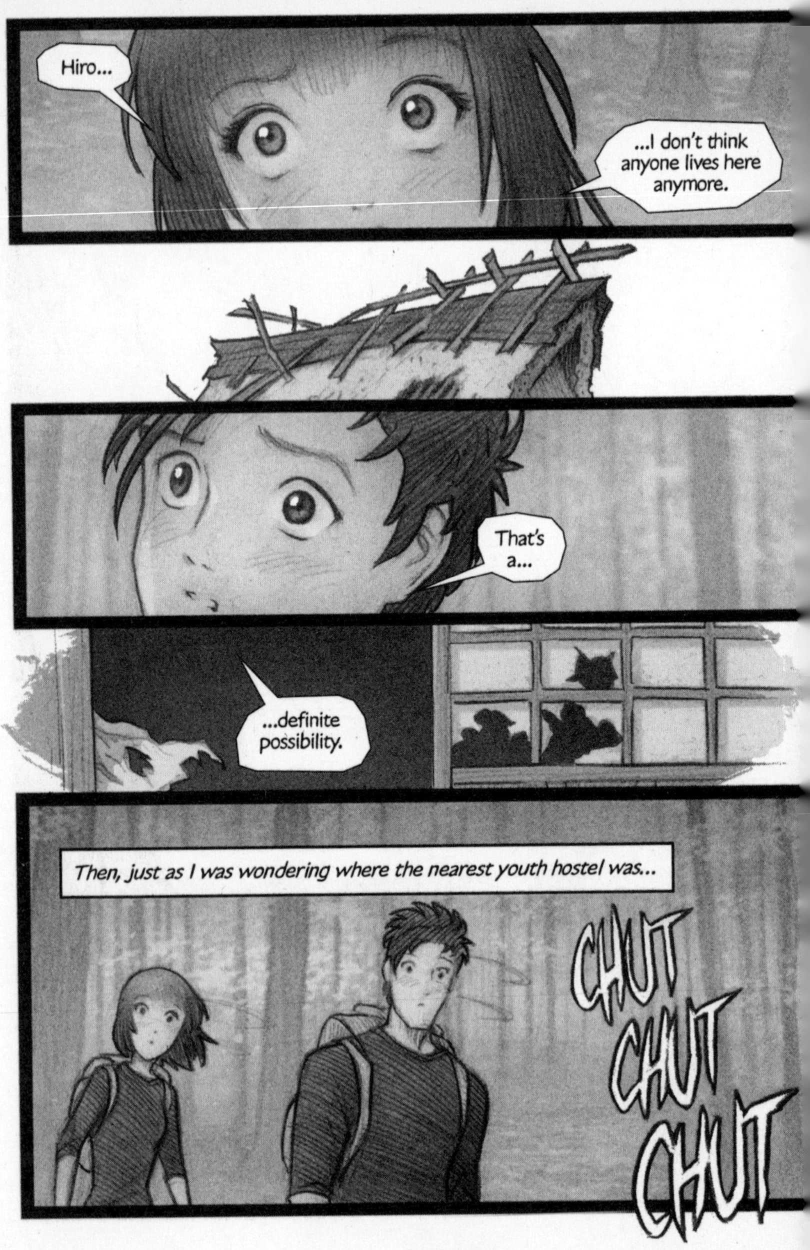

Hiro...
...I don't think anyone lives here anymore.
That's a...
...definite possibility.
Then, just as I was wondering where the nearest youth hostel was...
CHUT CHUT CHUT

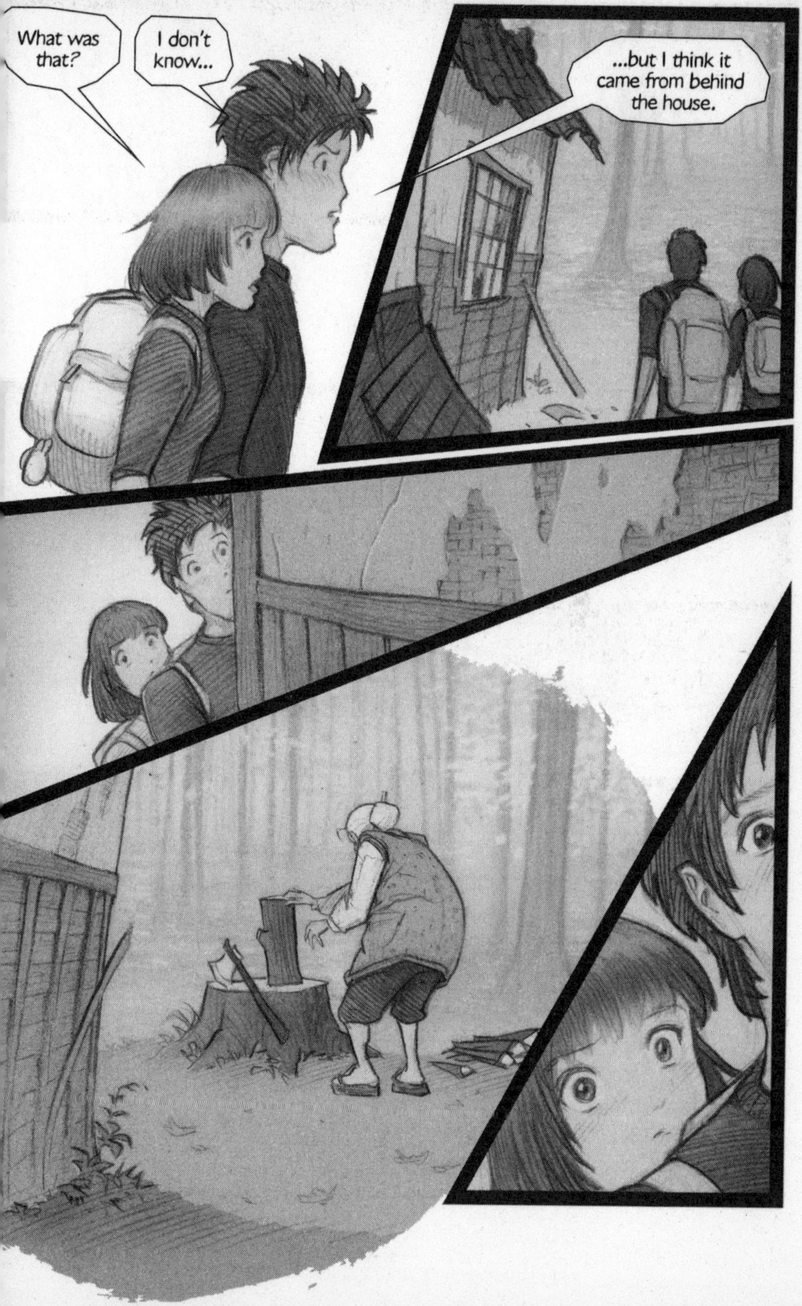
What was that?
I don't know...
...but I think it came from behind the house.

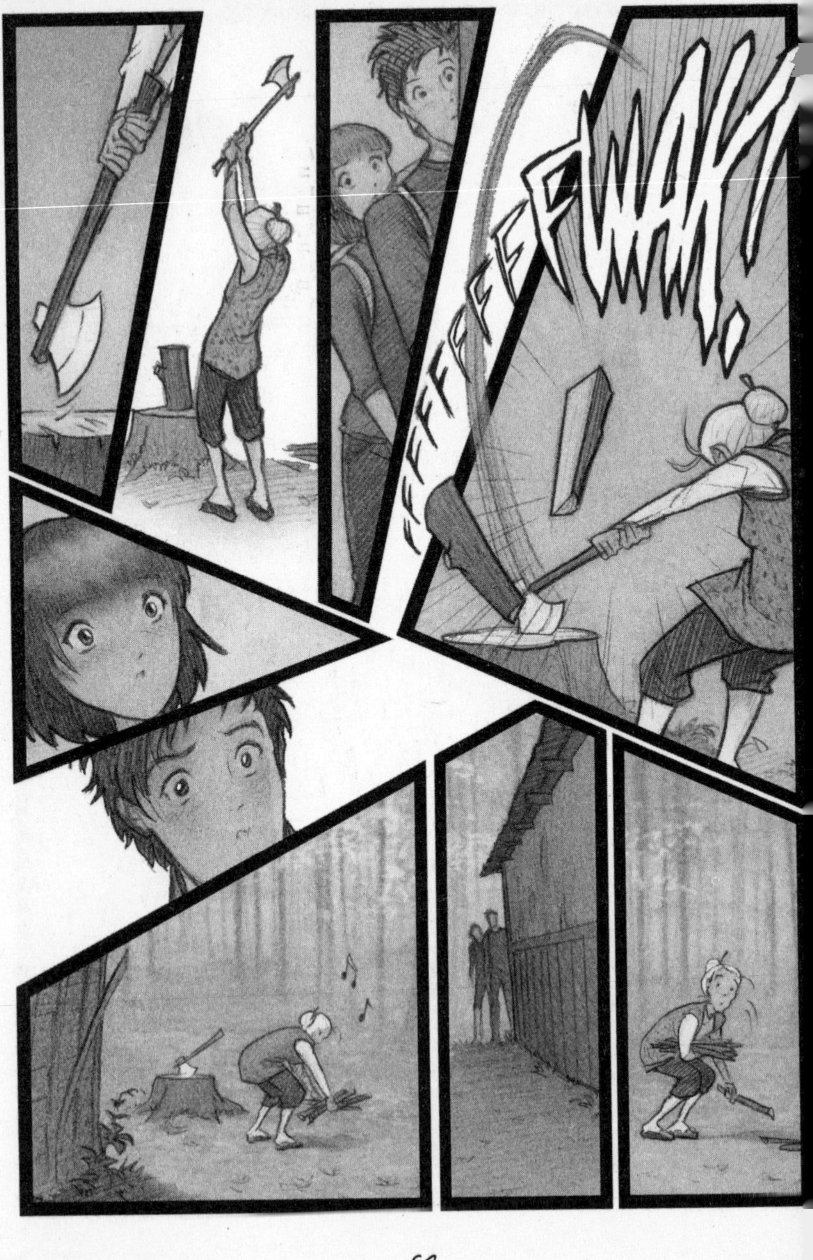
FFFFFFFFFWAK!

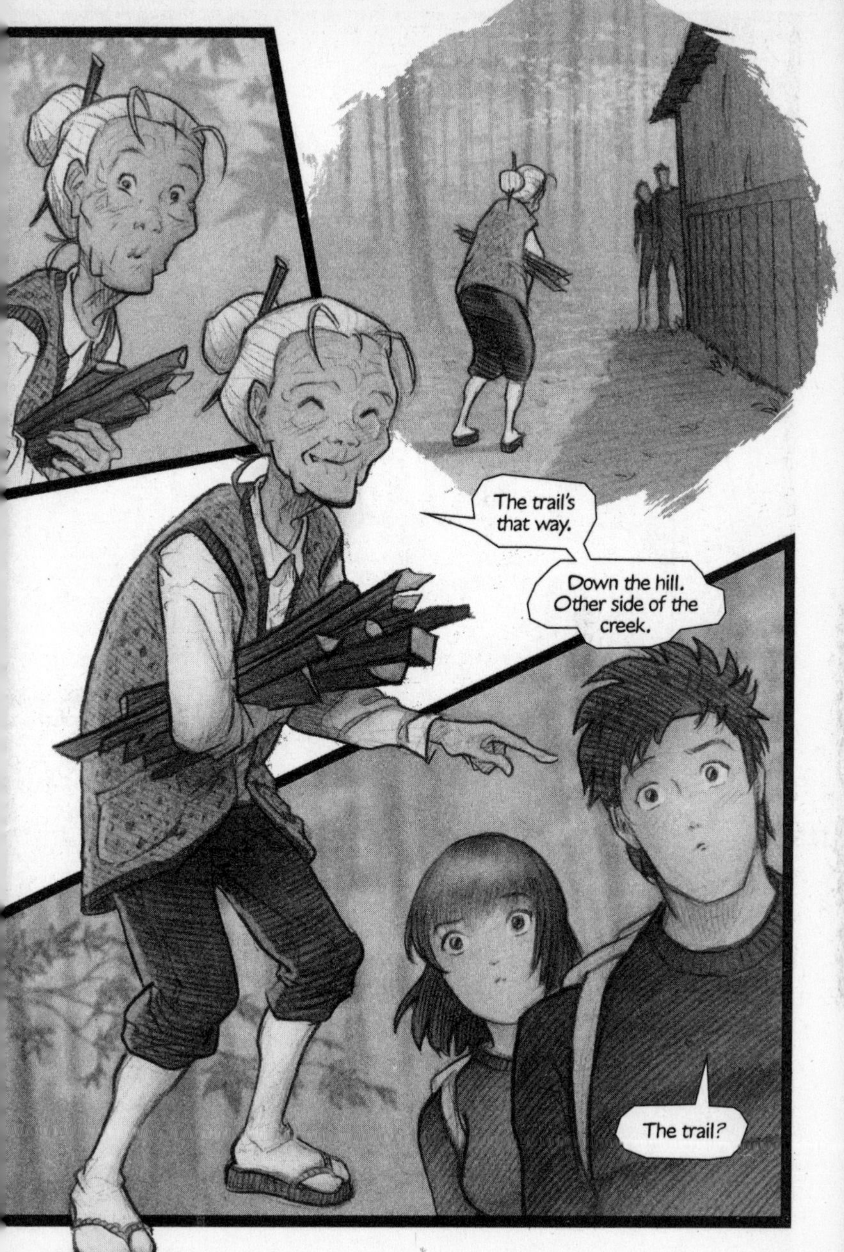
The trail's that way.
Down the hill. Other side of the creek.
The trail?

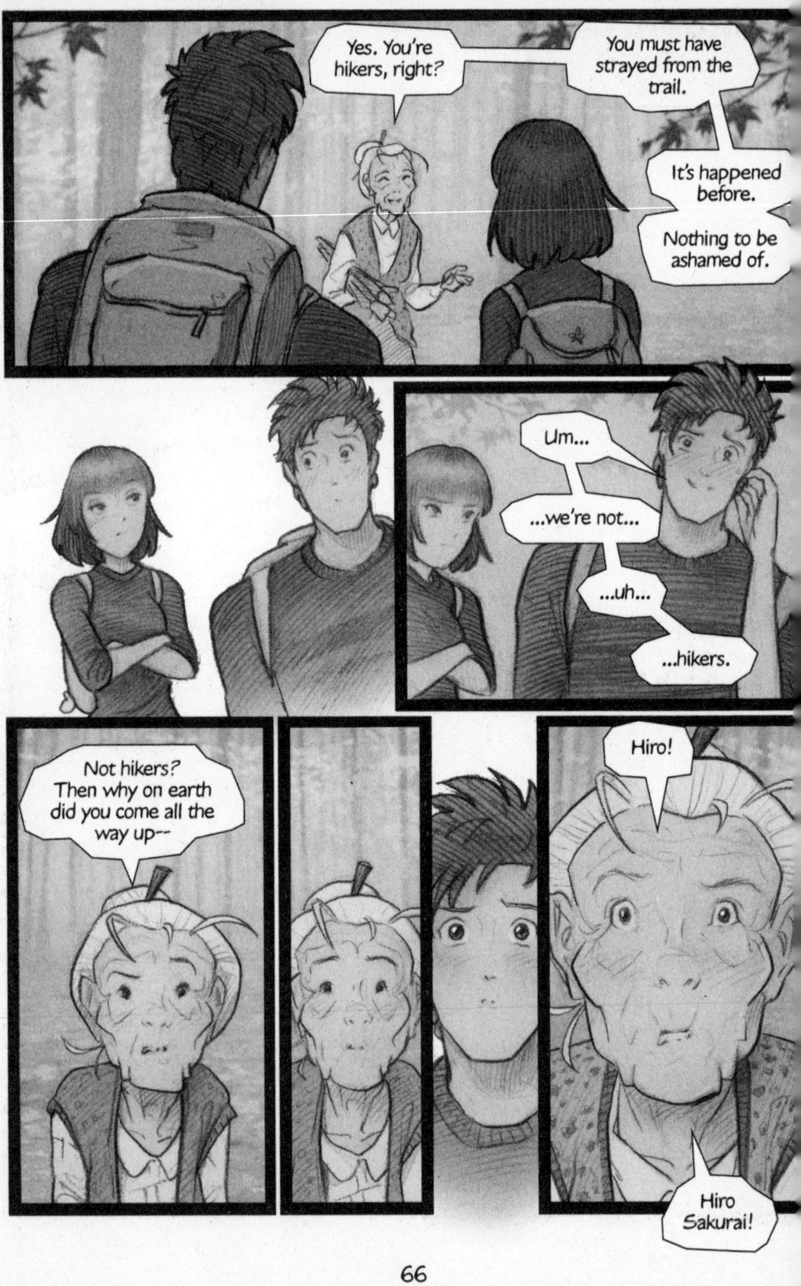
Yes. You're hikers, right?
You must have strayed from the trail.
It's happened before.
Nothing to be ashamed of.
Um...
...we're not...
...uh...
...hikers.
Not hikers? Then why on earth did you come all the way up--
Hiro!
Hiro Sakurai!

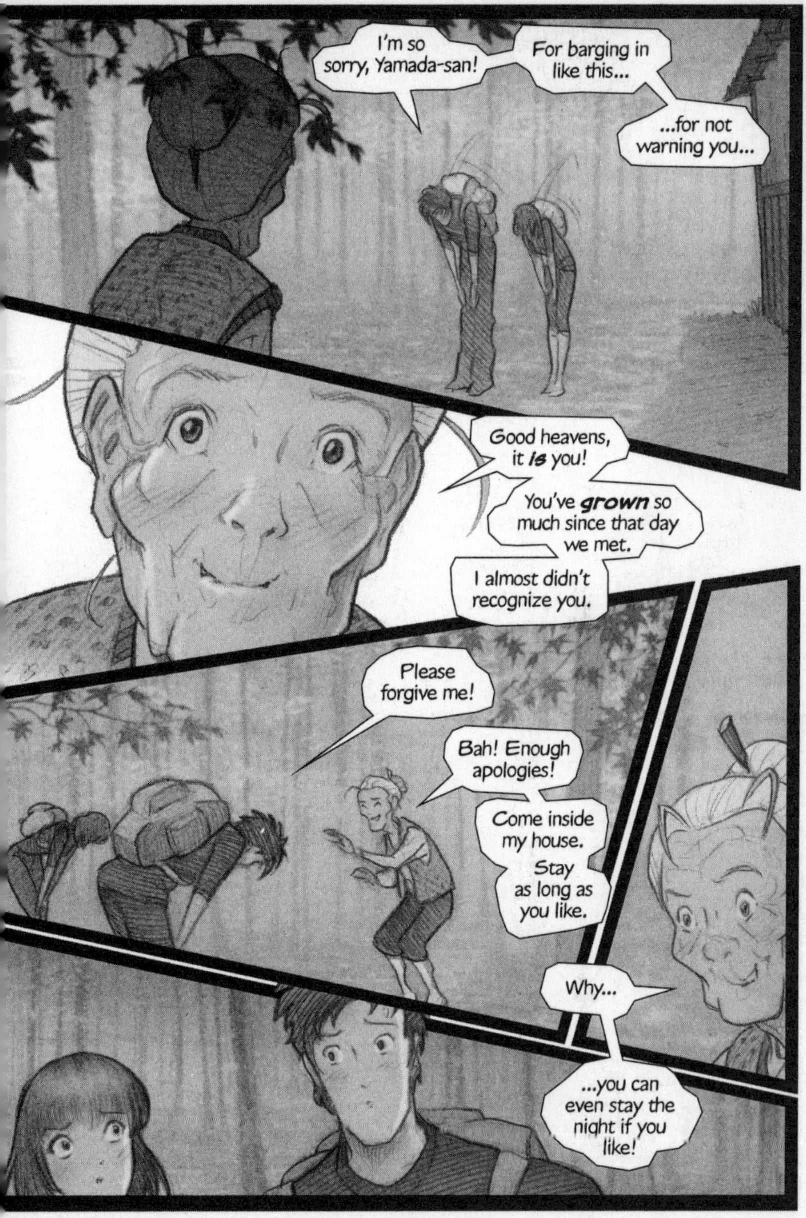
I'm so sorry, Yamada-san!
For barging in like this...
...for not warning you...
Good heavens, it *is* you!
You've **grown** so much since that day we met.
I almost didn't recognize you.
Please forgive me!
Bah! Enough apologies!
Come inside my house.
Stay as long as you like.
Why...
...you can even stay the night if you like!

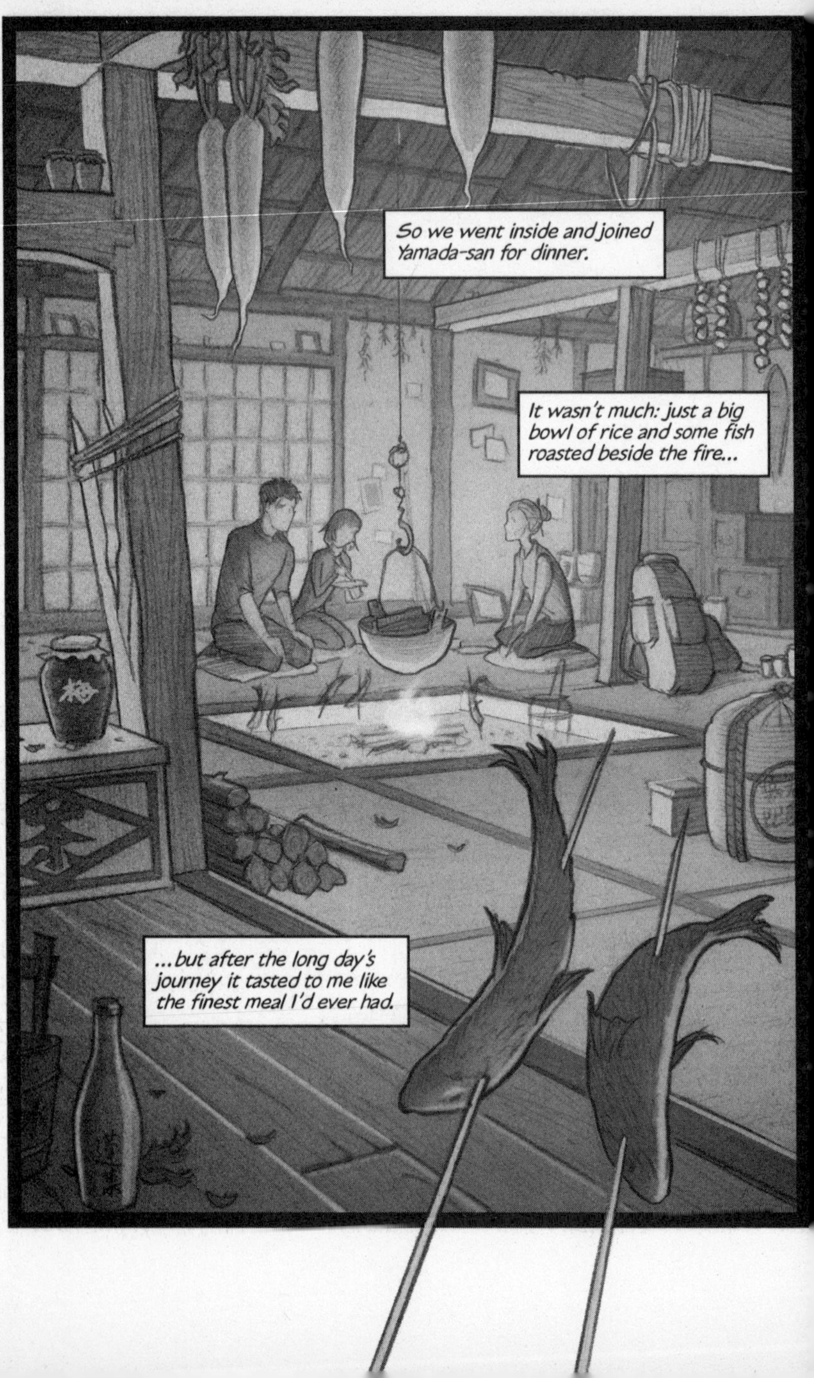
So we went inside and joined Yamada-san for dinner.
It wasn't much: just a big bowl of rice and some fish roasted beside the fire...
...but after the long day's journey it tasted to me like the finest meal I'd ever had.

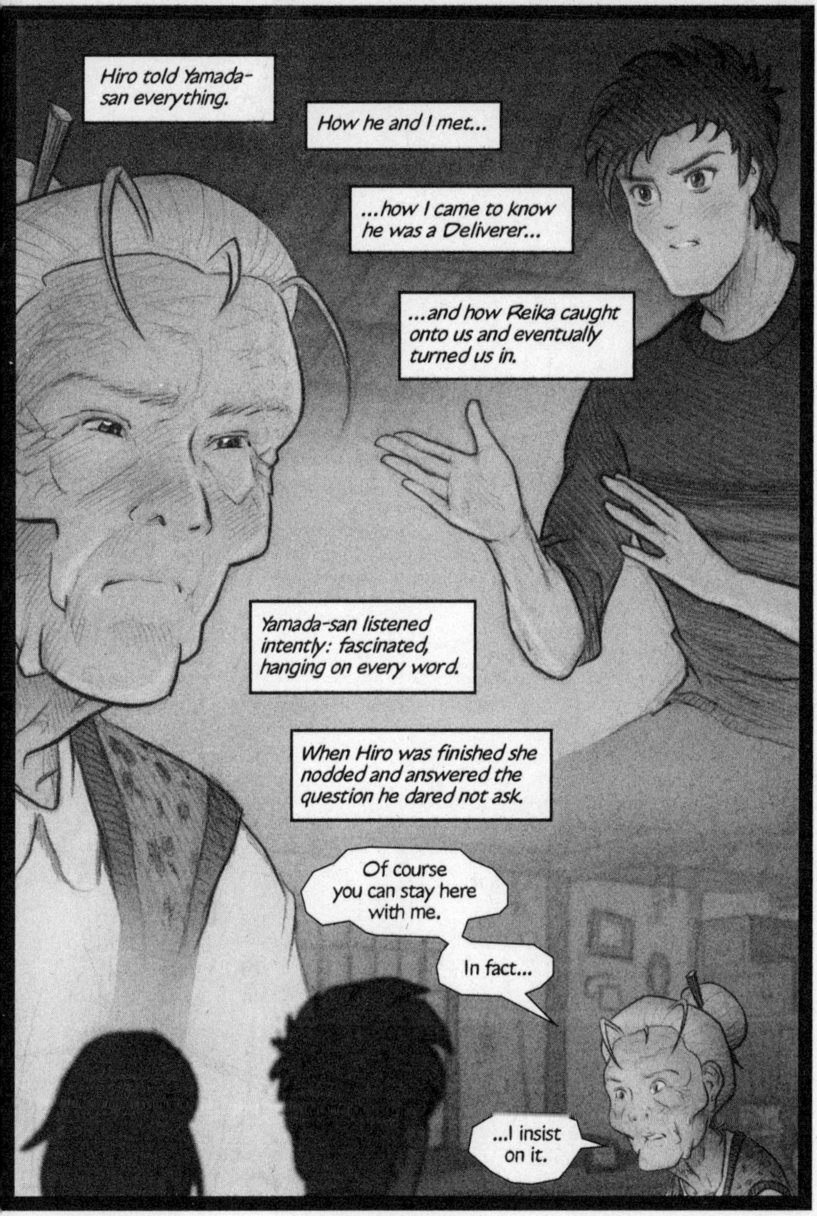
Hiro told Yamada-san everything.
How he and I met...
...how I came to know he was a Deliverer...
...and how Reika caught onto us and eventually turned us in.
Yamada-san listened intently: fascinated, hanging on every word.
When Hiro was finished she nodded and answered the question he dared not ask.
Of course you can stay here with me.
In fact...
...I insist on it.

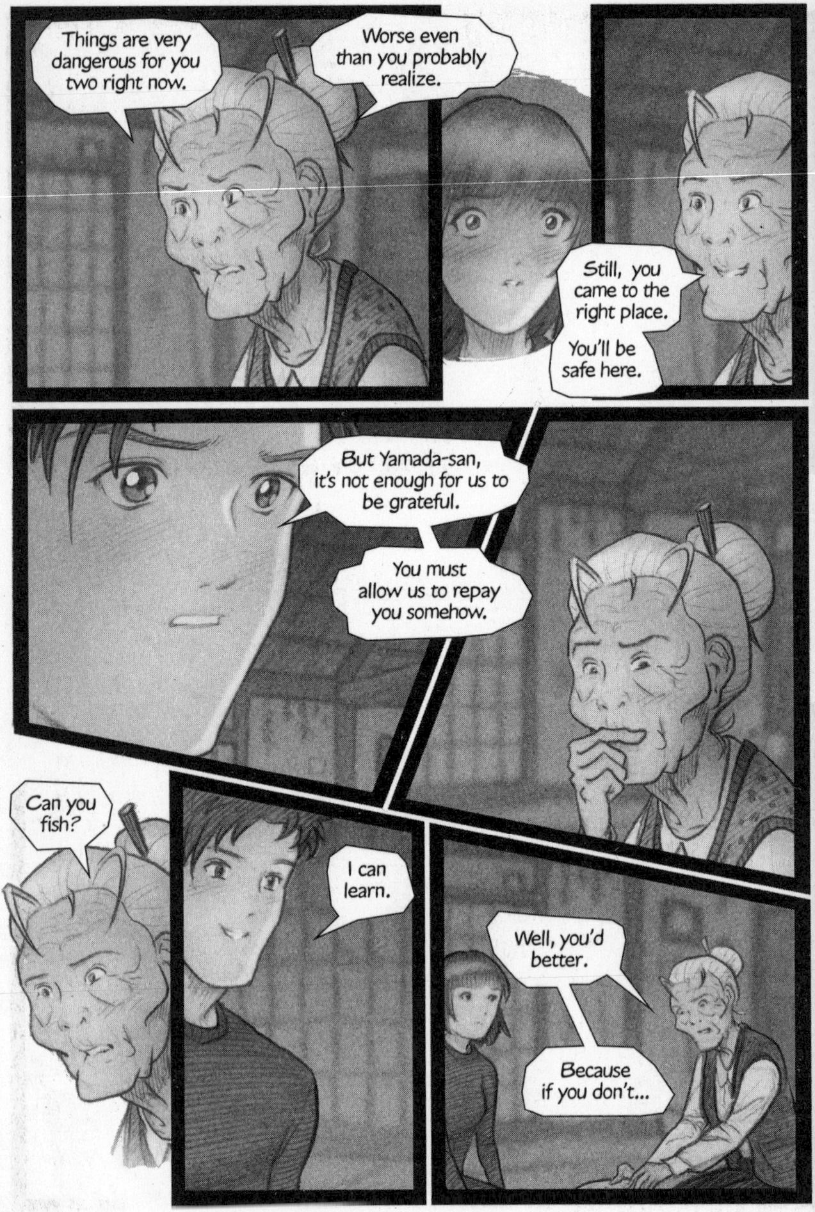
Things are very dangerous for you two right now.
Worse even than you probably realize.
Still, you came to the right place.
You'll be safe here.
But Yamada-san, it's not enough for us to be grateful.
You must allow us to repay you somehow.
Can you fish?
I can learn.
Well, you'd better.
Because if you don't...

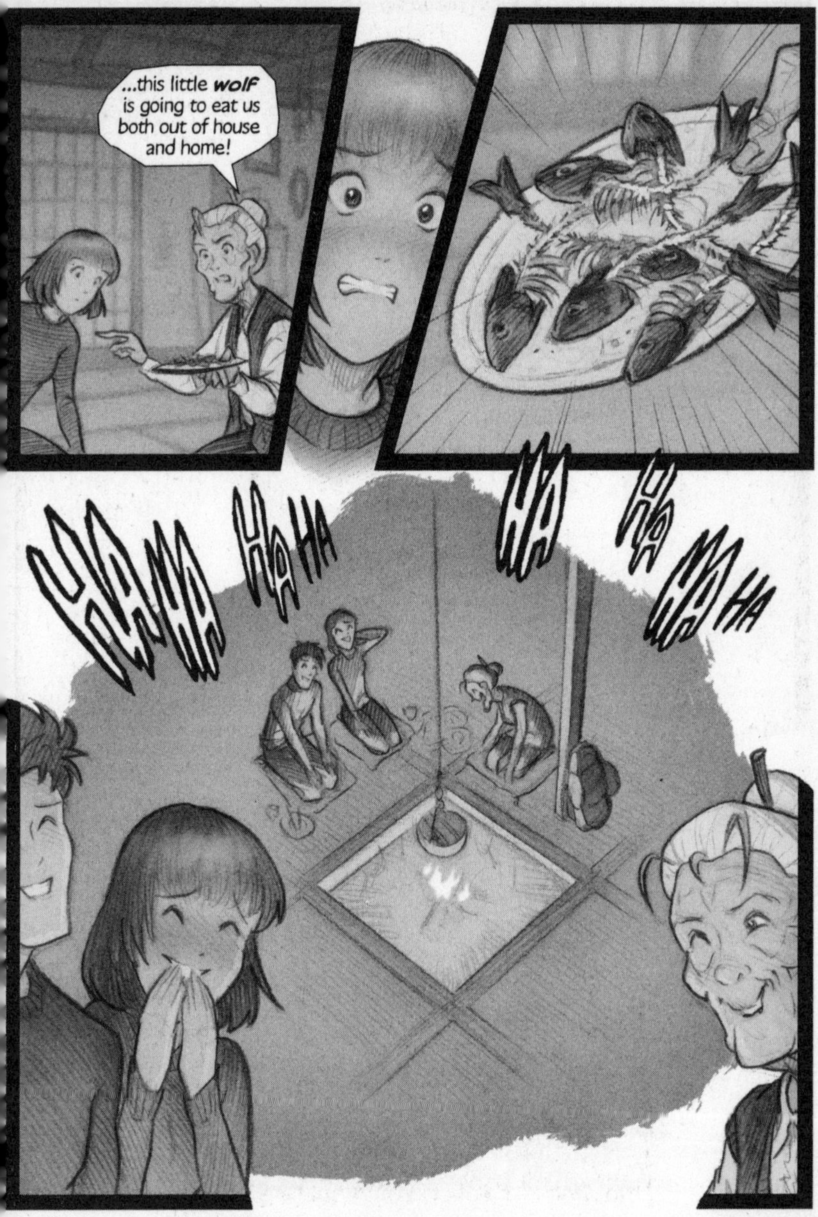
...this little **wolf** is going to eat us both out of house and home!
HAHAHA
HAHAHA
HA
HAHA
HAHAHA

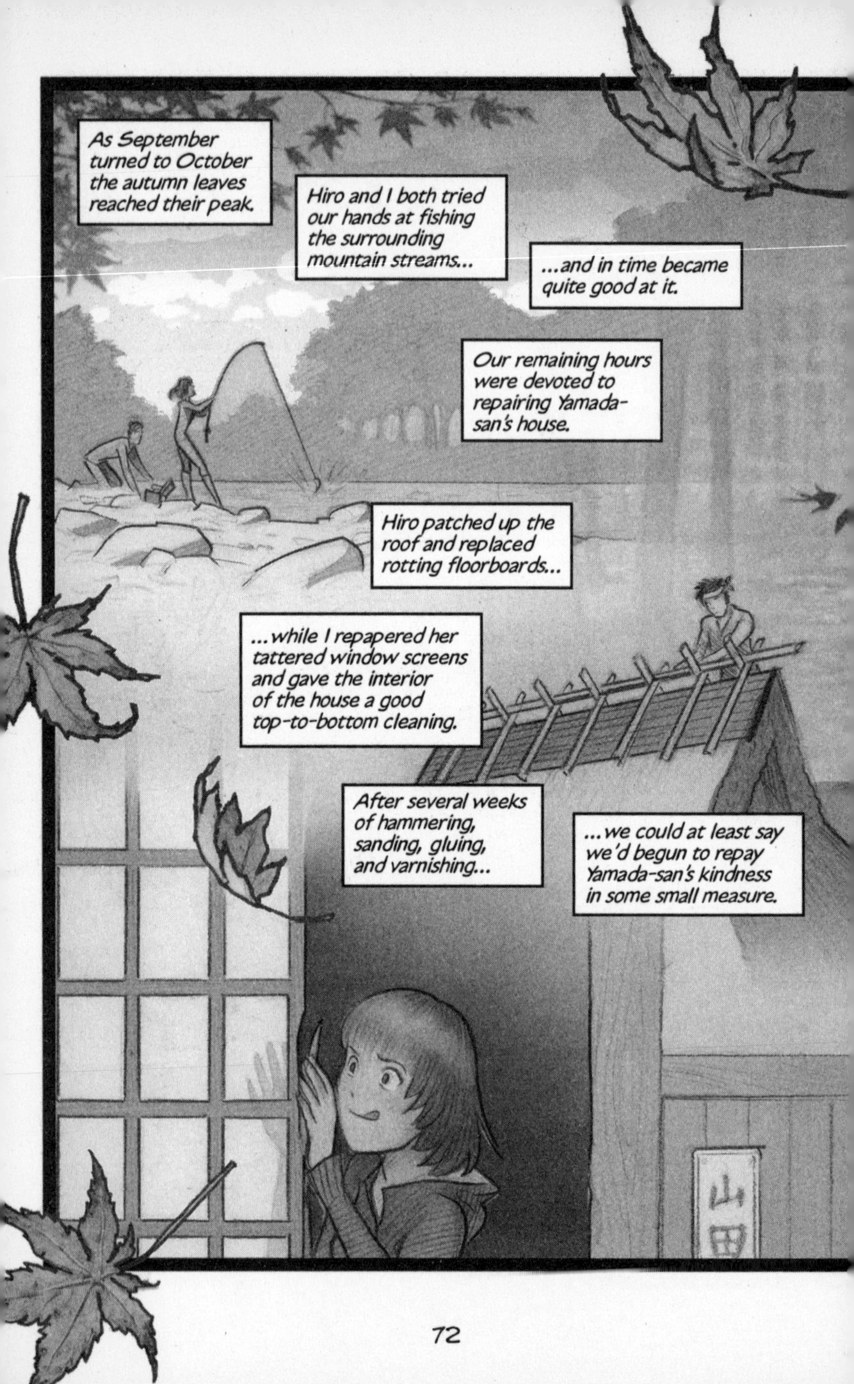
As September turned to October the autumn leaves reached their peak.
Hiro and I both tried our hands at fishing the surrounding mountain streams...
...and in time became quite good at it.
Our remaining hours were devoted to repairing Yamada-san's house.
Hiro patched up the roof and replaced rotting floorboards...
...while I repapered her tattered window screens and gave the interior of the house a good top-to-bottom cleaning.
After several weeks of hammering, sanding, gluing, and varnishing...
...we could at least say we'd begun to repay Yamada-san's kindness in some small measure.
山田

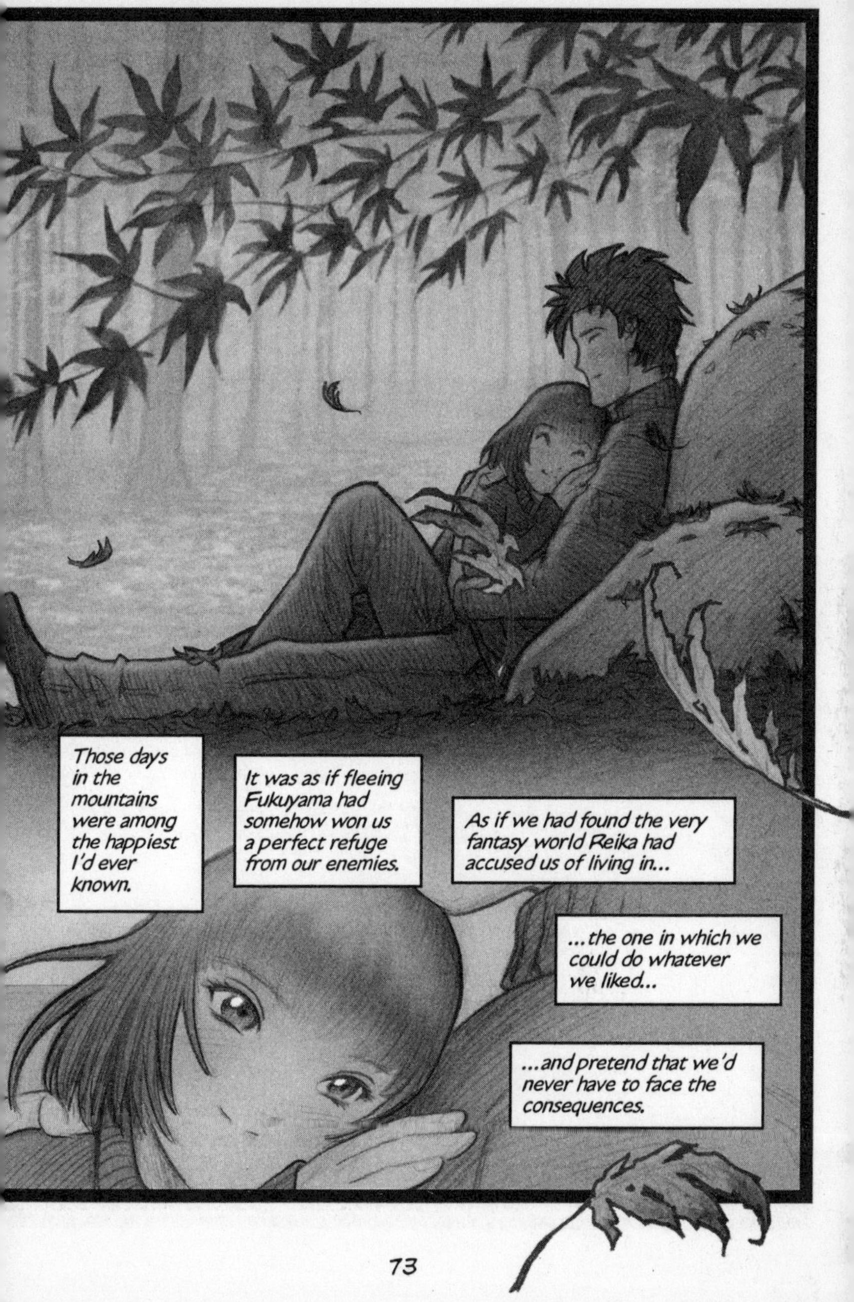
Those days in the mountains were among the happiest I'd ever known.
It was as if fleeing Fukuyama had somehow won us a perfect refuge from our enemies.
As if we had found the very fantasy world Reika had accused us of living in...
...the one in which we could do whatever we liked...
...and pretend that we'd never have to face the consequences.

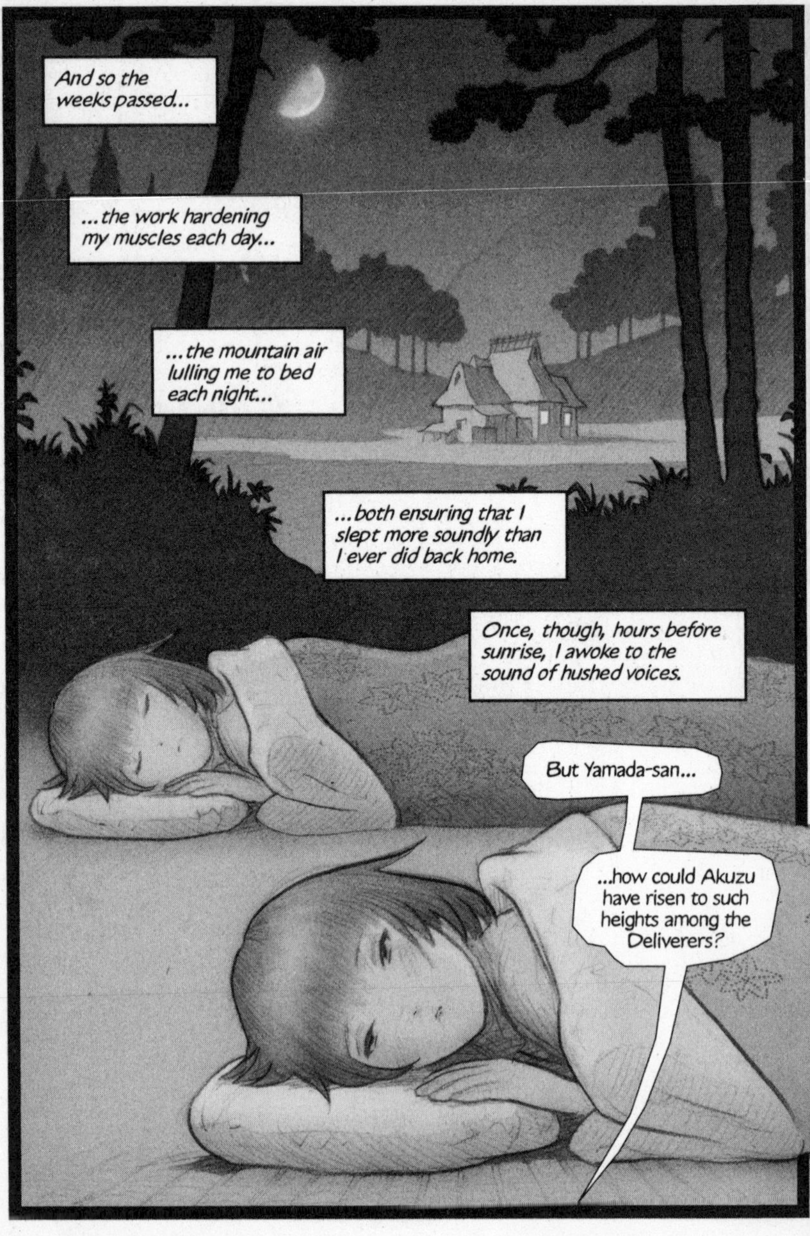
And so the weeks passed...
...the work hardening my muscles each day...
...the mountain air lulling me to bed each night...
...both ensuring that I slept more soundly than I ever did back home.
Once, though, hours before sunrise, I awoke to the sound of hushed voices.
But Yamada-san...
...how could Akuzu have risen to such heights among the Deliverers?

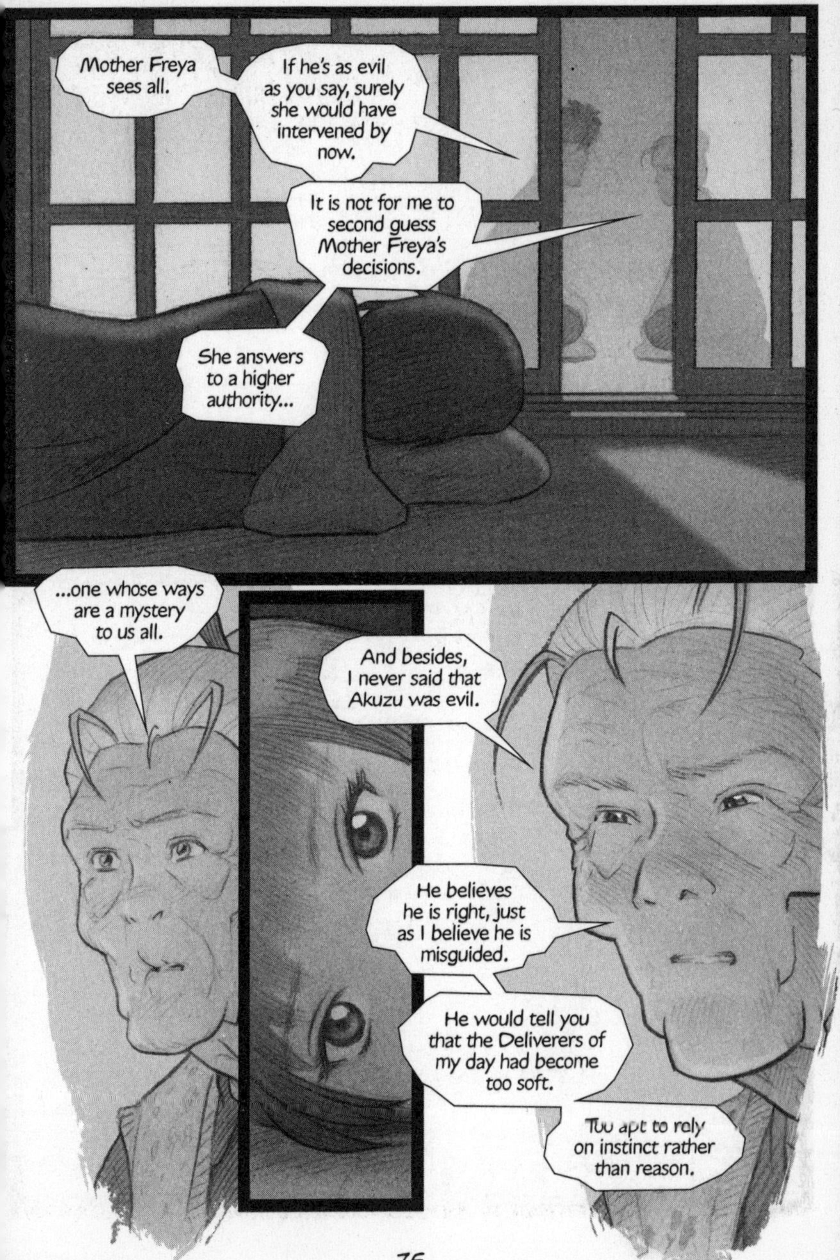

Mother Freya sees all.
If he's as evil as you say, surely she would have intervened by now.
It is not for me to second guess Mother Freya's decisions.
She answers to a higher authority...
...one whose ways are a mystery to us all.
And besides, I never said that Akuzu was evil.
He believes he is right, just as I believe he is misguided.
He would tell you that the Deliverers of my day had become too soft.
Too apt to rely on instinct rather than reason.

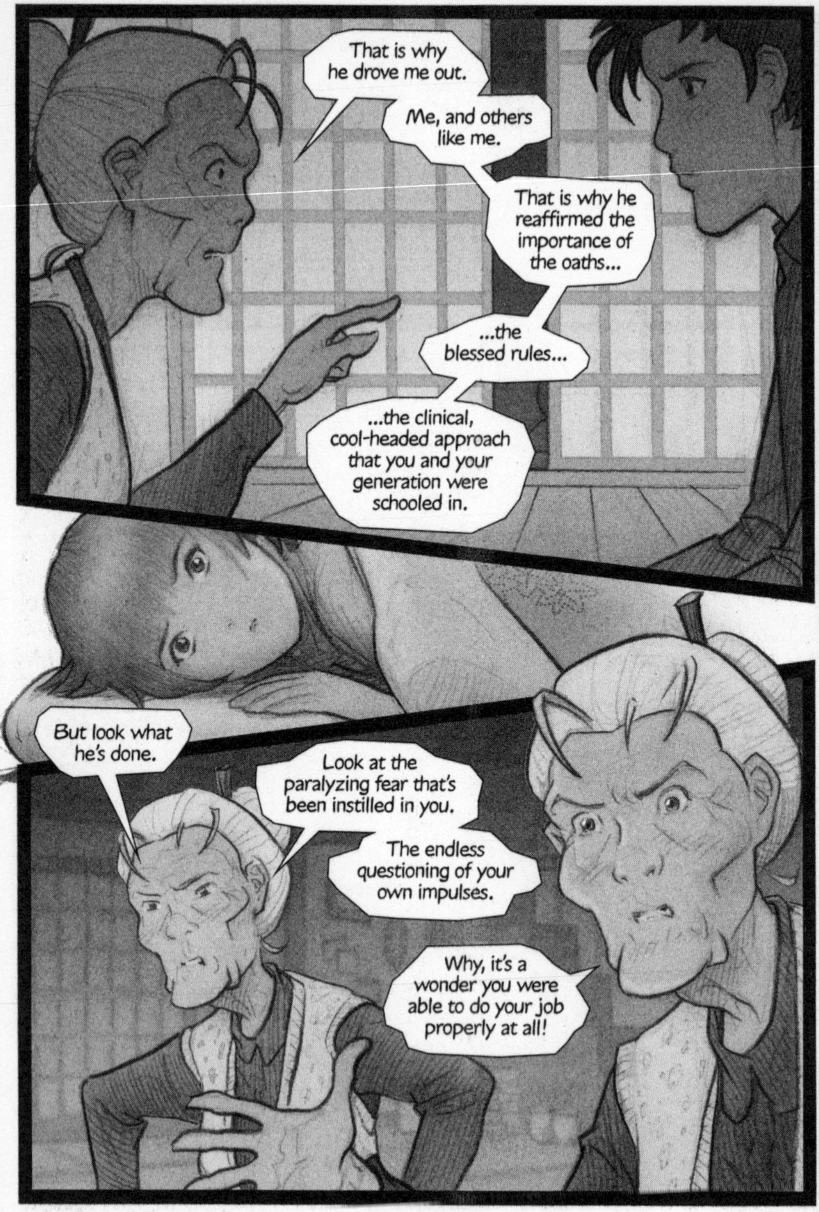
That is why he drove me out.
Me, and others like me.
That is why he reaffirmed the importance of the oaths...
...the blessed rules...
...the clinical, cool-headed approach that you and your generation were schooled in.
But look what he's done.
Look at the paralyzing fear that's been instilled in you.
The endless questioning of your own impulses.
Why, it's a wonder you were able to do your job properly at all!

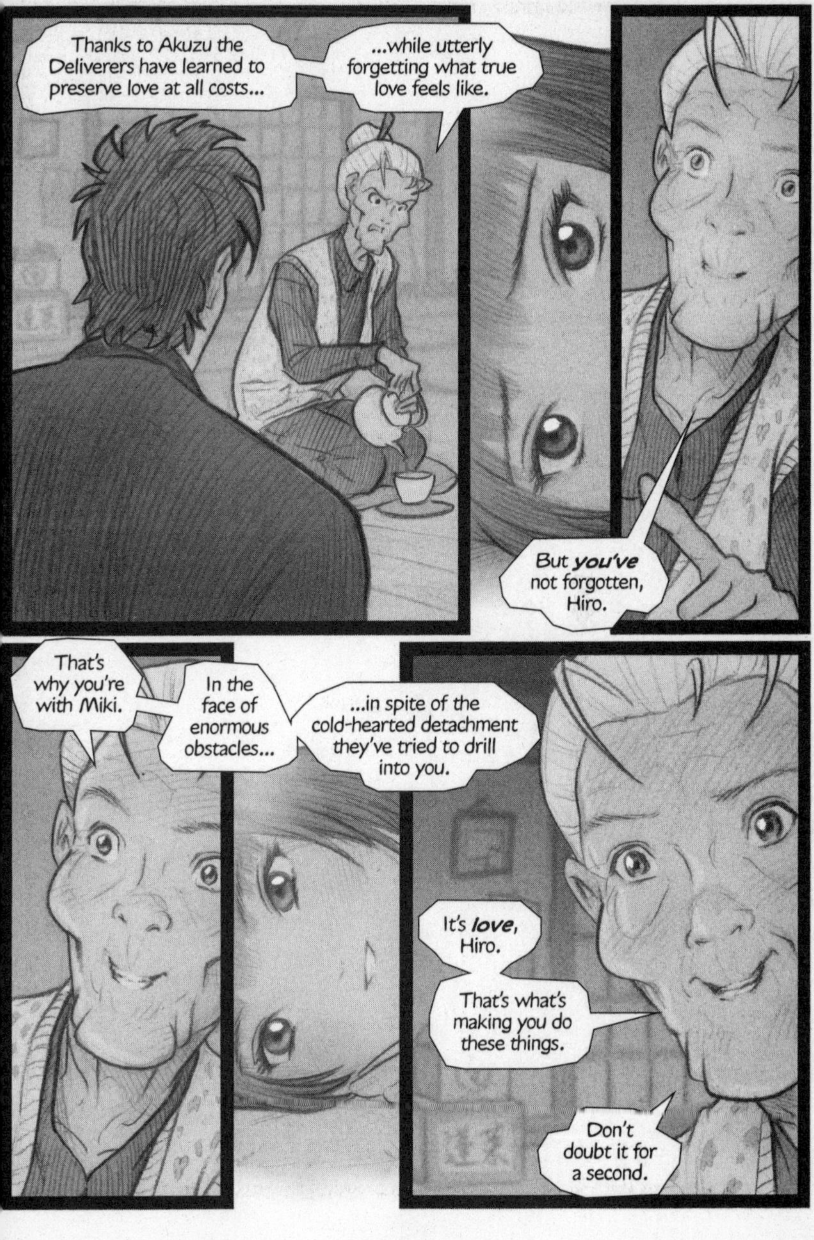
Thanks to Akuzu the Deliverers have learned to preserve love at all costs...
...while utterly forgetting what true love feels like.
But *you've* not forgotten, Hiro.
That's why you're with Miki.
In the face of enormous obstacles...
...in spite of the cold-hearted detachment they've tried to drill into you.
It's *love*, Hiro.
That's what's making you do these things.
Don't doubt it for a second.

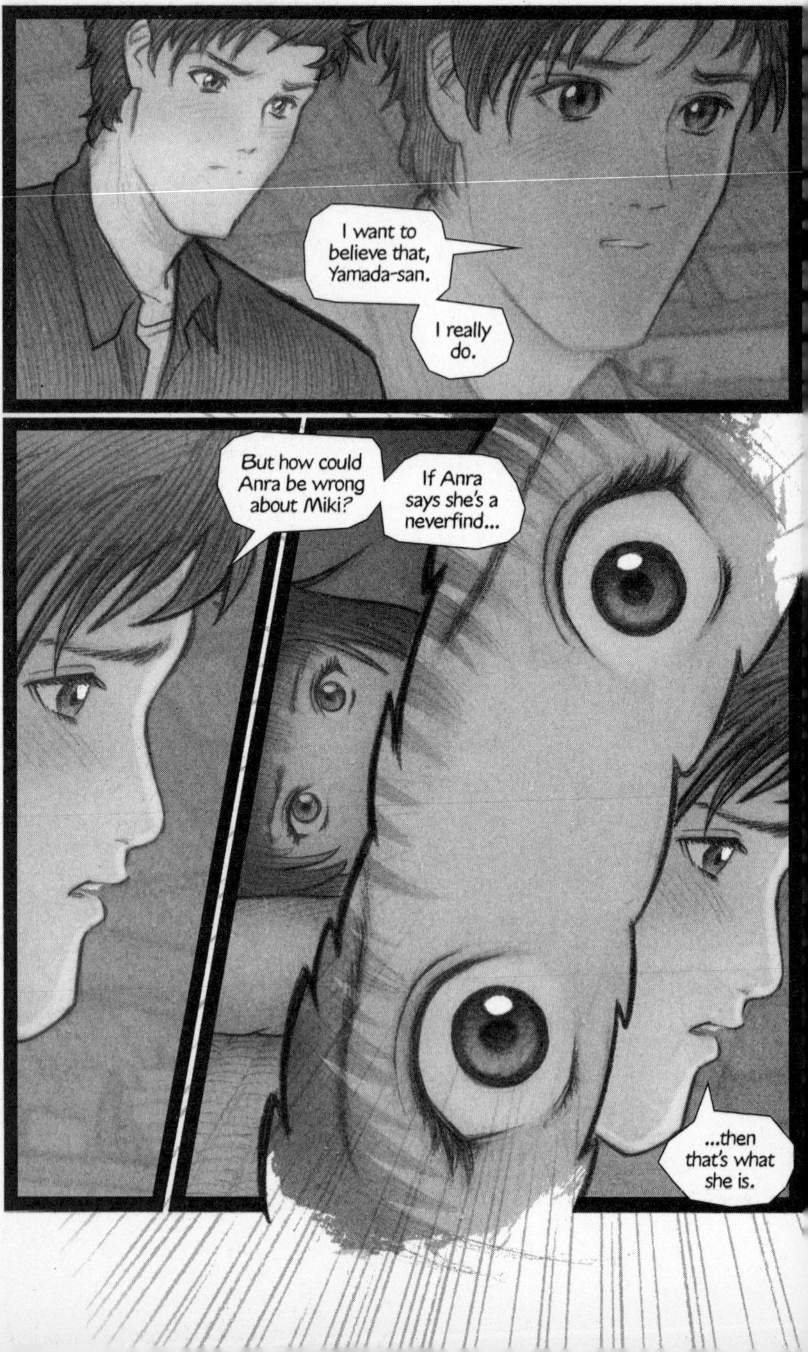
I want to believe that, Yamada-san.
I really do.
But how could Anra be wrong about Miki?
If Anra says she's a neverfind...
...then that's what she is.

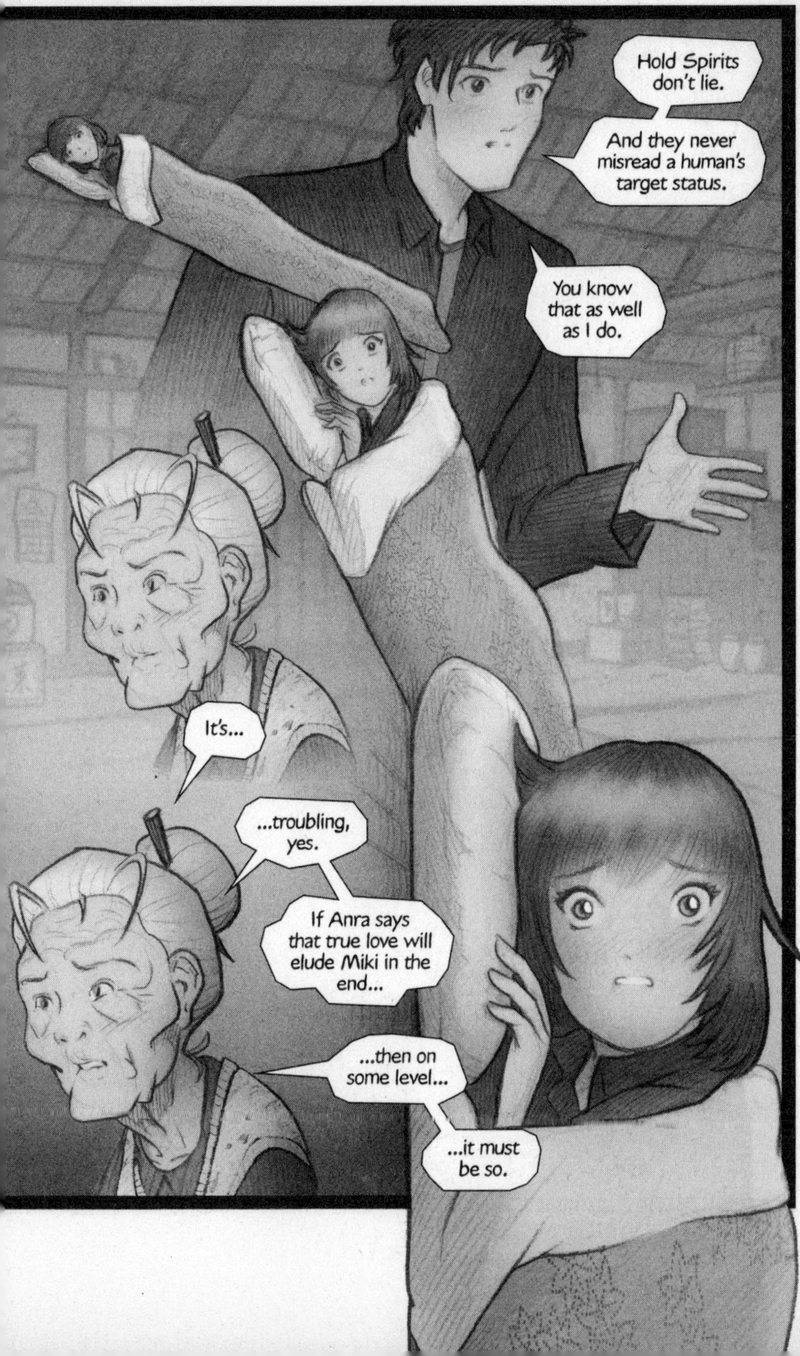
Hold Spirits don't lie.
And they never misread a human's target status.
You know that as well as I do.
It's...
...troubling, yes.
If Anra says that true love will elude Miki in the end...
...then on some level...
...it must be so.

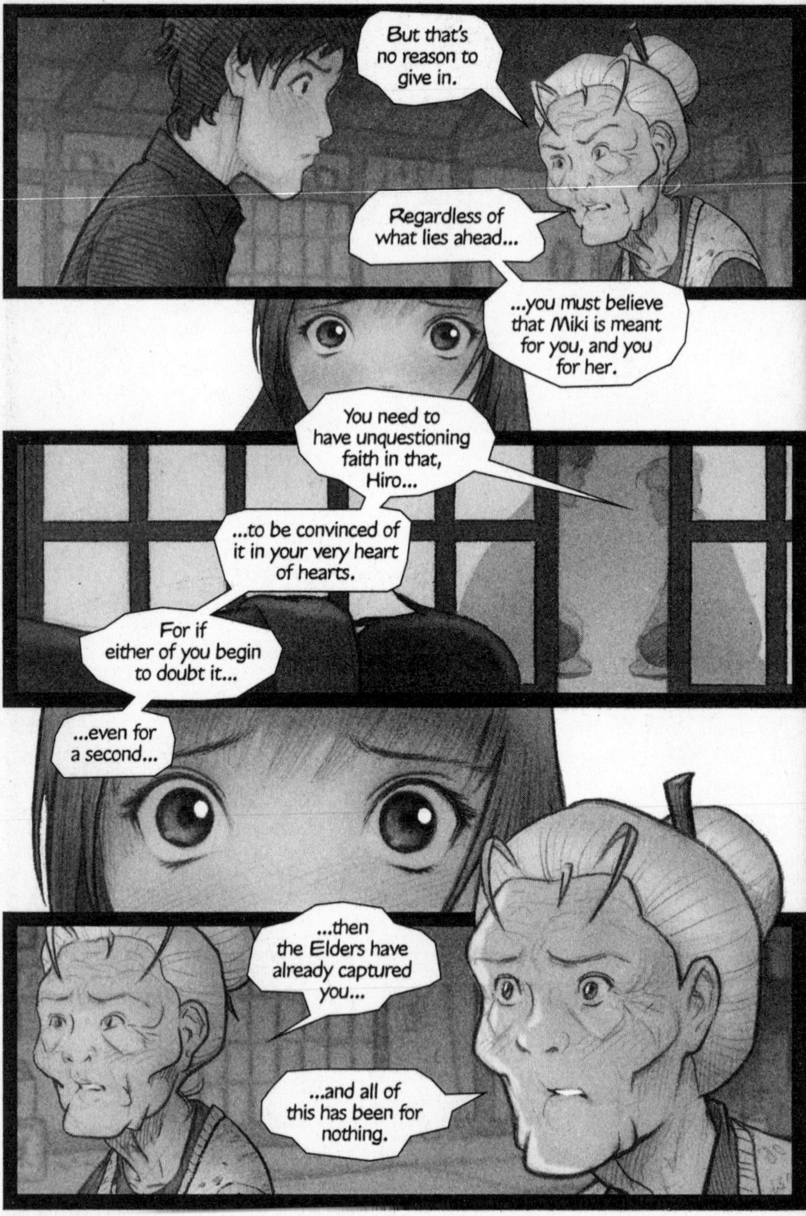
But that's no reason to give in.
Regardless of what lies ahead...
...you must believe that Miki is meant for you, and you for her.
You need to have unquestioning faith in that, Hiro...
...to be convinced of it in your very heart of hearts.
For if either of you begin to doubt it...
...even for a second...
...then the Elders have already captured you...
...and all of this has been for nothing.

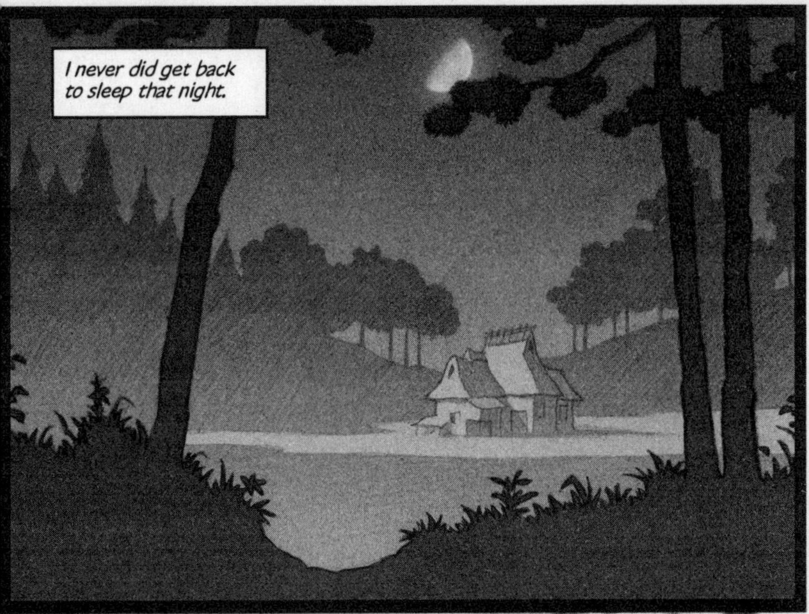
I never did get back to sleep that night.

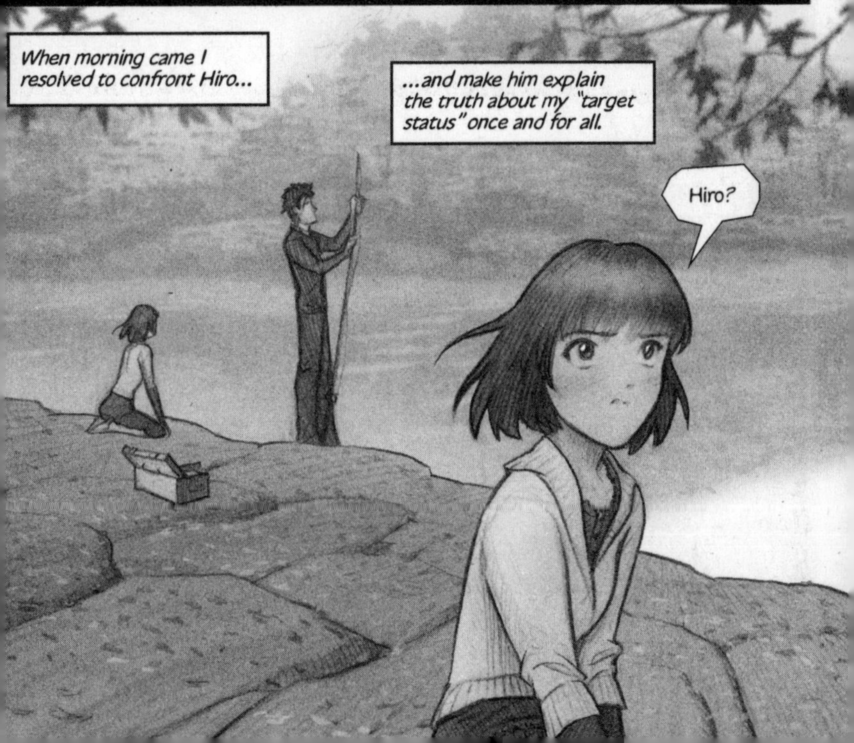
When morning came I resolved to confront Hiro...
...and make him explain the truth about my "target status" once and for all.
Hiro?

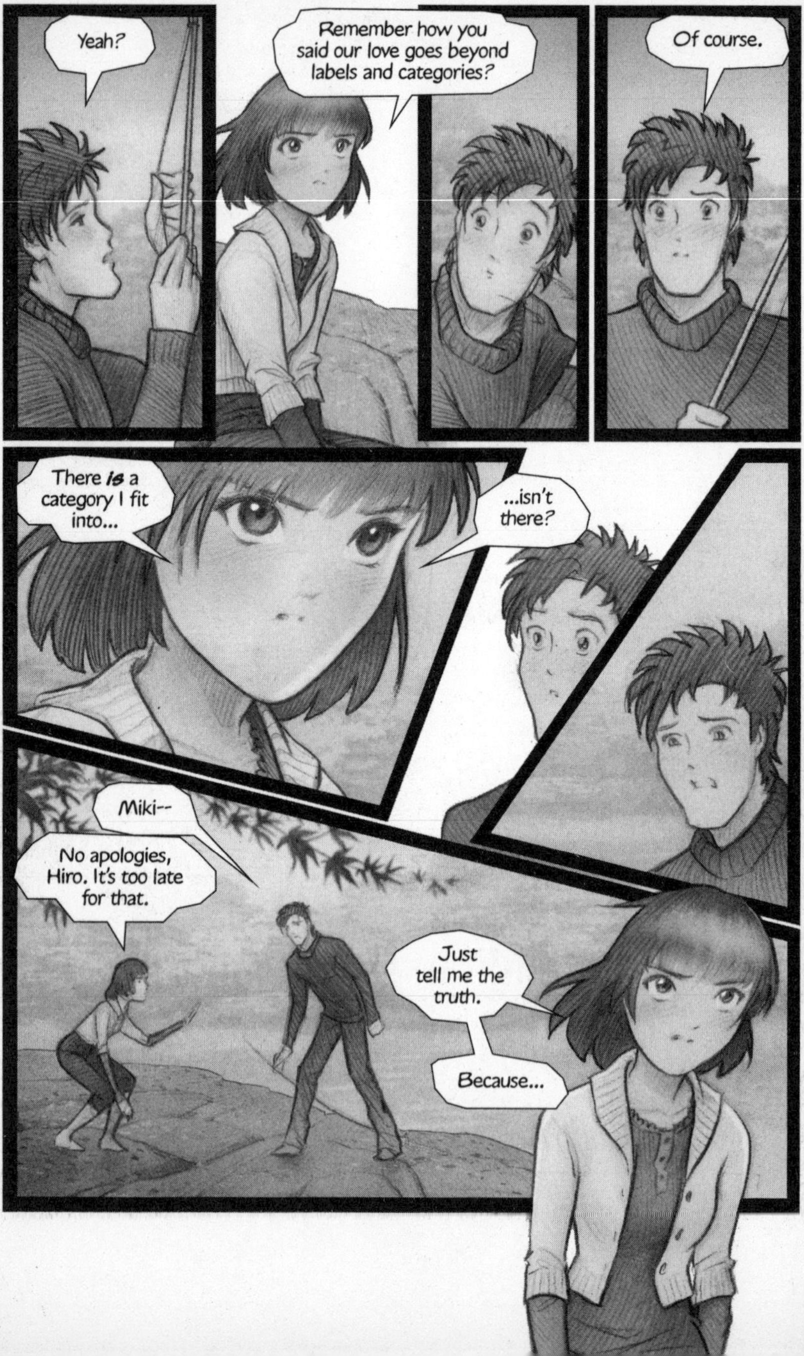
Yeah?
Remember how you said our love goes beyond labels and categories?
Of course.
There *is* a category I fit into...
...isn't there?
Miki--
No apologies, Hiro. It's too late for that.
Just tell me the truth.
Because...

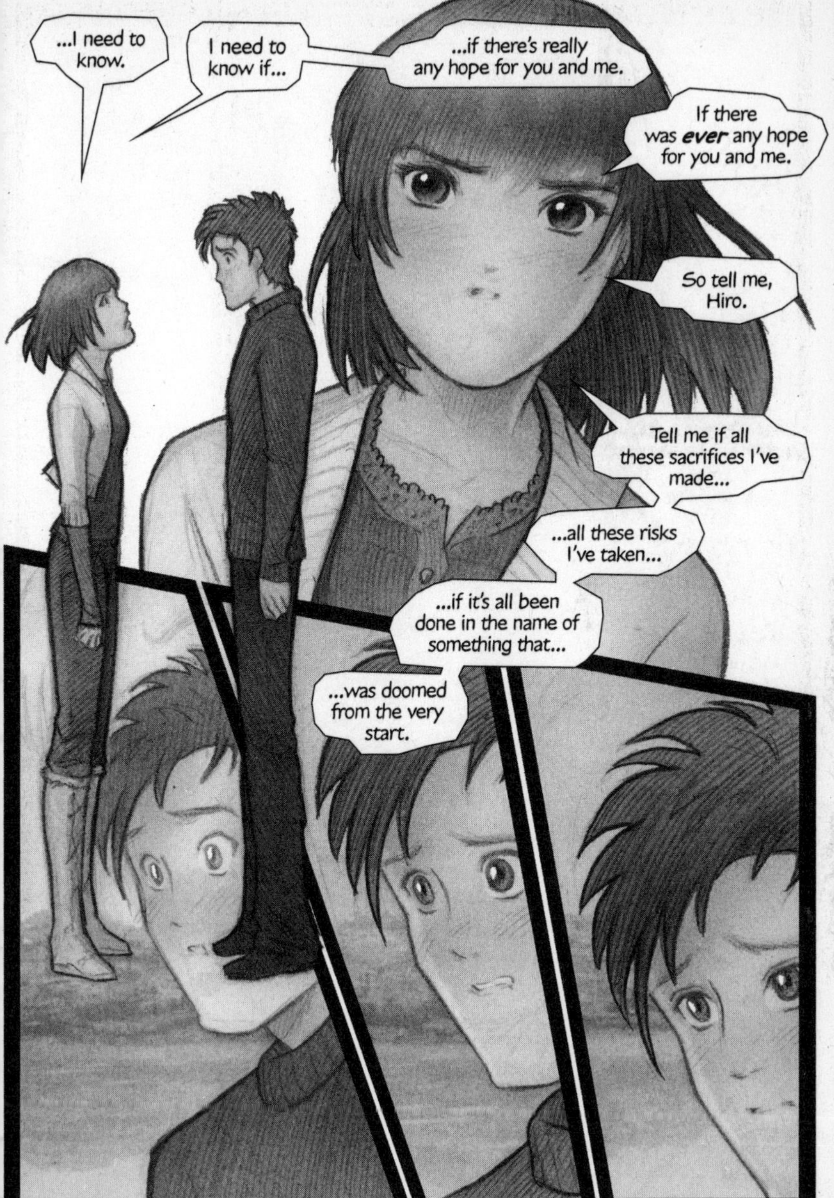
...I need to know.
I need to know if...
...if there's really any hope for you and me.
If there was *ever* any hope for you and me.
So tell me, Hiro.
Tell me if all these sacrifices I've made...
...all these risks I've taken...
...if it's all been done in the name of something that...
...was doomed from the very start.

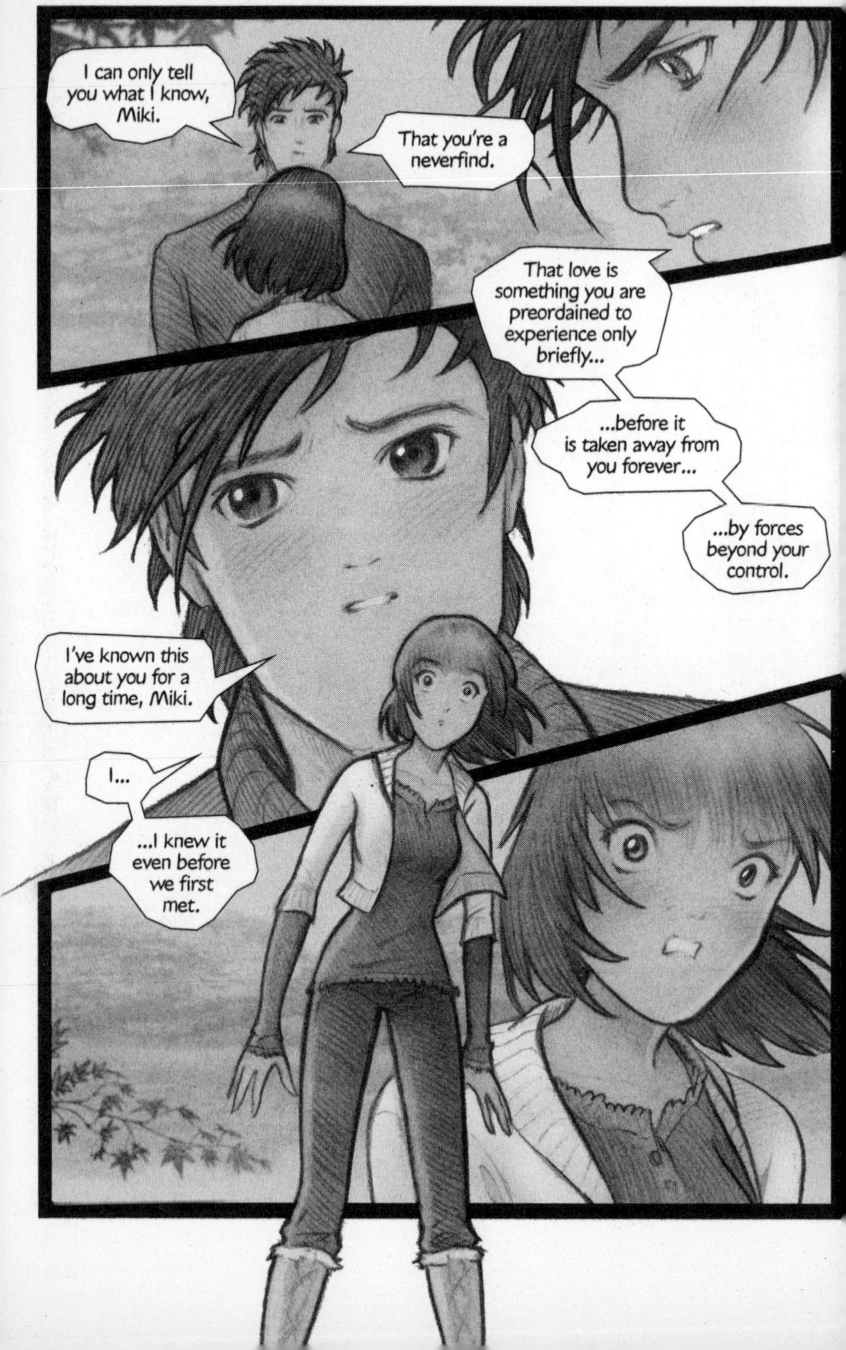
I can only tell you what I know, Miki.
That you're a neverfind.
That love is something you are preordained to experience only briefly...
...before it is taken away from you forever...
...by forces beyond your control.
I've known this about you for a long time, Miki.
I...
...I knew it even before we first met.

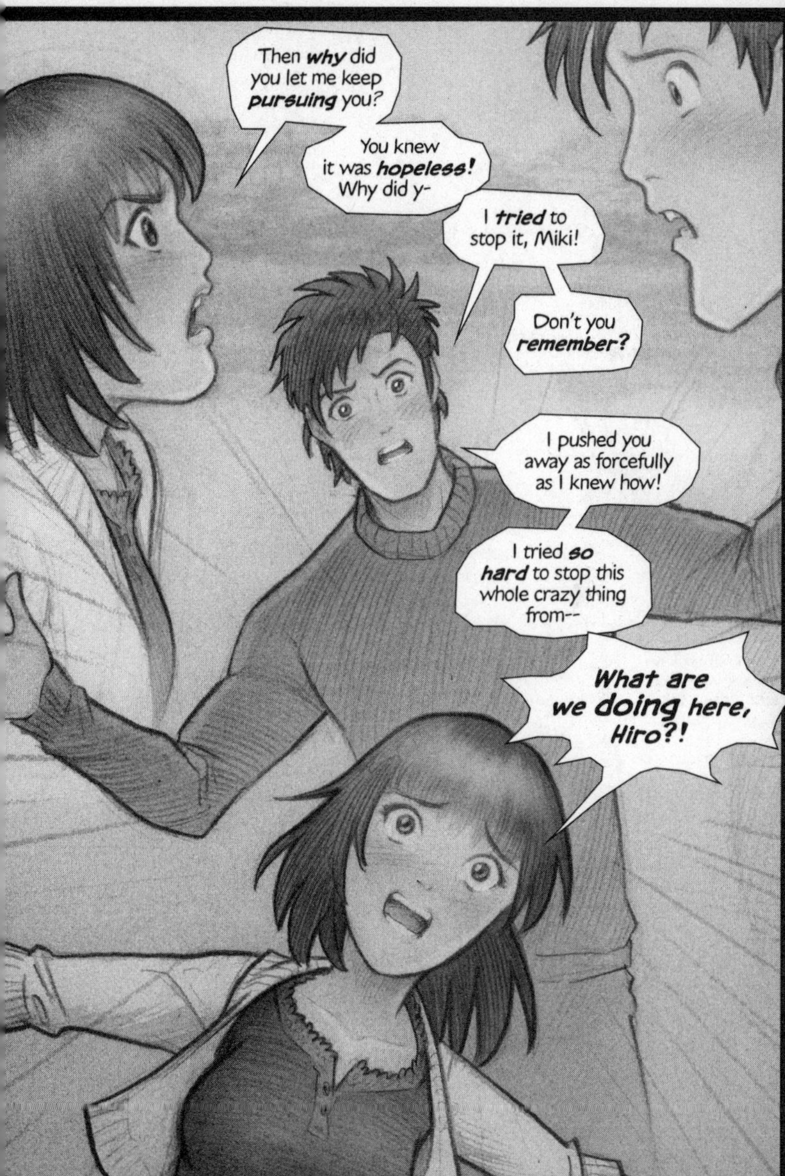
Then why did you let me keep pursuing you?
You knew it was hopeless! Why did y-
I tried to stop it, Miki!
Don't you remember?
I pushed you away as forcefully as I knew how!
I tried so hard to stop this whole crazy thing from--
What are we doing here, Hiro?!

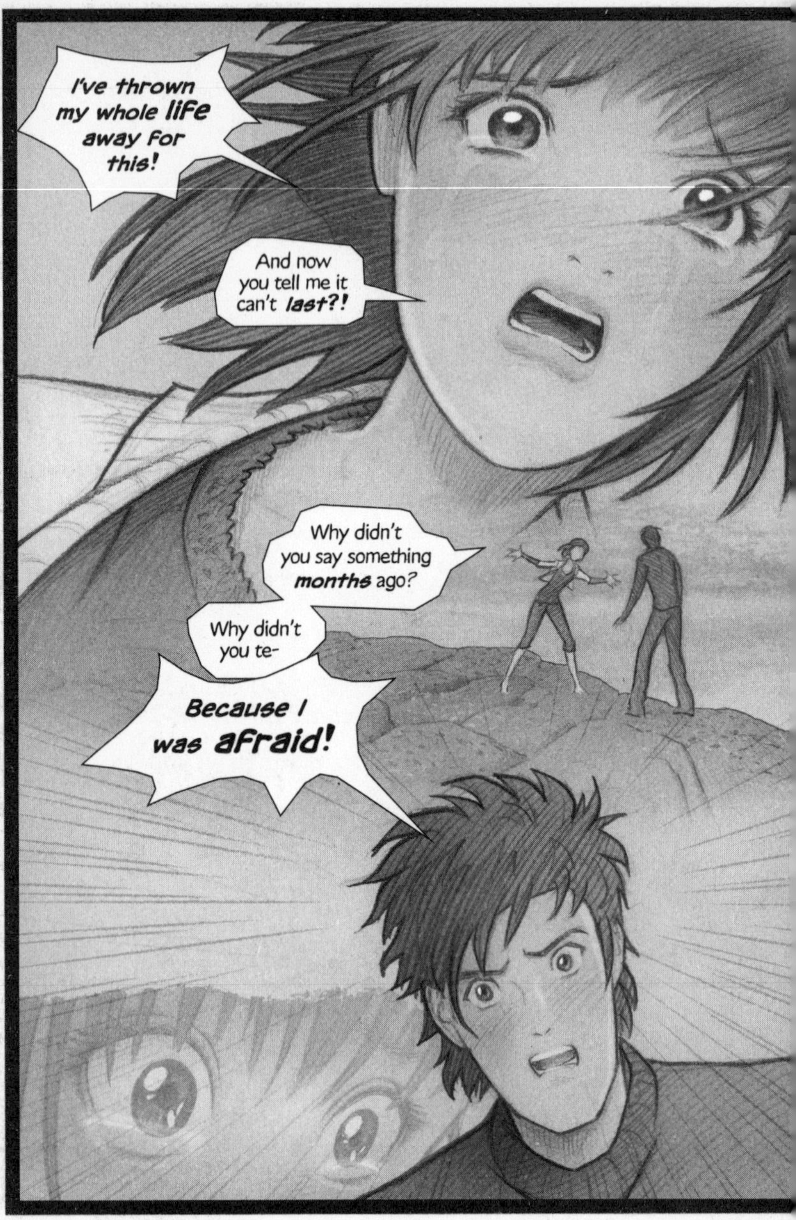
I've thrown my whole life away for this!
And now you tell me it can't last?!
Why didn't you say something months ago?
Why didn't you te-
Because I was afraid!

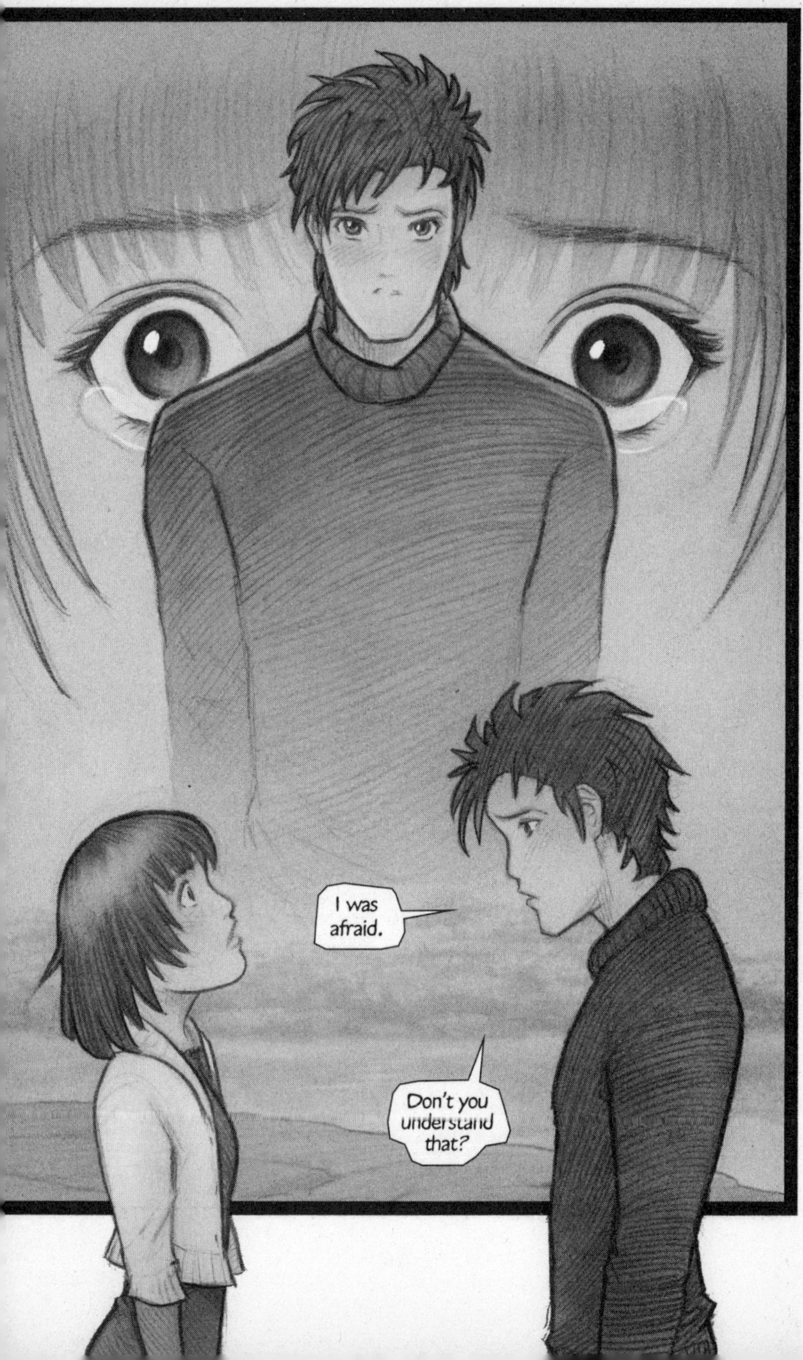
I was afraid.
Don't you understand that?

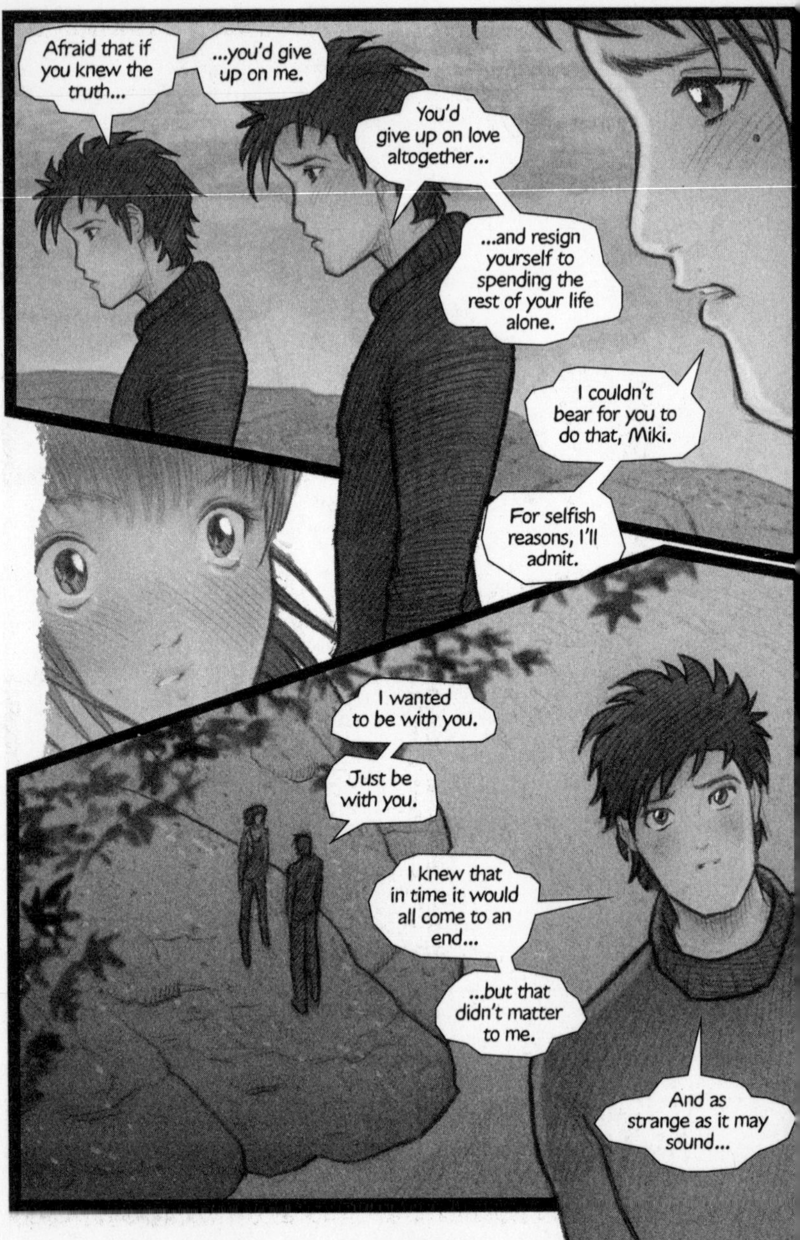
Afraid that if you knew the truth...
...you'd give up on me.
You'd give up on love altogether...
...and resign yourself to spending the rest of your life alone.
I couldn't bear for you to do that, Miki.
For selfish reasons, I'll admit.
I wanted to be with you.
Just be with you.
I knew that in time it would all come to an end...
...but that didn't matter to me.
And as strange as it may sound...

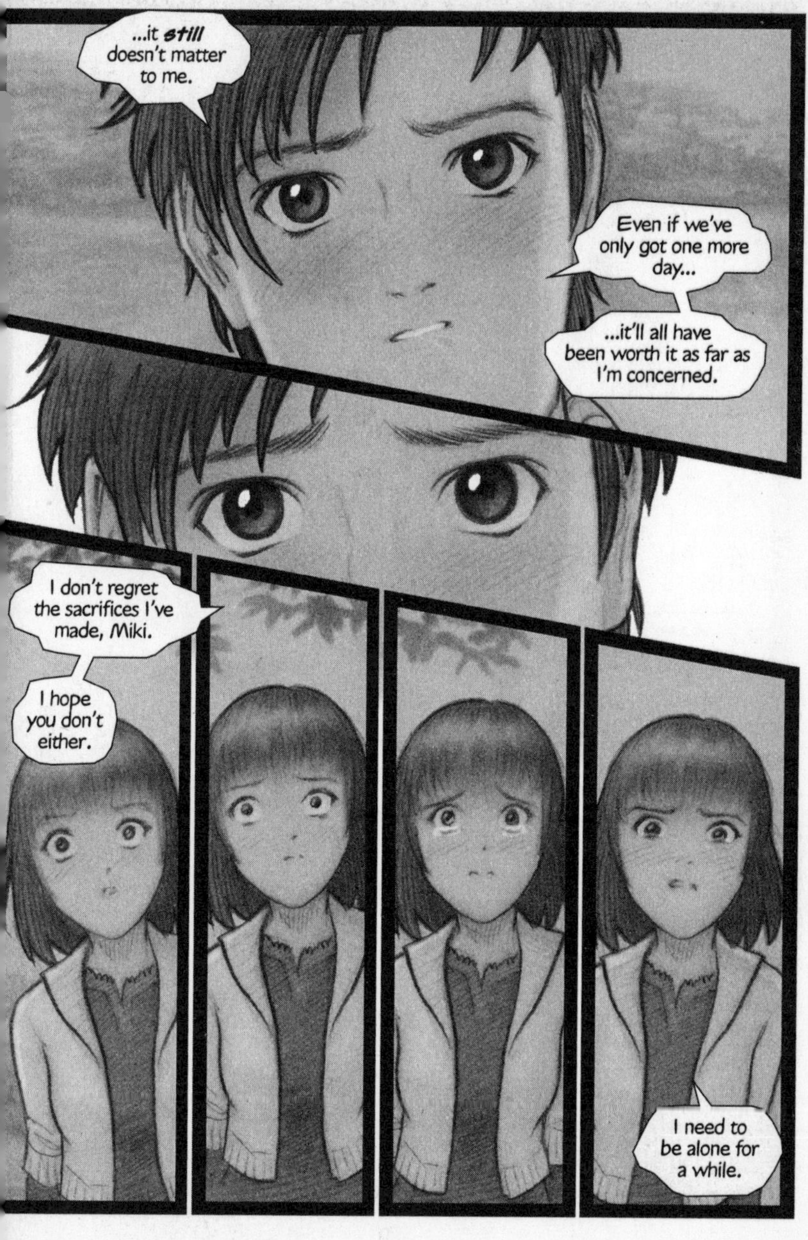
...it *still* doesn't matter to me.
Even if we've only got one more day...
...it'll all have been worth it as far as I'm concerned.
I don't regret the sacrifices I've made, Miki.
I hope you don't either.
I need to be alone for a while.

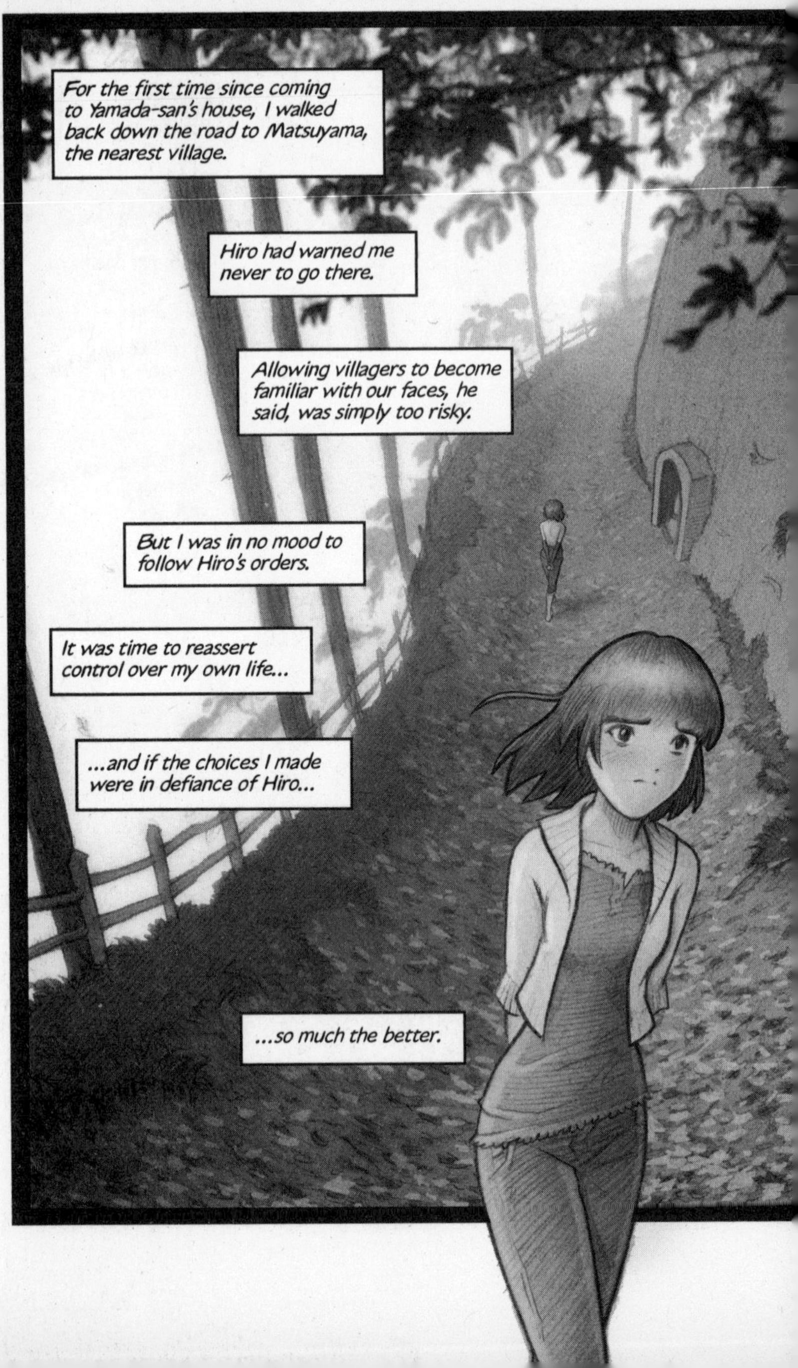
For the first time since coming to Yamada-san's house, I walked back down the road to Matsuyama, the nearest village.
Hiro had warned me never to go there.
Allowing villagers to become familiar with our faces, he said, was simply too risky.
But I was in no mood to follow Hiro's orders.
It was time to reassert control over my own life...
...and if the choices I made were in defiance of Hiro...
...so much the better.

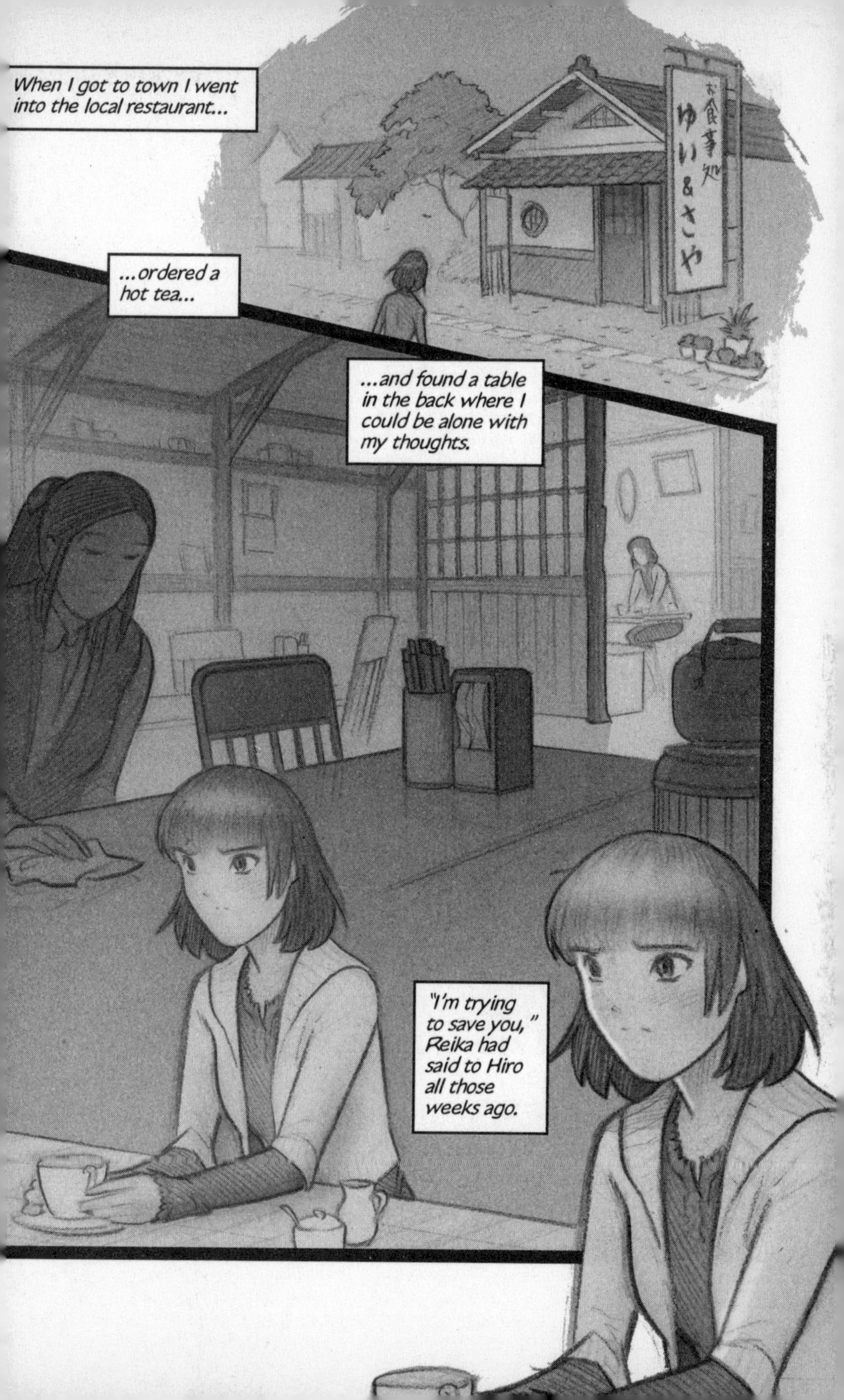
When I got to town I went into the local restaurant...
...ordered a hot tea...
...and found a table in the back where I could be alone with my thoughts.
"I'm trying to save you," Reika had said to Hiro all those weeks ago.

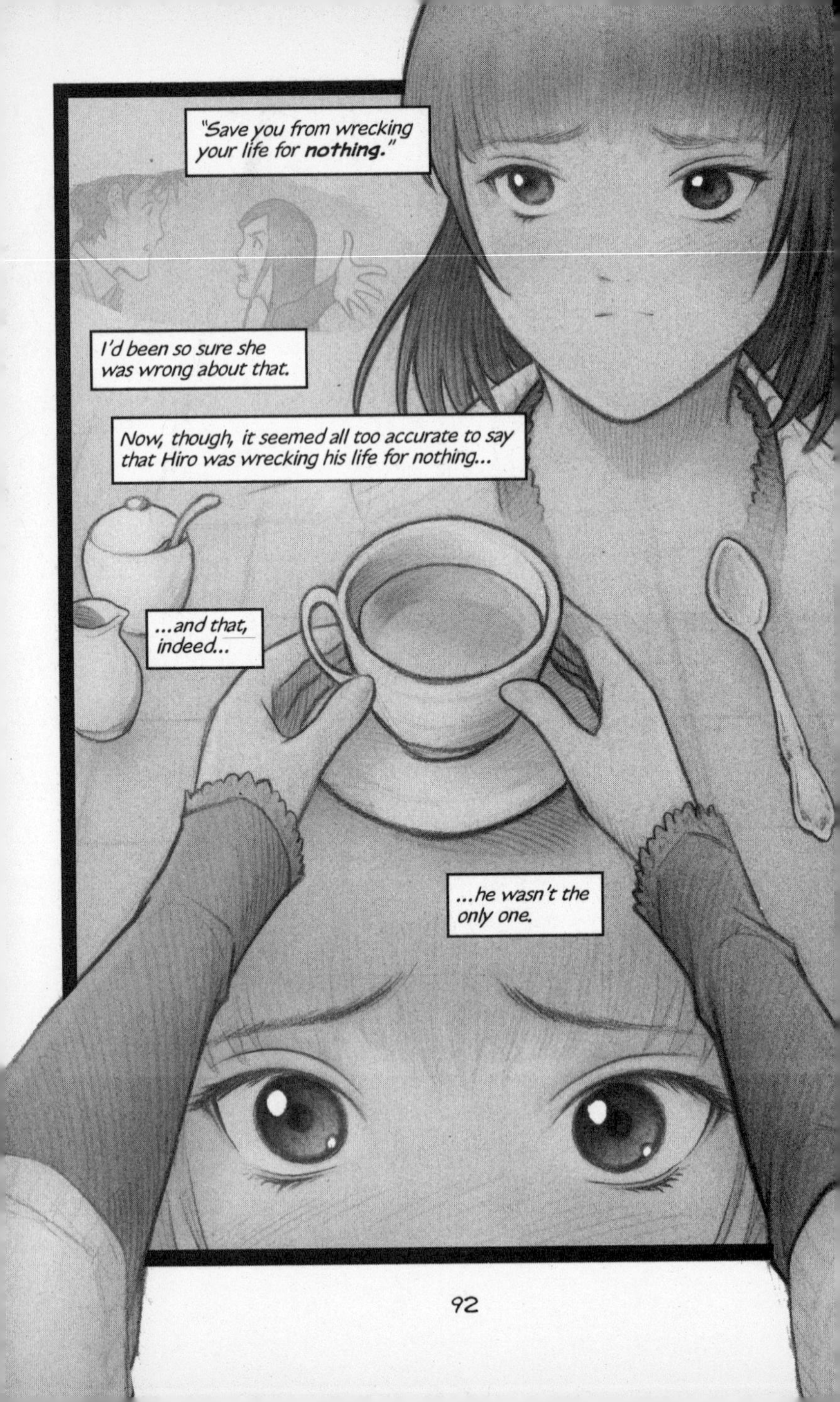
"Save you from wrecking your life for **nothing.**"
I'd been so sure she was wrong about that.
Now, though, it seemed all too accurate to say that Hiro was wrecking his life for nothing...
...and that, indeed...
...he wasn't the only one.

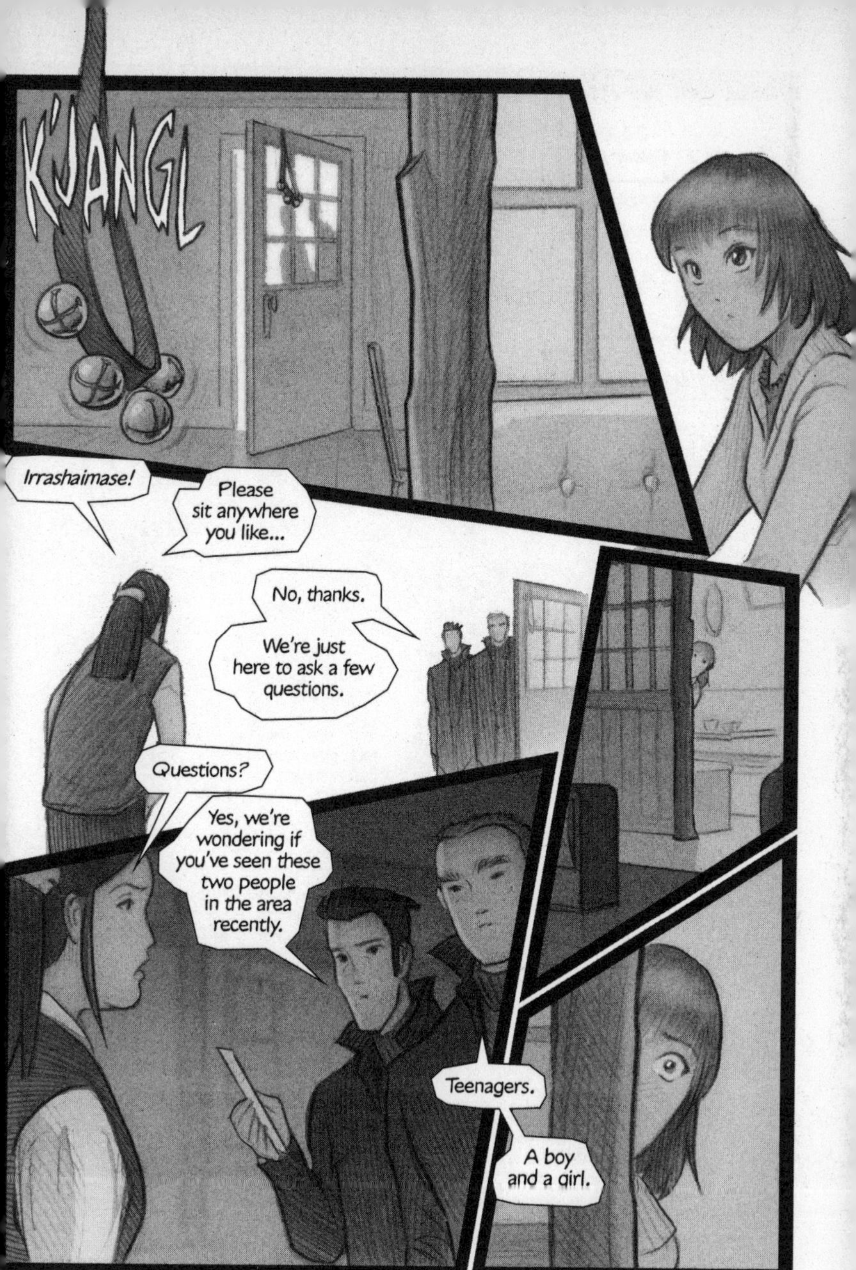
K'JANGL
Irrashaimase!
Please sit anywhere you like...
No, thanks.
We're just here to ask a few questions.
Questions?
Yes, we're wondering if you've seen these two people in the area recently.
Teenagers.
A boy and a girl.

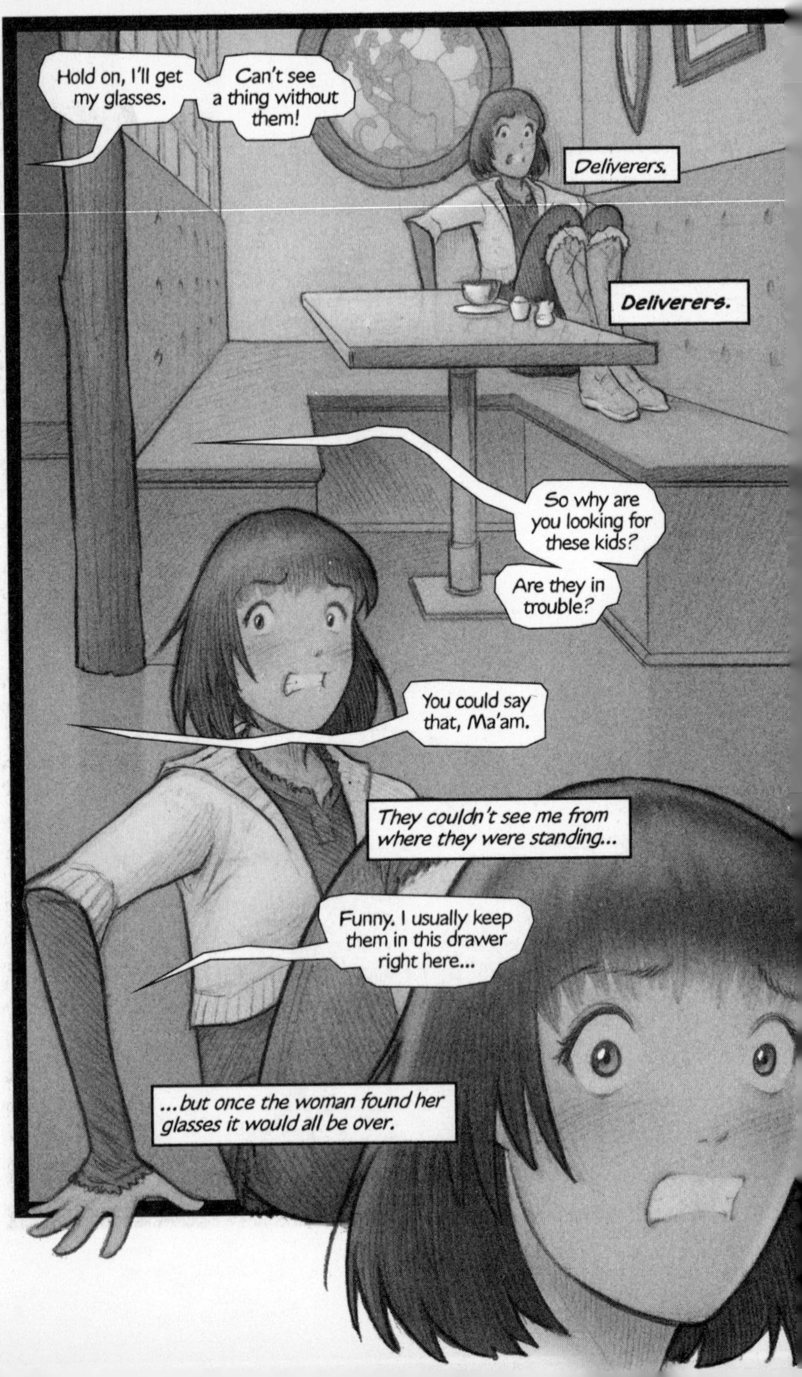
Hold on, I'll get my glasses.
Can't see a thing without them!
Deliverers.
Deliverers.
So why are you looking for these kids?
Are they in trouble?
You could say that, Ma'am.
They couldn't see me from where they were standing...
Funny. I usually keep them in this drawer right here...
...but once the woman found her glasses it would all be over.

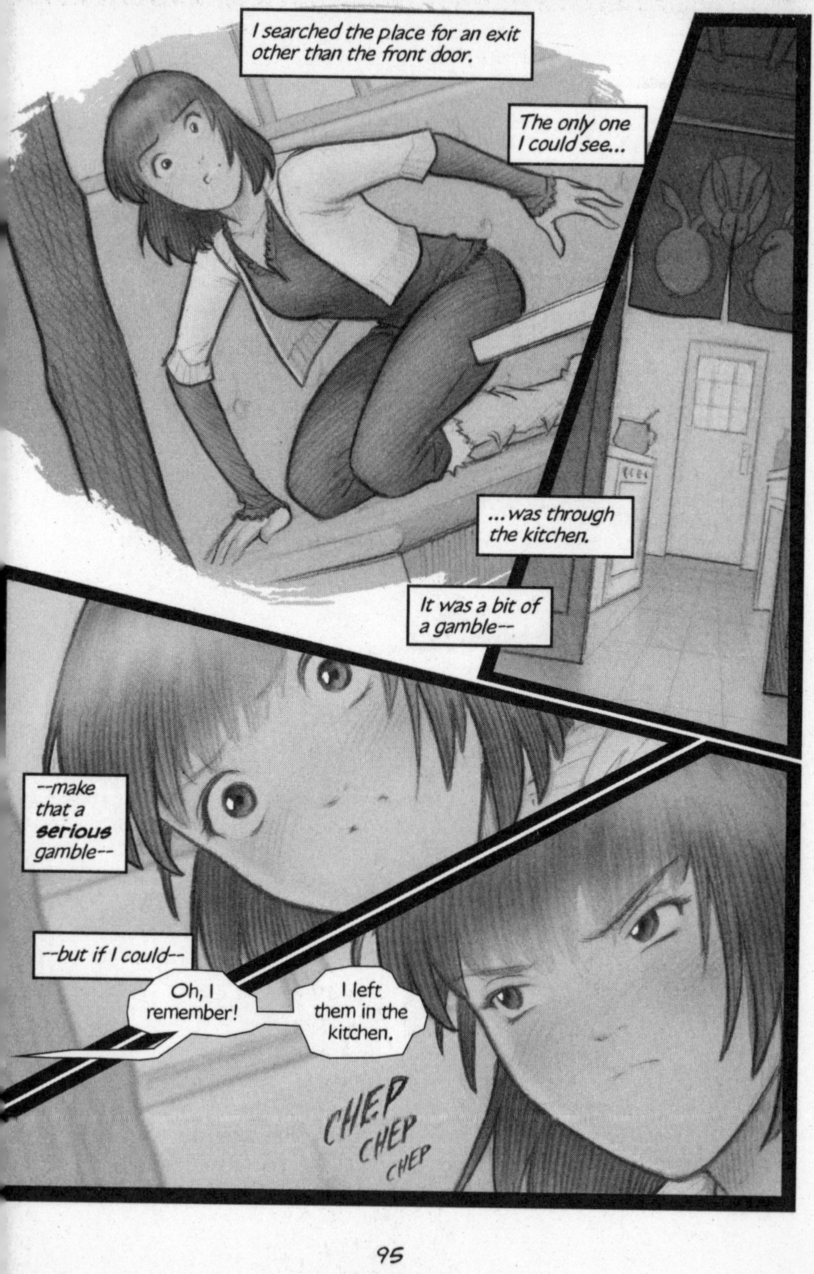
I searched the place for an exit other than the front door.
The only one I could see...
...was through the kitchen.
It was a bit of a gamble--
--make that a **serious** gamble--
--but if I could--
Oh, I remember!
I left them in the kitchen.
CHEP CHEP CHEP CHEP

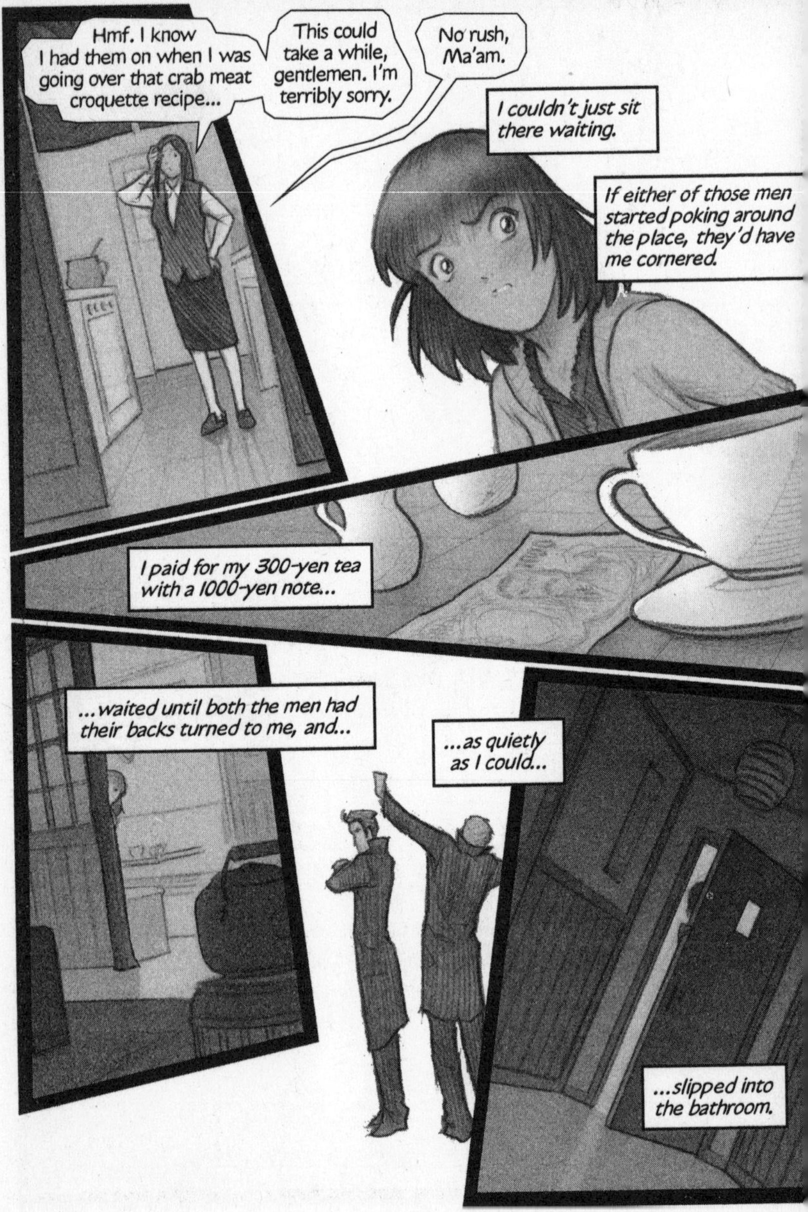
Hmf. I know I had them on when I was going over that crab meat croquette recipe...
This could take a while, gentlemen. I'm terribly sorry.
No rush, Ma'am.
I couldn't just sit there waiting.
If either of those men started poking around the place, they'd have me cornered.
I paid for my 300-yen tea with a 1000-yen note...
...waited until both the men had their backs turned to me, and...
...as quietly as I could...
...slipped into the bathroom.

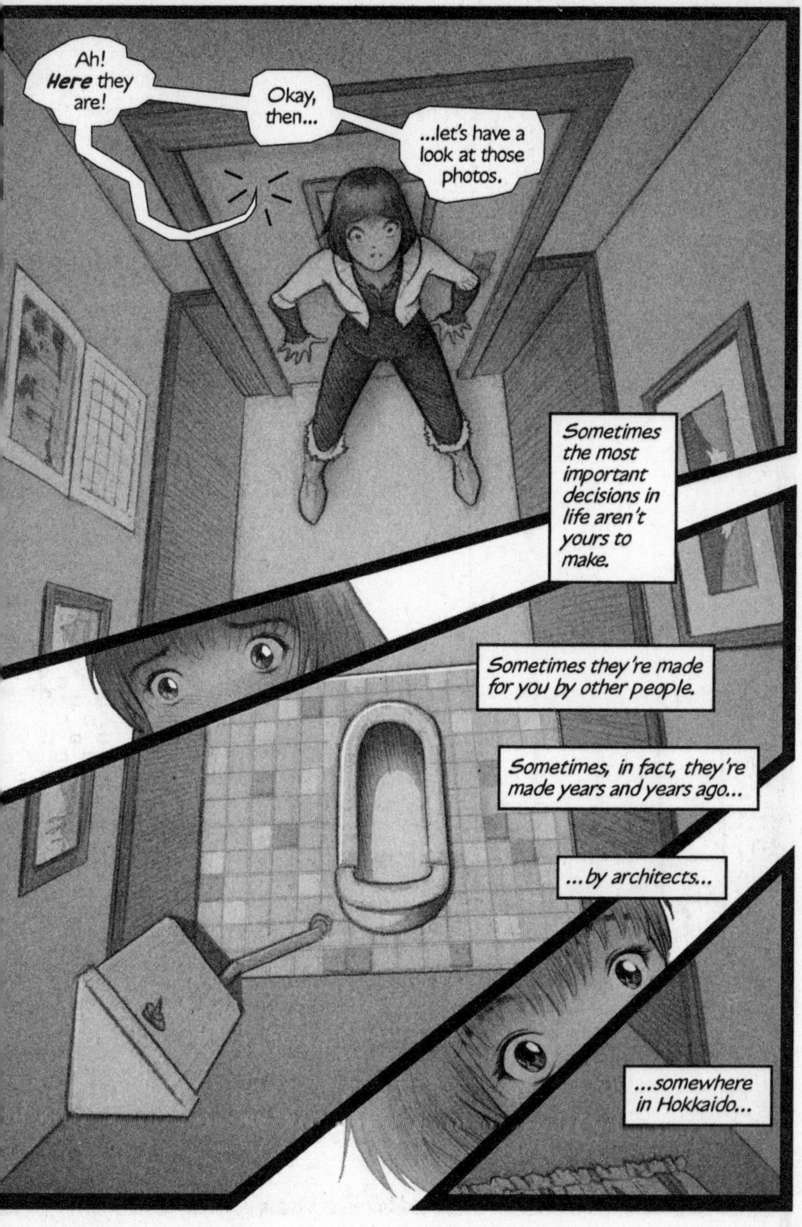
Ah! **Here** they are!
Okay, then...
...let's have a look at those photos.
Sometimes the most important decisions in life aren't yours to make.
Sometimes they're made for you by other people.
Sometimes, in fact, they're made years and years ago...
...by architects...
...somewhere in Hokkaido...

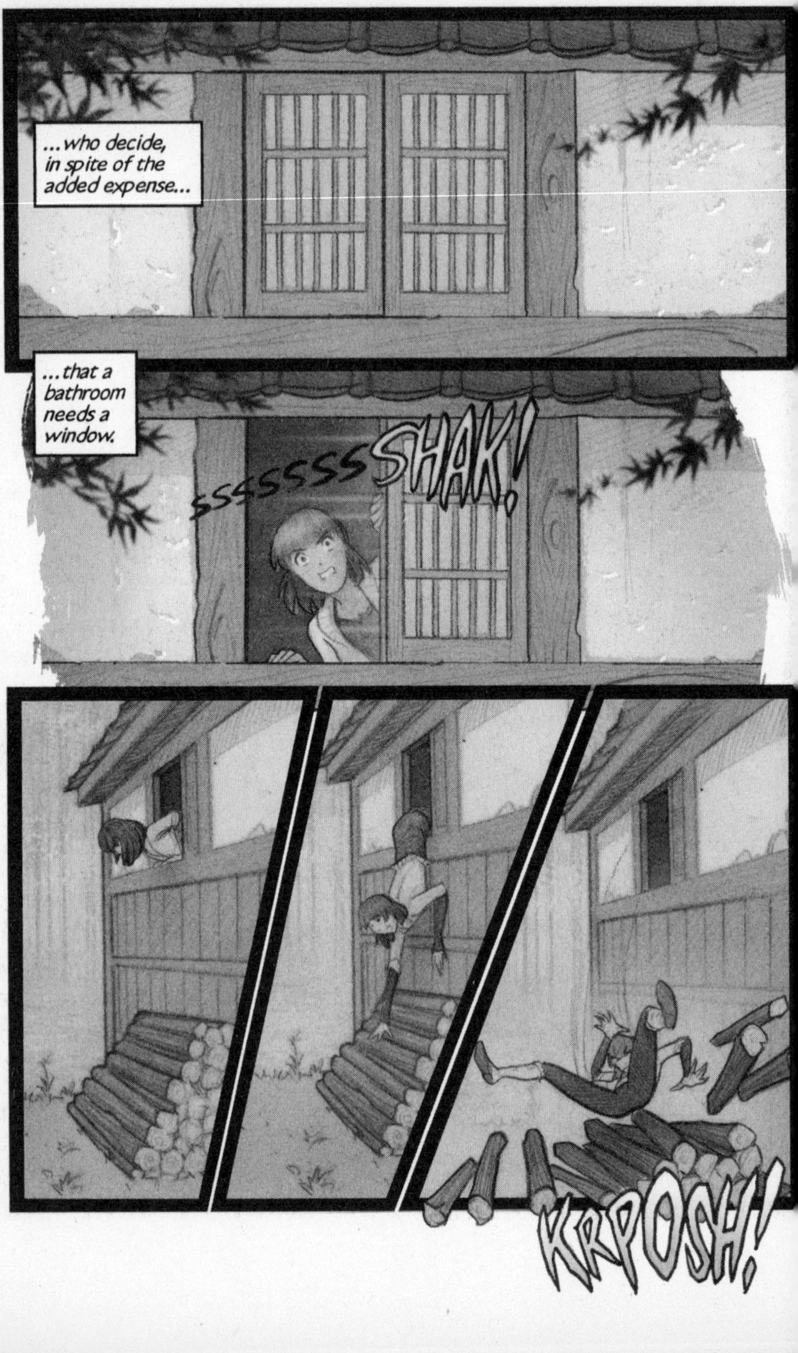

...who decide, in spite of the added expense...
...that a bathroom needs a window.
SSSSSSSSHAK!
KRPOSH!

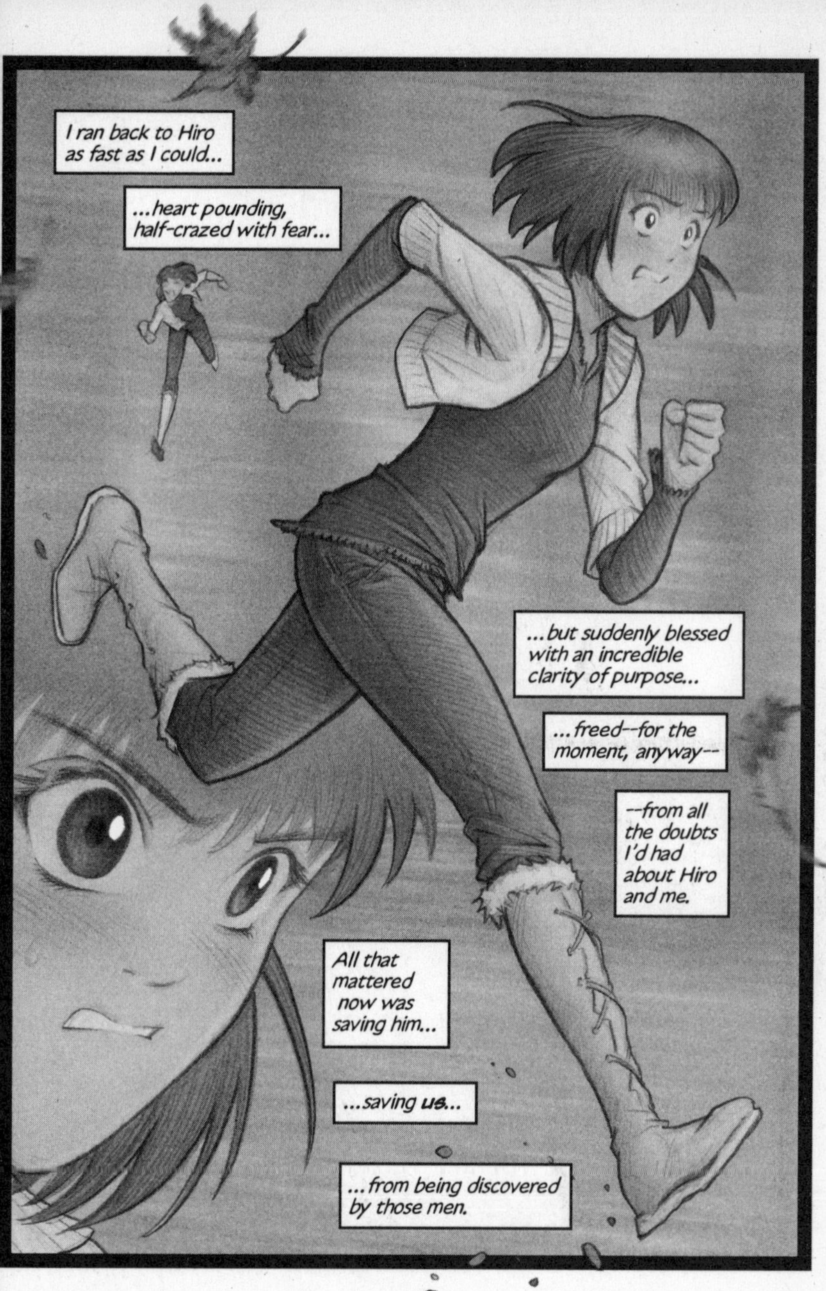
I ran back to Hiro as fast as I could...
...heart pounding, half-crazed with fear...
...but suddenly blessed with an incredible clarity of purpose...
...freed--for the moment, anyway--
--from all the doubts I'd had about Hiro and me.
All that mattered now was saving him...
...saving **us**...
...from being discovered by those men.

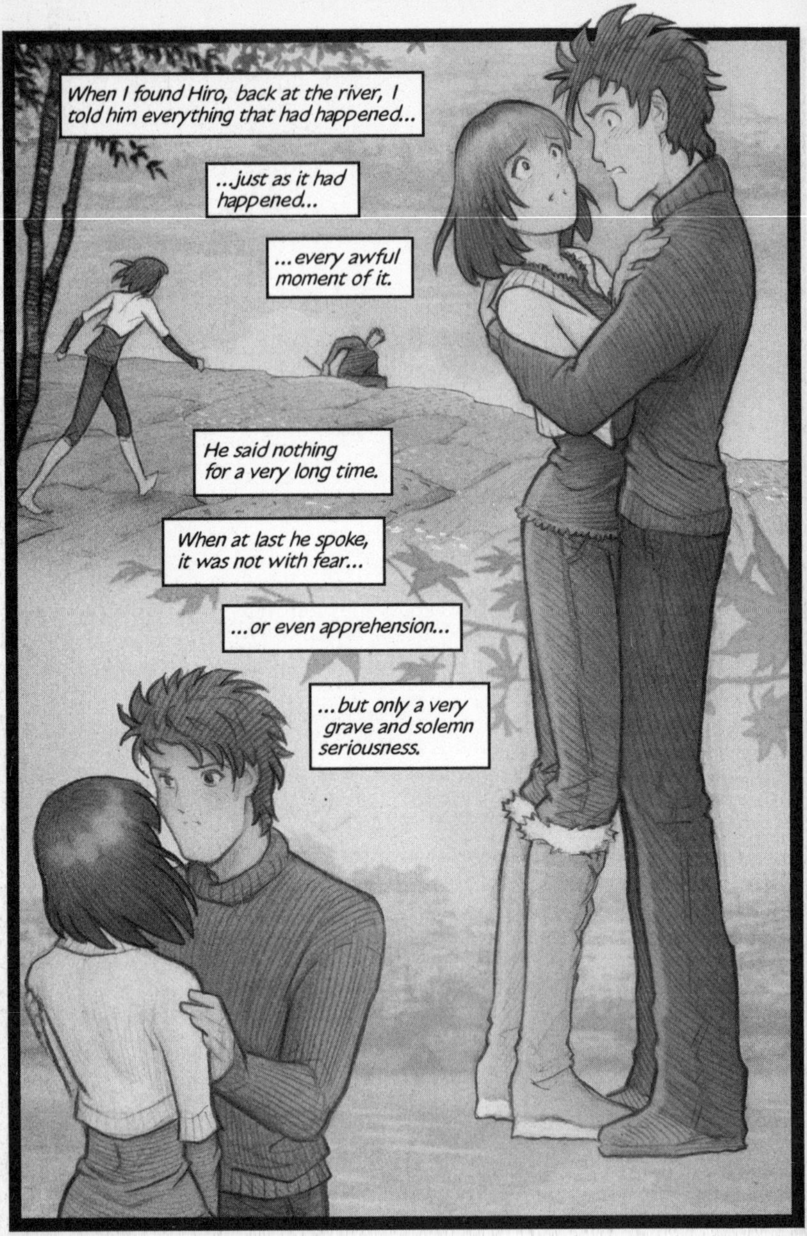
When I found Hiro, back at the river, I told him everything that had happened...
...just as it had happened...
...every awful moment of it.
He said nothing for a very long time.
When at last he spoke, it was not with fear...
...or even apprehension...
...but only a very grave and solemn seriousness.

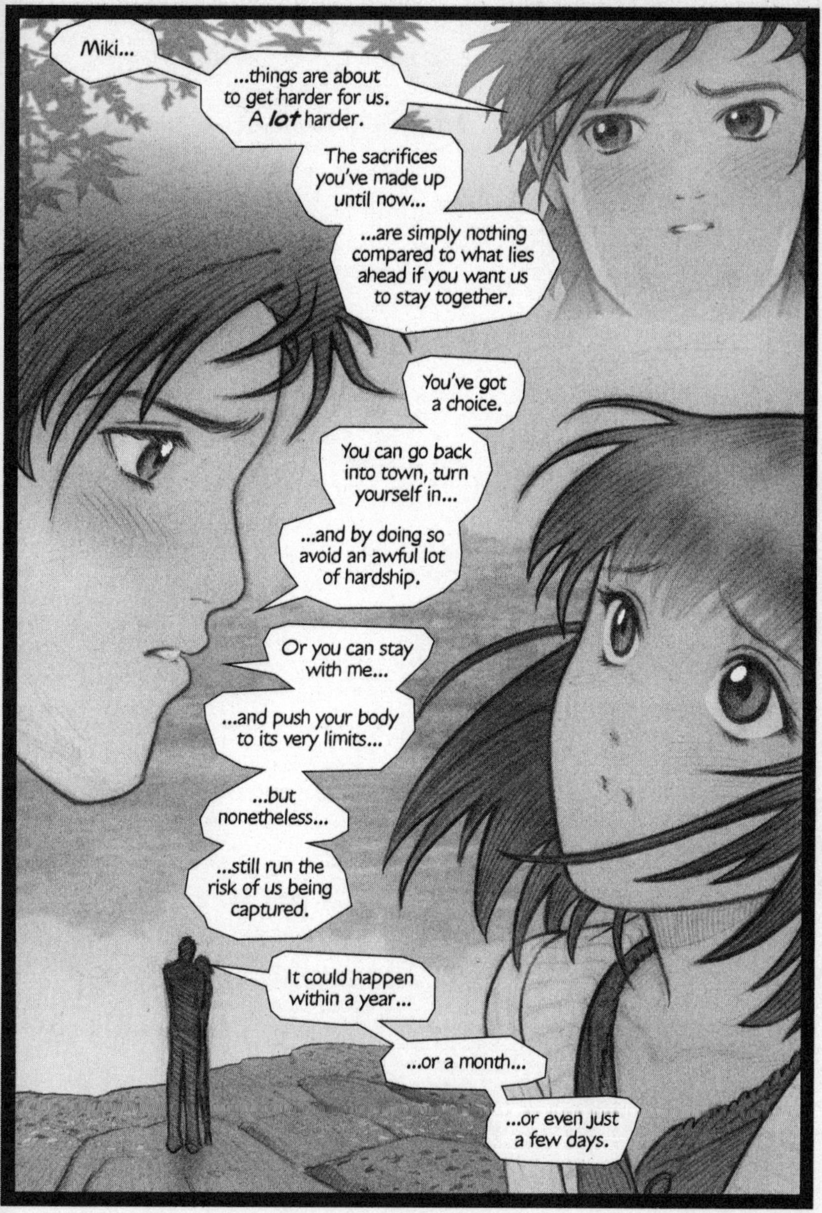
Miki...
...things are about to get harder for us. A *lot* harder.
The sacrifices you've made up until now...
...are simply nothing compared to what lies ahead if you want us to stay together.
You've got a choice.
You can go back into town, turn yourself in...
...and by doing so avoid an awful lot of hardship.
Or you can stay with me...
...and push your body to its very limits...
...but nonetheless...
...still run the risk of us being captured.
It could happen within a year...
...or a month...
...or even just a few days.

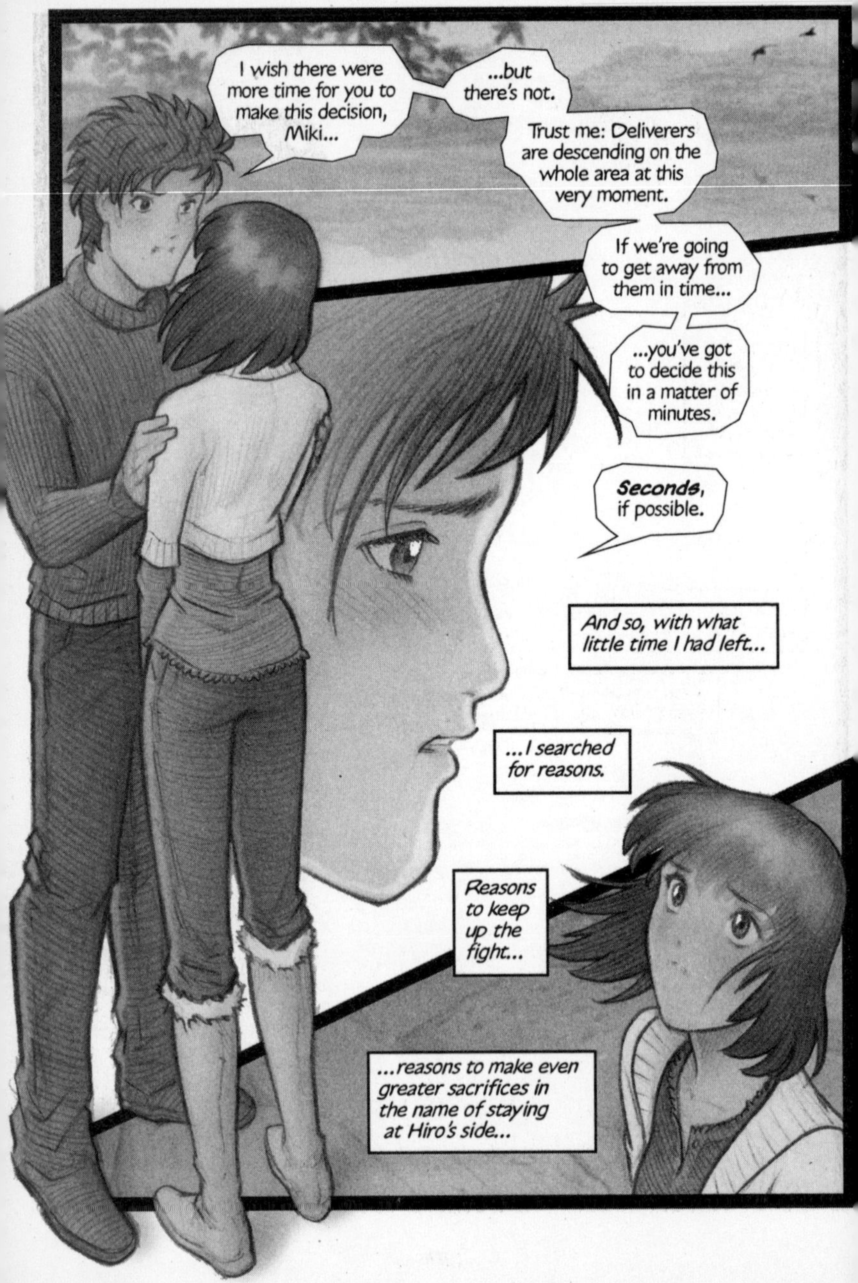

I wish there were more time for you to make this decision, Miki...
...but there's not.
Trust me: Deliverers are descending on the whole area at this very moment.
If we're going to get away from them in time...
...you've got to decide this in a matter of minutes.
Seconds, if possible.
And so, with what little time I had left...
...I searched for reasons.
Reasons to keep up the fight...
...reasons to make even greater sacrifices in the name of staying at Hiro's side...

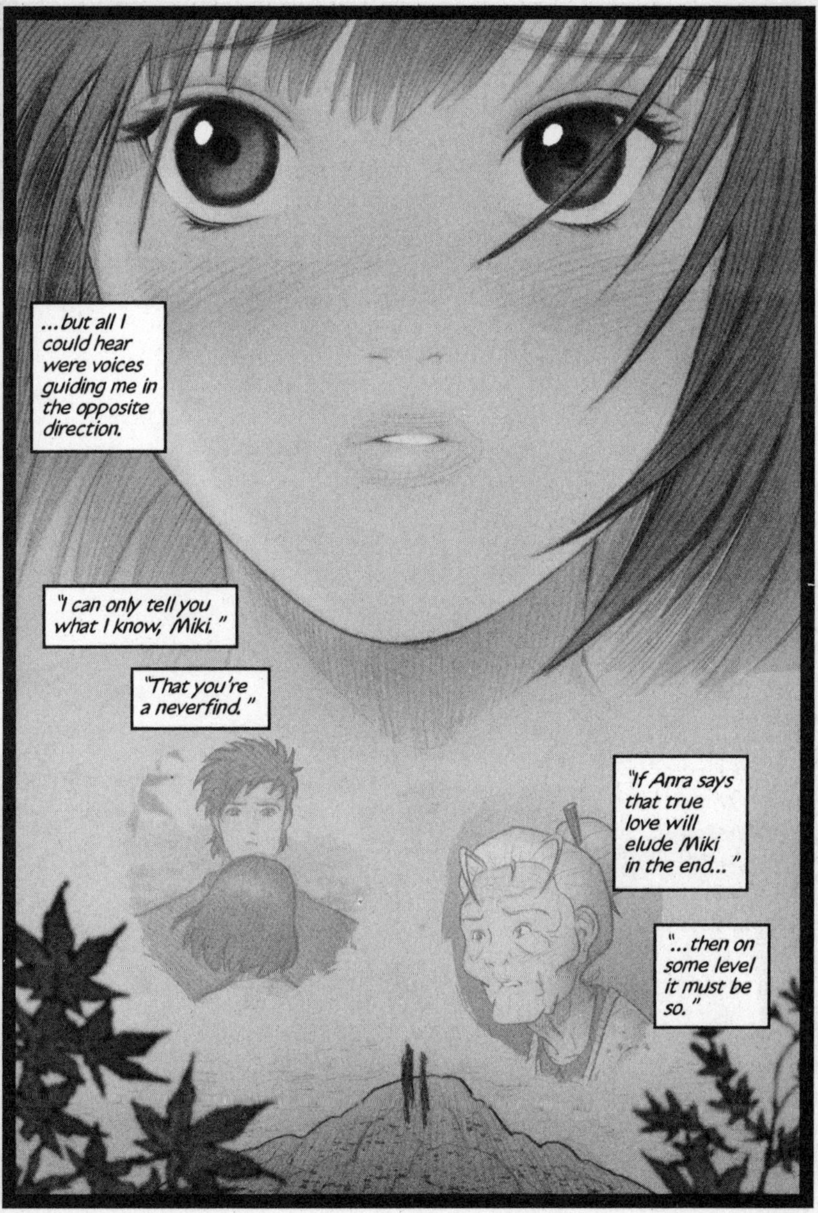
...but all I could hear were voices guiding me in the opposite direction.
"I can only tell you what I know, Miki."
"That you're a neverfind."
"If Anra says that true love will elude Miki in the end..."
"...then on some level it must be so."

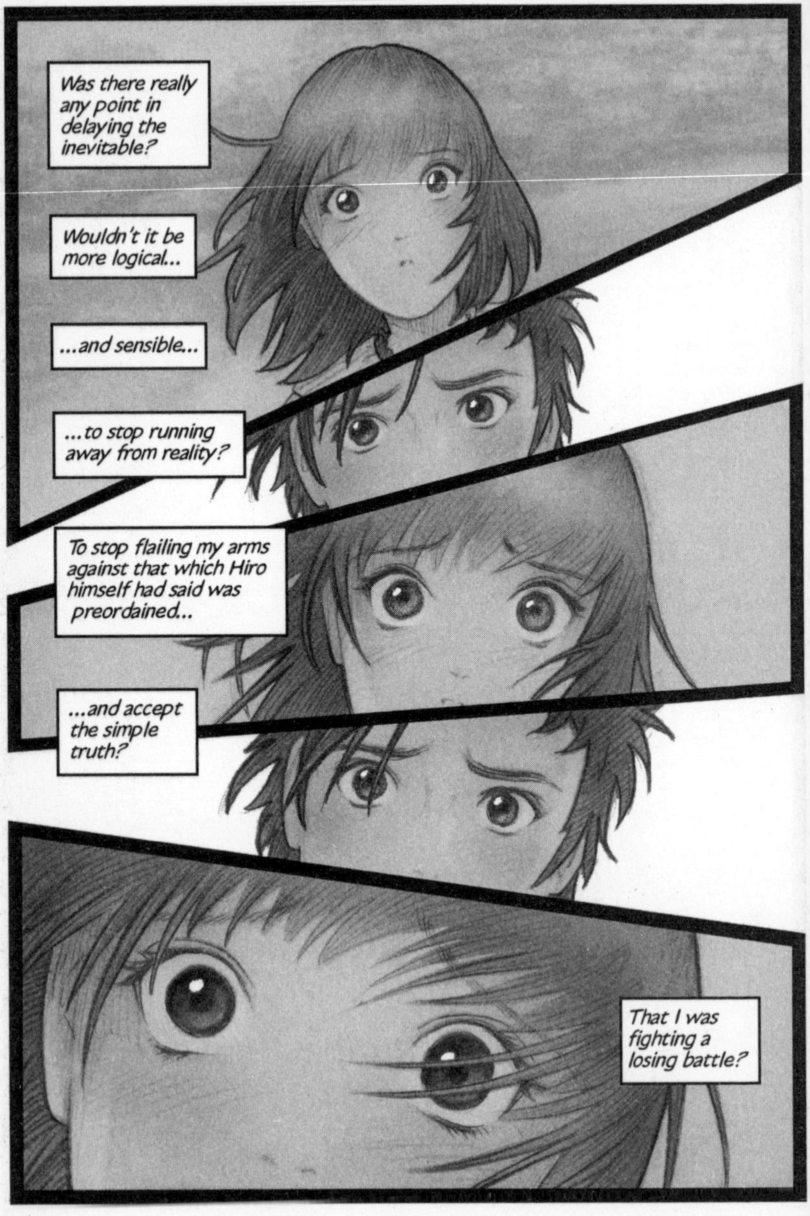
Was there really any point in delaying the inevitable?
Wouldn't it be more logical...
...and sensible...
...to stop running away from reality?
To stop flailing my arms against that which Hiro himself had said was preordained...
...and accept the simple truth?
That I was fighting a losing battle?

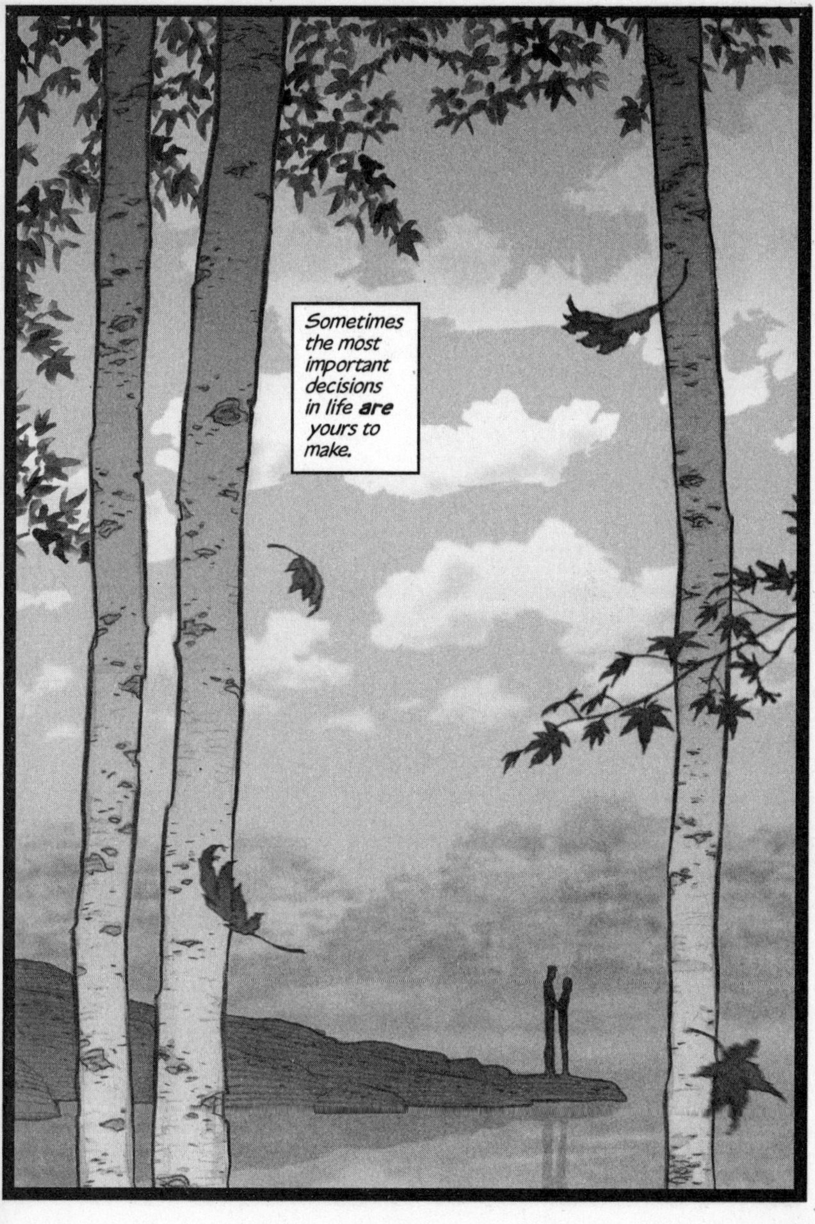
Sometimes the most important decisions in life **are** yours to make.

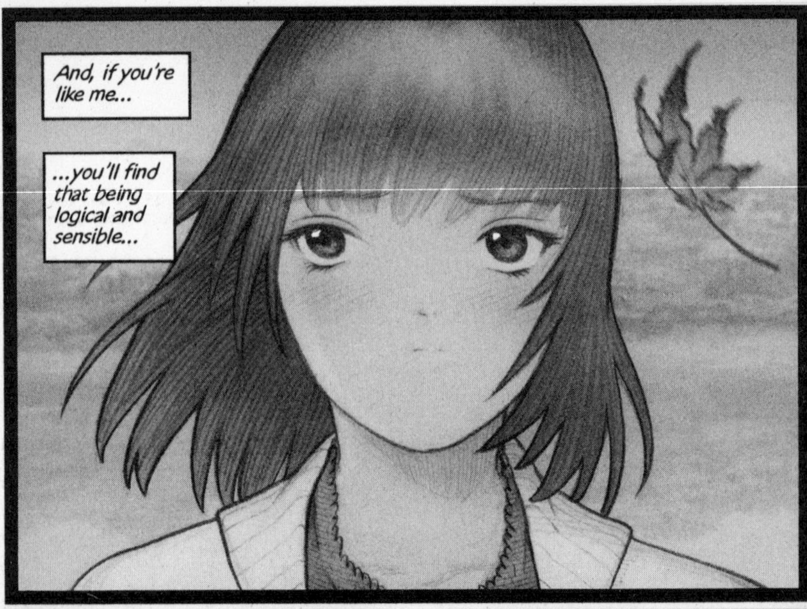
And, if you're like me...
...you'll find that being logical and sensible...

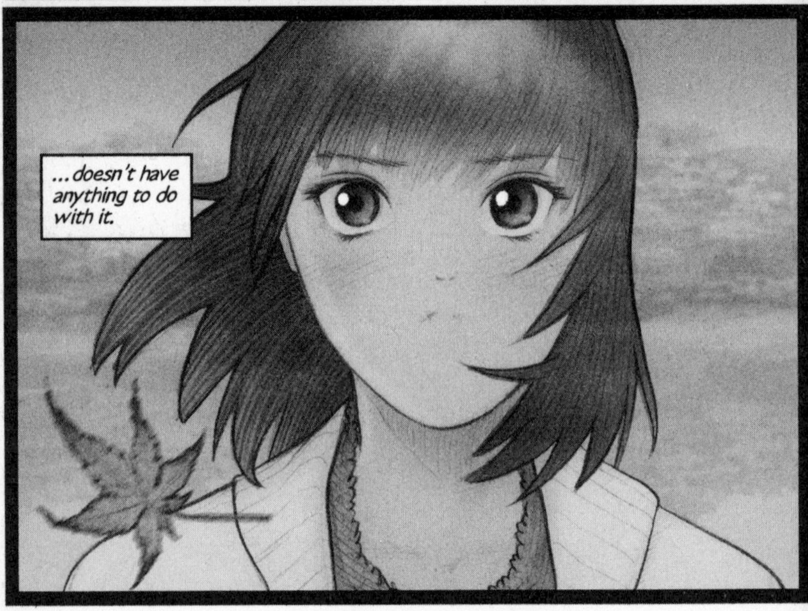
...doesn't have anything to do with it.

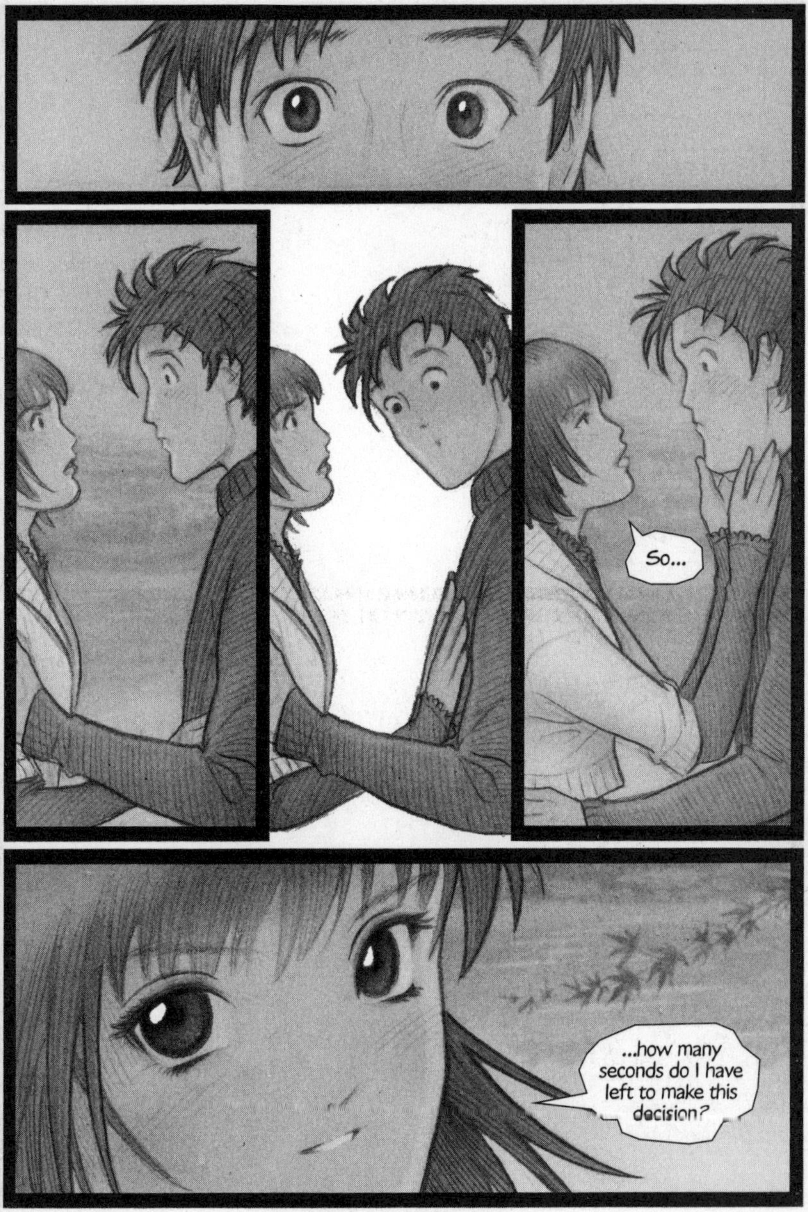
So...
...how many seconds do I have left to make this decision?

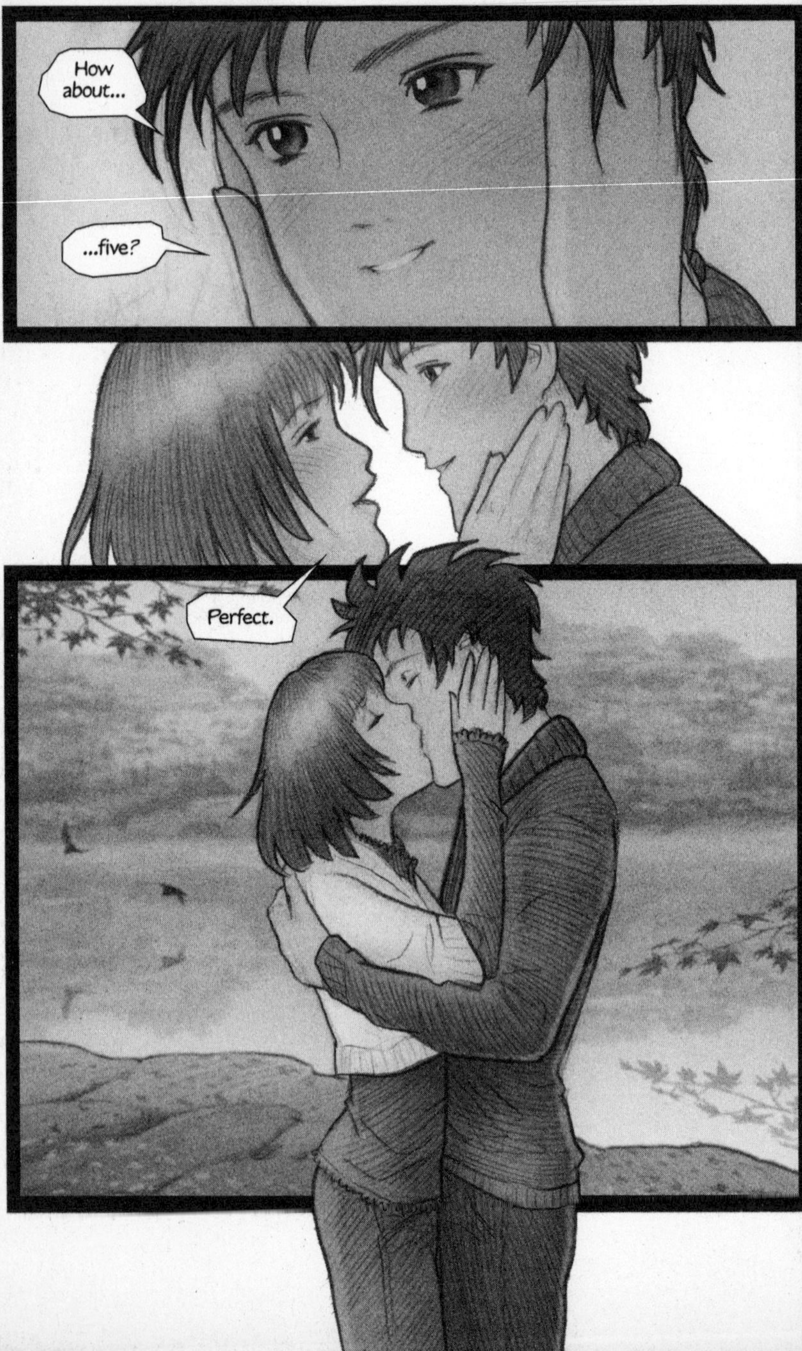
How about...
...five?
Perfect.

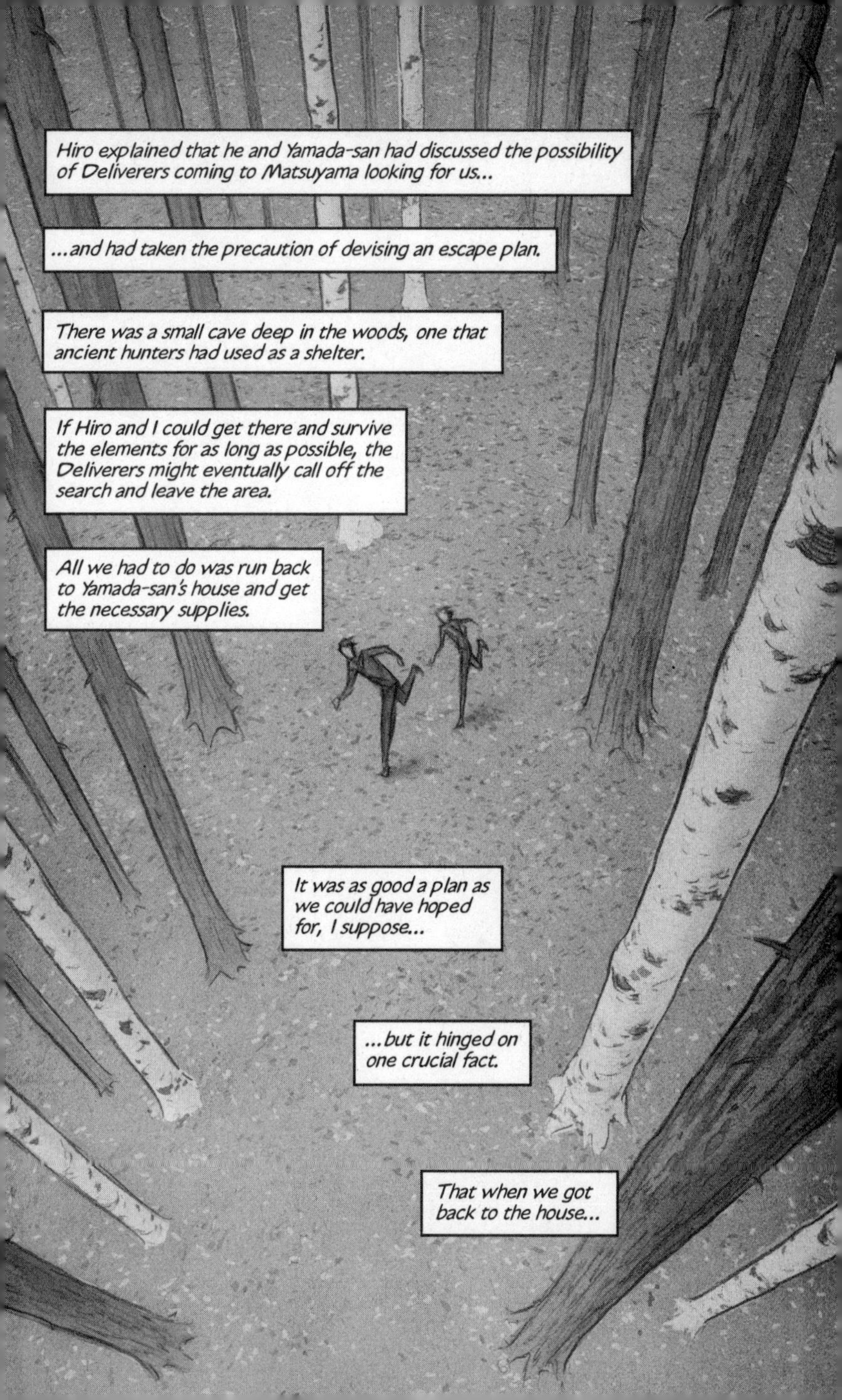
Hiro explained that he and Yamada-san had discussed the possibility of Deliverers coming to Matsuyama looking for us...
...and had taken the precaution of devising an escape plan.
There was a small cave deep in the woods, one that ancient hunters had used as a shelter.
If Hiro and I could get there and survive the elements for as long as possible, the Deliverers might eventually call off the search and leave the area.
All we had to do was run back to Yamada-san's house and get the necessary supplies.
It was as good a plan as we could have hoped for, I suppose...
...but it hinged on one crucial fact.
That when we got back to the house...

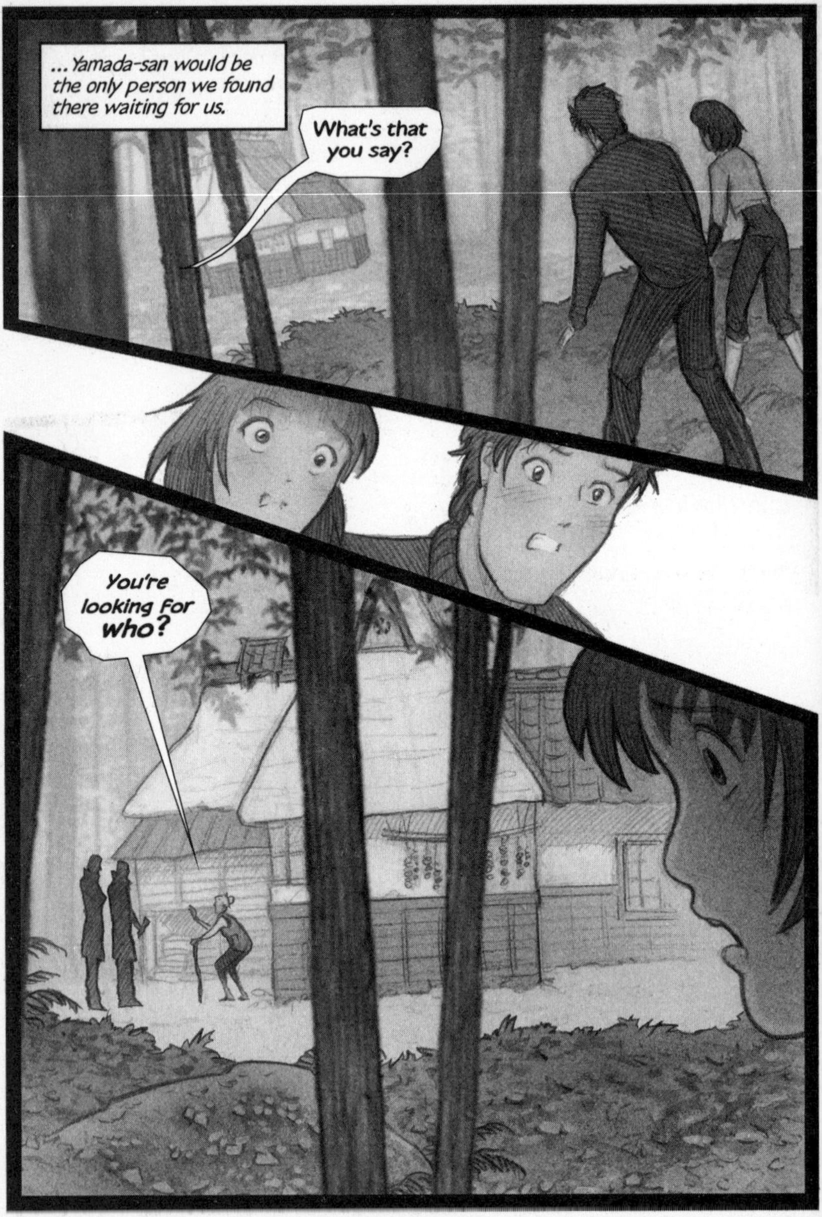
...Yamada-san would be the only person we found there waiting for us.
What's that you say?
You're looking for who?

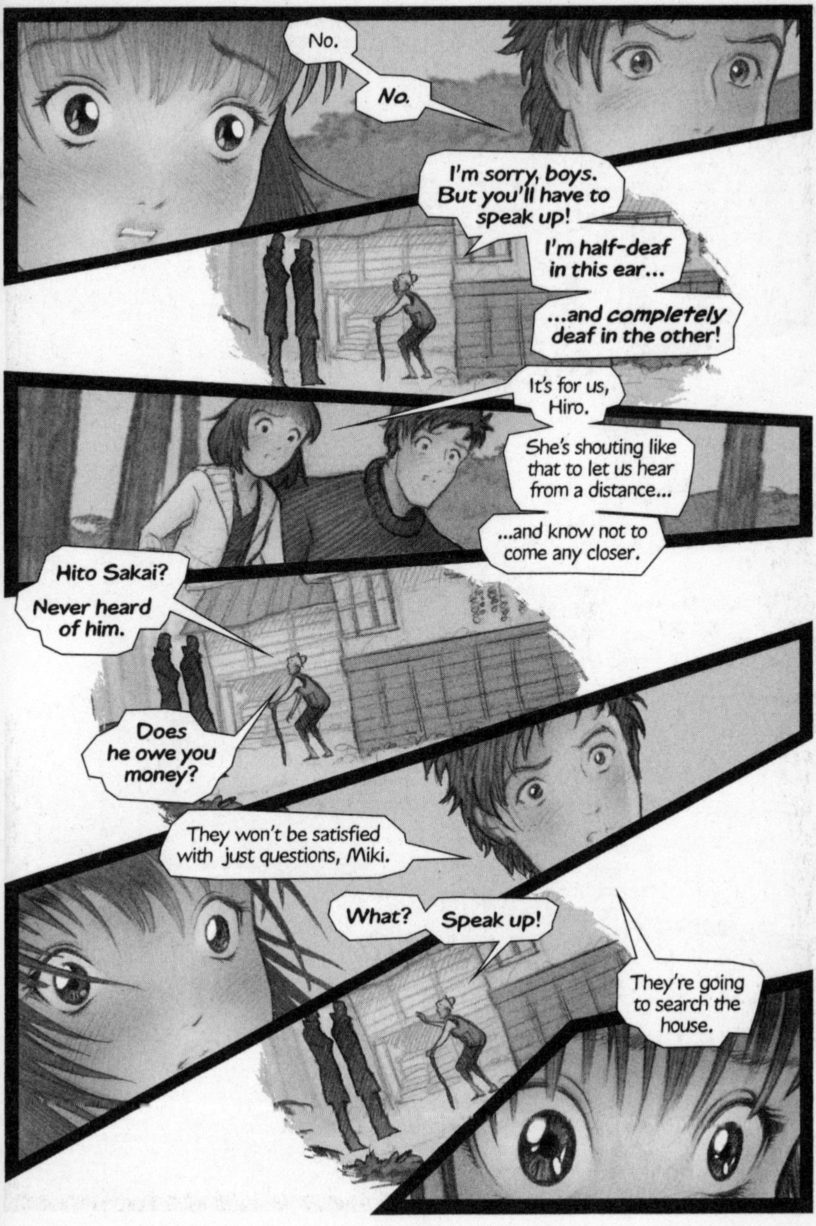
No.
No.
I'm sorry, boys. But you'll have to speak up!
I'm half-deaf in this ear...
...and *completely* deaf in the other!
It's for us, Hiro.
She's shouting like that to let us hear from a distance...
...and know not to come any closer.
Hito Sakai?
Never heard of him.
Does he owe you money?
They won't be satisfied with just questions, Miki.
What?
Speak up!
They're going to search the house.

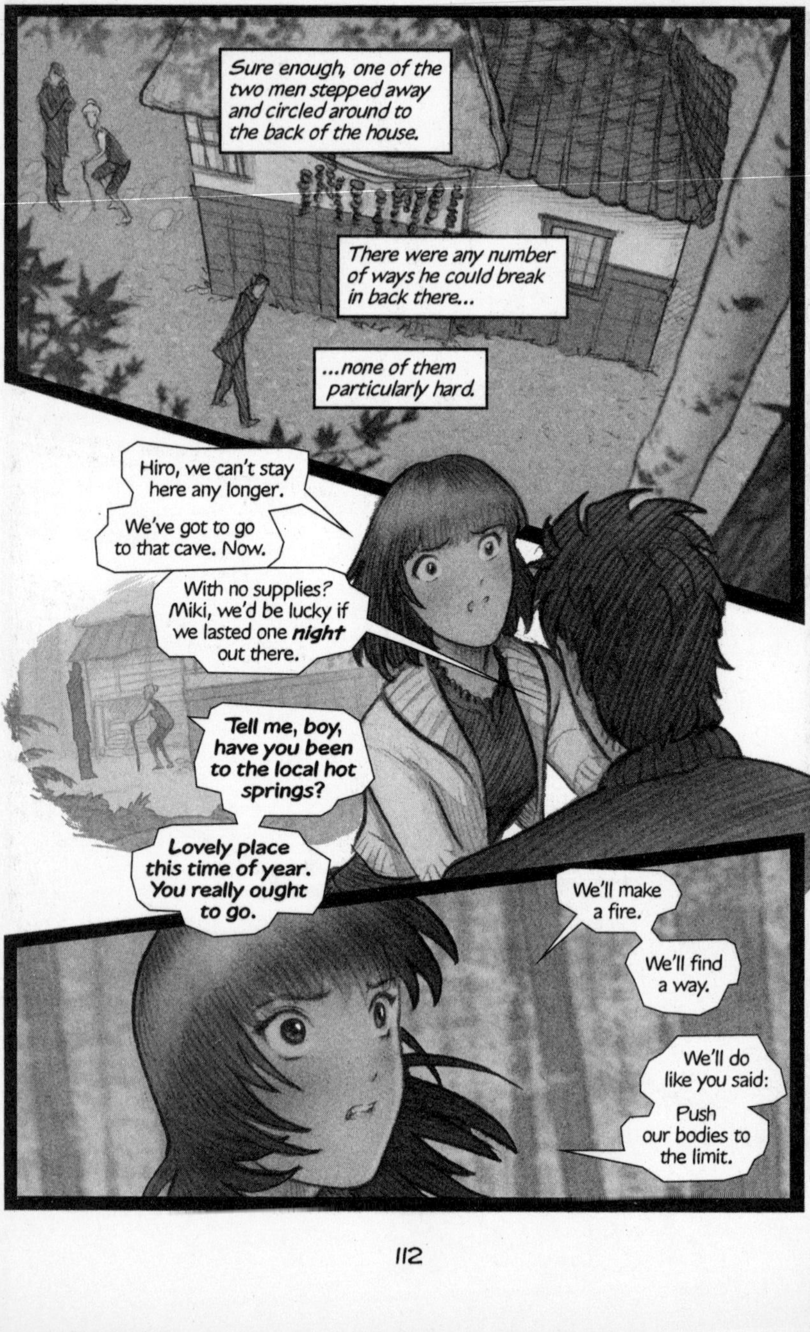

Sure enough, one of the two men stepped away and circled around to the back of the house.
There were any number of ways he could break in back there...
...none of them particularly hard.
Hiro, we can't stay here any longer.
We've got to go to that cave. Now.
With no supplies? Miki, we'd be lucky if we lasted one night out there.
Tell me, boy, have you been to the local hot springs?
Lovely place this time of year. You really ought to go.
We'll make a fire.
We'll find a way.
We'll do like you said:
Push our bodies to the limit.

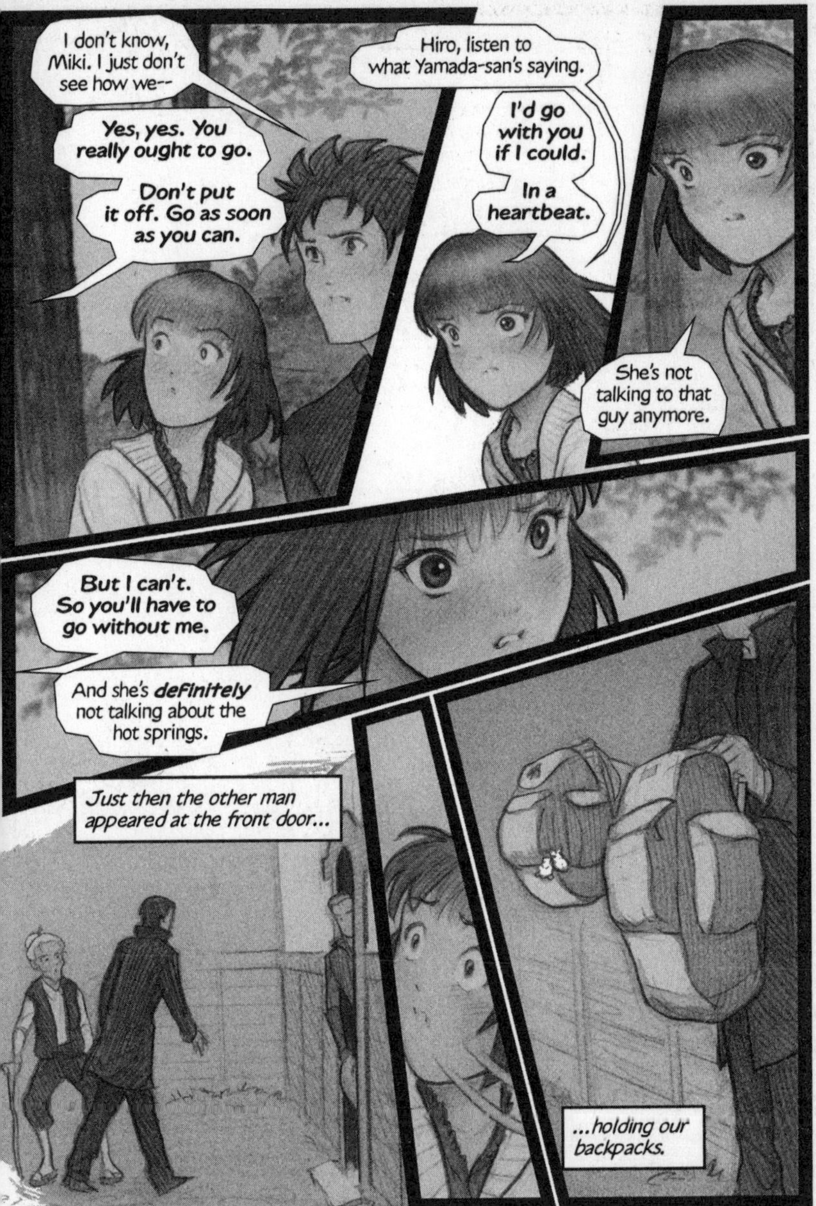
I don't know, Miki. I just don't see how we--
Yes, yes. You really ought to go.
Don't put it off. Go as soon as you can.
Hiro, listen to what Yamada-san's saying.
I'd go with you if I could.
In a heartbeat.
She's not talking to that guy anymore.
But I can't. So you'll have to go without me.
And she's *definitely* not talking about the hot springs.
Just then the other man appeared at the front door...
...holding our backpacks.

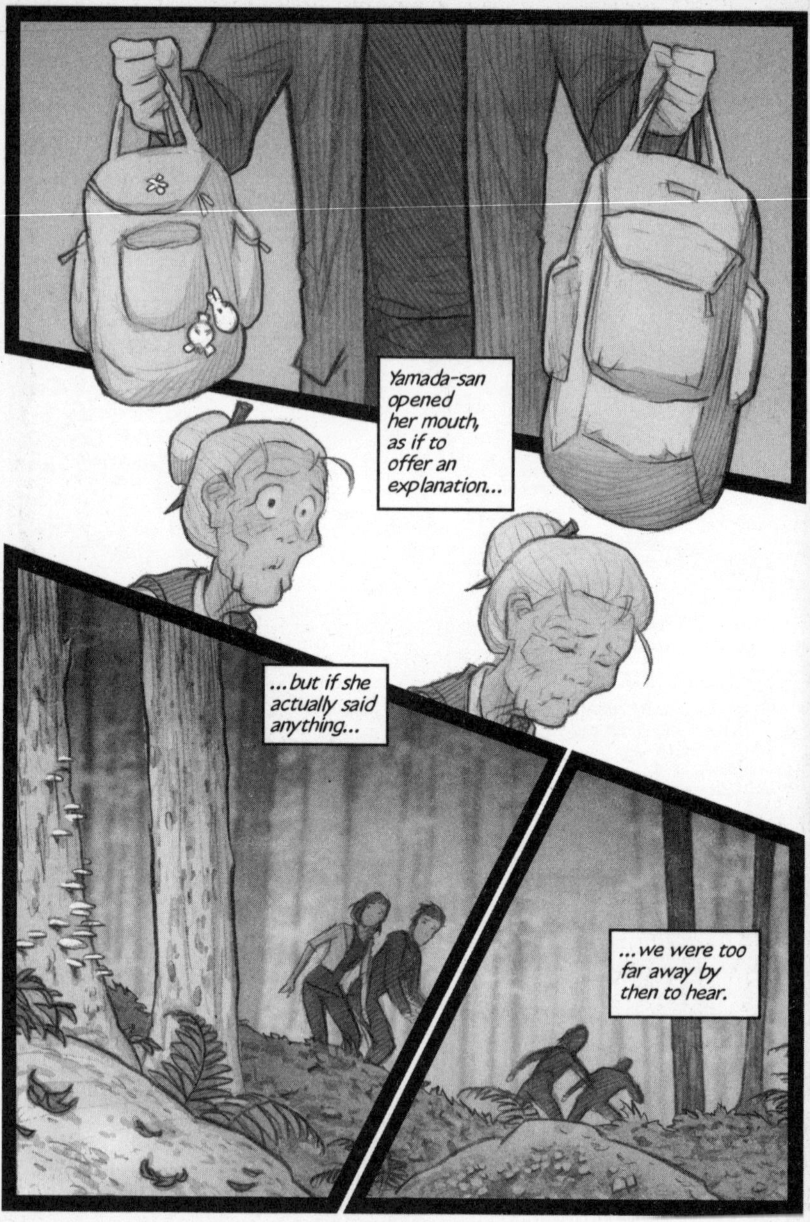

Yamada-san opened her mouth, as if to offer an explanation...
...but if she actually said anything...
...we were too far away by then to hear.

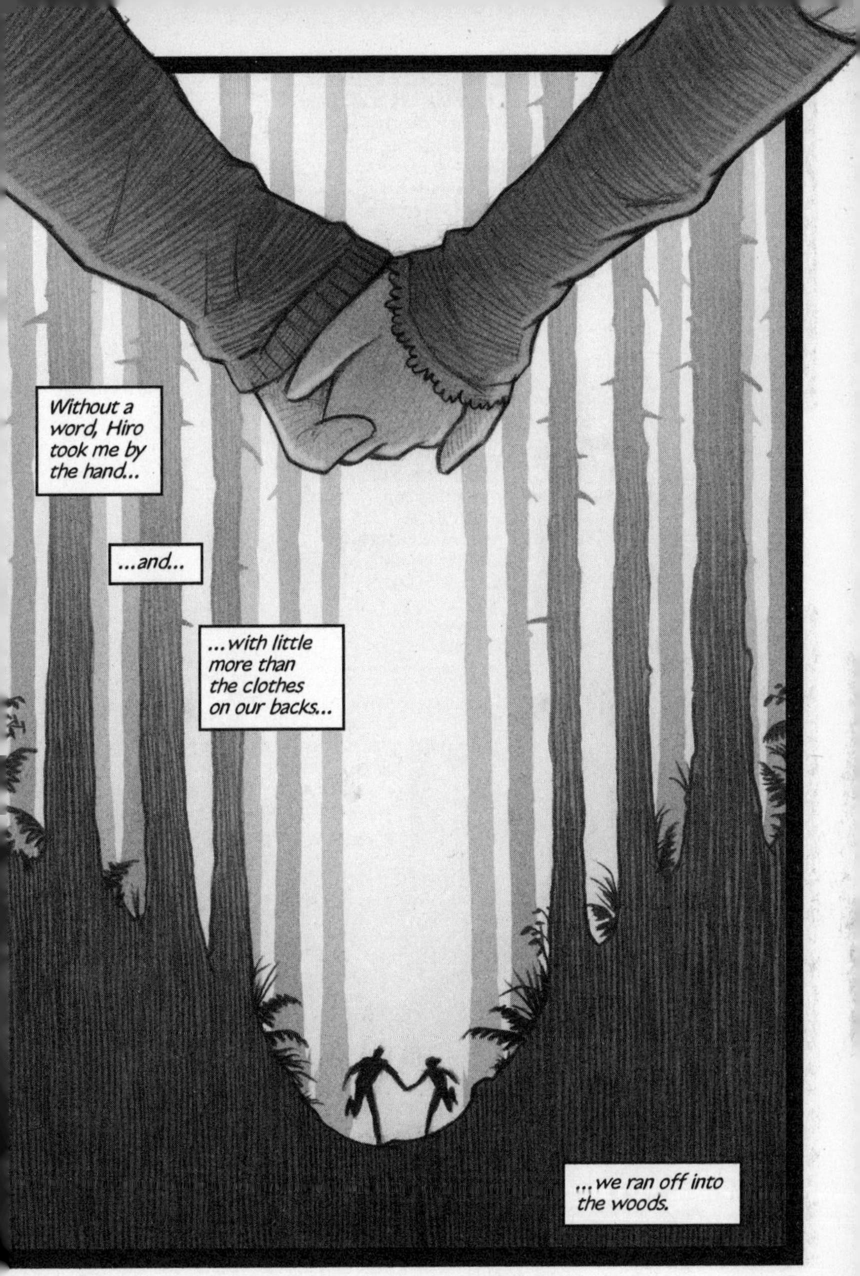
Without a word, Hiro took me by the hand...
...and...
...with little more than the clothes on our backs...
...we ran off into the woods.

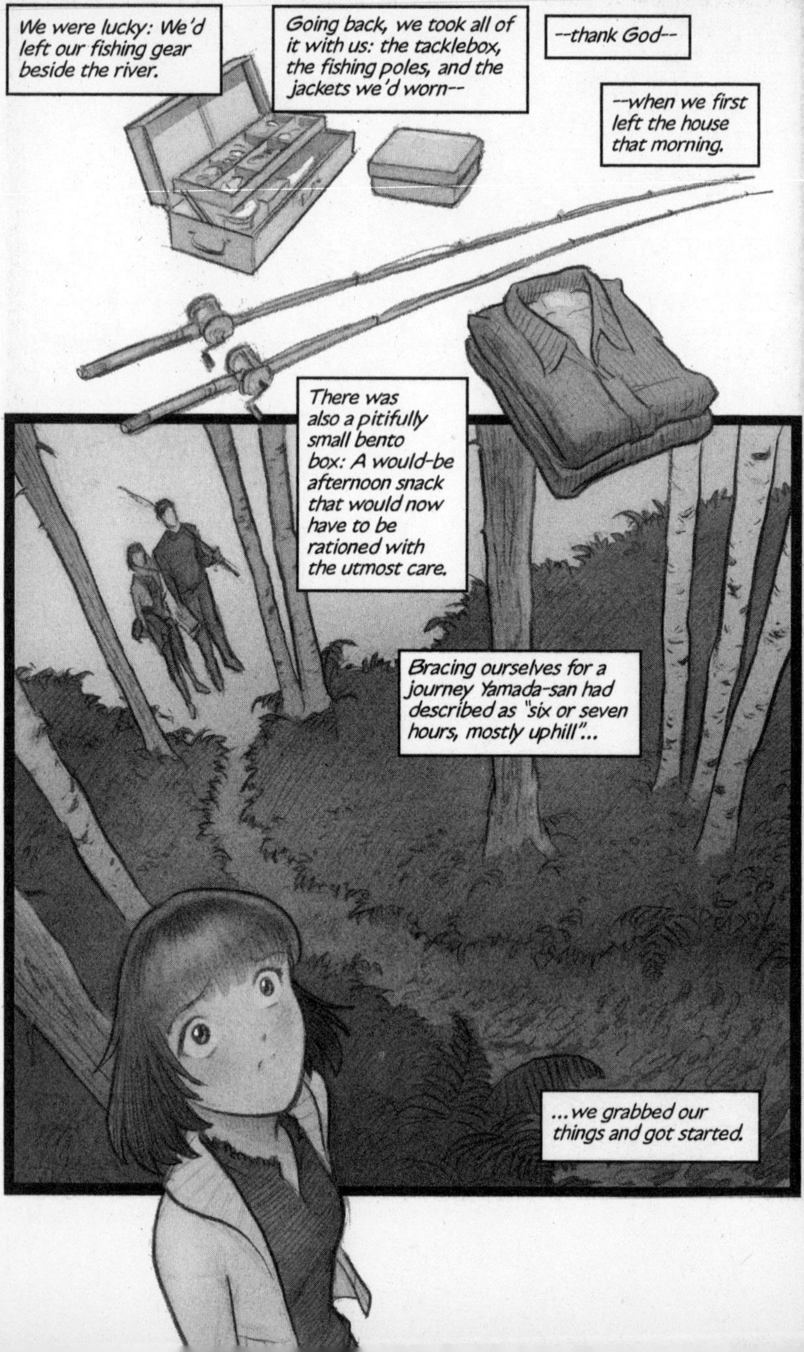
We were lucky: We'd left our fishing gear beside the river.
Going back, we took all of it with us: the tacklebox, the fishing poles, and the jackets we'd worn--
--thank God--
--when we first left the house that morning.
There was also a pitifully small bento box: A would-be afternoon snack that would now have to be rationed with the utmost care.
Bracing ourselves for a journey Yamada-san had described as "six or seven hours, mostly uphill"...
...we grabbed our things and got started.

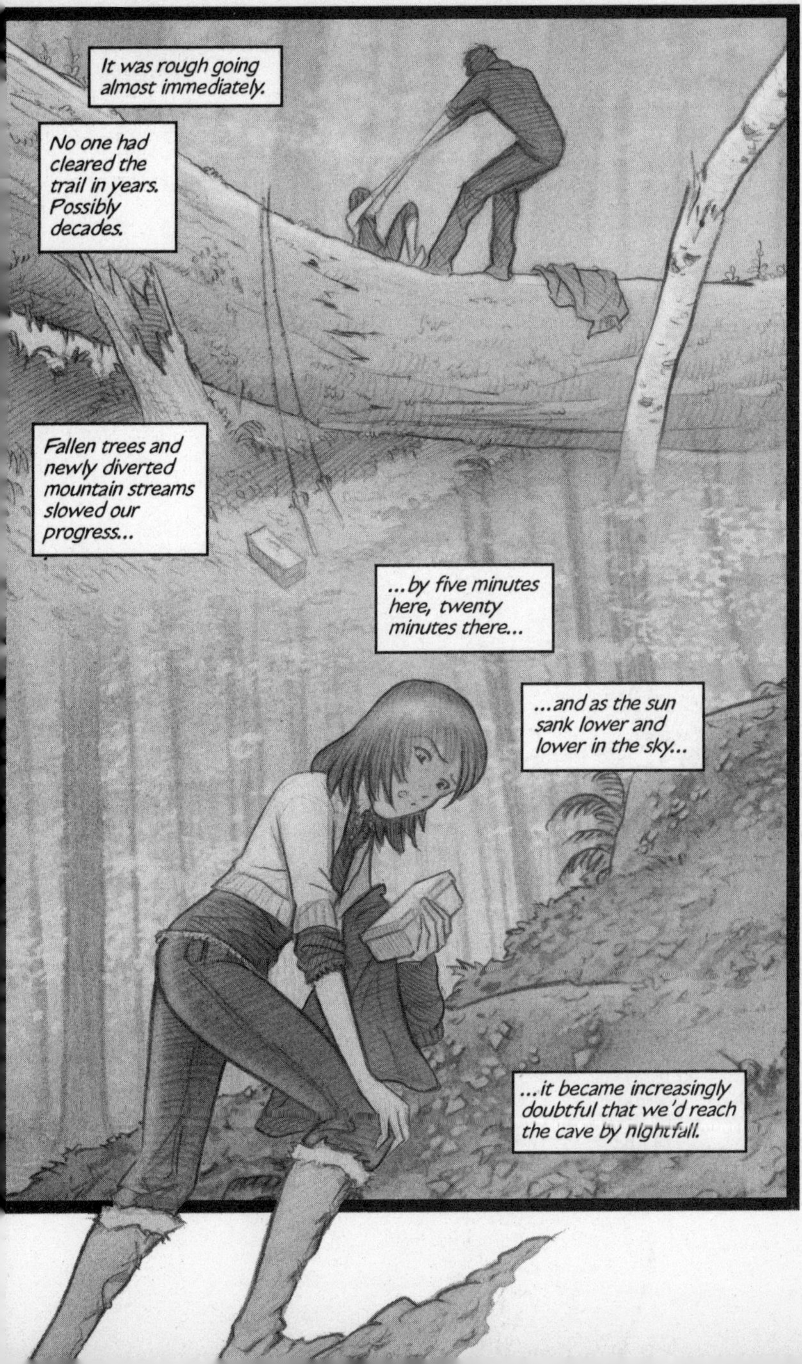
It was rough going almost immediately.
No one had cleared the trail in years. Possibly decades.
Fallen trees and newly diverted mountain streams slowed our progress...
...by five minutes here, twenty minutes there...
...and as the sun sank lower and lower in the sky...
...it became increasingly doubtful that we'd reach the cave by nightfall.

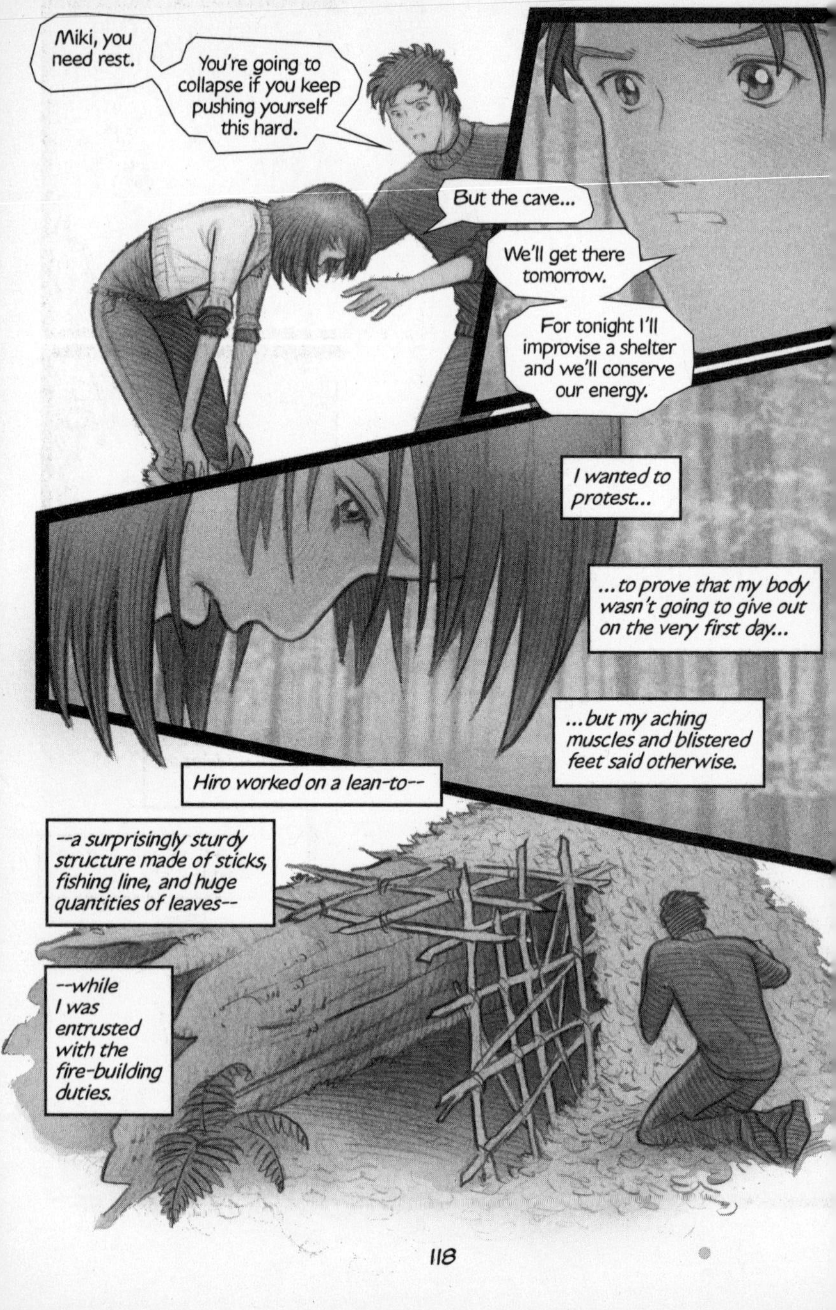
Miki, you need rest.
You're going to collapse if you keep pushing yourself this hard.
But the cave...
We'll get there tomorrow.
For tonight I'll improvise a shelter and we'll conserve our energy.
I wanted to protest...
...to prove that my body wasn't going to give out on the very first day...
...but my aching muscles and blistered feet said otherwise.
Hiro worked on a lean-to--
--a surprisingly sturdy structure made of sticks, fishing line, and huge quantities of leaves--
--while I was entrusted with the fire-building duties.

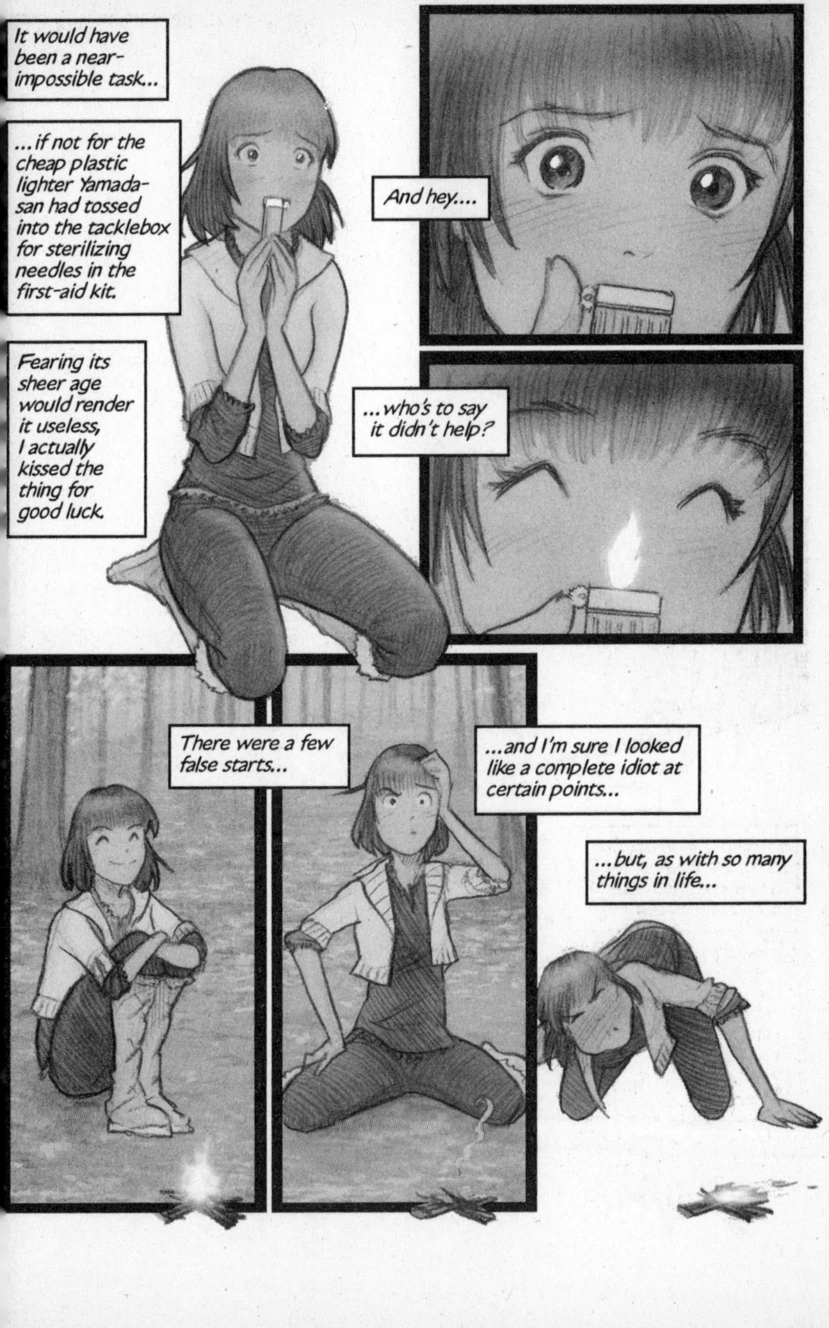
It would have been a near-impossible task...
...if not for the cheap plastic lighter Yamada-san had tossed into the tacklebox for sterilizing needles in the first-aid kit.
Fearing its sheer age would render it useless, I actually kissed the thing for good luck.
And hey....
...who's to say it didn't help?
There were a few false starts...
...and I'm sure I looked like a complete idiot at certain points...
...but, as with so many things in life...

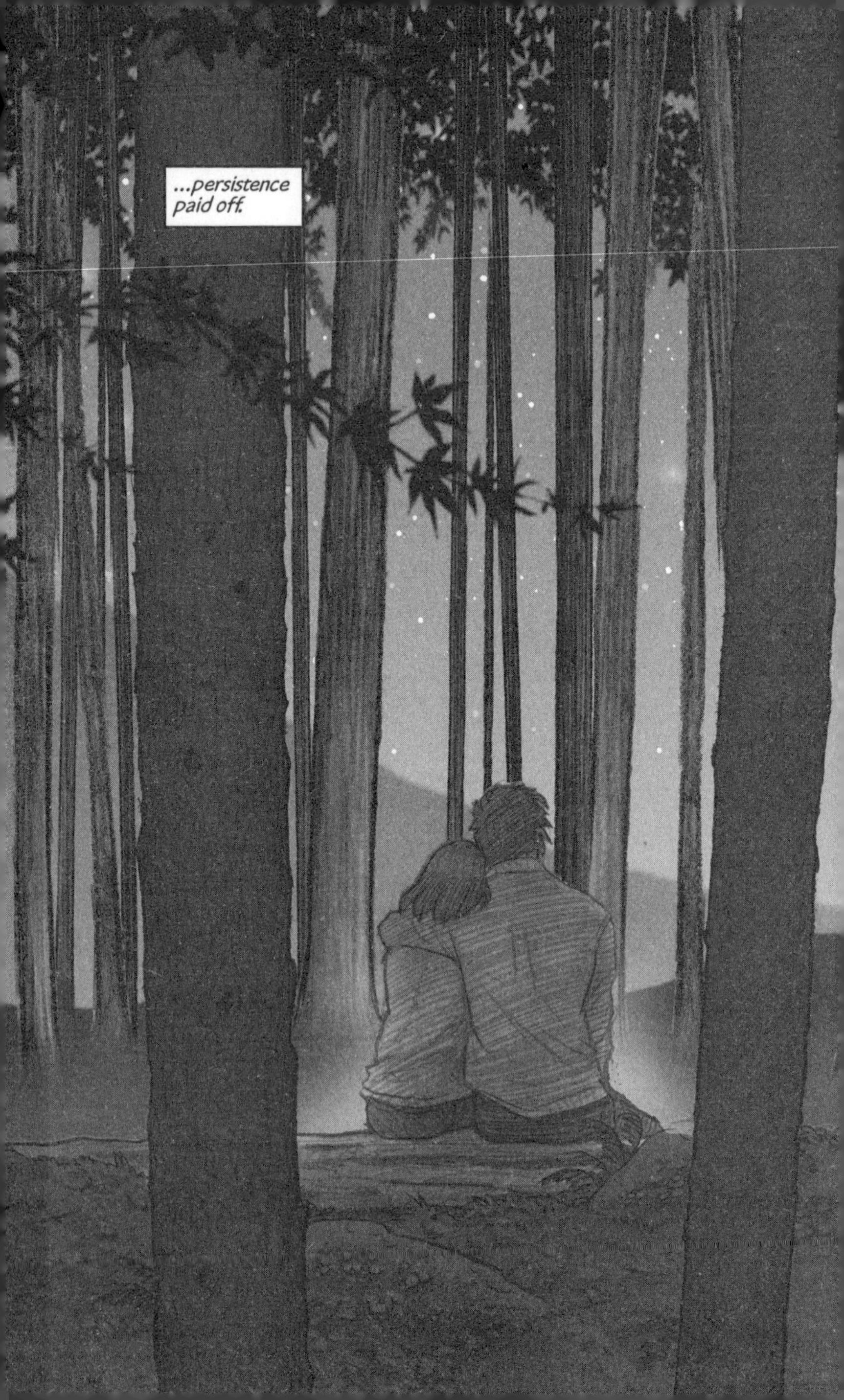
...persistence paid off.

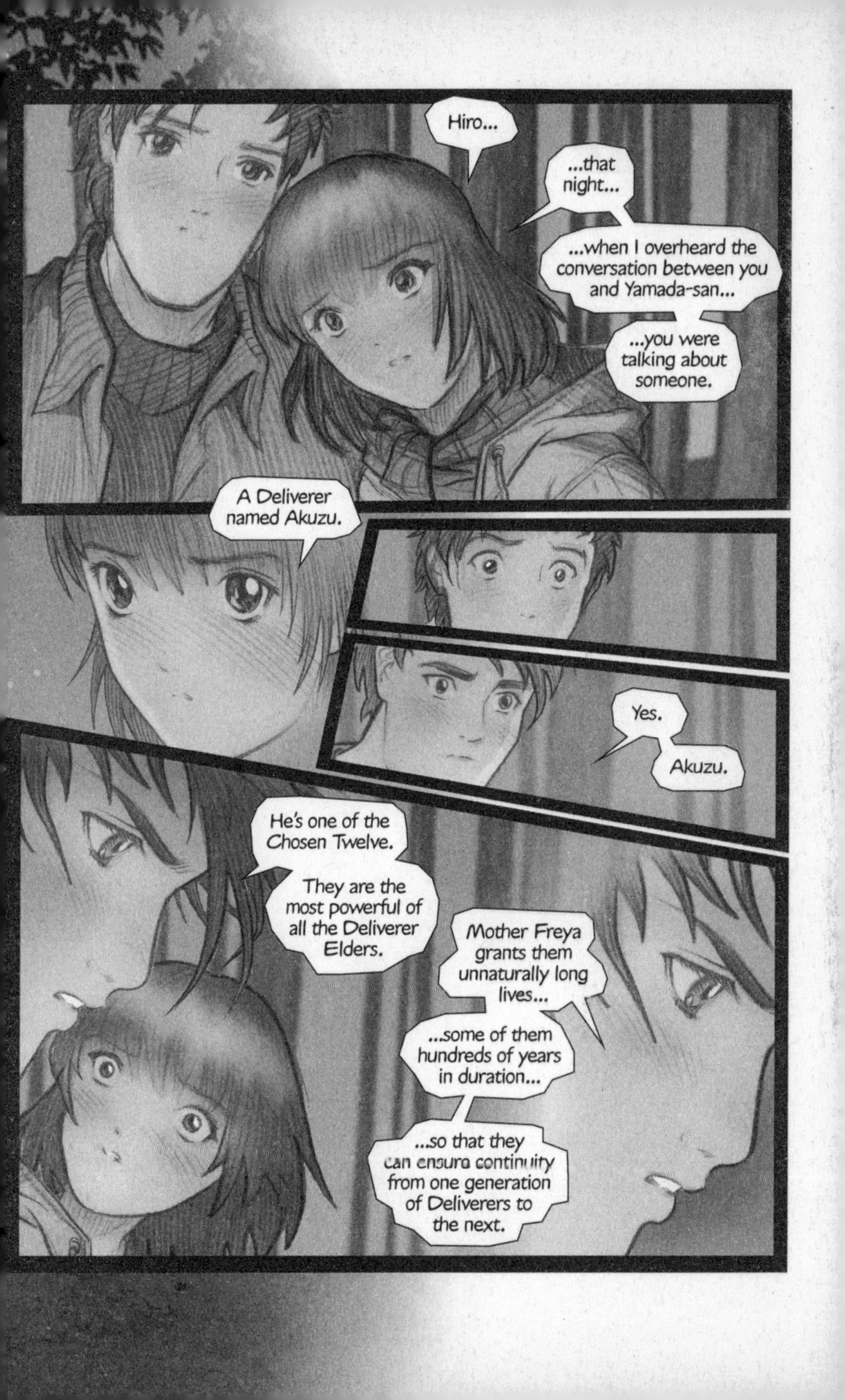
Hiro...
...that night...
...when I overheard the conversation between you and Yamada-san...
...you were talking about someone.
A Deliverer named Akuzu.
Yes.
Akuzu.
He's one of the Chosen Twelve.
They are the most powerful of all the Deliverer Elders.
Mother Freya grants them unnaturally long lives...
...some of them hundreds of years in duration...
...so that they can ensure continuity from one generation of Deliverers to the next.

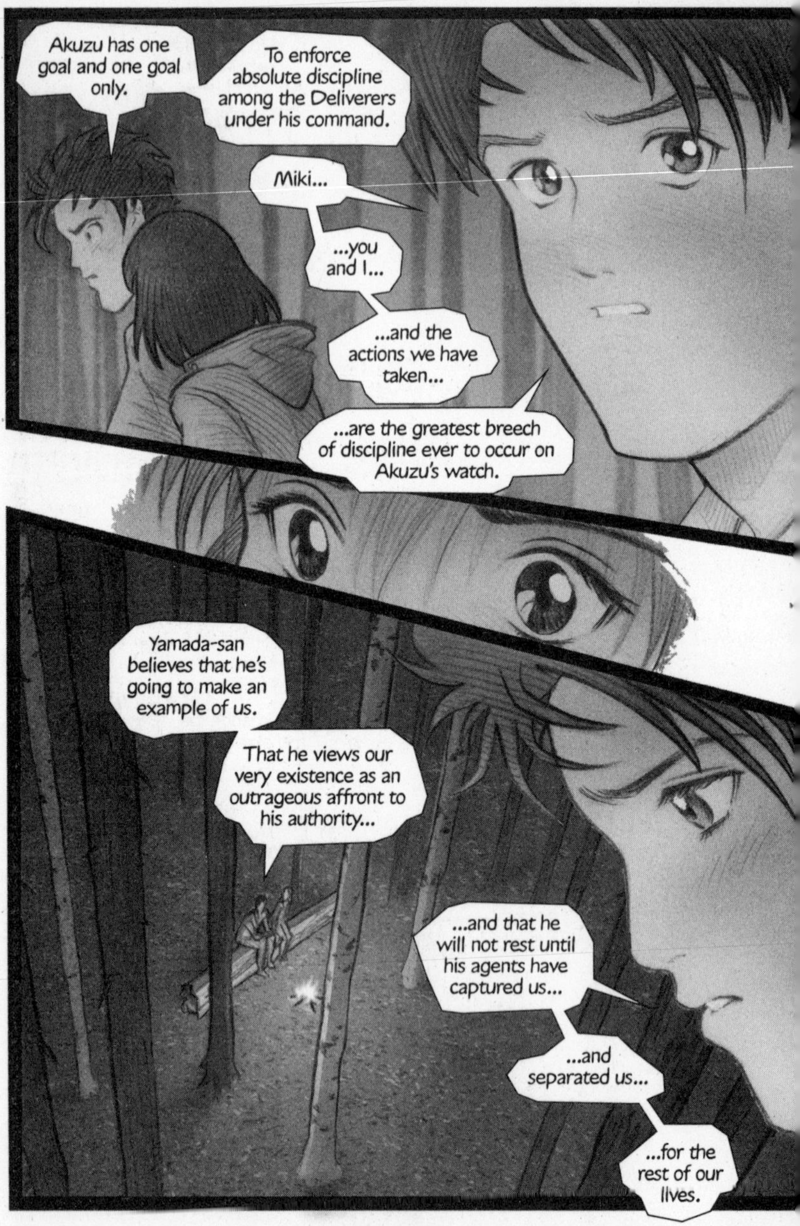
Akuzu has one goal and one goal only.
To enforce absolute discipline among the Deliverers under his command.
Miki...
...you and I...
...and the actions we have taken...
...are the greatest breech of discipline ever to occur on Akuzu's watch.
Yamada-san believes that he's going to make an example of us.
That he views our very existence as an outrageous affront to his authority...
...and that he will not rest until his agents have captured us...
...and separated us...
...for the rest of our lives.

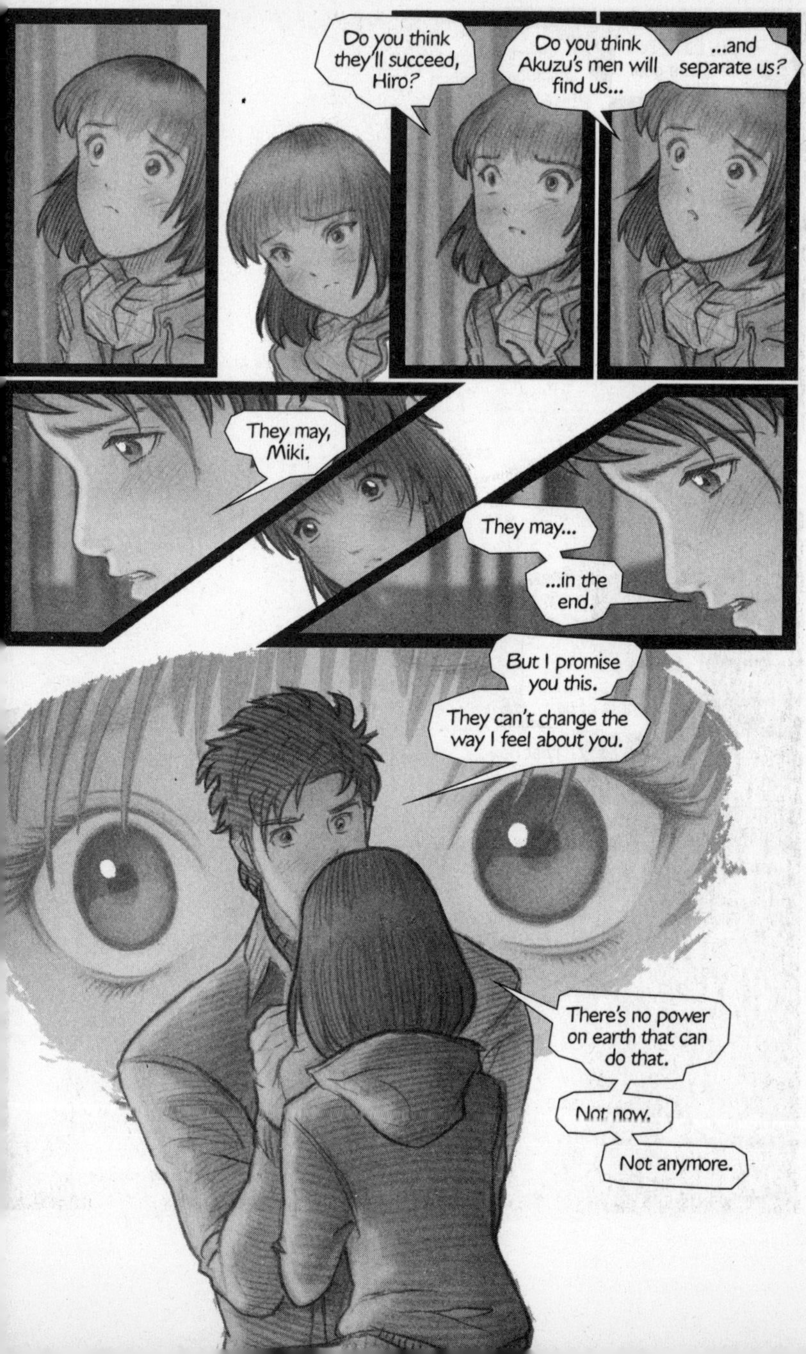
Do you think they'll succeed, Hiro?
Do you think Akuzu's men will find us...
...and separate us?
They may, Miki.
They may...
...in the end.
But I promise you this.
They can't change the way I feel about you.
There's no power on earth that can do that.
Not now.
Not anymore.

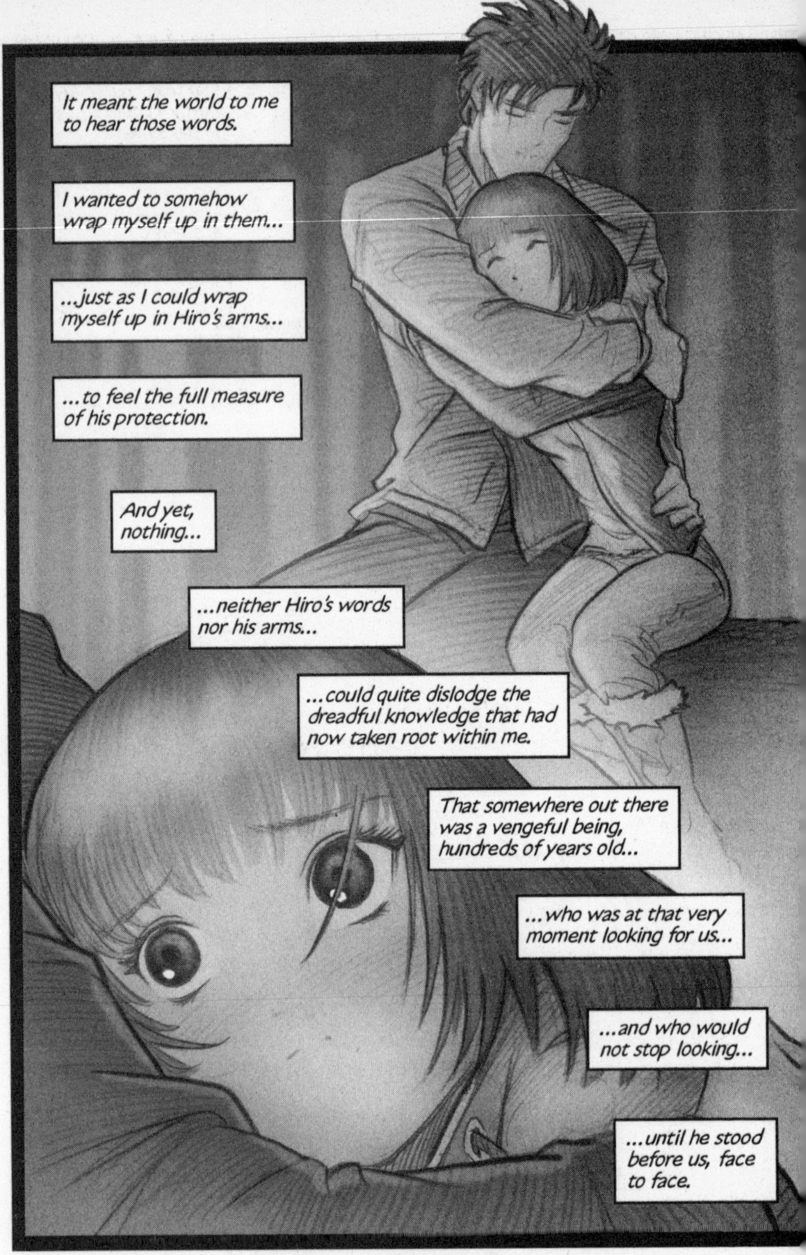
It meant the world to me to hear those words.
I wanted to somehow wrap myself up in them...
...just as I could wrap myself up in Hiro's arms...
...to feel the full measure of his protection.
And yet, nothing...
...neither Hiro's words nor his arms...
...could quite dislodge the dreadful knowledge that had now taken root within me.
That somewhere out there was a vengeful being, hundreds of years old...
...who was at that very moment looking for us...
...and who would not stop looking...
...until he stood before us, face to face.

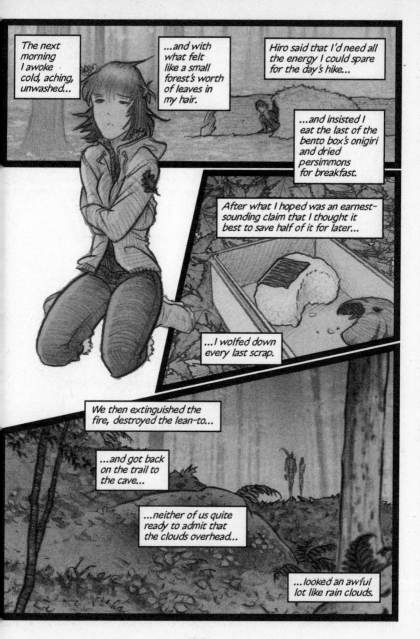

The next morning I awoke cold, aching, unwashed...

...and with what felt like a small forest's worth of leaves in my hair.

Hiro said that I'd need all the energy I could spare for the day's hike...

...and insisted I eat the last of the bento box's onigiri and dried persimmons for breakfast.

After what I hoped was an earnest-sounding claim that I thought it best to save half of it for later...

...I wolfed down every last scrap.

We then extinguished the fire, destroyed the lean-to...

...and got back on the trail to the cave...

...neither of us quite ready to admit that the clouds overhead...

...looked an awful lot like rain clouds.

125

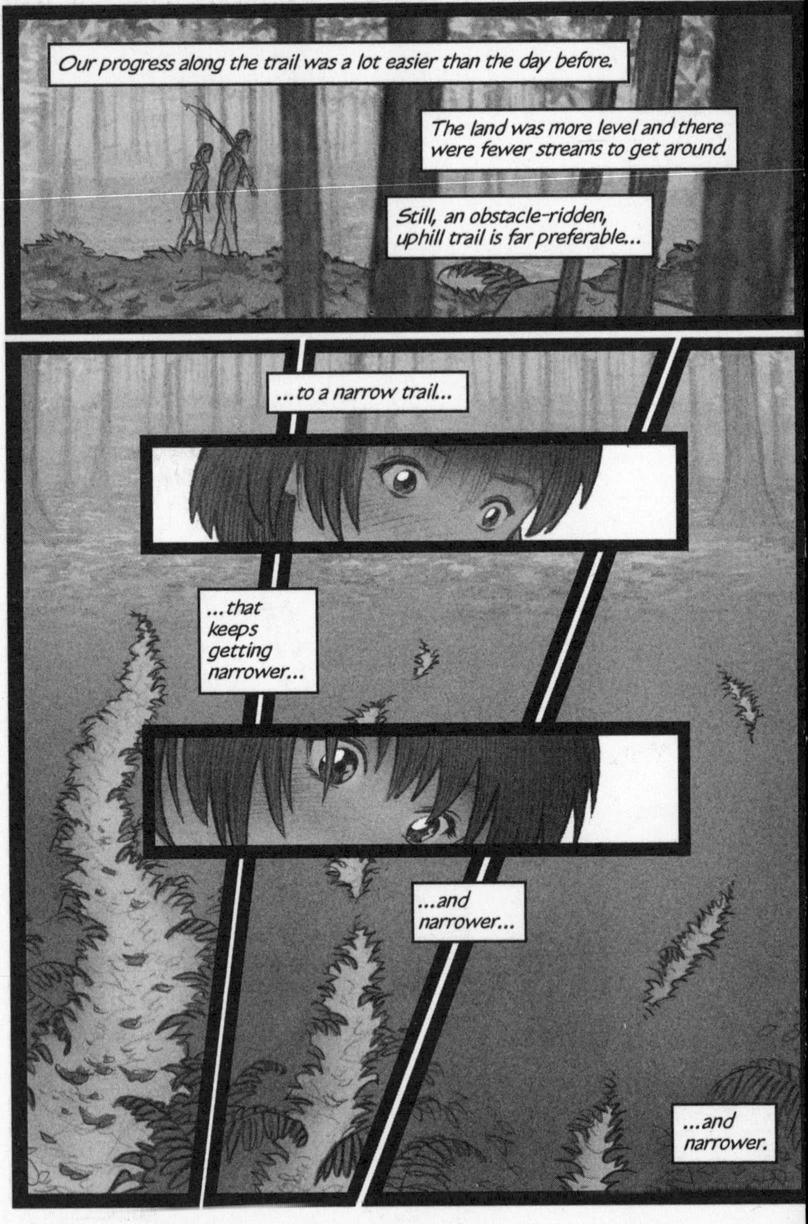
Our progress along the trail was a lot easier than the day before.
The land was more level and there were fewer streams to get around.
Still, an obstacle-ridden, uphill trail is far preferable...
...to a narrow trail...
...that keeps getting narrower...
...and narrower...
...and narrower.

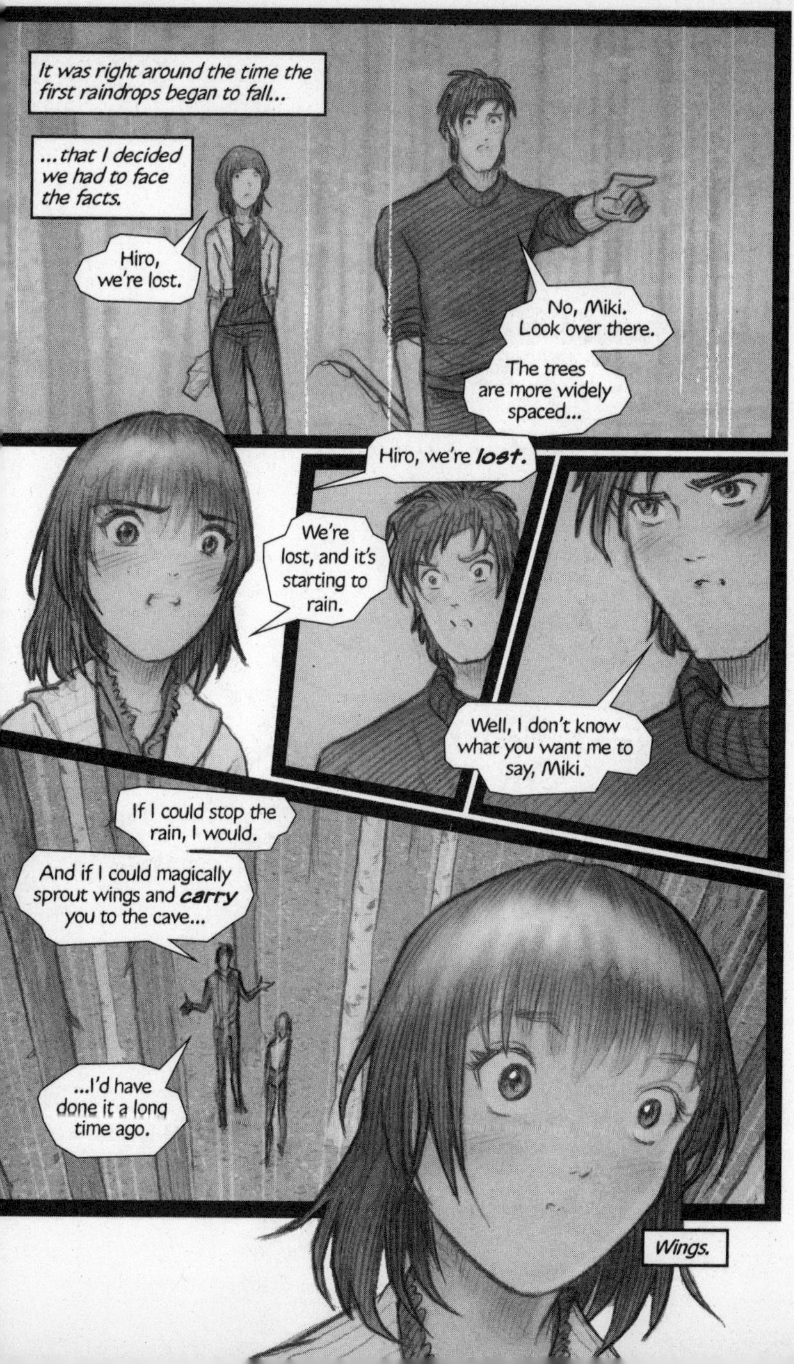
It was right around the time the first raindrops began to fall...
...that I decided we had to face the facts.
Hiro, we're lost.
No, Miki. Look over there.
The trees are more widely spaced...
Hiro, we're **lost.**
We're lost, and it's starting to rain.
Well, I don't know what you want me to say, Miki.
If I could stop the rain, I would.
And if I could magically sprout wings and **carry** you to the cave...
...I'd have done it a long time ago.
Wings.

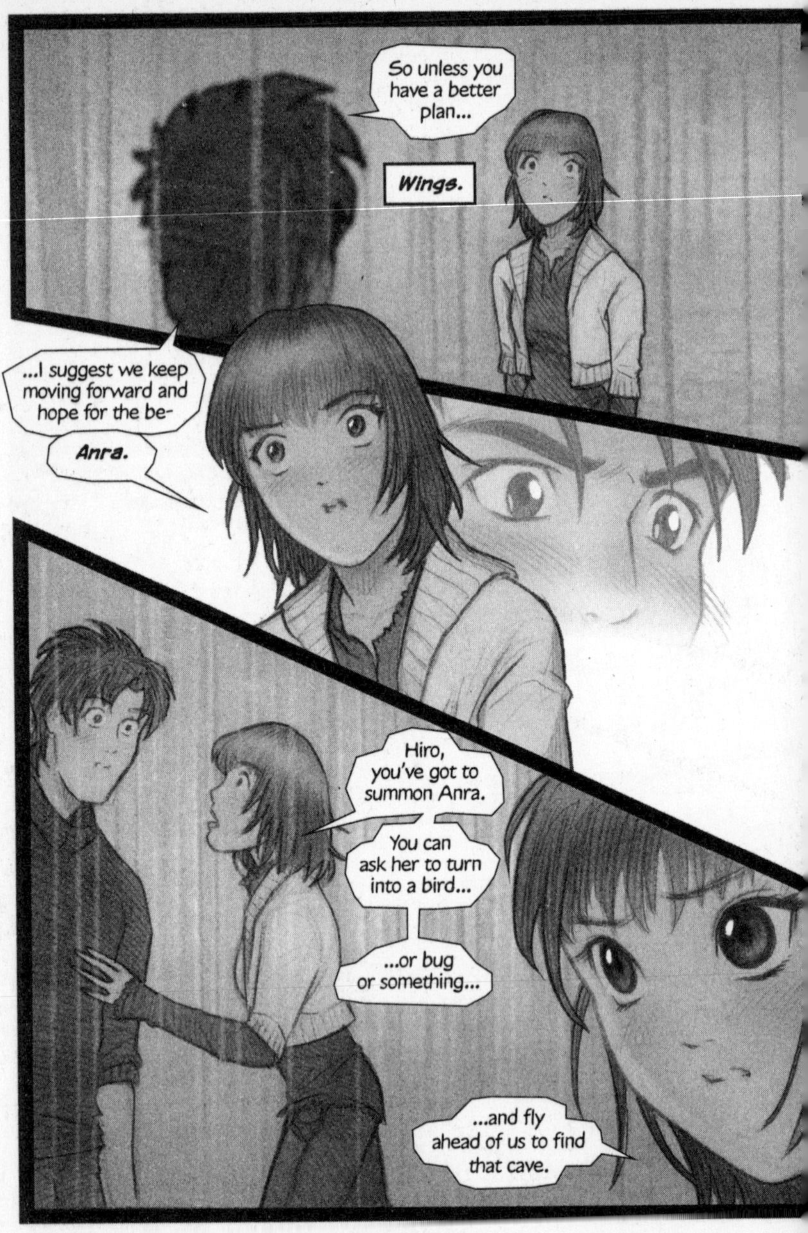
So unless you have a better plan...
Wings.
...I suggest we keep moving forward and hope for the be-
Anra.
Hiro, you've got to summon Anra.
You can ask her to turn into a bird...
...or bug or something...
...and fly ahead of us to find that cave.

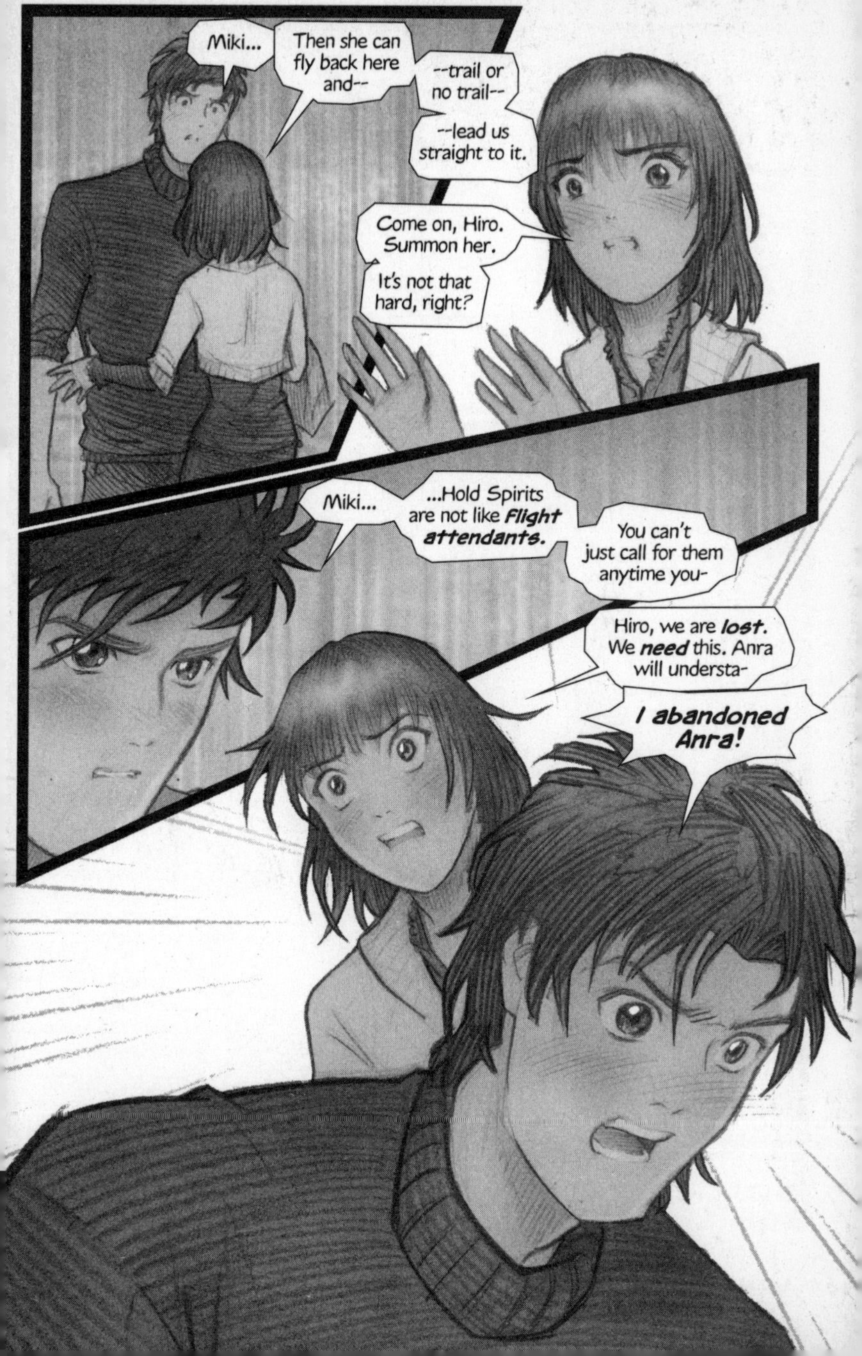
Miki...
Then she can fly back here and--
--trail or no trail--
--lead us straight to it.
Come on, Hiro. Summon her.
It's not that hard, right?
Miki...
...Hold Spirits are not like *Flight attendants.*
You can't just call for them anytime you-
Hiro, we are *lost.* We *need* this. Anra will understa-
I abandoned Anra!

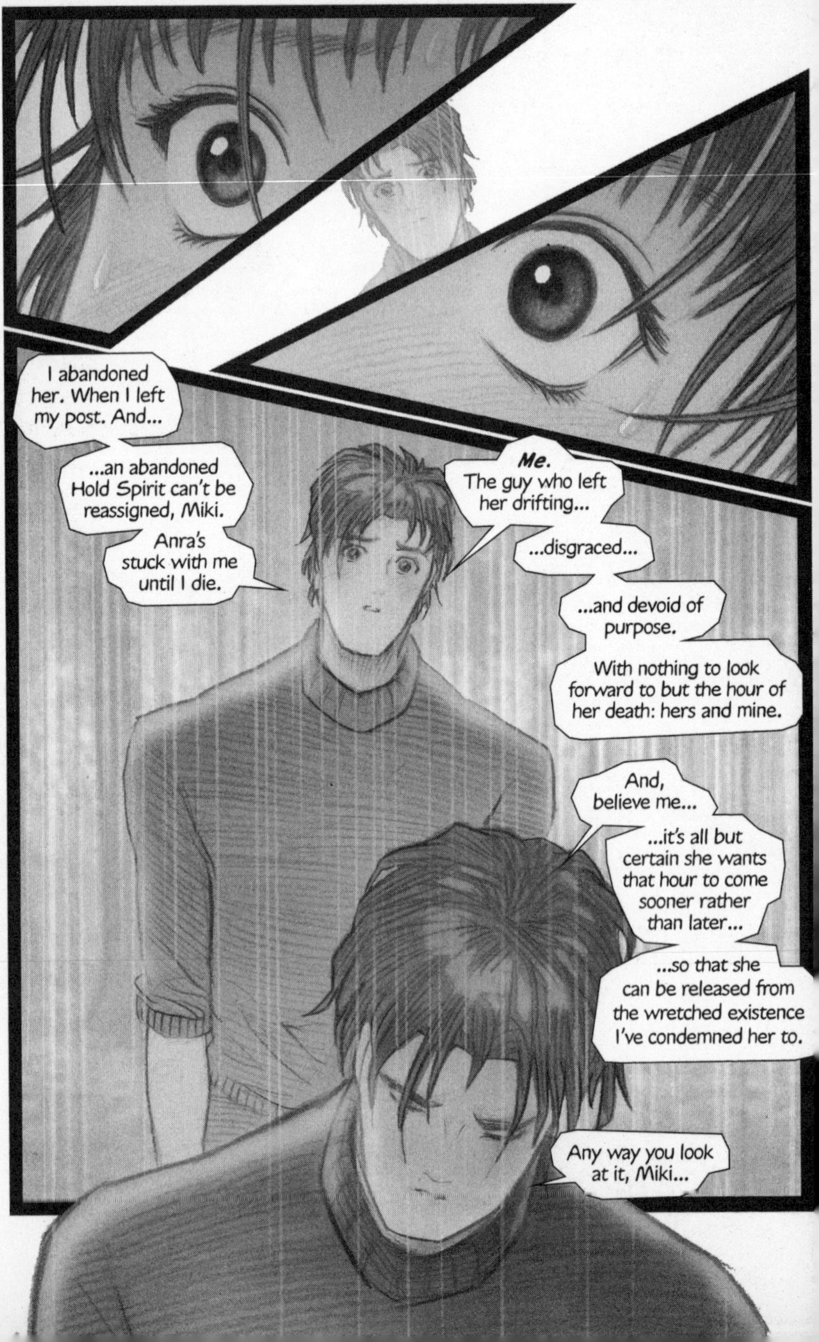
I abandoned her. When I left my post. And...
...an abandoned Hold Spirit can't be reassigned, Miki.
Anra's stuck with me until I die.
Me. The guy who left her drifting...
...disgraced...
...and devoid of purpose.
With nothing to look forward to but the hour of her death: hers and mine.
And, believe me...
...it's all but certain she wants that hour to come sooner rather than later...
...so that she can be released from the wretched existence I've condemned her to.
Any way you look at it, Miki...

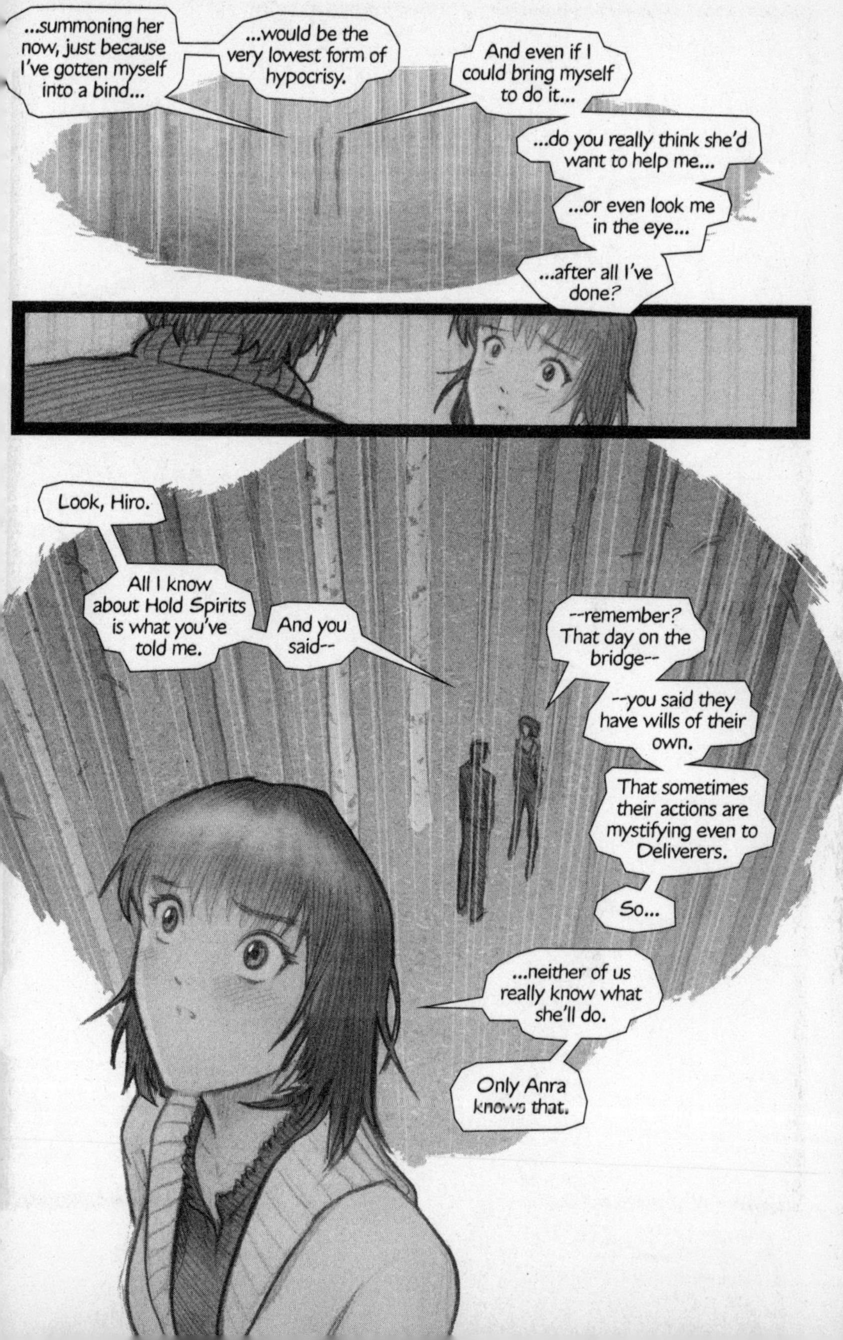
...summoning her now, just because I've gotten myself into a bind...
...would be the very lowest form of hypocrisy.
And even if I could bring myself to do it...
...do you really think she'd want to help me...
...or even look me in the eye...
...after all I've done?
Look, Hiro.
All I know about Hold Spirits is what you've told me.
And you said--
--remember? That day on the bridge--
--you said they have wills of their own.
That sometimes their actions are mystifying even to Deliverers.
So...
...neither of us really know what she'll do.
Only Anra knows that.

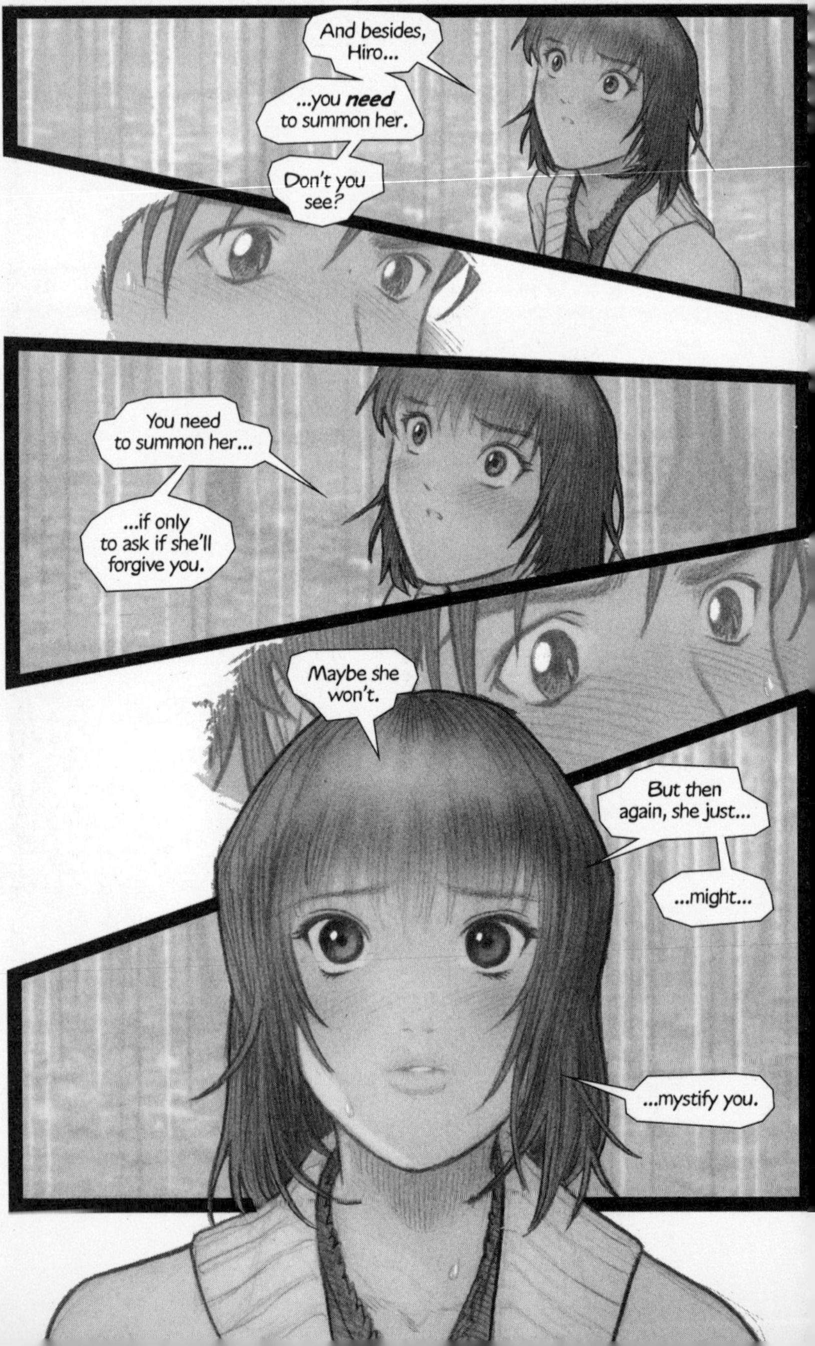

And besides, Hiro...
...you *need* to summon her.
Don't you see?
You need to summon her...
...if only to ask if she'll forgive you.
Maybe she won't.
But then again, she just...
...might...
...mystify you.

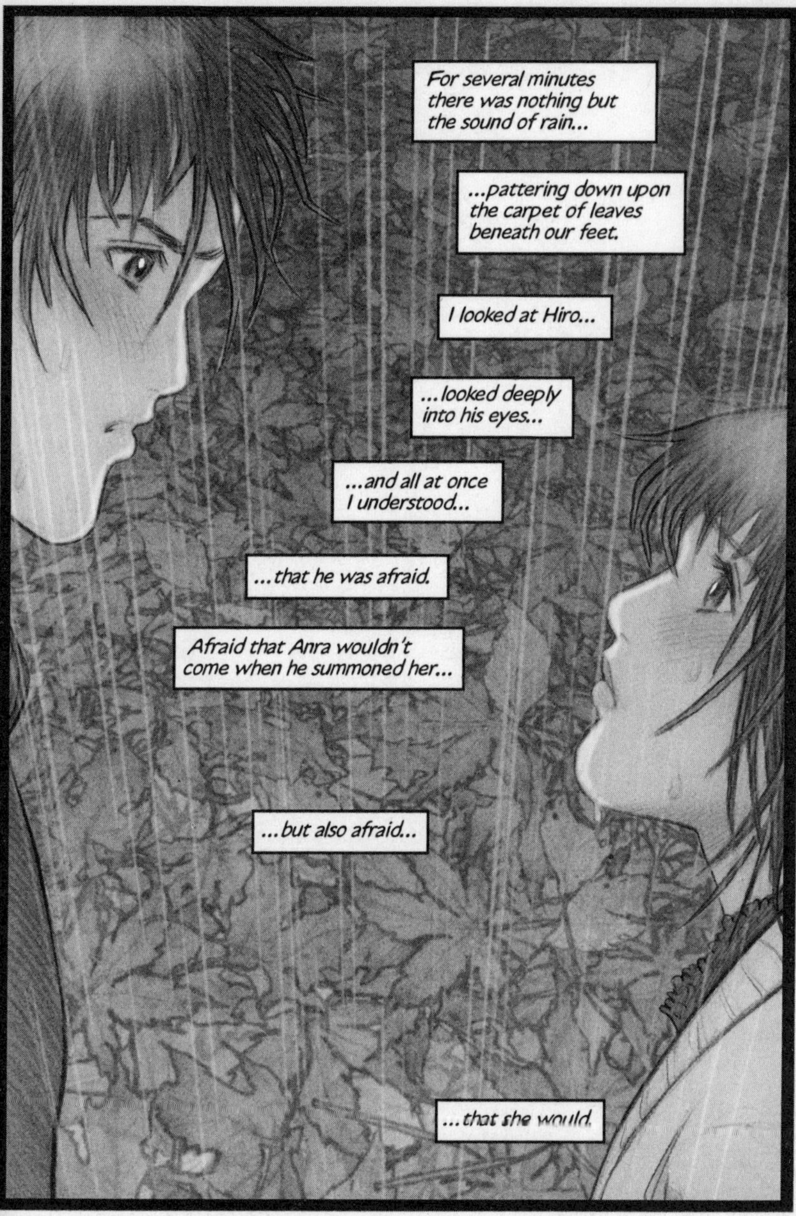
For several minutes there was nothing but the sound of rain...
...pattering down upon the carpet of leaves beneath our feet.
I looked at Hiro...
...looked deeply into his eyes...
...and all at once I understood...
...that he was afraid.
Afraid that Anra wouldn't come when he summoned her...
...but also afraid...
...that she would.

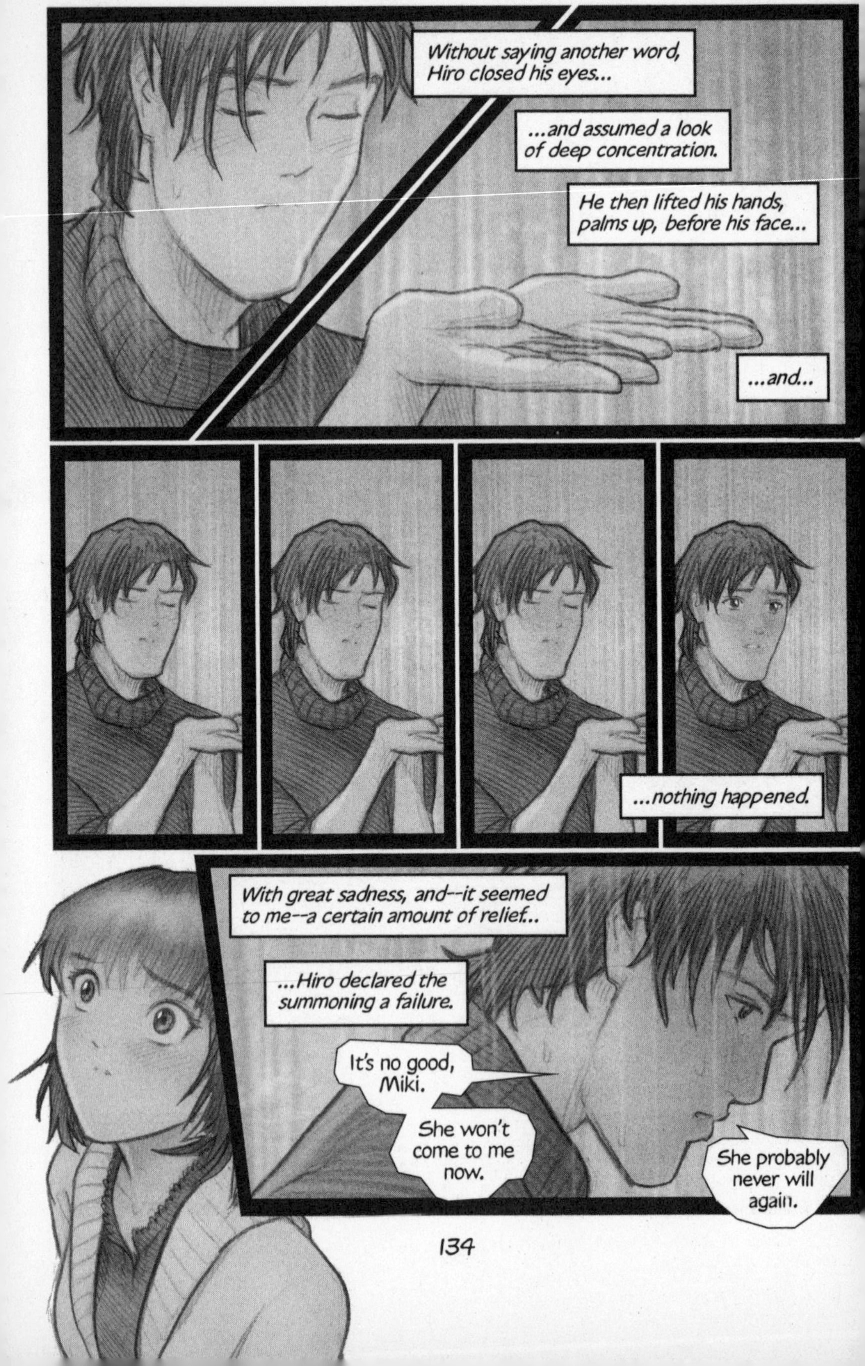
Without saying another word, Hiro closed his eyes...
...and assumed a look of deep concentration.
He then lifted his hands, palms up, before his face...
...and...
...nothing happened.
With great sadness, and--it seemed to me--a certain amount of relief...
...Hiro declared the summoning a failure.
It's no good, Miki.
She won't come to me now.
She probably never will again.

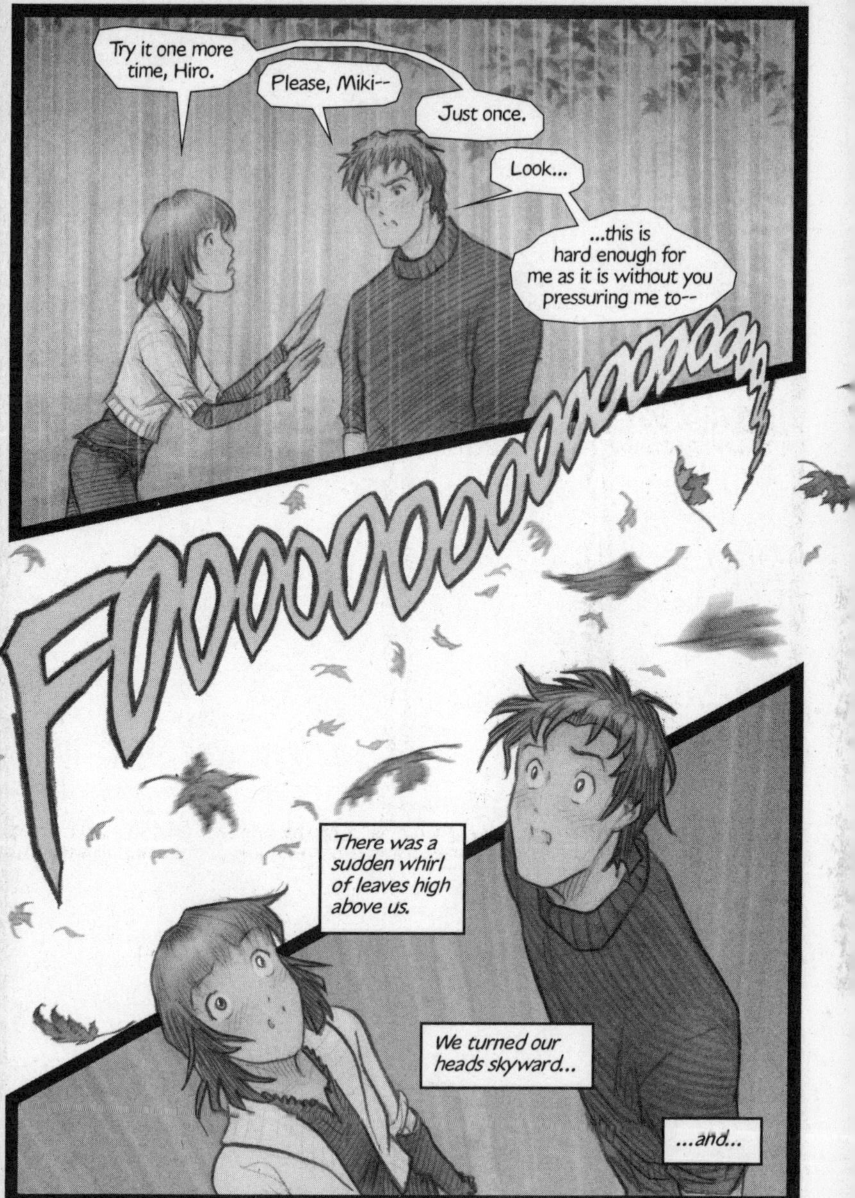
Try it one more time, Hiro.
Please, Miki--
Just once.
Look...
...this is hard enough for me as it is without you pressuring me to--
FOOOOOOOOOOOOOOOOOOOOO
There was a sudden whirl of leaves high above us.
We turned our heads skyward...
...and...

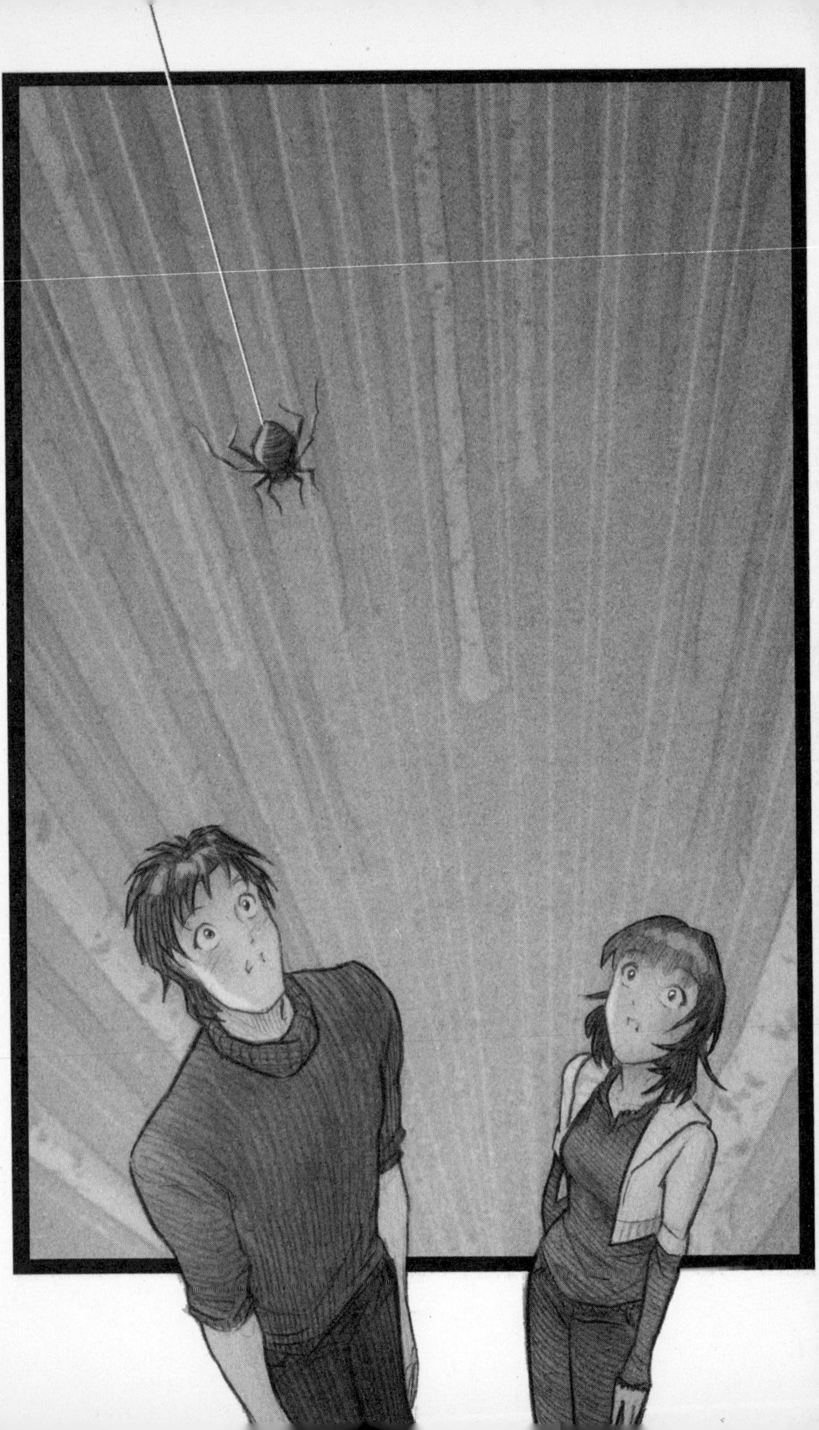

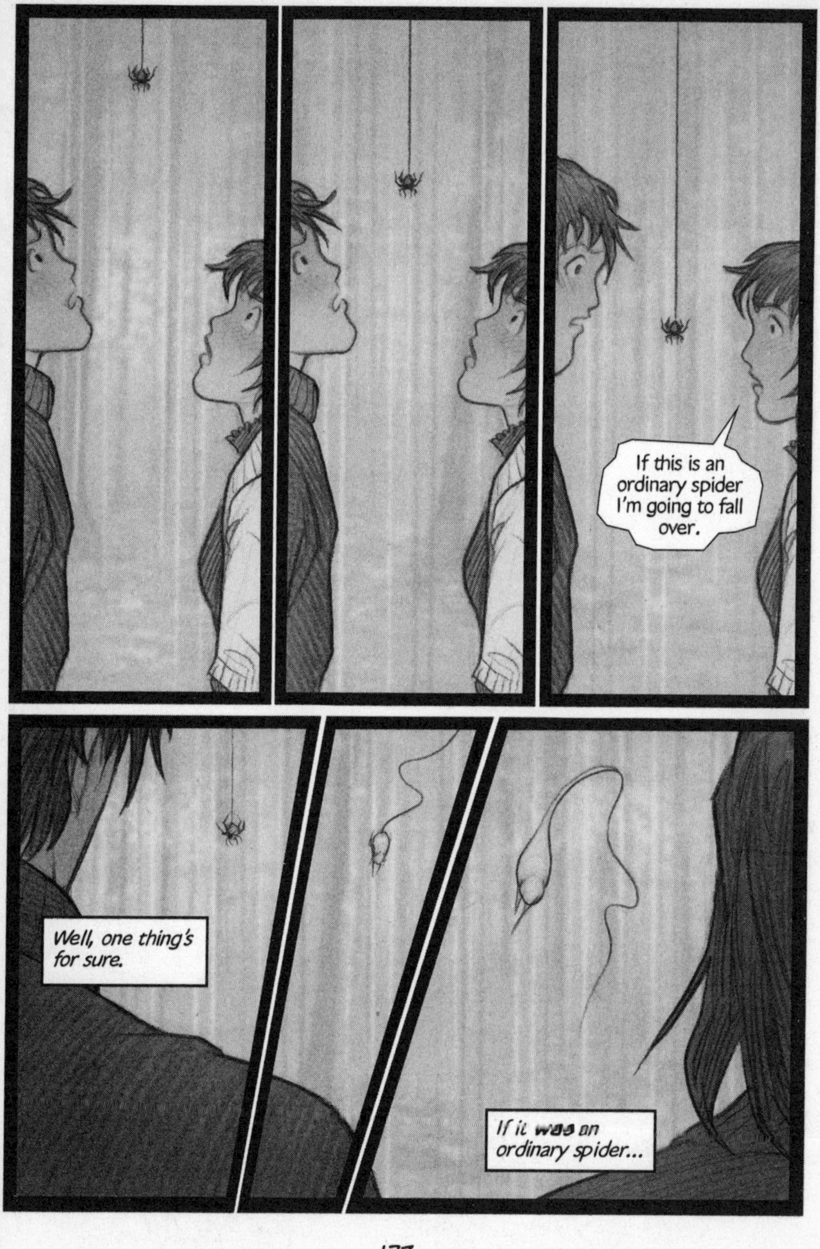
If this is an ordinary spider I'm going to fall over.
Well, one thing's for sure.
If it was an ordinary spider...

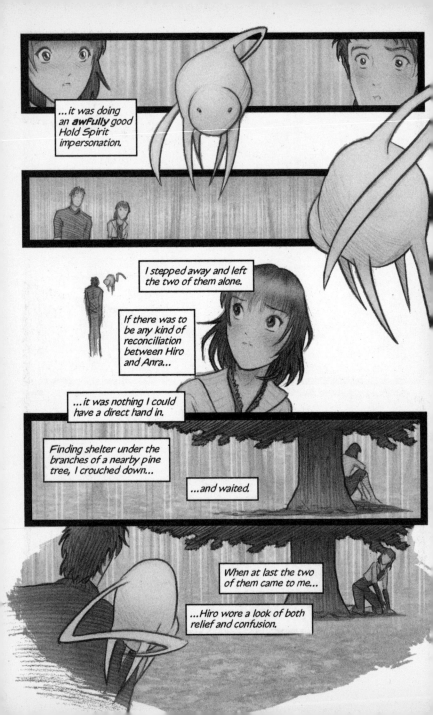

...it was doing an **awfully** good Hold Spirit impersonation.

I stepped away and left the two of them alone.

If there was to be any kind of reconciliation between Hiro and Anra...

...it was nothing I could have a direct hand in.

Finding shelter under the branches of a nearby pine tree, I crouched down...

...and waited.

When at last the two of them came to me...

...Hiro wore a look of both relief and confusion.

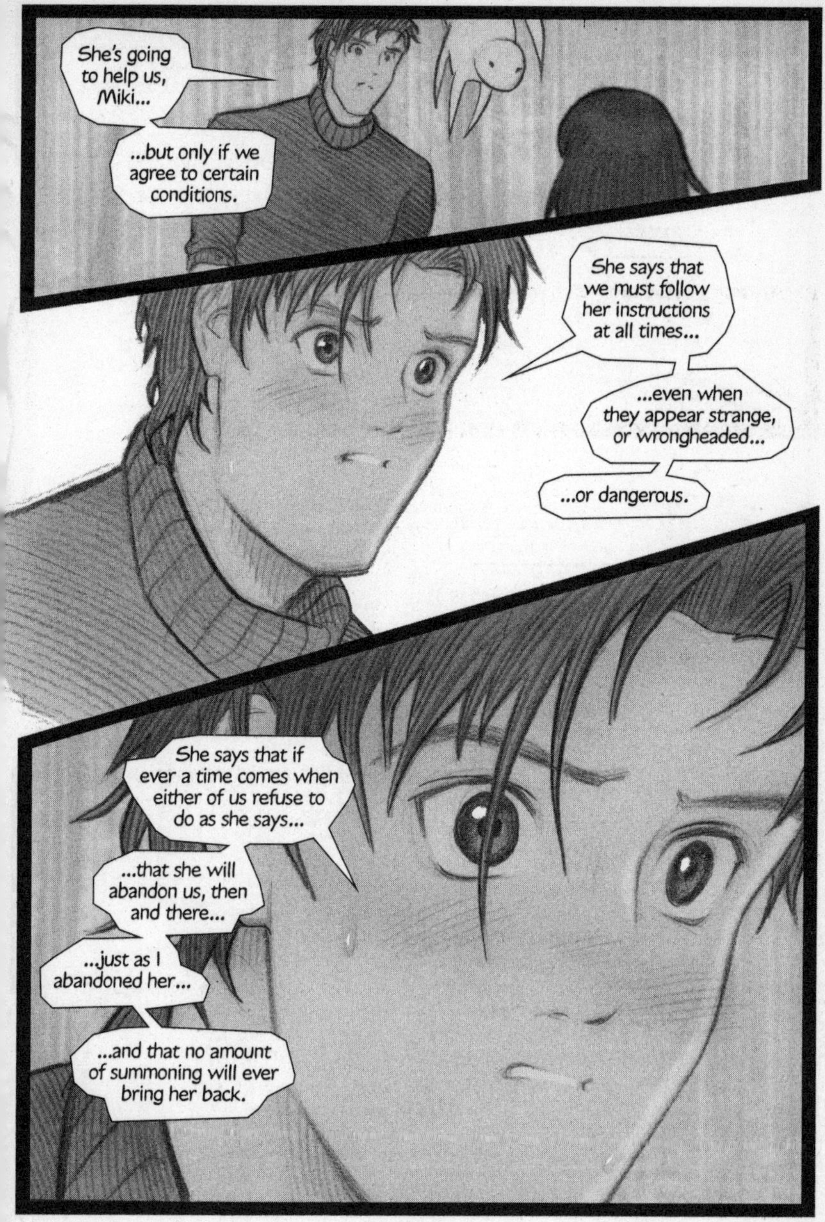
She's going to help us, Miki...
...but only if we agree to certain conditions.
She says that we must follow her instructions at all times...
...even when they appear strange, or wrongheaded...
...or dangerous.
She says that if ever a time comes when either of us refuse to do as she says...
...that she will abandon us, then and there...
...just as I abandoned her...
...and that no amount of summoning will ever bring her back.

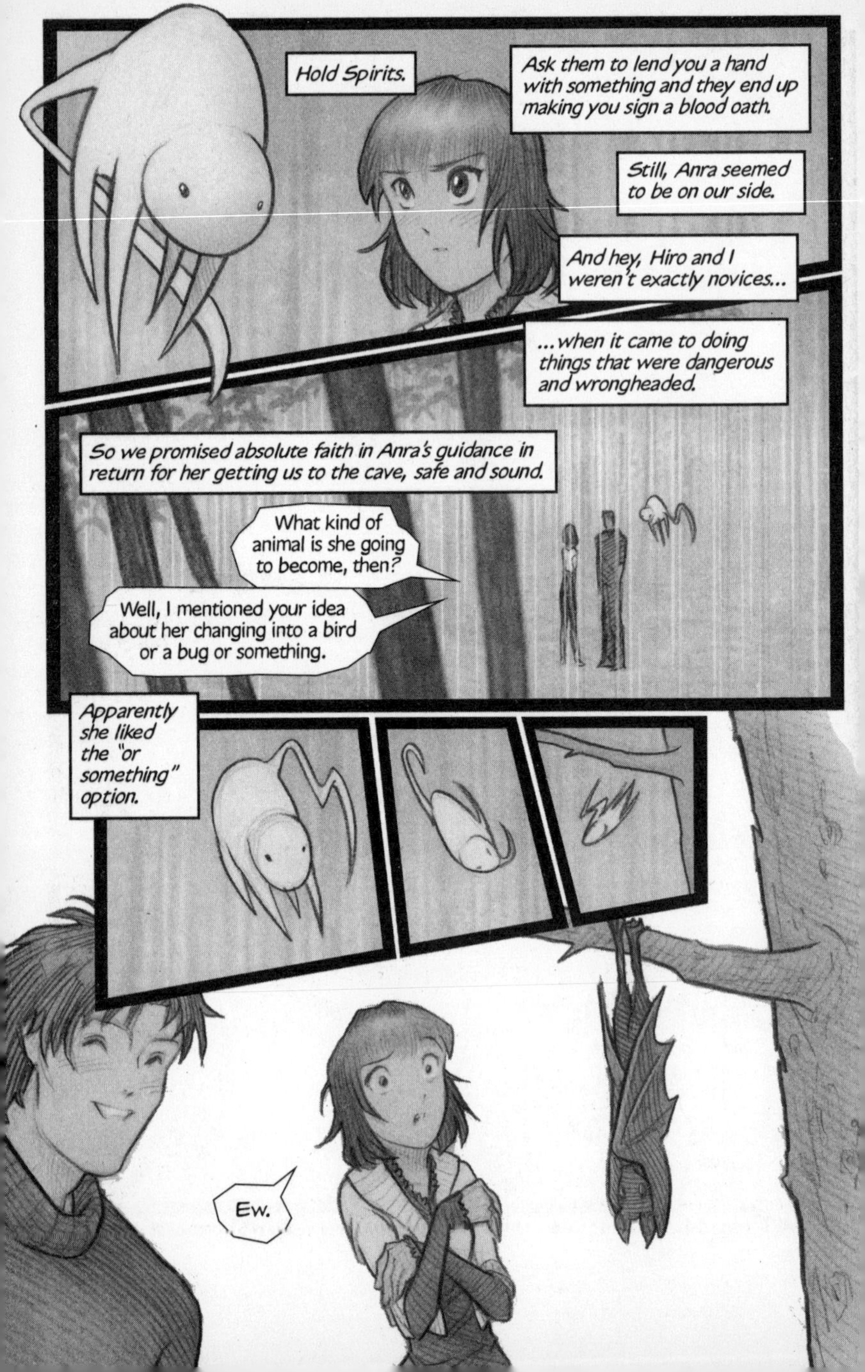
Hold Spirits.
Ask them to lend you a hand with something and they end up making you sign a blood oath.
Still, Anra seemed to be on our side.
And hey, Hiro and I weren't exactly novices...
...when it came to doing things that were dangerous and wrongheaded.
So we promised absolute faith in Anra's guidance in return for her getting us to the cave, safe and sound.
What kind of animal is she going to become, then?
Well, I mentioned your idea about her changing into a bird or a bug or something.
Apparently she liked the "or something" option.
Ew.

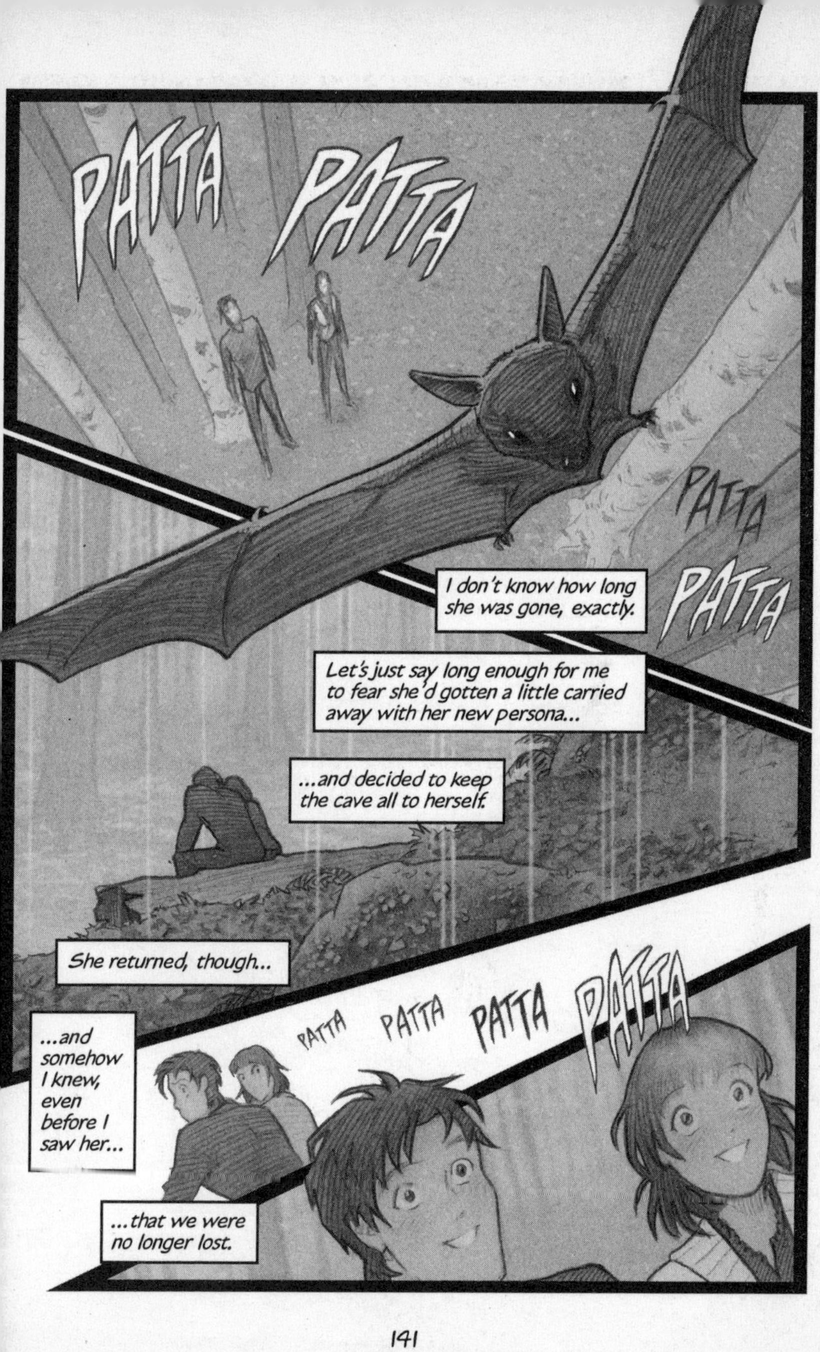
PATTA PATTA
PATTA
PATTA
I don't know how long she was gone, exactly.
Let's just say long enough for me to fear she'd gotten a little carried away with her new persona...
...and decided to keep the cave all to herself.
She returned, though...
...and somehow I knew, even before I saw her...
PATTA PATTA PATTA PATTA
...that we were no longer lost.

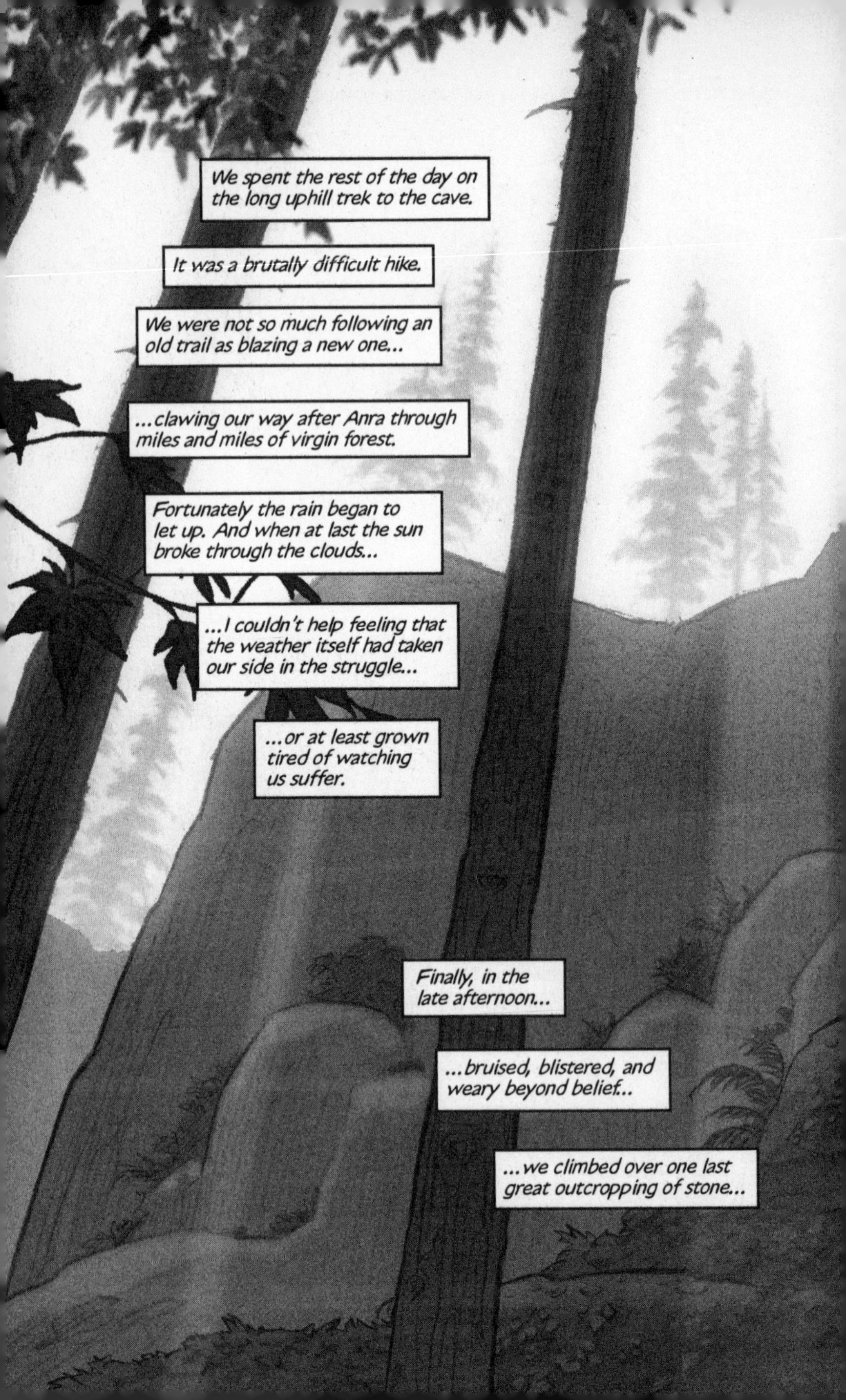

We spent the rest of the day on the long uphill trek to the cave.
It was a brutally difficult hike.
We were not so much following an old trail as blazing a new one...
...clawing our way after Anra through miles and miles of virgin forest.
Fortunately the rain began to let up. And when at last the sun broke through the clouds...
...I couldn't help feeling that the weather itself had taken our side in the struggle...
...or at least grown tired of watching us suffer.
Finally, in the late afternoon...
...bruised, blistered, and weary beyond belief...
...we climbed over one last great outcropping of stone...

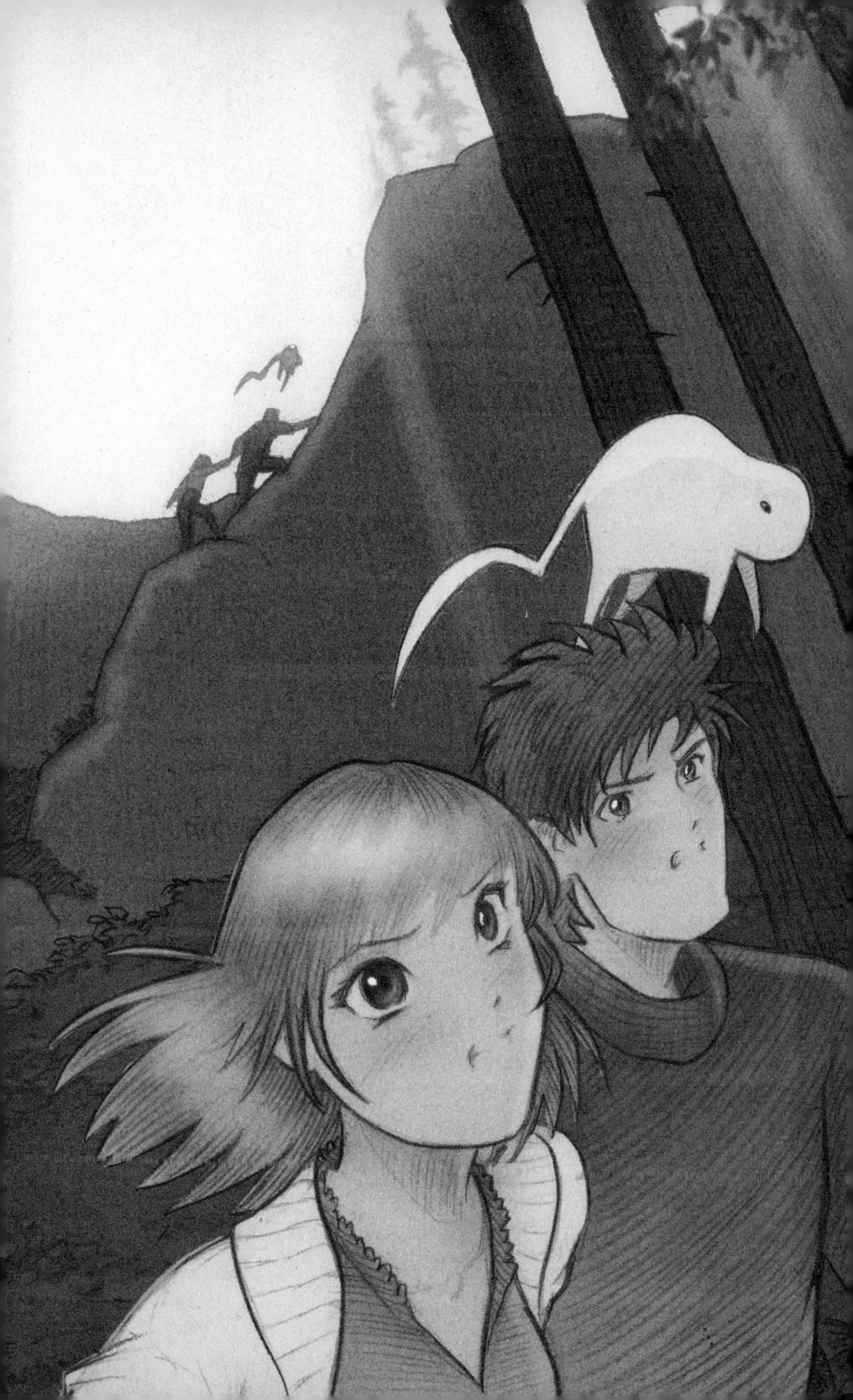

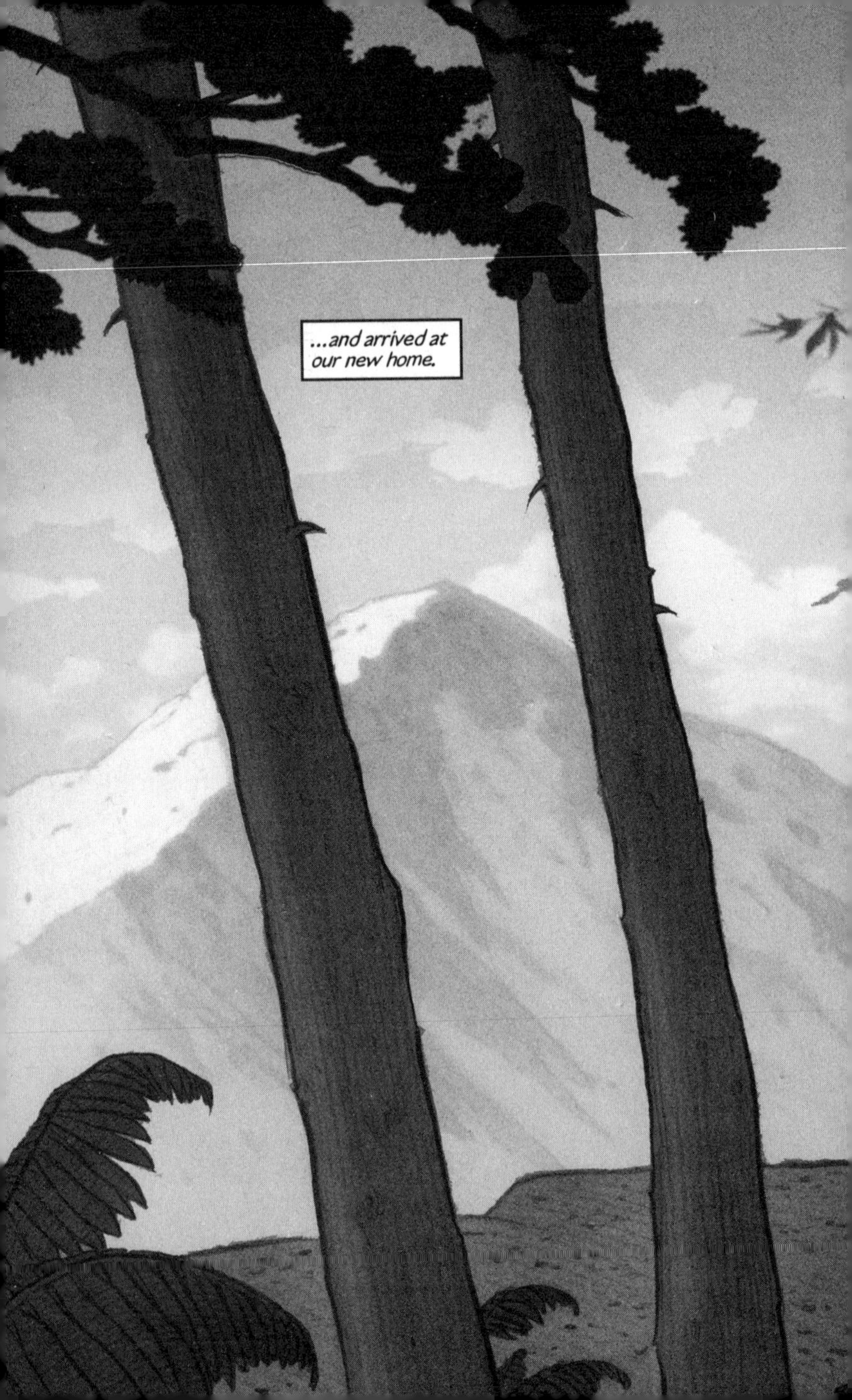
...and arrived at our new home.

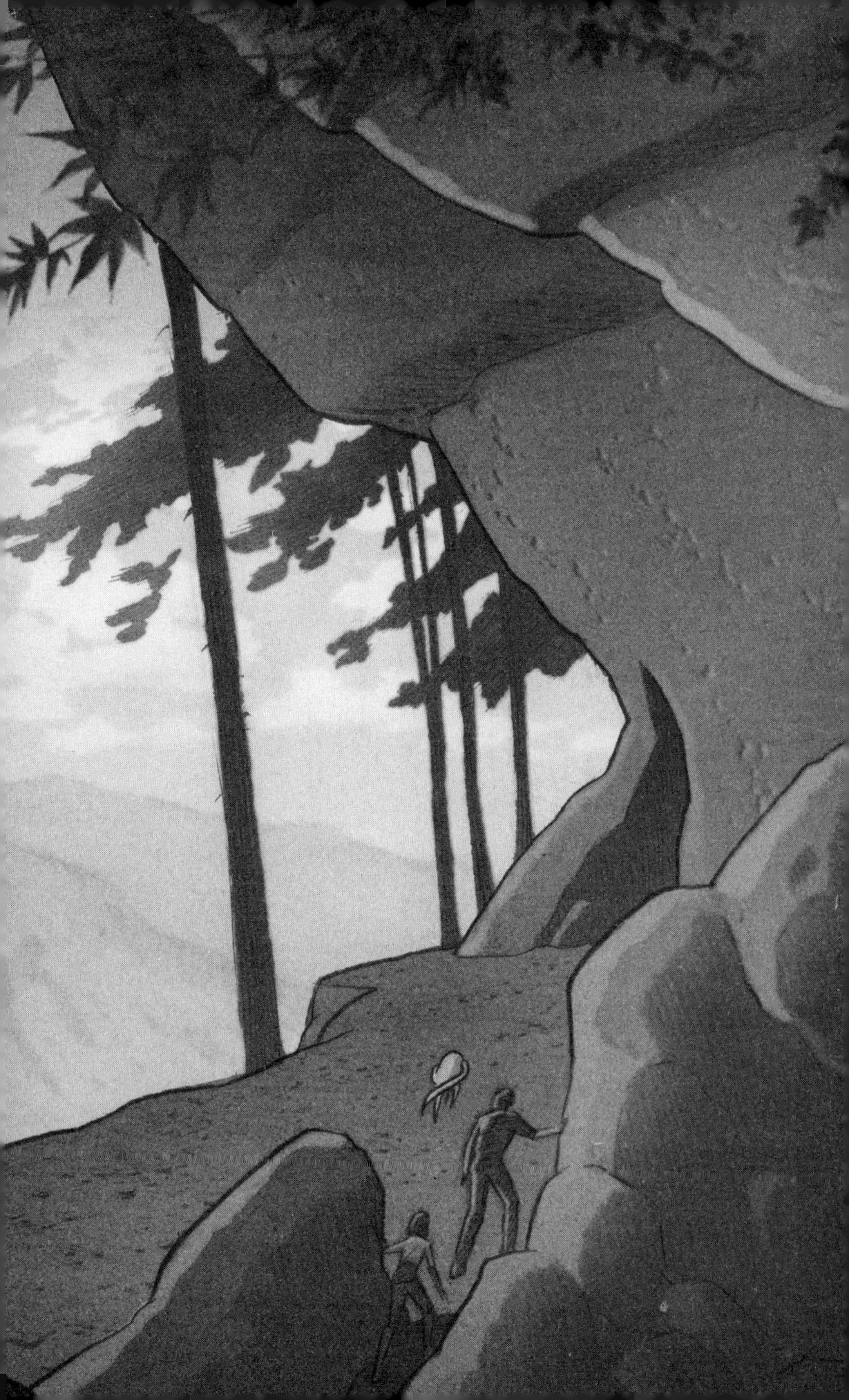

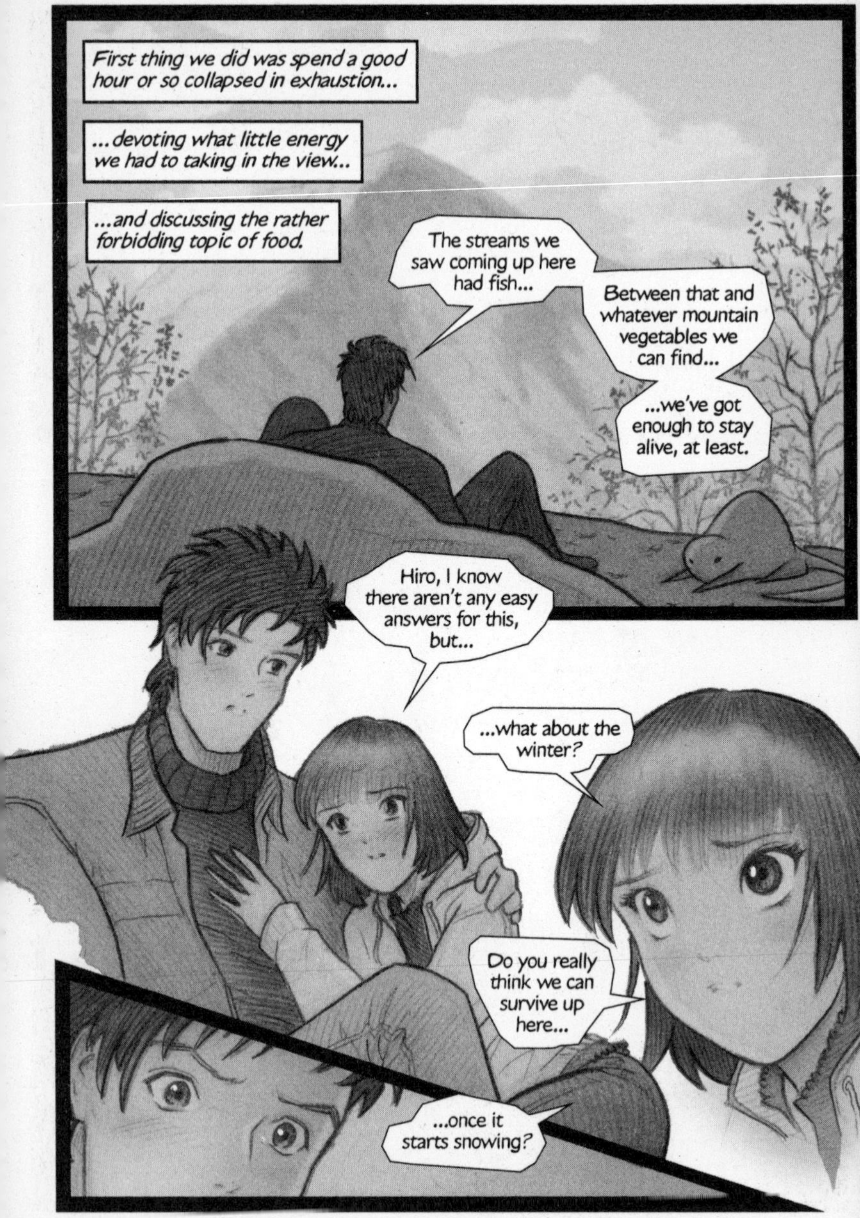
First thing we did was spend a good hour or so collapsed in exhaustion...
...devoting what little energy we had to taking in the view...
...and discussing the rather forbidding topic of food.
The streams we saw coming up here had fish...
Between that and whatever mountain vegetables we can find...
...we've got enough to stay alive, at least.
Hiro, I know there aren't any easy answers for this, but...
...what about the winter?
Do you really think we can survive up here...
...once it starts snowing?

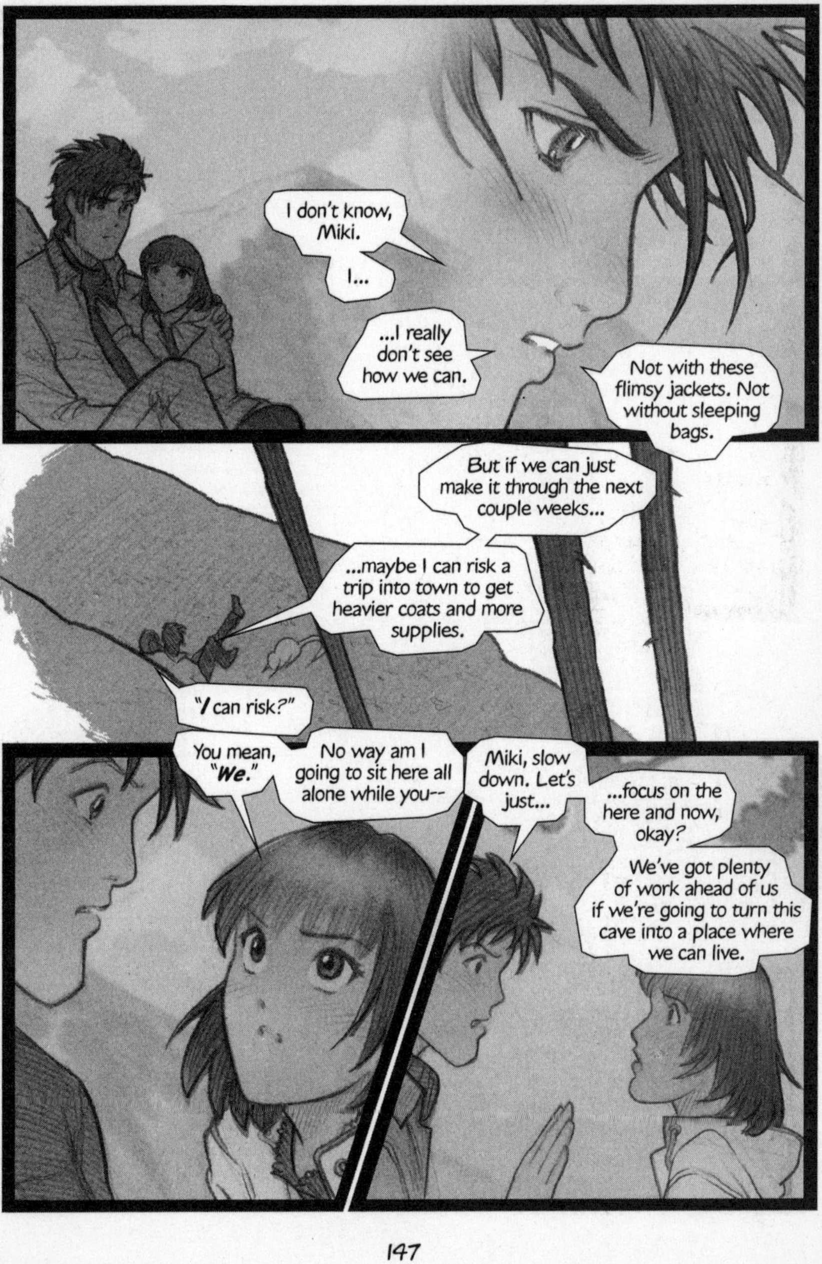

I don't know, Miki.
I...
...I really don't see how we can.
Not with these flimsy jackets. Not without sleeping bags.
But if we can just make it through the next couple weeks...
...maybe I can risk a trip into town to get heavier coats and more supplies.
"*I* can risk?"
You mean, "***We***."
No way am I going to sit here all alone while you--
Miki, slow down. Let's just...
...focus on the here and now, okay?
We've got plenty of work ahead of us if we're going to turn this cave into a place where we can live.

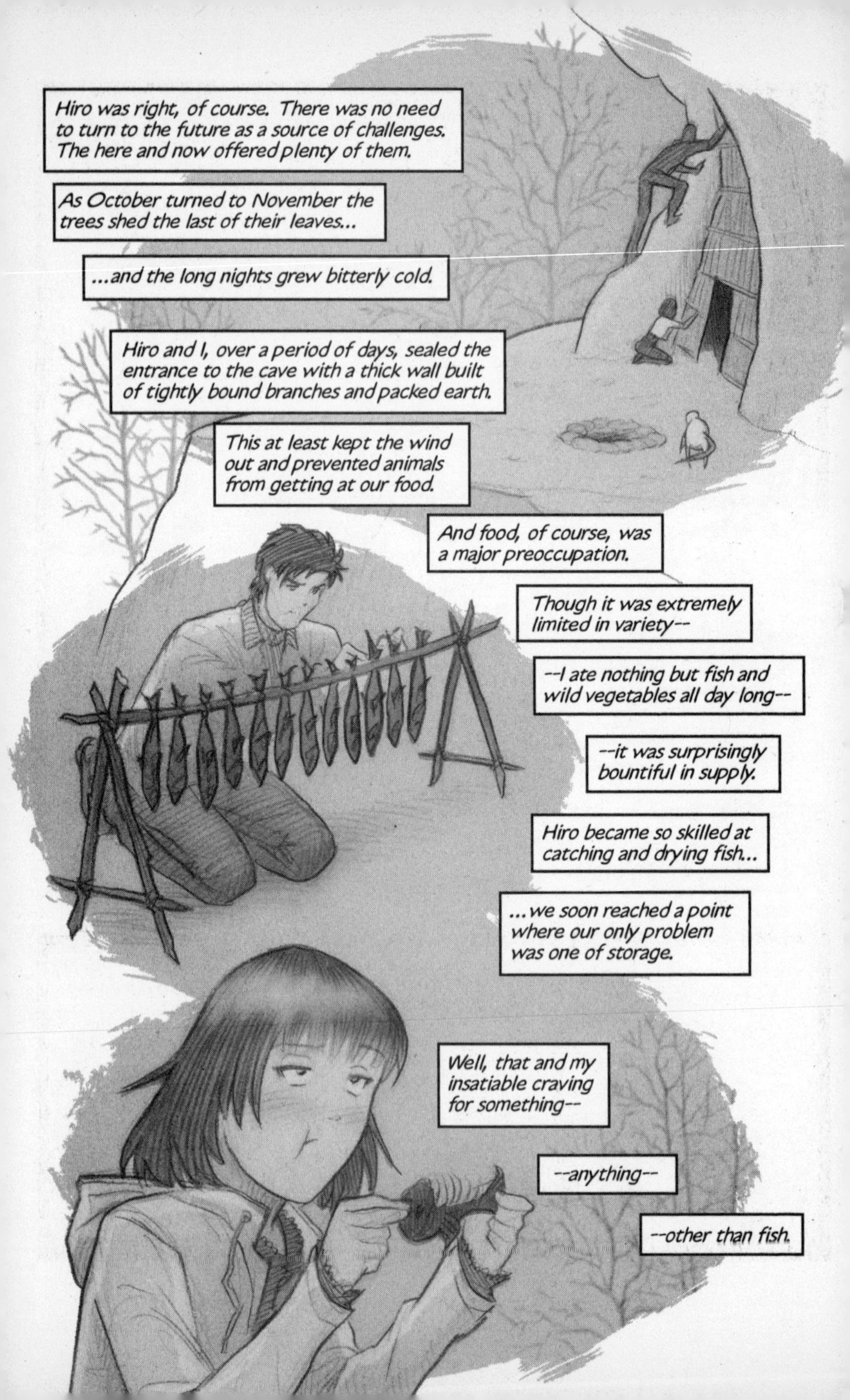
Hiro was right, of course. There was no need to turn to the future as a source of challenges. The here and now offered plenty of them.
As October turned to November the trees shed the last of their leaves...
...and the long nights grew bitterly cold.
Hiro and I, over a period of days, sealed the entrance to the cave with a thick wall built of tightly bound branches and packed earth.
This at least kept the wind out and prevented animals from getting at our food.
And food, of course, was a major preoccupation.
Though it was extremely limited in variety--
--I ate nothing but fish and wild vegetables all day long--
--it was surprisingly bountiful in supply.
Hiro became so skilled at catching and drying fish...
...we soon reached a point where our only problem was one of storage.
Well, that and my insatiable craving for something--
--anything--
--other than fish.

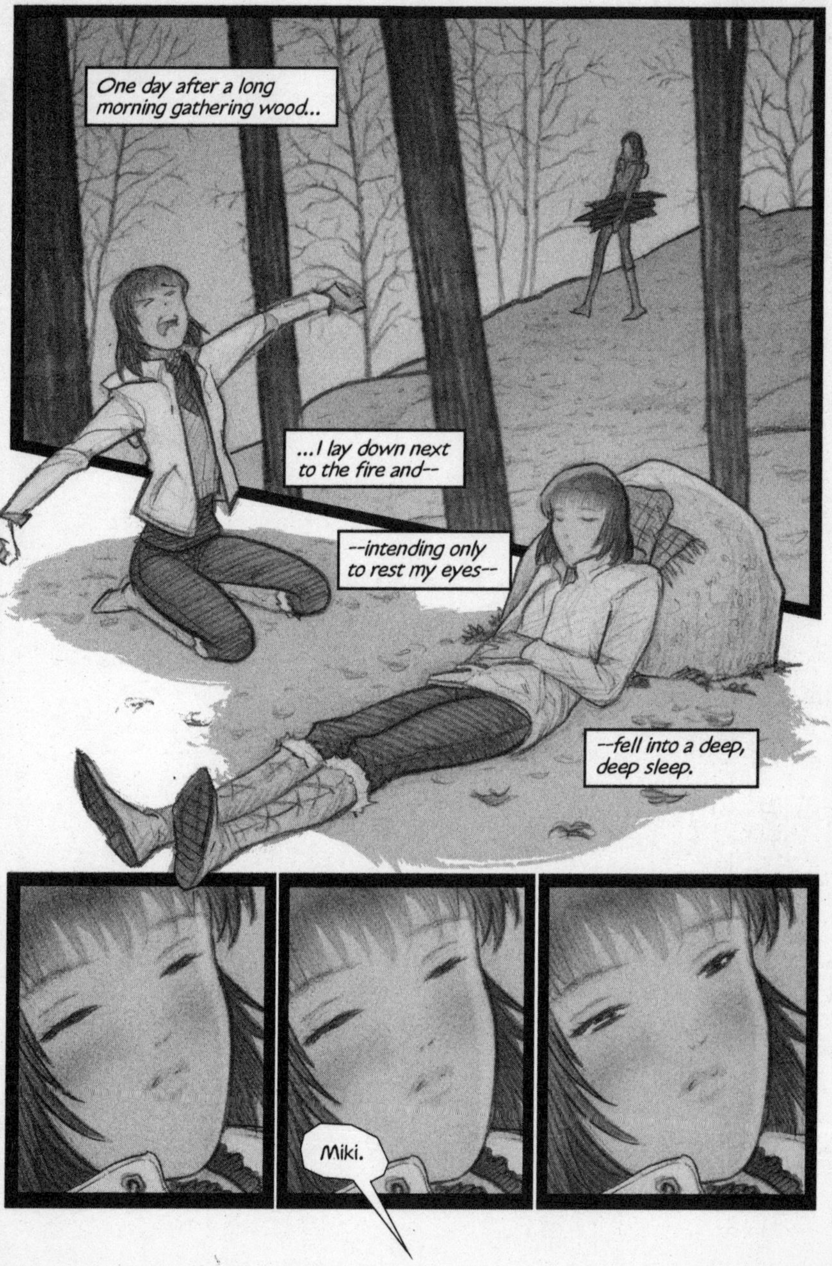
One day after a long morning gathering wood...
...I lay down next to the fire and--
--intending only to rest my eyes--
--fell into a deep, deep sleep.
Miki.

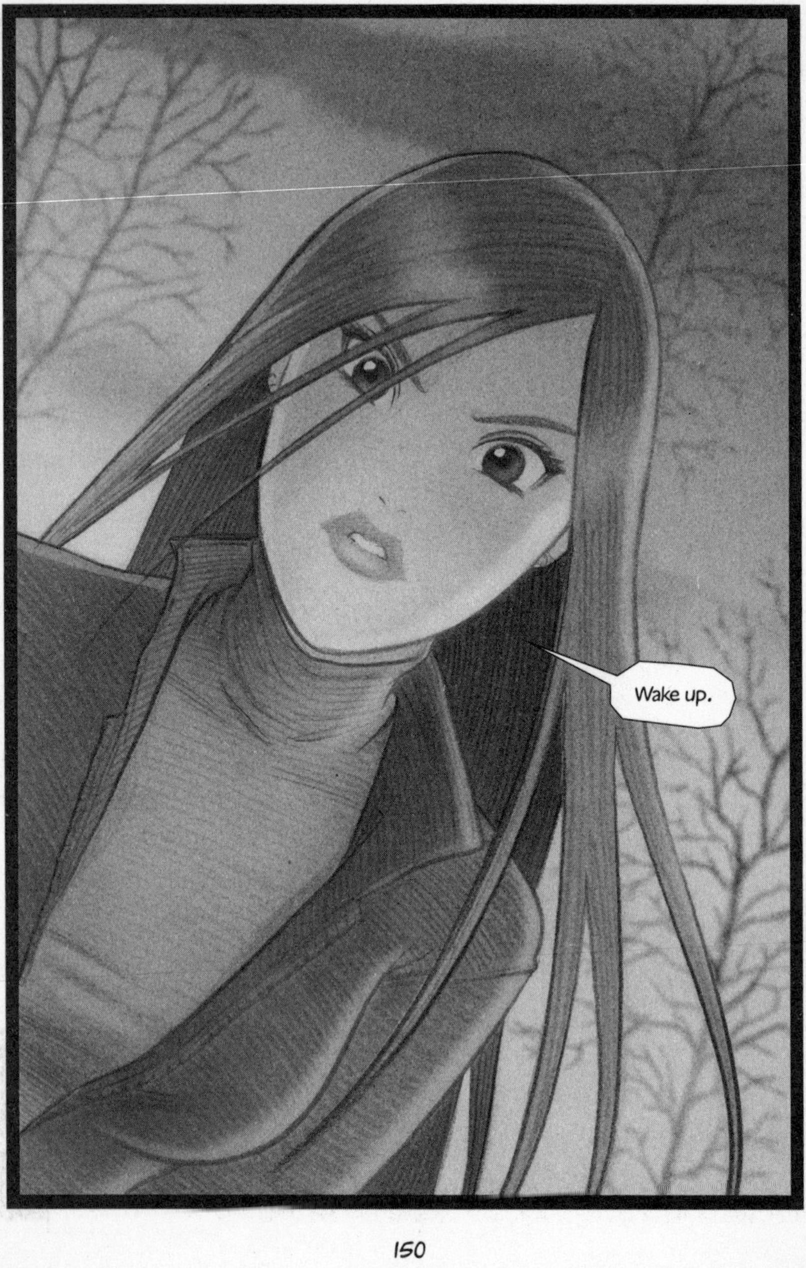
Wake up.

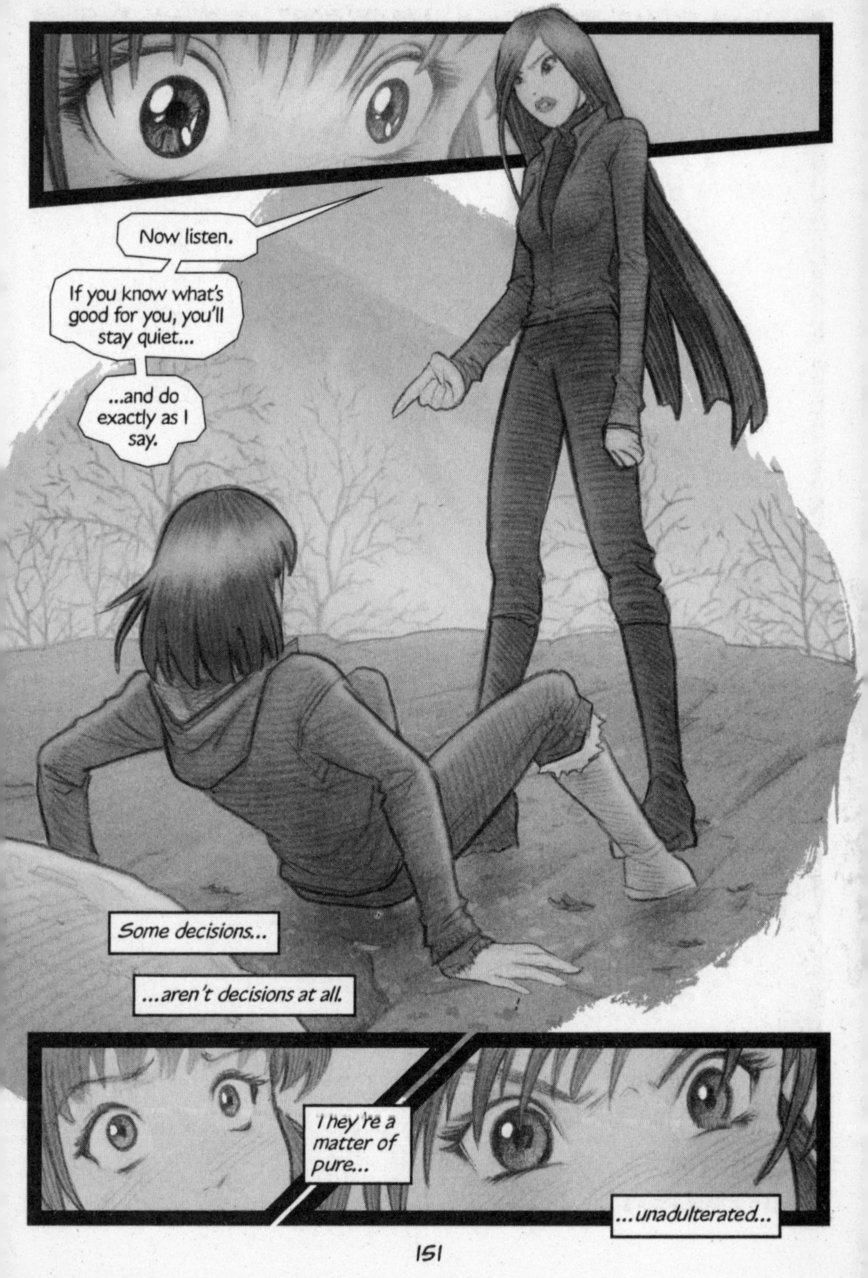
Now listen.
If you know what's good for you, you'll stay quiet...
...and do exactly as I say.
Some decisions...
...aren't decisions at all.
They're a matter of pure...
...unadulterated...

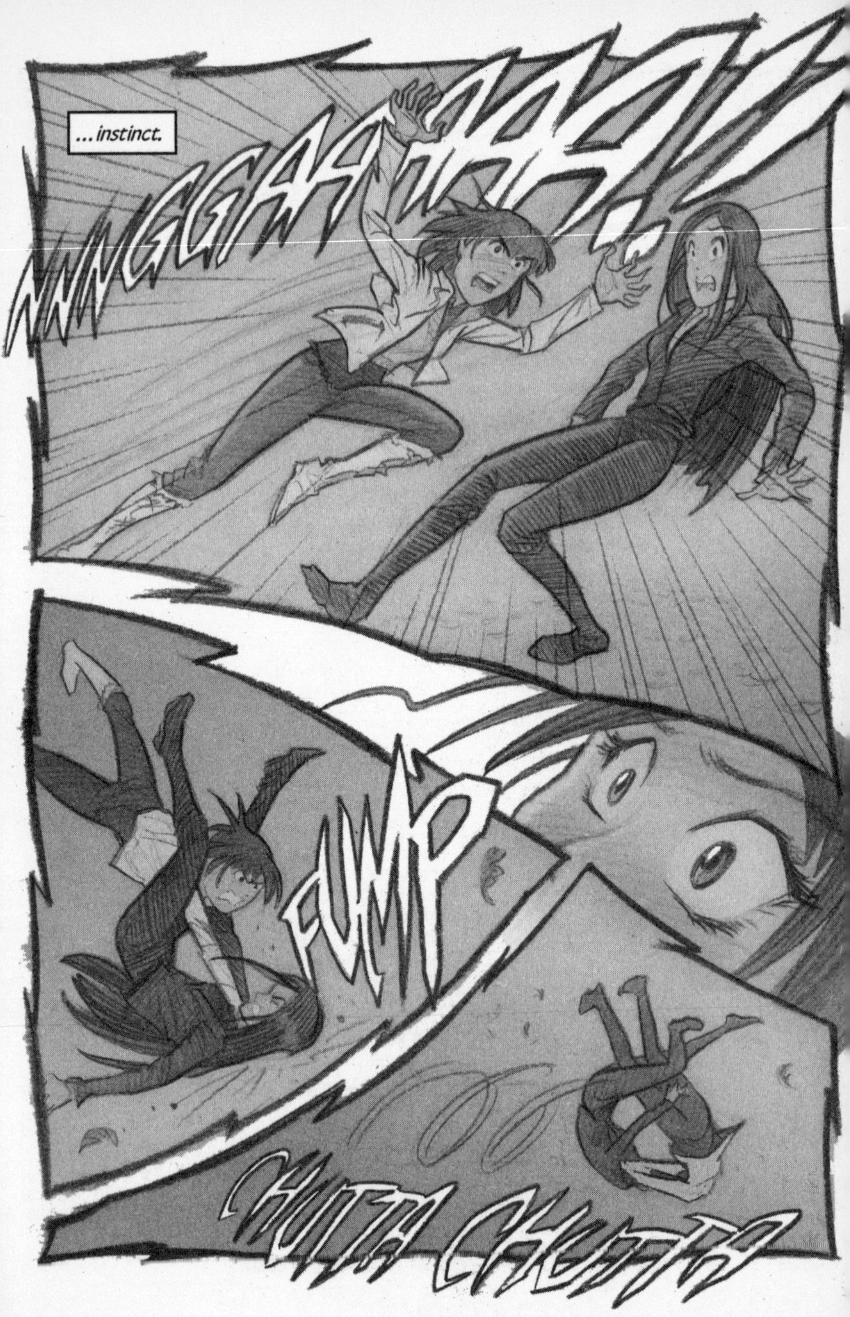
...instinct.
FUMP

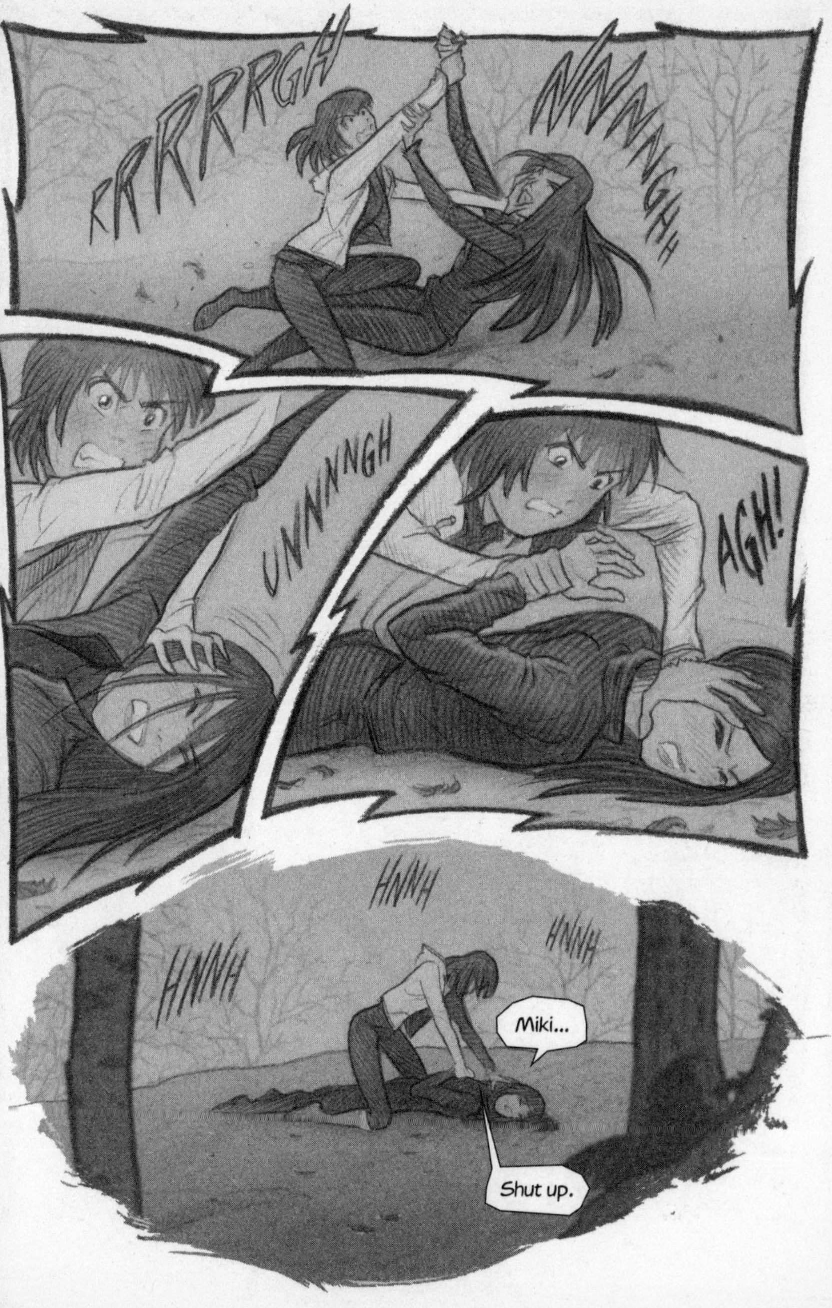
KRRRRRGH
NNNNNGHH
UNNNNGH
AGH!
HNNH
HNNH
HNNH
Miki...
Shut up.

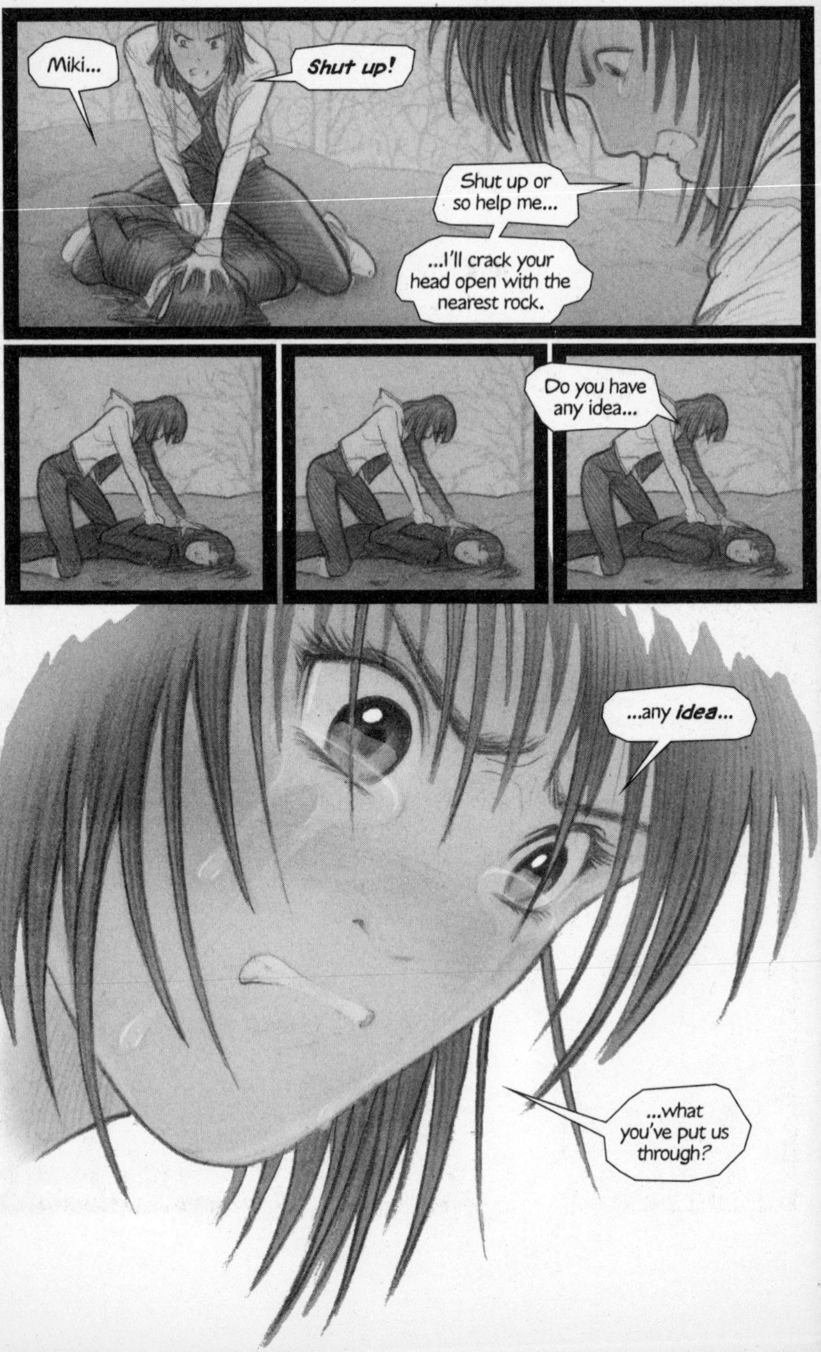
Miki...
Shut up!
Shut up or so help me...
...I'll crack your head open with the nearest rock.
Do you have any idea...
...any idea...
...what you've put us through?

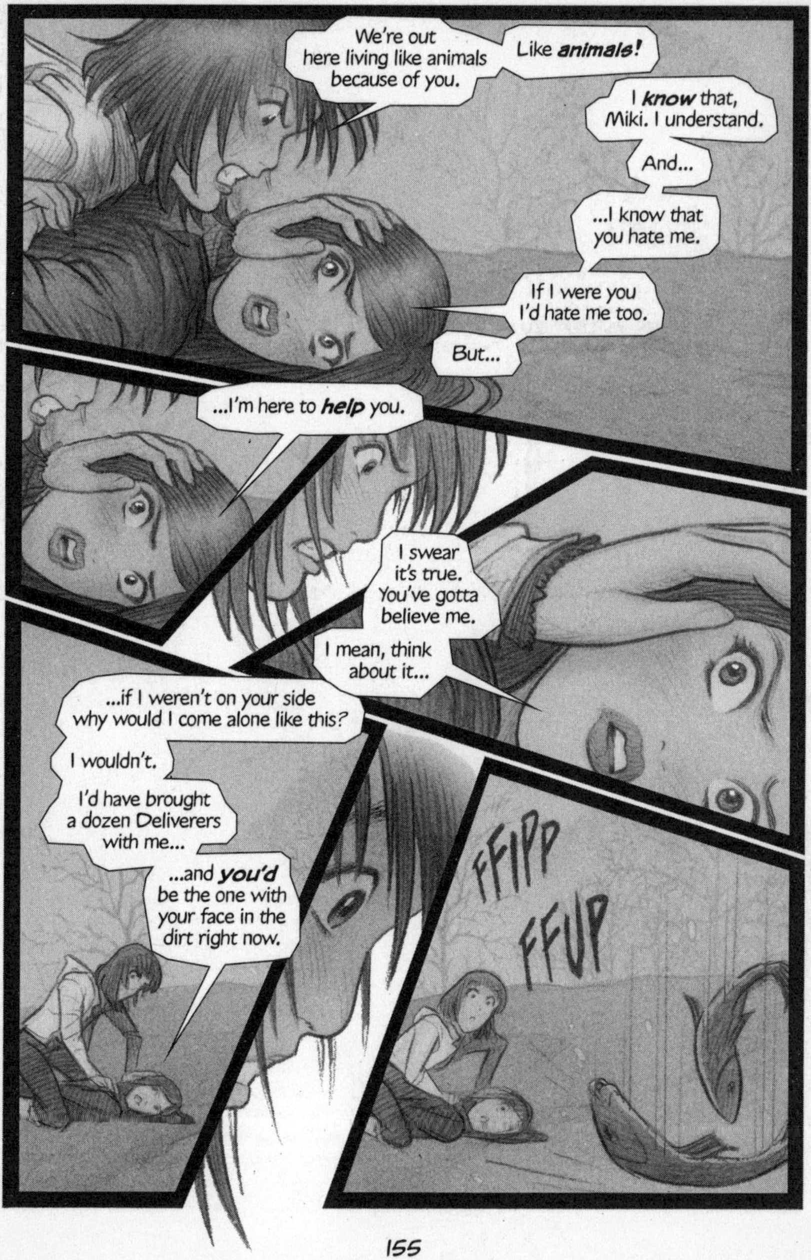
We're out here living like animals because of you.
Like ***animals!***
I ***know*** that, Miki. I understand.
And...
...I know that you hate me.
If I were you I'd hate me too.
But...
...I'm here to ***help*** you.
I swear it's true. You've gotta believe me.
I mean, think about it...
...if I weren't on your side why would I come alone like this?
I wouldn't.
I'd have brought a dozen Deliverers with me...
...and ***you'd*** be the one with your face in the dirt right now.
FFIPP
FFUP

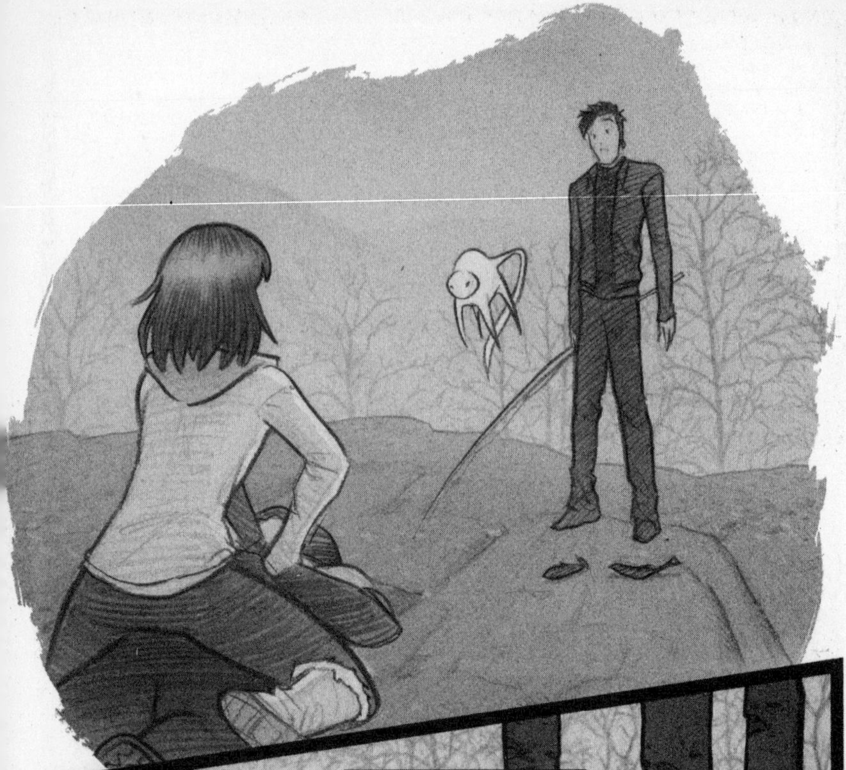

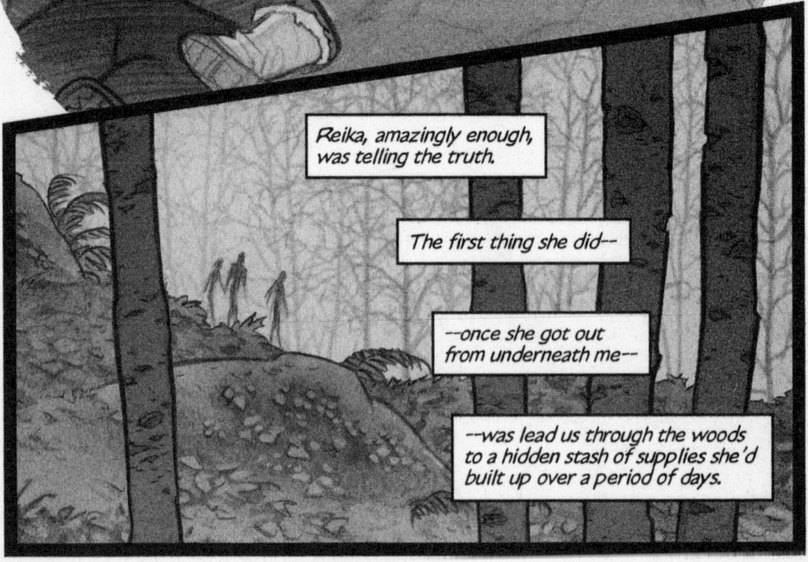
Reika, amazingly enough, was telling the truth.
The first thing she did--
--once she got out from underneath me--
--was lead us through the woods to a hidden stash of supplies she'd built up over a period of days.

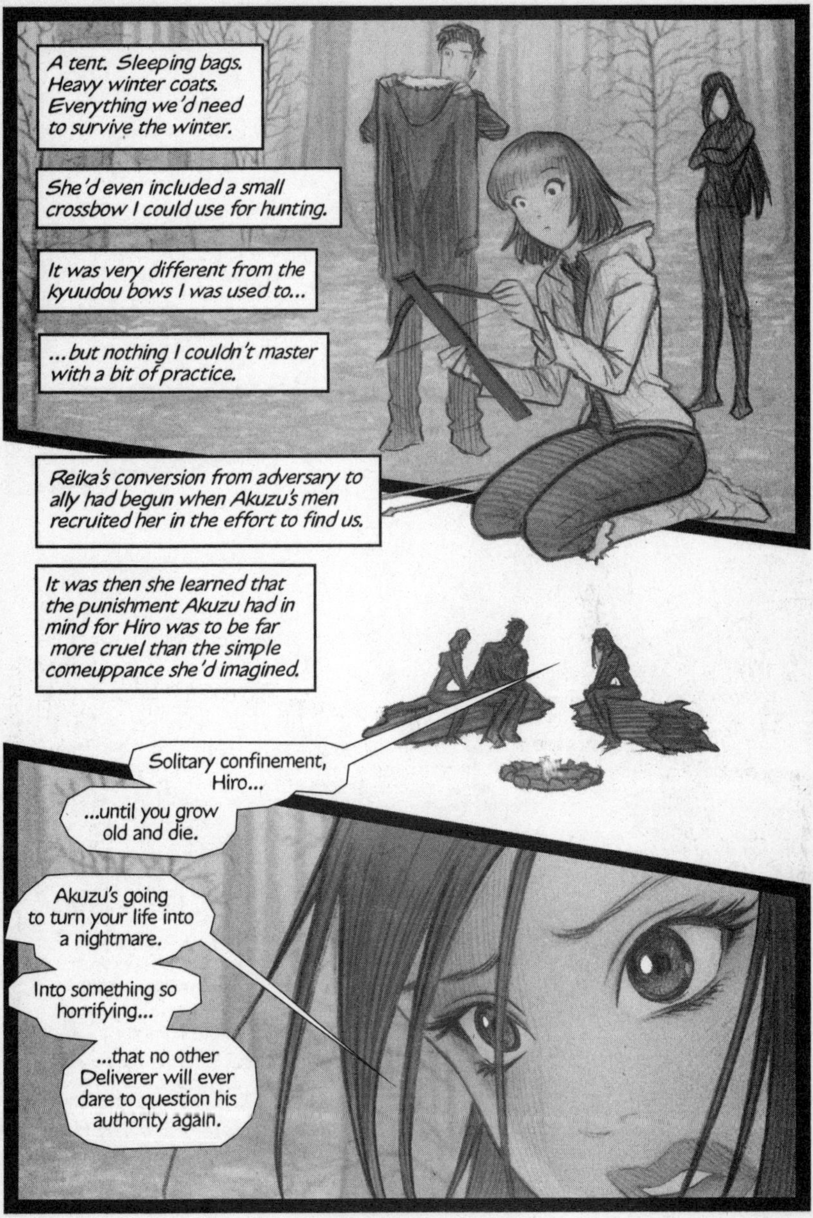
A tent. Sleeping bags. Heavy winter coats. Everything we'd need to survive the winter.
She'd even included a small crossbow I could use for hunting.
It was very different from the kyuudou bows I was used to...
...but nothing I couldn't master with a bit of practice.
Reika's conversion from adversary to ally had begun when Akuzu's men recruited her in the effort to find us.
It was then she learned that the punishment Akuzu had in mind for Hiro was to be far more cruel than the simple comeuppance she'd imagined.
Solitary confinement, Hiro...
...until you grow old and die.
Akuzu's going to turn your life into a nightmare.
Into something so horrifying...
...that no other Deliverer will ever dare to question his authority again.

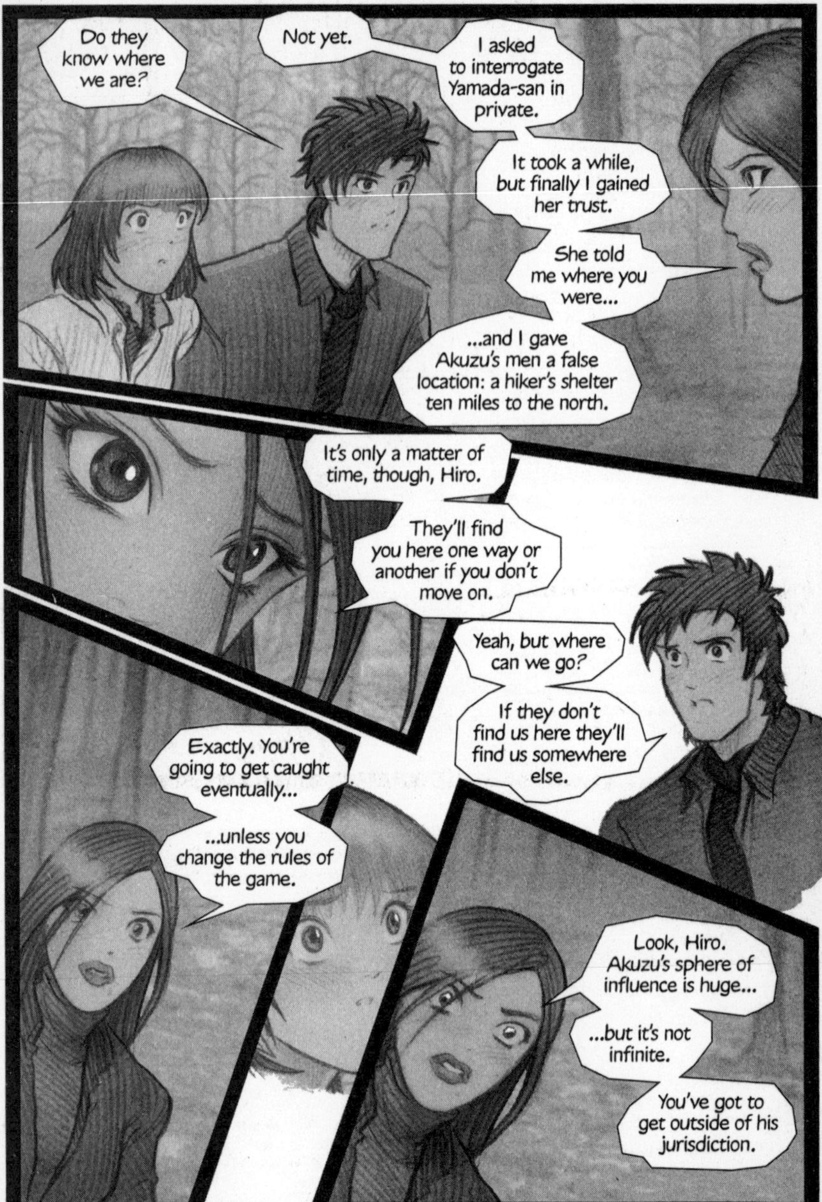
Do they know where we are?
Not yet.
I asked to interrogate Yamada-san in private.
It took a while, but finally I gained her trust.
She told me where you were...
...and I gave Akuzu's men a false location: a hiker's shelter ten miles to the north.
It's only a matter of time, though, Hiro.
They'll find you here one way or another if you don't move on.
Yeah, but where can we go?
If they don't find us here they'll find us somewhere else.
Exactly. You're going to get caught eventually...
...unless you change the rules of the game.
Look, Hiro. Akuzu's sphere of influence is huge...
...but it's not infinite.
You've got to get outside of his jurisdiction.

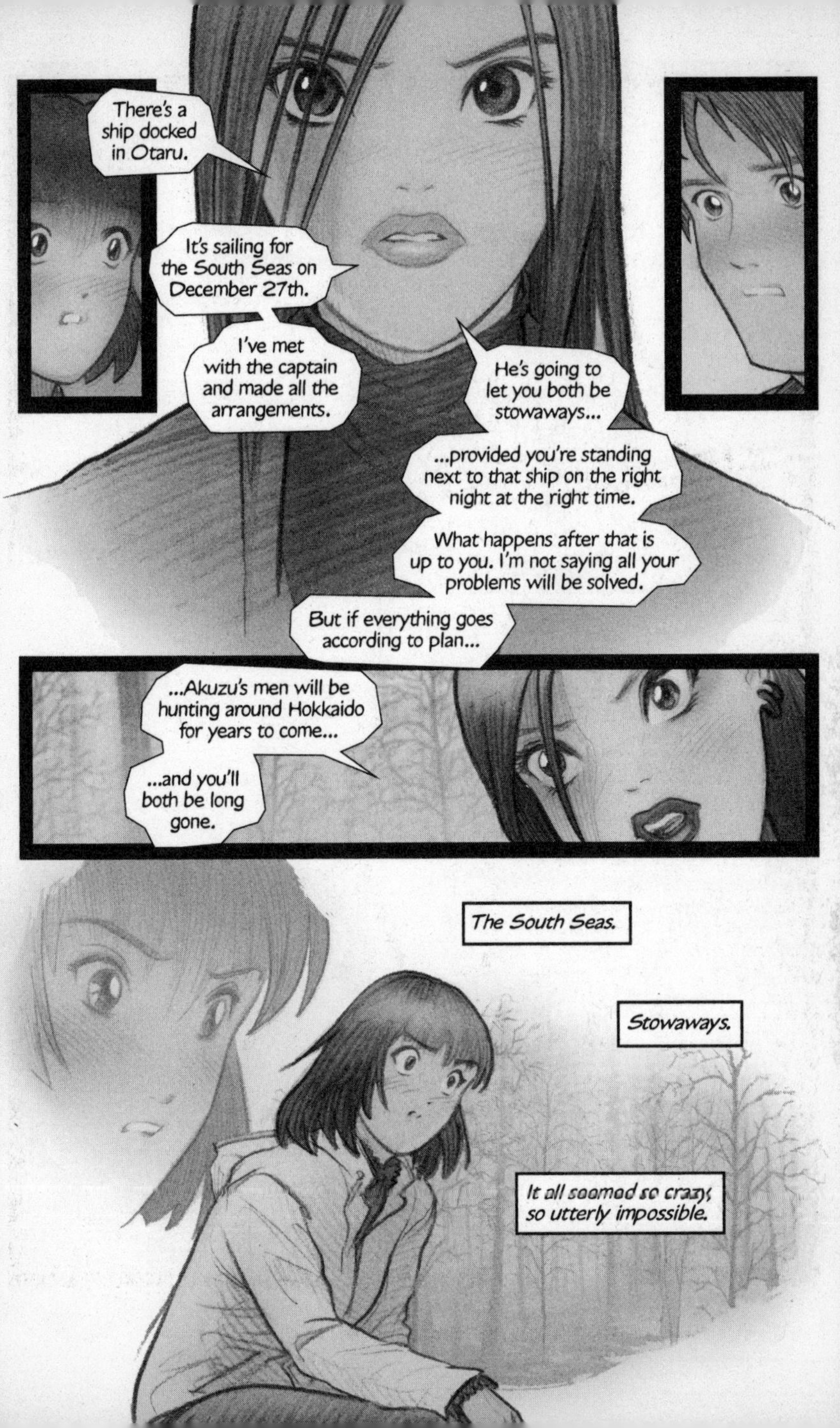
There's a ship docked in Otaru.
It's sailing for the South Seas on December 27th.
I've met with the captain and made all the arrangements.
He's going to let you both be stowaways...
...provided you're standing next to that ship on the right night at the right time.
What happens after that is up to you. I'm not saying all your problems will be solved.
But if everything goes according to plan...
...Akuzu's men will be hunting around Hokkaido for years to come...
...and you'll both be long gone.
The South Seas.
Stowaways.
It all seemed so crazy, so utterly impossible.

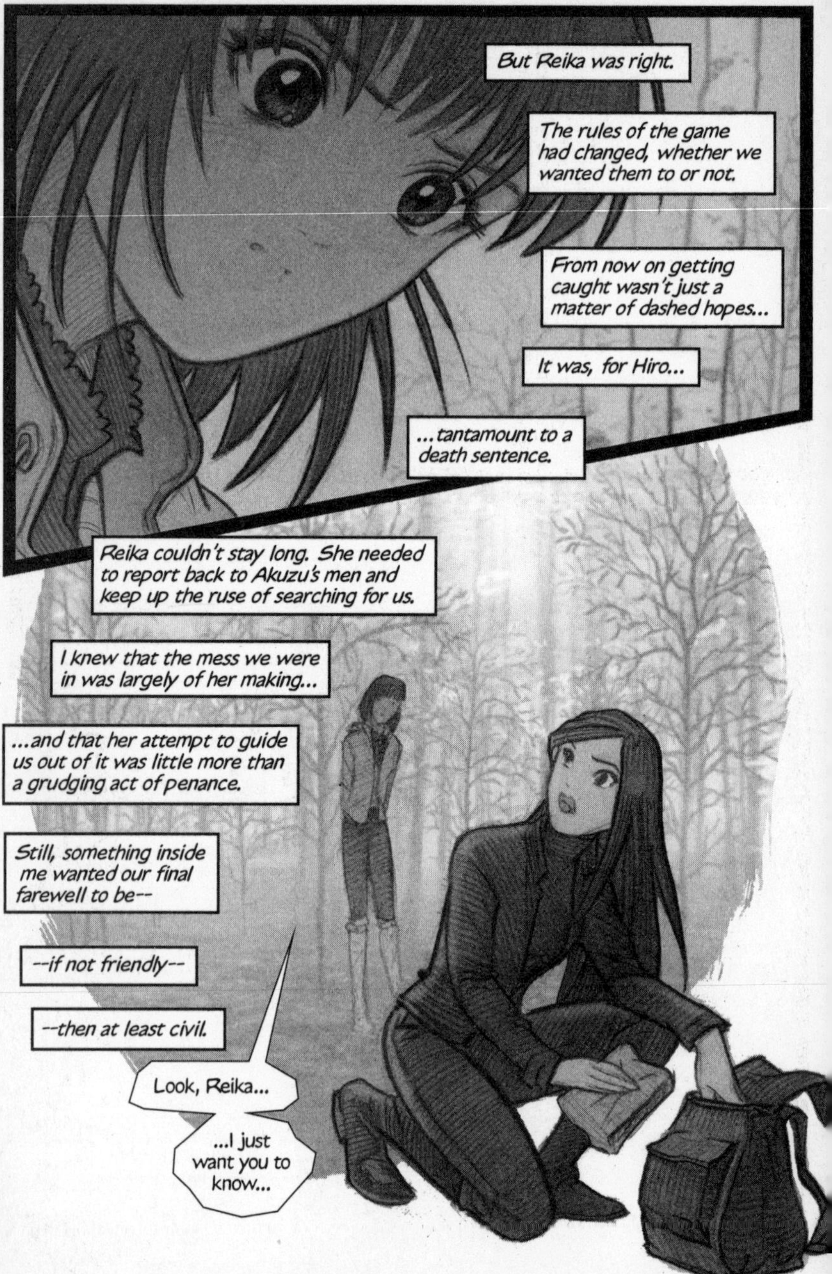
But Reika was right.
The rules of the game had changed, whether we wanted them to or not.
From now on getting caught wasn't just a matter of dashed hopes...
It was, for Hiro...
...tantamount to a death sentence.
Reika couldn't stay long. She needed to report back to Akuzu's men and keep up the ruse of searching for us.
I knew that the mess we were in was largely of her making...
...and that her attempt to guide us out of it was little more than a grudging act of penance.
Still, something inside me wanted our final farewell to be--
--if not friendly--
--then at least civil.
Look, Reika...
...I just want you to know...

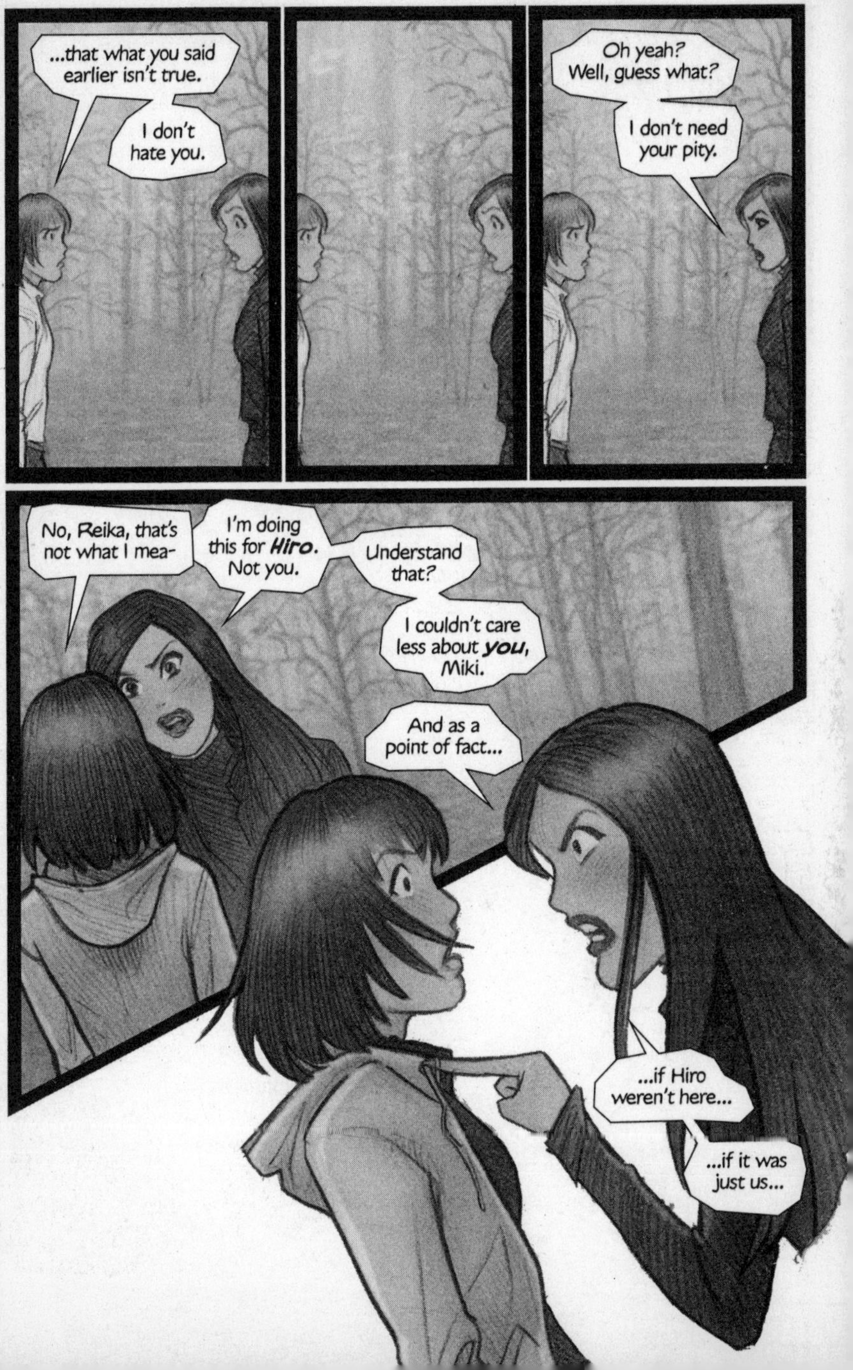
...that what you said earlier isn't true.
I don't hate you.
Oh yeah? Well, guess what?
I don't need your pity.
No, Reika, that's not what I mea-
I'm doing this for *Hiro*. Not you.
Understand that?
I couldn't care less about *you*, Miki.
And as a point of fact...
...if Hiro weren't here...
...if it was just us...

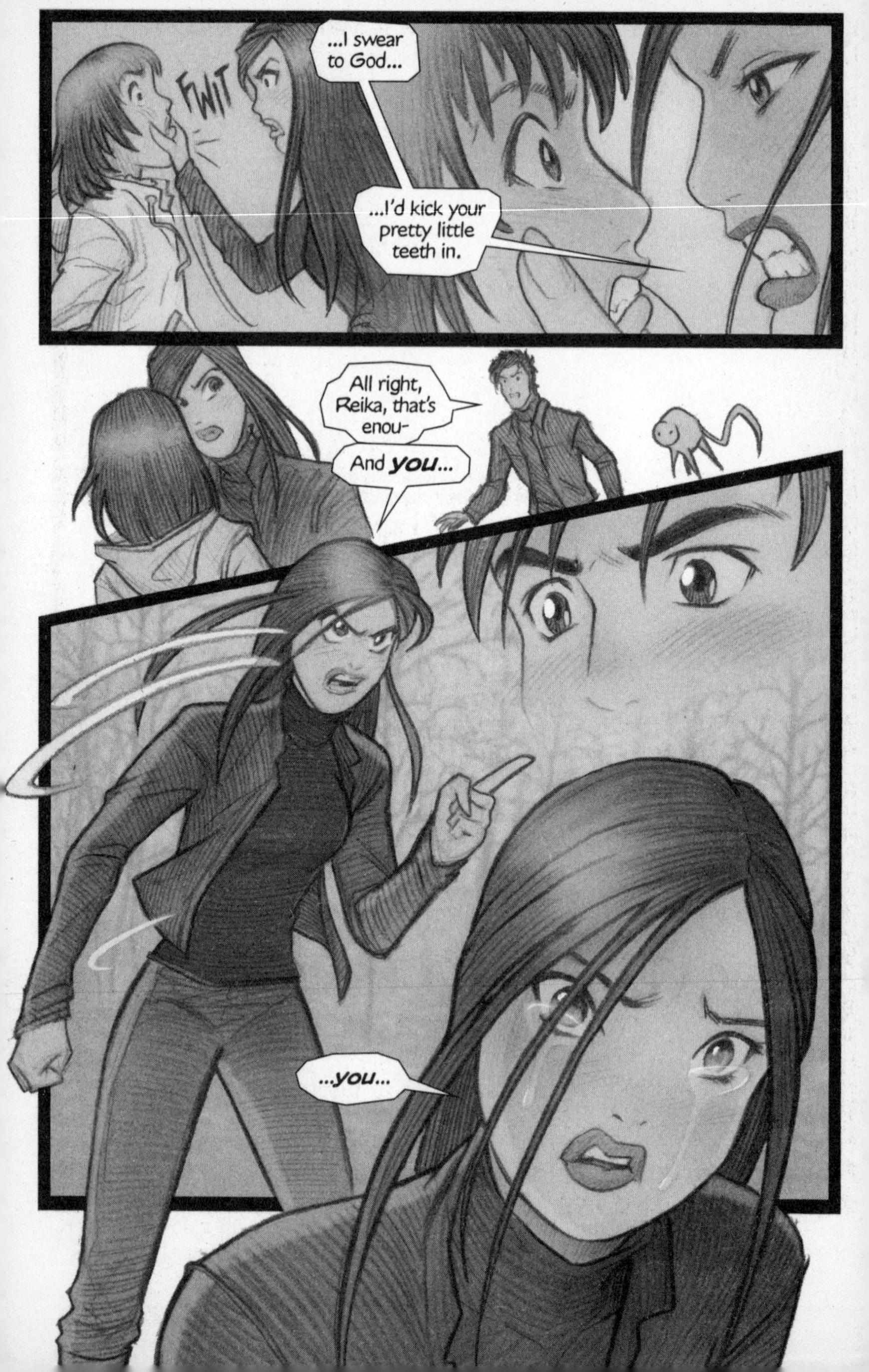
FWIT
...I swear to God...
...I'd kick your pretty little teeth in.
All right, Reika, that's enou-
And *you*...
...*you*...

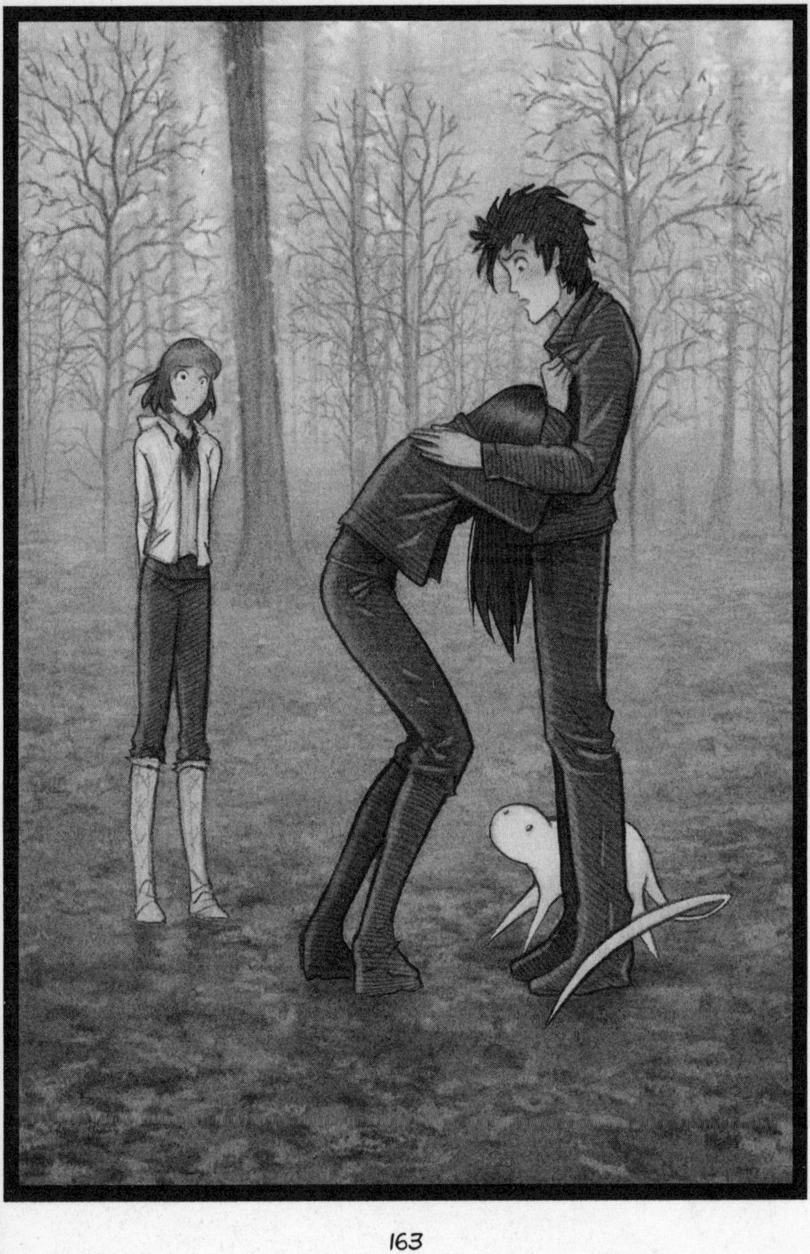

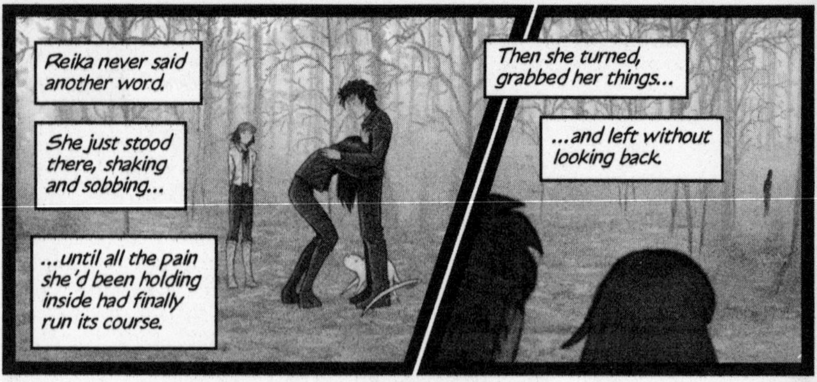
Reika never said another word.
She just stood there, shaking and sobbing...
...until all the pain she'd been holding inside had finally run its course.
Then she turned, grabbed her things...
...and left without looking back.

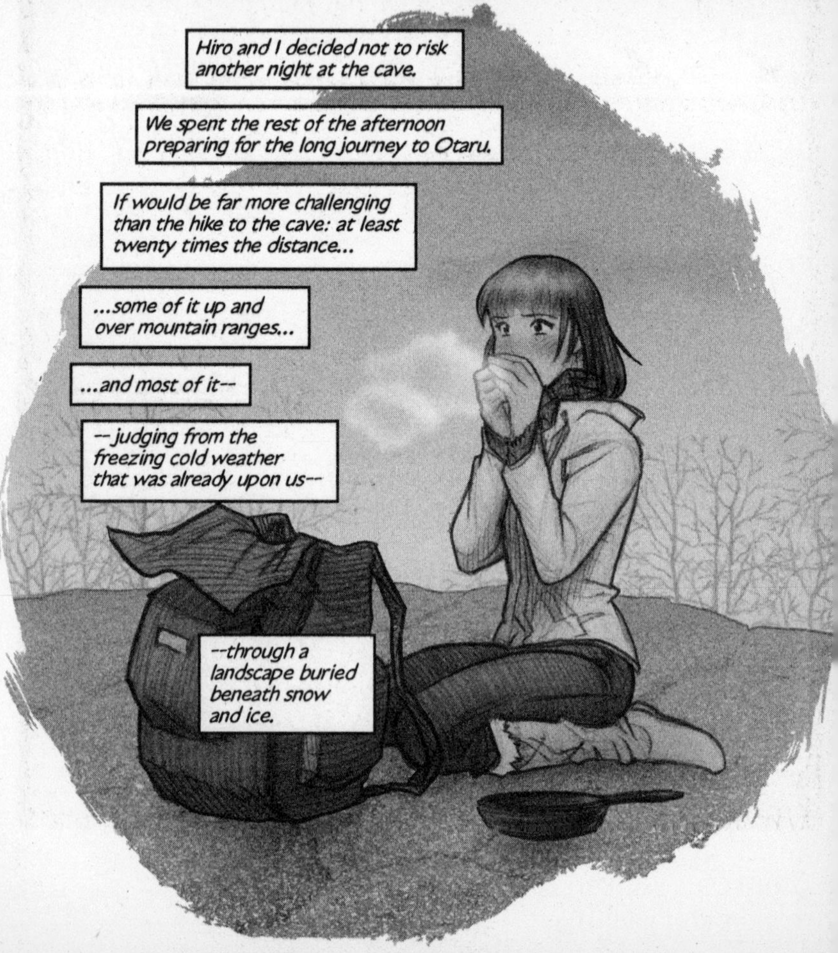
Hiro and I decided not to risk another night at the cave.
We spent the rest of the afternoon preparing for the long journey to Otaru.
If would be far more challenging than the hike to the cave: at least twenty times the distance...
...some of it up and over mountain ranges...
...and most of it--
--judging from the freezing cold weather that was already upon us--
--through a landscape buried beneath snow and ice.

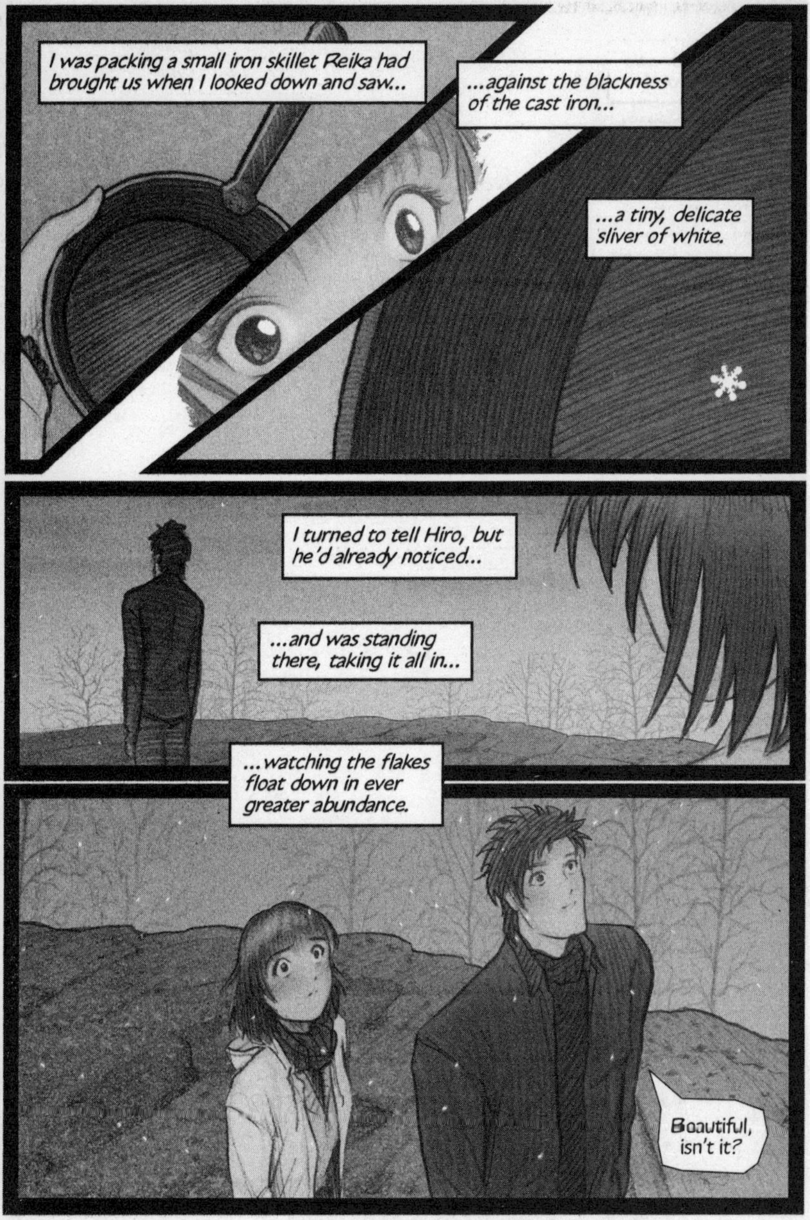
I was packing a small iron skillet Reika had brought us when I looked down and saw...
...against the blackness of the cast iron...
...a tiny, delicate sliver of white.
I turned to tell Hiro, but he'd already noticed...
...and was standing there, taking it all in...
...watching the flakes float down in ever greater abundance.
Beautiful, isn't it?

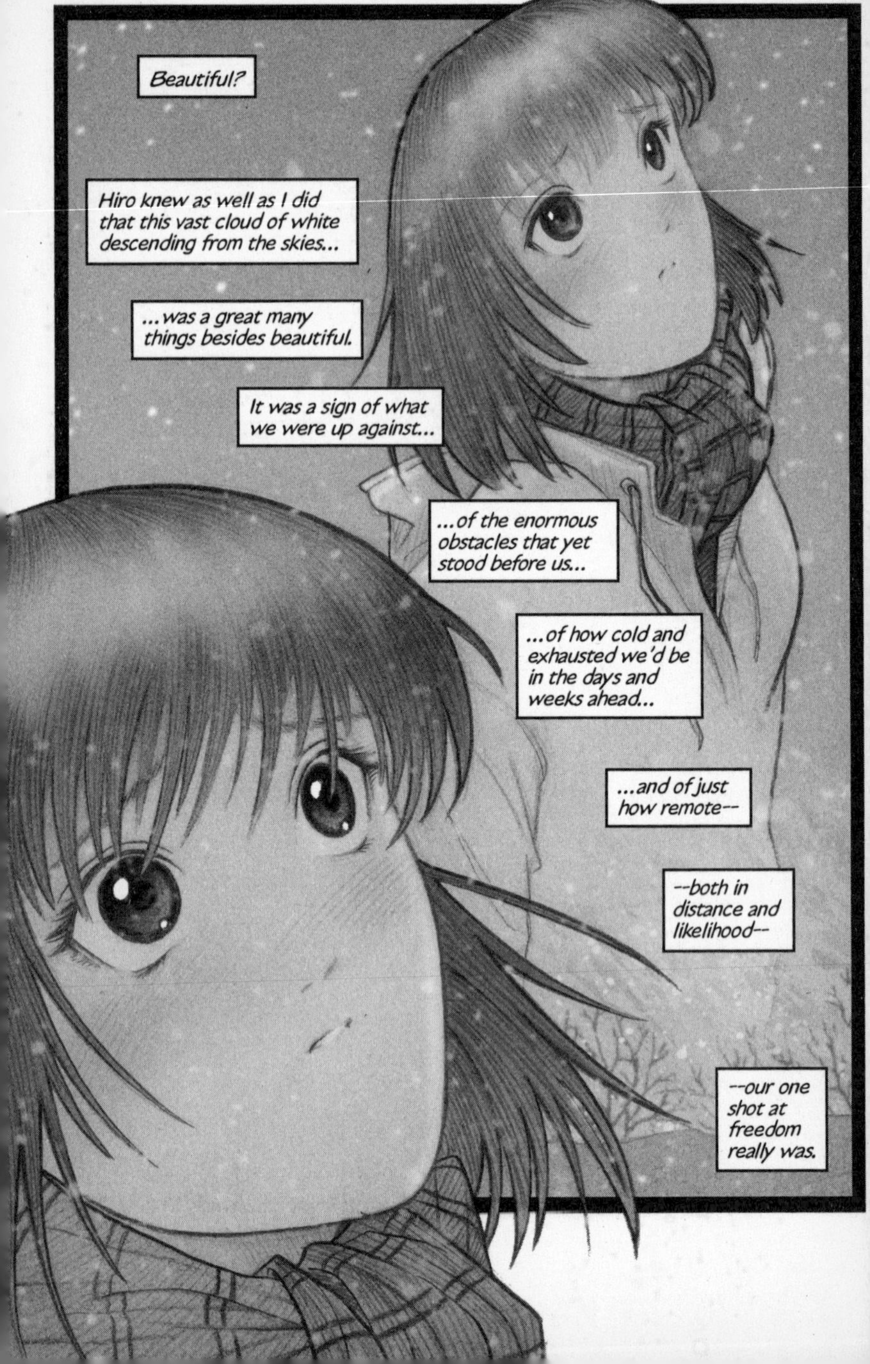
Beautiful?
Hiro knew as well as I did that this vast cloud of white descending from the skies...
...was a great many things besides beautiful.
It was a sign of what we were up against...
...of the enormous obstacles that yet stood before us...
...of how cold and exhausted we'd be in the days and weeks ahead...
...and of just how remote--
--both in distance and likelihood--
--our one shot at freedom really was.

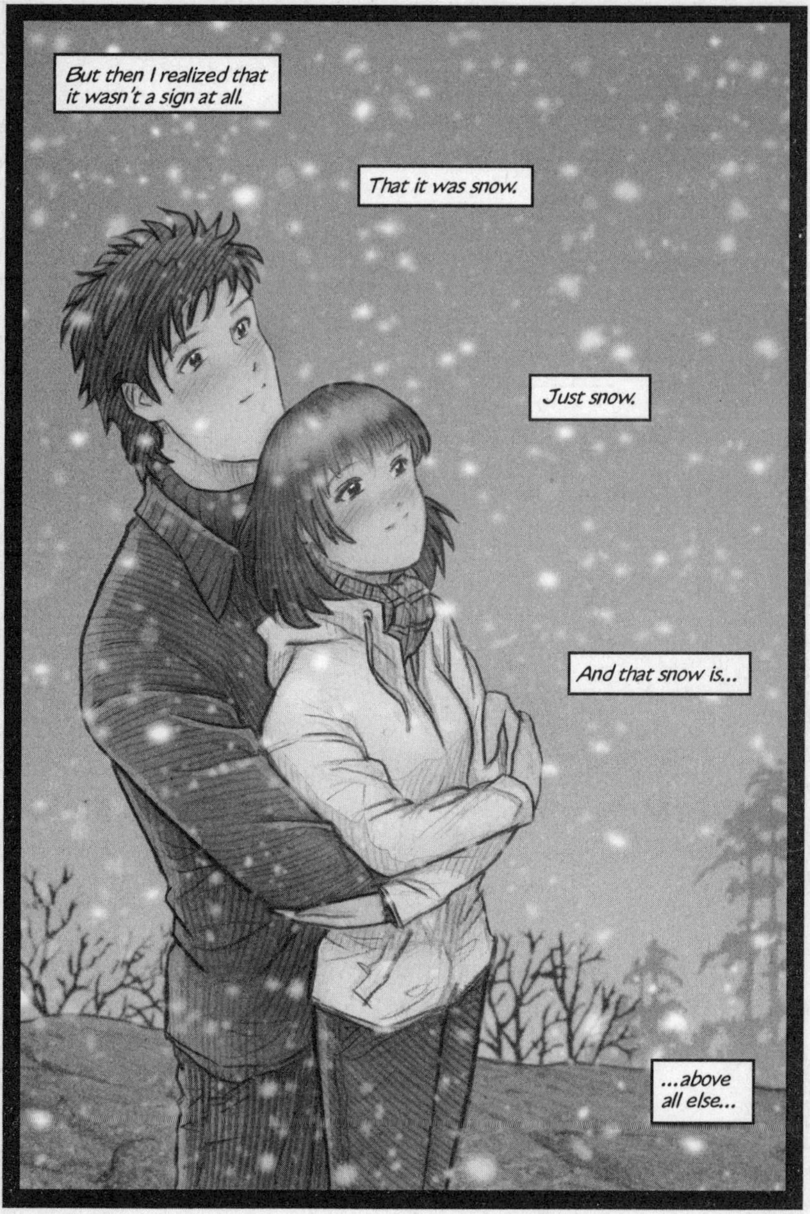
But then I realized that it wasn't a sign at all.
That it was snow.
Just snow.
And that snow is...
...above all else...

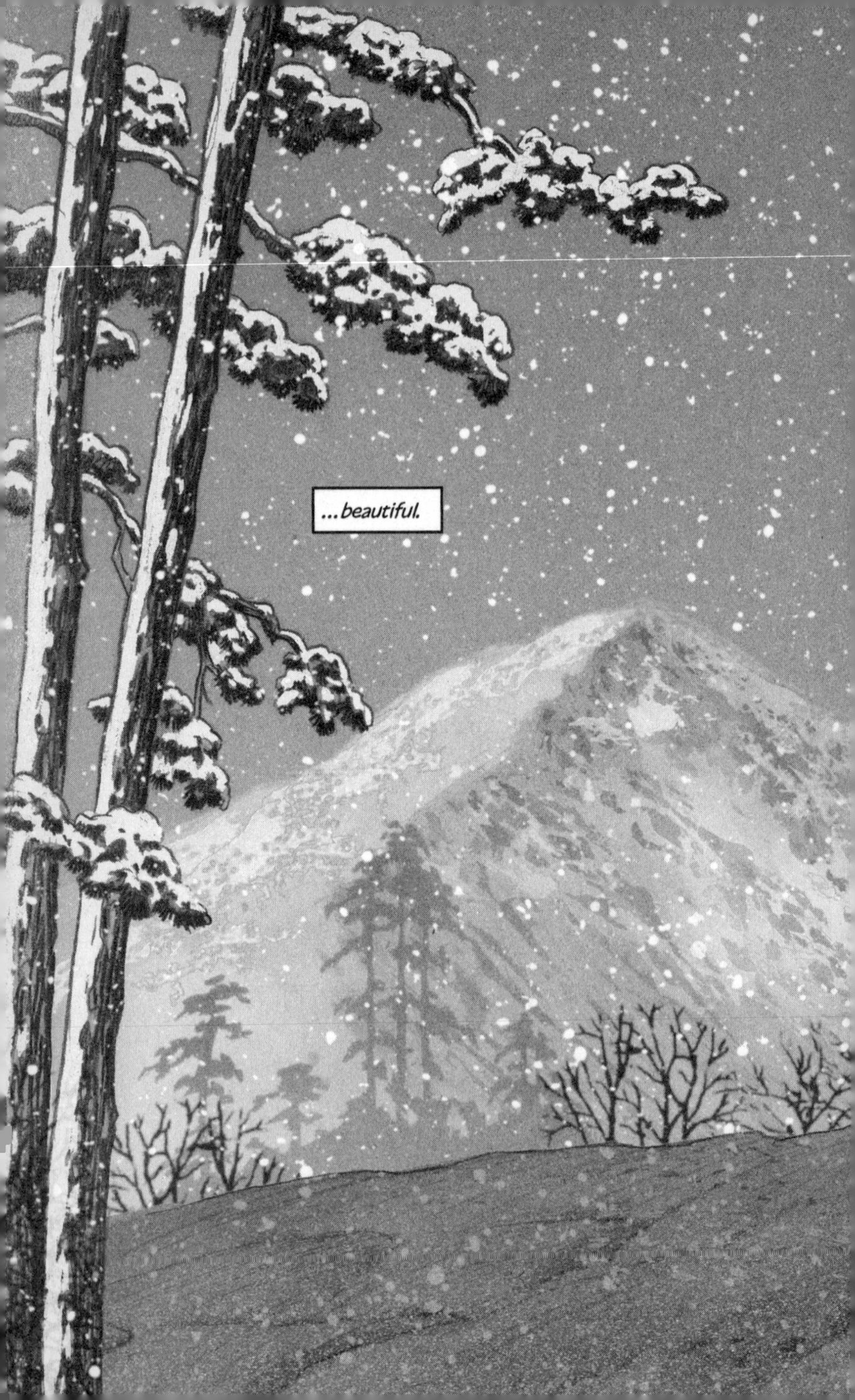
...beautiful.

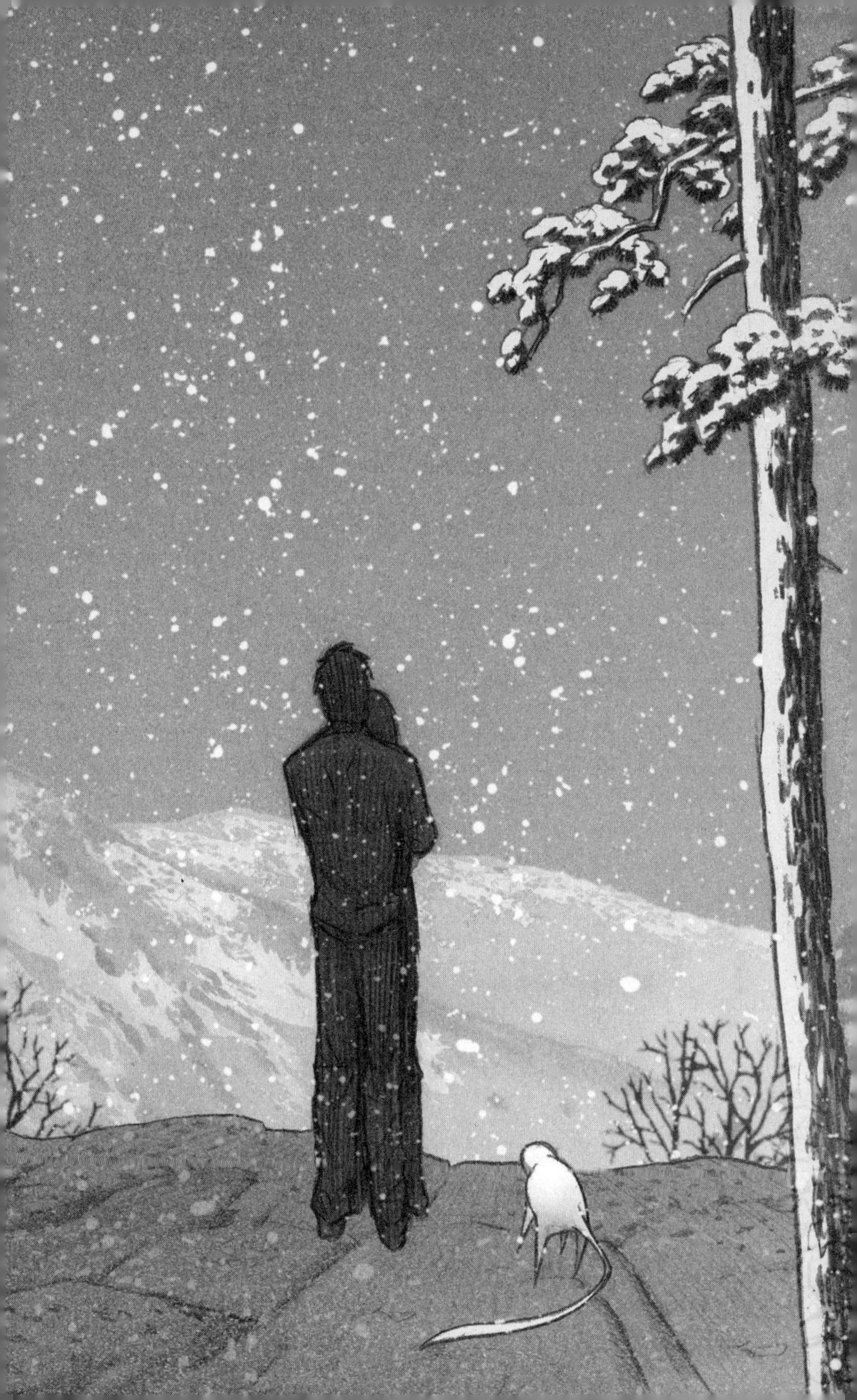

For my son, Matthew

HarperTeen is an imprint of HarperCollins Publishers.

Miki Falls: Autumn
Copyright © 2007 by Mark Crilley
All rights reserved. Printed in the United States of America.
No part of this book may be used or reproduced in any manner whatsoever
without written permission except in the case of brief
quotations embodied in critical articles and reviews.
For information address HarperCollins Children's Books,
a division of HarperCollins Publishers,
1350 Avenue of the Americas,
New York, NY 10019.
www.harperteen.com
Library of Congress Catalog Card Number: 2007931804
ISBN 978-0-06-084618-3
❖
First Edition

Is Miki finally safe?
Keep reading to find out more!

Turn the page for a preview of

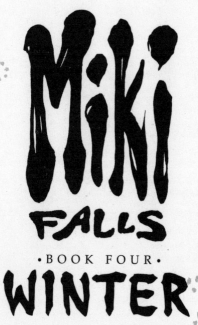

MiKi
FALLS
· BOOK FOUR ·
WINTER

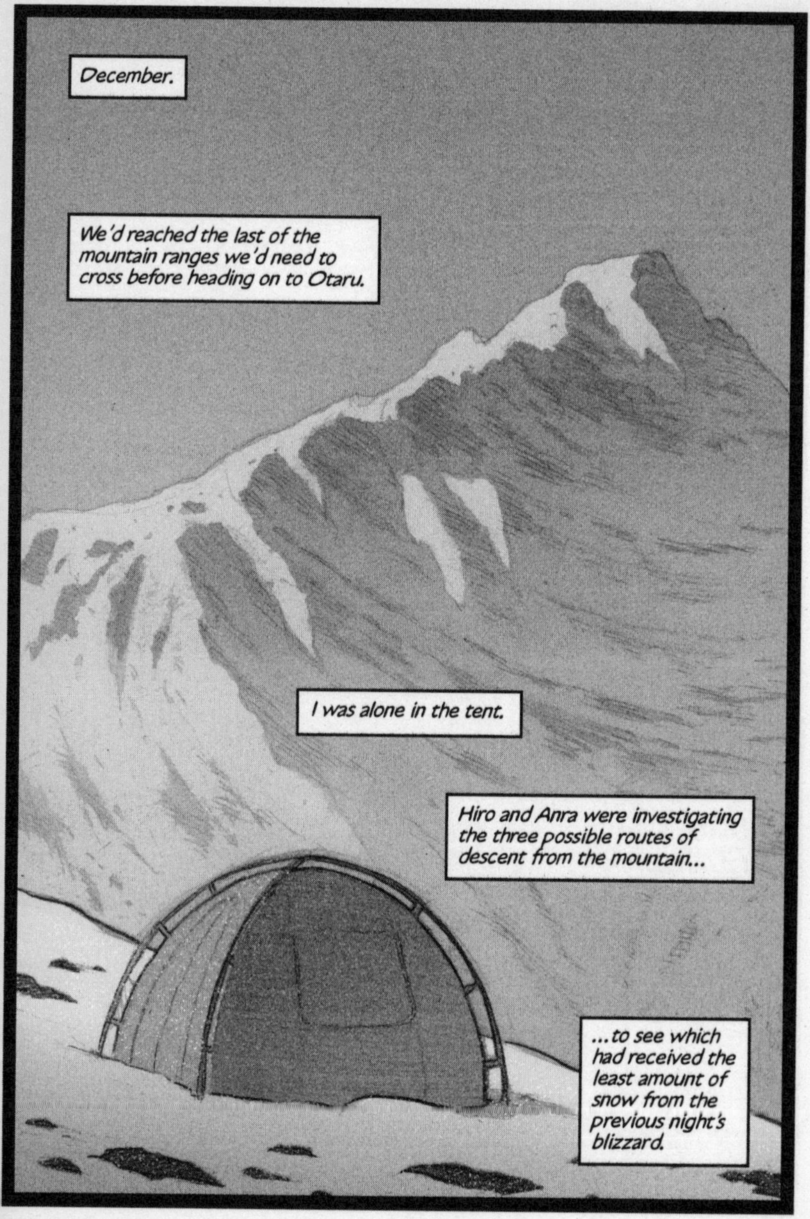
December.
We'd reached the last of the mountain ranges we'd need to cross before heading on to Otaru.
I was alone in the tent.
Hiro and Anra were investigating the three possible routes of descent from the mountain...
...to see which had received the least amount of snow from the previous night's blizzard.

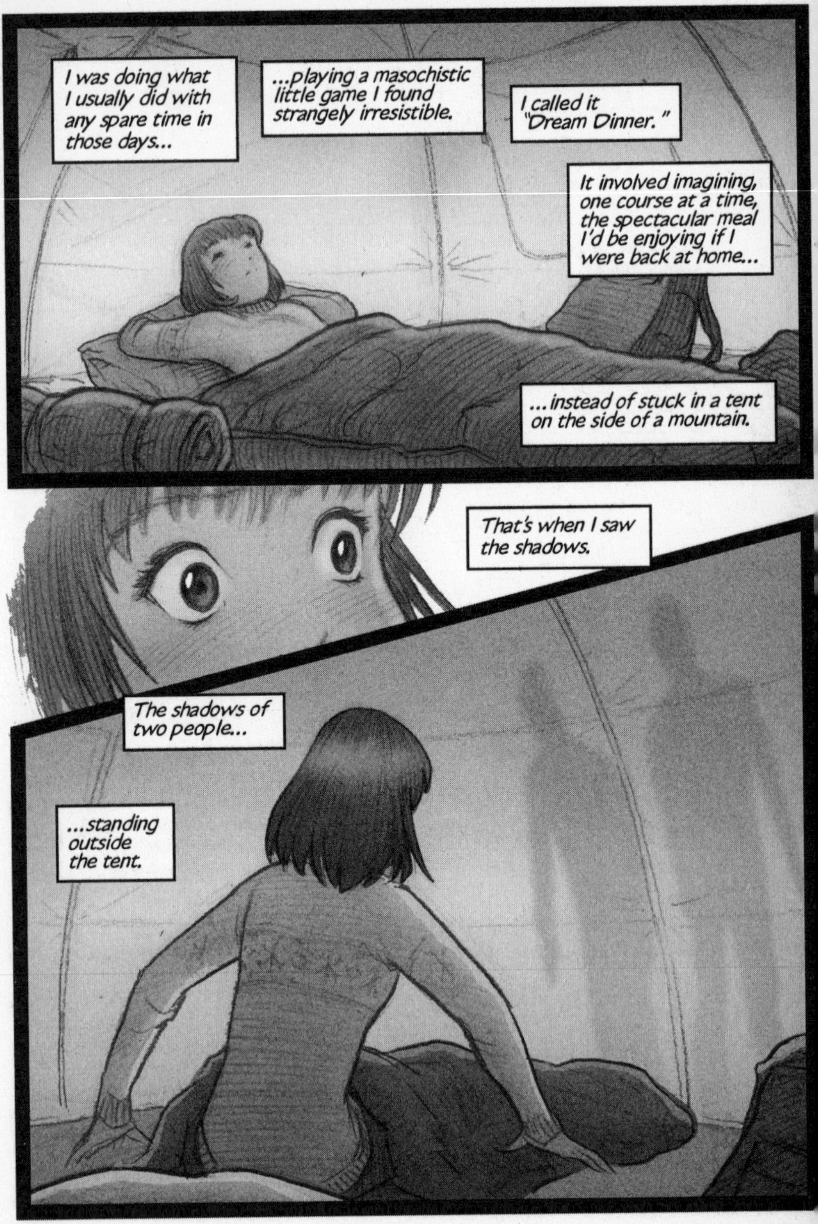

I was doing what I usually did with any spare time in those days...
...playing a masochistic little game I found strangely irresistible.
I called it "Dream Dinner."
It involved imagining, one course at a time, the spectacular meal I'd be enjoying if I were back at home...
...instead of stuck in a tent on the side of a mountain.
That's when I saw the shadows.
The shadows of two people...
...standing outside the tent.

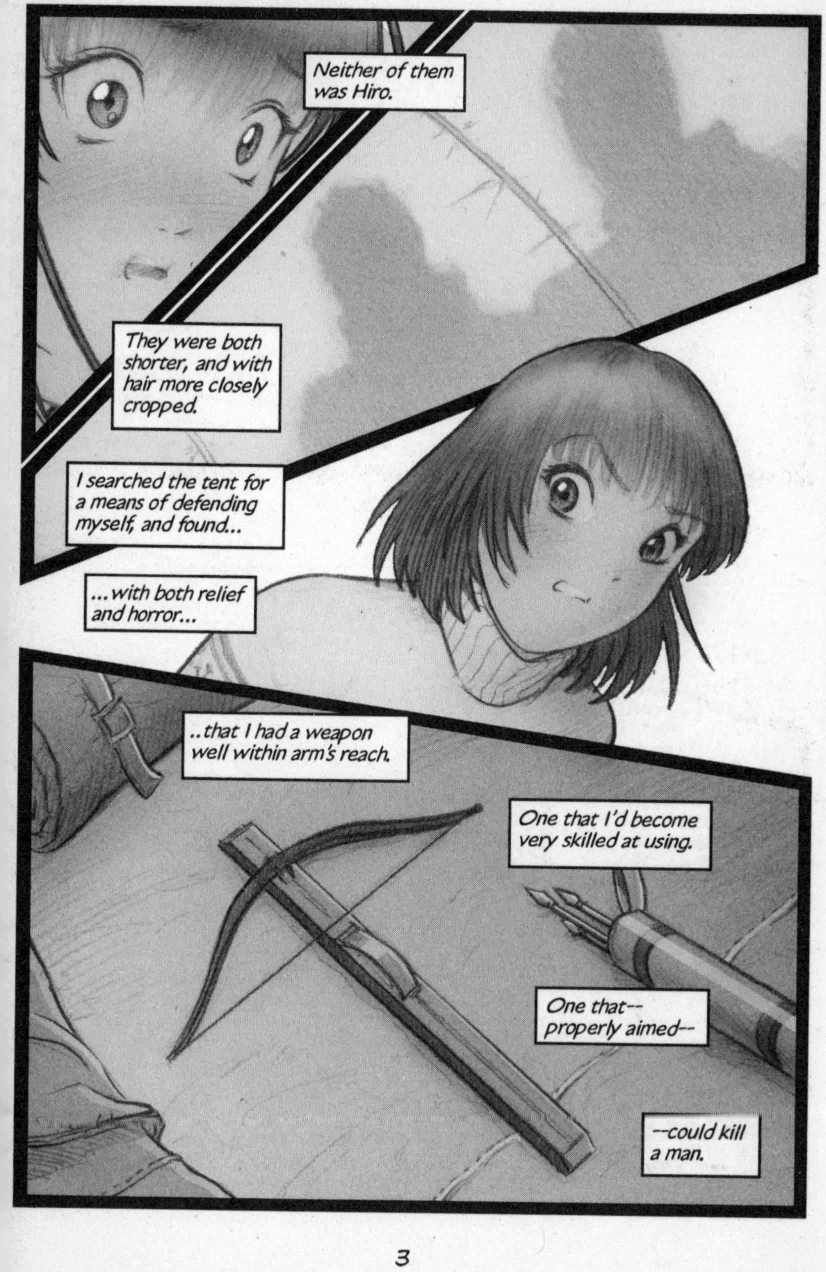
Neither of them was Hiro.
They were both shorter, and with hair more closely cropped.
I searched the tent for a means of defending myself, and found...
...with both relief and horror...
..that I had a weapon well within arm's reach.
One that I'd become very skilled at using.
One that-- properly aimed--
--could kill a man.